THE GIRL WHO DARED TO ENDURE

THE GIRL WHO DARED TO THINK 6

BELLA FORREST

Nightlight

1

Before the Tower, humanity took chances.

They plunged into the unknown with both feet, some bearing the brunt of failure, while others snagged the fruit of success. Both paths were taught so that others could learn, grow, and build. They had the courage to explore, the intelligence to question, the spark to create, and the daring to risk it all for the simple opportunity to try. Their bravery paved the way for those behind them, inspiring the following generations to build upon what they'd created, expand even farther out, so that the unknown could become known.

Once, humanity had been filled with pioneers. Now, humanity seemed content to put its head down and survive.

But not me. Not anymore. Not after I had discovered the truth: the AI designed to keep the Tower safe, Scipio, was actually being manipulated by a group of people called legacies. They had been trying to dismantle and control him since the beginning of the Tower. And right now, I was in the quarters of one of their leaders

—possibly even *the* leader of their organization—in the process of recovering Jasper and Rose, two AI fragments that had once been part of Scipio but had been stolen by the legacies as part of their plan to control him.

We had recovered Rose from a sentinel the legacies had stolen and used to attack innocent people, and had found the program damaged as a result of the torture the legacies had put her through. But Leo, the AI modeled after Lionel Scipio and currently inhabiting the body of my boyfriend, Grey, had managed to stabilize her, and we had sent her after Jasper, who was trapped in the head of the IT Department's personal terminal, panicked by the thought that she was torturing him like she had Rose.

But something had gone wrong, and we'd ended up having to physically break into her private quarters in order to recover both programs. We couldn't afford to leave them in our enemy's hands—not just because they were sentient beings being tortured, but also because if we wanted to fix the damage the legacies had done to Scipio, we would need them. They were a part of his code, and without them, he was degrading.

So I had lied to the council, telling them that my quarters had suffered a computer glitch that reset my entire apartment. I'd used it to lure Sadie Monroe, the head of IT—and possible leader of a legacy family—there. Then my friends and I attacked her, stole her net (and the ID credentials attached to it) to access her room, and broke in. As far as capital offenses went, it was pretty bad. If we were caught by the council, I'd be kicked off, and every last one of us would be put into the expulsion chambers.

But that was nothing compared to what would happen if the legacies found out what we were doing, which was why we had gone to extreme lengths to cover our trail.

The first step was using a medication called Spero to erase Sadie's memory of the attack, and then a mild sedative to adjust her perception of the amount of time she spent in the apartment. But since we had a limited number of pills, and she was the head of her own department, we couldn't keep her for too long, or people would notice. Which meant moving fast.

Then, there was the fun bonus hurdle that everything in a councilor's quarters was recorded, and we didn't have time to get rid of the recordings of our comings and goings. Instead, we planned to replicate the same tactic we had used to lure Sadie from her department, and reset her quarters. It would erase all of the data on her terminal, and hopefully she would believe it was another glitch related to the one in my quarters. If we were successful in stealing Jasper, we hoped that she would *further* believe that he'd been somehow erased in the process.

But we had to be careful. Because if the legacies found out that we stole Jasper, they would realize that we knew about the fragment AIs. And that we had one of them. In which case they would come after us with everything they had.

And I couldn't defend us all from an enemy whose face I didn't even know.

Which was what made this mission all the more integral. Sadie was clearly one of them—the legacy net in the back of her neck had proved that—and we were banking on her files containing information about who she was working with. That, along with recovering Jasper and Rose, was of paramount importance to me, because with that, I could finally begin to root out the corruption of the legacies.

And even though we had slapped together an insane plan and leapt through all of these impossible hoops, things had been going great. I had been stealing files from Sadie's desk while Leo had been working on Jasper and Rose. For some reason, Jasper was the one who had attacked Rose when she entered his system—and was still attacking her—and given our limited timeframe, Leo had started downloading both of them onto some hard drives, rather than trying to separate them immediately. He'd also been grabbing all of Sadie's computer files. Everything had been just freaking perfect.

Until it had stopped being so.

I exchanged a nervous look with Leo and then looked back to the shut bedroom door: a thin and weak barrier against anyone who wanted in. "How did he know we were here?" I asked, my voice barely a level above a breath. It had to be; my throat already felt tight, the memory of drowning in blood causing a visceral reaction in me.

The sensation was understandable, though. Somewhere on the other side of the door, walking in a strong and confident manner down the curved hall of Sadie's apartment, was the man who had cut my throat only yesterday, and five of his friends. He and I had crossed paths several times, and each time, he had only grown more dangerous. The last time I'd seen him, I'd been looking into his eyes as he stabbed the knife into my carotid artery.

He was a legacy who had tried to kill me—and now he was here. It only confirmed in my mind that he and Sadie were working together, but in what way? Was he in charge? Was it her? Or someone else?

And why was he here? Did he happen to notice Sadie's net transmission in the brief moment when I had removed the neural blocker to gain access to her apartment? I knew the legacies had a way of monitoring the system, so it wasn't that far outside of our belief that they could have. But it had only been active for a few seconds, while we gained access to the room. Did he actually *know* we were there, or was he there for something else? Fear crept along my skin, and my stomach quivered with uncertainty.

"I don't know," Leo replied in answer to my question, his voice also as soft as possible. "But Jasper and Rose are still downloading," he said, tightening his grip on his gun. "Even if they aren't here for us, they *are* going to notice that something is off as soon as they go in her office. We left the desk a mess."

He was right. Even if they weren't here for us, they'd soon notice the general state of disarray I'd left the office in when I was searching for anything we could use against Sadie. As soon as they did, they'd investigate, and it wouldn't take them long to find us. I needed more information on where they were before I could figure out what to do next. Focusing on the door, I considered it for a moment. I couldn't hear anything going on out there, and now that we weren't in the office, we had no way of monitoring their location. Running had lost us that advantage, and I felt stupid for having done it in the first place, but it was too late to take that back now. I had to deal with the situation in front of me.

That meant knowing if they were here for us, or if this was an unfortunate coincidence. If it was the latter, then we had the element of surprise and could capitalize on it. If it was the former, then it made things worlds more complicated. They'd be ready with weapons, prepared for a fight, and had us outnumbered two to one. We had guns—instruments of destruction that no one else in the Tower had access to—and Leo could more than hold his own in a fight, but they still had more people than we did, and that could make all the difference.

And if they were prepared for us—or any intruder, really—then that might mean they were being monitored. If any one of them managed to send out a message to Sadie or anyone else about what we were doing or who we were, then all of our planning would result in nothing, and we would be caught and executed. Either by the legacies or by the council.

I couldn't let that happen. So if they were here for us, or even if they saw us, we would have to stop them immediately. Not a single one could escape, or we risked the legacies learning what we had done, and who we had stolen.

But I didn't mind that conclusion, because I didn't want them to escape. Especially not Baldy, their leader. He had information we needed, like who was running everything, who was helping them, and what they were planning to do. Those were answers I craved more than anything, as they would lead to the person responsible for the deaths of too many people, including my mother. It would stop the attack on Scipio and give us time to recover the remaining fragments so we could repair him. It would finally allow us to take the Tower in the direction that the founder, Lionel Scipio, had intended.

"Can you crack the door open just a little bit?" I whispered to Leo, deciding I needed to hear what they were doing. Before I could even come up with a plan, I had to know why they were here, and where they were.

Leo nodded and moved over to the door, and I followed, holding open the bag I had so he could get at the tools inside. He turned and started working, and it took him a few agonizing seconds to pry the cover from the door control that activated the motor. I watched impatiently as he disconnected a few wires from some of the glowing crystals and then dragged the tips of them together, experimenting. On combination number three, something sparked, and the door lifted up a few inches from the floor.

A male voice that I recognized as Baldy's wafted through, but it was too muddled to discern what he was saying. I hesitated, and then slid down onto the ground. I hated making myself even the slightest bit visible, in case they were just around the bend, but I had to know what was going on. I glanced under the door first, to make sure there were no shoes waiting on the other side or in the vicinity, and then pressed my ear to the gap. Holding my breath to keep from making any noise, I strained to hear what he was saying. Even my heartbeat seemed too loud in my ears, but I closed my eyes and focused.

"—down, I'm here," he said, his voice growing louder in my ears. "We got slowed at a checkpoint because Sadie couldn't make it, but it's fine. All we have to do is grab it, and we'll be on our way. It's a little weird though. Alara isn't responding to me."

He paused, and I waited for someone to respond while puzzling over what he was talking about. Who was Alara? Why would he be expecting her to respond?

Then I realized that Alara was probably the name of Sadie's virtual assistant. Rose had knocked it out when we sent her in after Jasper, which was the only thing that had made this mission possible. If Sadie's assistant had been online, it would've killed us before we even got past the first room, with or without Sadie's net.

But back to the important thing: it was clear that Baldy was transmitting to someone over the net, and from his words, it sounded like he was here by coincidence. And to pick something up. If we were lucky, that something would be in one of the other rooms before the office, and they would get it and go without questioning things too much.

If we weren't lucky, there was still a chance. If we could make it to the office before they did, grab the hard drives with our AI friends, and start the reset process, then they would be caught in the chaos of the automated systems removing the furniture and bringing the walls down. Having it happen when they were there would certainly lend credence to the idea that it was a glitch. But that was even riskier, because we were planning to leave using an escape hatch, and if we didn't make it in time, or got injured by the furniture as it rushed by overhead, there was a chance Baldy and the others would see us and know what was happening.

I'd do it—and give up my chance at taking them out—but only if we could do it safely.

I kept listening, and heard: "No, I'm not sure what's going on. That bitch Champion registered some sort of complaint that Sadie had to attend to." There was a pause, and I found myself wondering who was at the other end. Accomplice, or someone in charge? "No, I don't know the details. She authorized me to come up here and get it anyway, so calm down. It's just a small deviation, not a complete disaster. I'll get it down to you in a few minutes."

Oh, this was good—very good. As long as whatever they had to get was in another room and not the office, we would be fine. We could just wait here for them to get what they came for and leave, and then be on our way.

As soon as I thought it, though, I realized I was about thirty-two shades of *wrong*. Of course they were going into Sadie's office —the only thing they'd be here for was something computer-related, as she was the head of the IT Department, and the office was the only place where electronics and files were kept. If they noticed the mess on the desk or the three hard drives that had been slaved together and attached to the terminal, they would start to suspect something was wrong and investigate.

Once again, I found myself considering making a run for the office and trying to initiate the reset before they got there. Their voices sounded far enough away, and if Leo and I could just get there, get Jasper and Rose and the stuff we had planned to steal, then start the process...

But if we were spotted while he was still on a net call with someone... If he managed to get word out that the Champion of the Knights was in the head of IT's quarters illegally... It was so very risky, and I hovered on the edge of the decision. If he ended the call soon, then it might be worth a try.

My hand tightened on my gun, the urge to tell Leo to open the door and get ready to move nearly overpowering as their footsteps thundered closer—still heading toward us, and toward the office, and making me reconsider the plan again. If we made a run for the office, and they caught us in the halls before we could make it there, chances were they could knock us off our feet using a burst of pressurized air from their pulse shields. If that were to happen, we'd lose control over the situation very quickly. Going into the halls to try to reach the office before them was too desperate and too risky. I had to think of something else. Maybe coming up from behind them and shooting them in the back. Maybe—

I opened my eyes as I realized that Baldy hadn't said anything for a long time. He must've ended his conversation with whoever was on the net. On the one hand, that was good for us; now that he wasn't transmitting, we could do something about him. On the other, it meant I had missed my opportunity to try to make it to the office before them.

"So how mad was he when you told him?" asked a feminine voice. I recognized it, too—as the one Baldy had been talking to right before he'd cut my throat. My fingers immediately itched to touch the spot, to remind myself that my neck was whole and unbroken, but I kept them firmly around the gun, straining to hear.

"I don't want to talk about it, Claire," Baldy replied tightly. But then, a heartbeat later, he exploded into, "That stupid order to keep that intrusive little bitch alive is a mistake, and we all know it."

Claire made a consoling noise. "I know, I know," she said soothingly. "She chased us from our home, and she's been getting into stuff left and right. But he wants her alive for some reason, and you have to respect that."

He went quiet, which only made the sound of stomping feet grow louder. I fought against the fear the noise created, focusing instead on their words. They were clearly talking about me, as I was the one who had accidently stumbled into their home when we were trying to recover some items we needed from the Attic. That was when he had cut my throat, as a cover for their escape. But the fact that they really didn't want me dead left me feeling two things.

The first being abject fear. They might have orders to keep me alive, but they clearly didn't like it. If they found us here and got the upper hand, who knew if they would let me live a second time. They might not, if they realized what I was here for—and how much I knew.

The second thing I noticed was that Baldy had mentioned a

"he." That meant there was a leader over Baldy... but was he over Sadie? Or was Sadie over him? Or were they partners?

I waited for them to say more about it, but to my dismay, the next thing I heard was Claire's voice saying, "What the hell... Why is Sadie's desk a mess?"

2

My heart seemed to go very quiet in my chest, and I had to put a hand over it just to make sure it was still beating. Stomach churning, I squeezed the pommel of the gun tighter and waited for his reply.

When it finally came, it filled me with some relief, but not much. "I don't know," he replied uncertainly. "Maybe she lost something and was in the process of looking for it when she had to leave?"

That was good. They were jumping to a reasonable idea instead of immediately arriving at the conclusion that someone was here. And why wouldn't they? The councilor's quarters were supposed to be the most secure places in the Tower. None of them had been breached.

Although, given the ease with which I was able to do it (ha!), maybe that record wasn't as pristine as I had been told. I wasn't arrogant enough to assume that my team was the only one to come up with a plan to get in.

Still, it made sense that they wouldn't immediately leap to that conclusion.

But that didn't mean they wouldn't get there eventually. We needed to move—now—away from them, before they questioned it. We could come up with a plan once we had some distance between us.

I started to sign my plan to Leo in Callivax—the hand language of the Divers—but stopped when I heard Claire's reply. "I don't know. Something feels off about this."

Dammit, Claire, I thought bitterly. *Why'd you have to be a* smart *bad guy?*

"What? Do you want to check it out?" If Claire replied, it must have been via a head nod, because I heard Baldy give an irritated sigh a few seconds later. "He's going to be angry at the delay, but yeah, take a look around. I'm sure it's nothing, but you're right. Something feels off."

"Thank you," she replied gratefully. "I'll take Callum. You just focus on getting what we came here for."

I didn't hear a reply from Baldy—only the sound of footsteps heading right toward us. And there were no other rooms between us and the office for them to check first. They had already noticed the mess, but if they noticed the hard drives and figured out that Jasper and Rose were being downloaded, too, they would *definitely* know someone was here. As soon as they did, we would lose any opportunity of surprising them, and it could give them a chance to call someone and let them know we were here.

Not. Good.

I was up and moving before I even had a chance to think, signing to Leo in Callivax that two of them were coming, and froze when I realized I wasn't exactly sure how to proceed. I knew how to use the gun, but I wasn't skilled in the type of combat necessary for it. I wasn't sure where the best place to stand was, what tactics to use. The gun was familiar in my hand, thanks to the legacy net.

Someone in the past had had experience with firearms, and that experience had translated to me—but only so much of it.

Panic surged through me as I realized that my earlier confidence in having the guns might have been misplaced. Leo's eyes were trained on my hands, but as the boots grew louder, I knew I wouldn't be able to figure out the right move. Should we stand next to the door, opposite it, flip up the mattress and hide behind it, use our lashes to get to the ceiling... My eyes darted around the room as I considered the multitude of choices, and it suddenly occurred to me that I had no comprehension of gun *strategy*. A wave of frustration and fear rolled over me, and I struggled to find the best answer.

Suddenly, a buzz shot through my skull thanks to my net, and my panic doubled. I didn't have time to be sucked away from reality and taken by yet another memory. The episodes left me blind to the real world when they occurred, and if I was locked in one when the door opened, they'd have me. I struggled against it, pressing one hand to my mouth to cover my gasp. Leo started to rush over, but I waved him back with my free arm.

To my surprise, though, no memory took me away. It was difficult to explain, but I felt some sort of past personality extending something like a handshake in a light, tentative brush across my brain. The touch was questioning, inquisitive, curious, but also confident and sure, as if it were saying, *Girl, do you need a little help?* My immediate response was that I did, and the next thing I felt was a wave of confidence suddenly translating into me.

No, it was more than that. It was like someone else was just under my skin, controlling my very responses. Leo's brown eyes widened as I suddenly straightened. Now, as I surveyed the room, it was like I could see the various positions I could take, and the new impulse inside of me directed me to the bed. I followed it and took a kneeling position on the bed, my arms extended straight toward the door.

Leo cocked his head at me, but the controlling force didn't bat a single eyelash as I lined up the shot. A deep calm seemed to settle over my muscles, and I couldn't help but question it. I had been nervous seconds ago, but now I felt confident. Maybe too confident. What if I was just imagining the net doing this? It had certainly never done anything like this before.

My questions didn't affect the calm, though, and I didn't move.

A shadow appeared on the edge of the gap, then, and grew as the figure beyond stopped just on the other side of the door. My grip on the gun tightened. The barrier between us started to rise, and I tracked its progress with my gun as legs clad in the gray of an IT uniform slid into view. My heart thudded against my chest as a chest appeared next—female, given the ampleness.

That meant Claire. A person with a name. A person with a family. A person, full stop.

But the legacy net told me what had to be done, and time slowed as her neck appeared, slim and pretty. It reminded me that she had been there when my throat was cut—and had done nothing to stop Baldy. My finger tightened on the trigger.

Her eyes came next, then, and I exhaled and squeezed. There was a sharp *bang*, and the gun kicked in my hand, but the memory held my hand firm.

She barely had a chance to register my presence before the bullet caught her in the center of her forehead. The force of it threw her back against the wall, and I was up and moving before she had even started sliding down it. I wanted to stare, to process what I had just done to another human being without giving them the decency of a warning or a fair fight, but there were two big problems with that. First, they didn't deserve a fair fight, and second, the strange legacy memory was fully in control.

I'd had almost nothing to do with it. I had been shocked when I felt myself pulling the trigger.

I knew that should frighten me, but I felt like I *could* control it, as long as I didn't try to fight it. The goal was now made simple: kill the other legacies, except for Baldy, before they could net anyone that we were here. Baldy, I wanted alive, to see what I could get out of him. But the rest had to die. Then we would get Jasper and Rose and the files, reset the room, and get the heck out of here.

I crossed the room in three short steps and emerged into the hall. Sure enough, a large man with cropped blond hair was staring at Claire's slumped form with confusion and alarm. I pointed the gun at him and squeezed the trigger twice, and he jerked as the bullets hit him on the left side of his chest, within an inch of each other. I knew I had hit him in the heart. Blood spurted, hitting the wall, but the net kept me strangely calm.

I motioned for Leo to follow, and then moved down the hall. "Claire?" Baldy called from up ahead in the office, a worried note in his voice. "What was that?"

The hall was curved, but the distance between the two rooms was short, and as I swung into view, I saw a man, blond as well, but lankier and shorter than Callum, leaning on the doorframe. His eyes widened when he saw me coming, and he started fumbling at his belt. Some cruel part of the legacy net let him struggle even as I closed the distance between us—or maybe it was wise, I wasn't sure—but as soon as he began to pull the familiar shape of the pulse shield out of its holster, I squeezed the trigger.

The bullet exploded from the end of the gun in a flash of fire, and I heard the wet sound of it striking a moment before the back of his skull exploded all over the wall and doorframe.

"Sam!" Baldy shouted, his voice suddenly panicked. "We're under attack! Weapons!"

My hand went up behind me, and I realized that the legacy net was forcing me to sign to Leo that he should go right while I went left. I felt him grab my hand, pulling me to a stop, and realized that he wanted me to let him go first. But the net wasn't allowing it, and I twisted my wrist free and plunged through the doorway, arms and gun extended in front of me.

Something dark and gray raced up a set of stairs in the corner of the room that led to the dais, and I homed in on it, shooting the person twice in the back before I consciously ascertained that it wasn't Baldy. His hair was way too long.

Another shot sounded to my right, completely unexpected, and I looked over to see Leo standing at the threshold, his gun pointed at a woman who had been hiding in the corner. I saw the pulse shield in her hand and realized that she had been about to shoot me with it. Leo had stopped her. His face was grim as he turned his focus back to the desk, and the legacy net echoed the movement.

It was already forcing me forward, racing toward the desk. Everyone was dead except for Baldy, but if he managed to net someone and let them know we were here before I got to him... I ducked as he swung up from where he had been hiding, his hand filled with a white pulse shield. I dove low, even as Leo shot from behind me. The bullet caught Baldy in the shoulder, flinging his arm up and back, and he cried out in pain and then disappeared behind the desk as he fell.

I was up and around it in three seconds, horrified at the thought that he could already be netting someone. Sure enough, he had his wrist up, and his flat, circular indicator was glowing, telling me that he'd touched it. He looked up at me with alarm as I slid to a knee beside him.

Reaching out, I grabbed a fistful of his uniform and hauled him up, my gun pointed right at his head. It was in my heart to squeeze the trigger right then and there; after all, he'd played a part in so much death in the Tower. And the personality in the net that was guiding my actions urged me to do just that. But even as my finger started to squeeze the trigger, I beat it back, forcing the tension in my finger to relax.

I drew the gun back, and a vicious hatred filled his eyes. "You!" he spat.

"Me," I agreed, and then slammed the butt of the gun down

against his temple, feeling the blow all the way down to my hip. There was a sharp crack, and he went limp. Fingers at his neck told me that he was still alive, though, and I felt a grim sense of satisfaction.

It was quickly replaced by a sense of weakness as the net stopped buzzing, the weird memory/personality sensation dissipating. I sagged, suddenly shaky from the onslaught of adrenaline, and took a moment to catch my breath.

As I did, I realized that I had just killed four people in quick succession.

And we didn't have a moment to waste. We had a minute—maybe two—to cover their deaths up before the system confirmed that they had died and the alarms went off. If we could disable their nets before that, then they wouldn't show up as alive or dead, because the net would be too damaged to transmit their life signs and the system wouldn't have confirmation one way or the other. That meant cutting or burning them out, and one was far faster than the other.

"Leo?" I said, straightening up and switching the gun to my other hand so I could draw my baton.

I wasn't surprised to find him right there next to me, brown eyes brimming with concern. "You okay?" he asked.

I nodded and wiped my mouth with the back of my hand, suddenly remembering the way the man's head had exploded when I shot him but managing to hold it together despite my churning stomach. "Yeah, but we have to hurry. I need you to remove Baldy's net so they can't track him, and he can't net anyone. I'm going to fry the other ones before the system can register they are dead. How long until Jasper and Rose are downloaded?"

He turned and looked at the monitor, and I saw a flashing blue status bar on the screen, two-thirds of the way full. "Four minutes," he replied. "I'll get to work on this guy. You get the others. We'll move the bodies to the emergency exit and hide them there."

I nodded, recognizing the wisdom in his words. Each department lead's apartment had an emergency escape route in case the Tower fell, maximizing the opportunity for some humans to survive, and utilizing Sadie's was the only way for us to get out undetected, as there were no sensors inside them. I knew from the reset of my own quarters that Sadie's personal items would be sorted out—which was why I was planning to destroy the desk, to cover the fact that I had stolen her files—so it stood to reason the bodies would remain as well. We had to remove them, or Sadie would find them when she got back and know something had gone down. Hiding them upstairs, in the escape tunnel, was the best thing we could do until we could deal with them. Not to mention, we could probably leave them there indefinitely. I doubted Sadie used her escape tunnel, so she wouldn't think to look inside it for some time.

As long as we took care of the nets first. I slid the bag over my shoulder and handed it to Leo. Then I moved to the first body—the woman in the corner—flipped her over, charged my baton, placed the tip at the back of her neck, and expended the electrical charge. Her body flopped like a fish for several seconds as I held it there, and I cringed against the horrific feeling it produced.

I relaxed slightly when it was over, but the feeling was brief. I turned to the next one.

One down, I thought as I approached it with grim purpose. *Three more to go.*

3

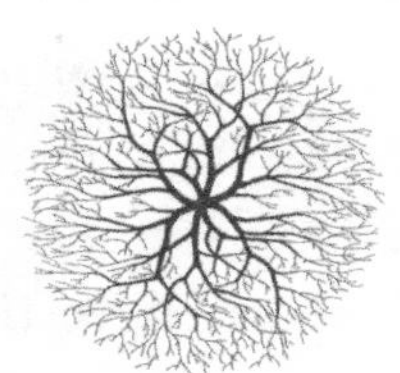

It only took Jasper and Rose four minutes to download, but it took Leo and me seven to neutralize the nets and carry the bodies to the escape tunnel. Luckily, it wasn't far from the office. Unluckily, that extra three minutes ate into the precious time Jasper and Rose had on the slaved hard drives. Jasper's program was mindlessly attacking Rose's, and it was using up a lot of power to do it—which was why we had the hard drives slaved together, for more power, and why we had only half an hour to get them to a more secure place, like a terminal. Transporting them was risky, because if the hard drive battery units gave out, we could lose Rose and Jasper forever.

But staying definitely wasn't an option.

We raced through the rest of what we needed to do after we deposited Baldy's unconscious form up in the escape tunnel, giving him an extra zap with the baton to make sure he *stayed* unconscious. Leo handled cleaning up the blood, using a few of Sadie's sheets, while I swept everything I had taken from Sadie's desk into the bag, my motions jerky and quick. Each second that dragged by felt like a second too long. As soon as I was done, I left Leo and fled to the emergency exit, while he set off the virus that would convince Sadie's assistant that she was dead, and that it needed to initiate the reset of her apartment and files.

And though I was alone for several seconds in the hall, I had no time to worry about Leo's safety. I quickly stripped out of the IT uniform that Dinah, our ally inside of IT, had given me, and donned my own uniform, complete with lashes. Leo showed up a moment later and helped me, and a few precious minutes later we were running down the hall and into a shaft that led upward, Baldy strapped to my back. We didn't have time for Leo to change as well, as his gear was still in the bag, so it was up to me and my harness to carry him. I utilized my lashes to climb, the gears in the gyros better equipped to handle the double weight, while Leo used a rung ladder.

"Did it work?" I asked him as I began my ascent, keeping my voice low.

"It did. I almost got clocked by a piece of furniture making my way back to you."

I couldn't find any humor in his statement. My nerves were already fraying from the sudden dip in adrenaline, so I focused instead on the climb, relieved that at the very least we had covered our tracks.

The shaft led to a hatch nearly a hundred feet up, and I let Leo go through first so he could help me out. Once we were on the roof, we paused to spray our faces—and Baldy's—with Quess's invention, which would obscure our features from the facial recognition software, and I gave Leo a minute to put on his uniform, and then we were moving again, opening up the large door to the hall. Once we were in the hall, I started using my lashes, throwing the thin lines out rhythmically, one right after the other. This was the only way I could carry Baldy such a distance without collapsing halfway there from the weight—and it was much faster than running.

We'd already taken too long as it was. Even now, the legacies could've noticed that Baldy was missing. He was supposed to meet someone, so there was a finite amount of time before they started looking for him. I wanted him back in my quarters before they noticed. Before they came looking. If they weren't already doing so.

My eyes scanned the corridors as we flew through them, searching for any sign of movement, but the Attic was, as always, devoid of human life. It didn't make me feel any better, however, and when we finally reached the storage room that would lead back to the Citadel, I almost quivered with relief.

It was too soon to feel it, though. I still had to get Sadie out of my quarters, and Jasper and Rose had to be downloaded before the hard drives ran out of power. AIs needed an energy source at all times, or they would die. It was why Scipio had backup source upon backup source, powered both by the hydro-turbines and the energy harvested from the sun.

When we got to the end of the hall, I slowly lowered myself to the ground just as Leo went for the door. My boots hit the floor, and in my impatience to get this whole mess over and done with, I disconnected the line prematurely—and my knees immediately buckled under Baldy's weight. Leo moved to help, but I waved him off as I took two staggering steps, trying to catch my balance. I smiled triumphantly at him a second later, managing to center myself, and then toppled right over onto my side, Baldy's extra weight too much to handle after moving all of those bodies.

We hit the ground with a thud, and I heard Leo tsk and move over. There was a jerking against my back as he disconnected Baldy from where we had hooked him onto my uniform, and I took a moment, feeling weak and sweaty, my muscles aching and burning from the exertion.

Then Leo's hand filled my vision, and I took it, gingerly

allowing him to pull me up. "I netted Maddox, and she's on her way," he reported softly, his hands going to the back of his neck. I realized he had pulled the neural scrambler off to do so and was in the process of putting it back on. I prayed that the activity hadn't been enough for anyone to triangulate his position. If they did, and saw two Knights randomly lashing through the halls of the Attic in the vid files, one with an unconscious man on her back, the legacies might piece together that Baldy's disappearance and Sadie's quarters simultaneously being reset was not a coincidence.

And that we were responsible.

"Good," I replied softly. "Help me get Baldy over to the hatch."

Leo shook his head and took off the bag he had carried. "I'll stay here with him," he replied as he knelt down and opened up the bag. I watched him pull out the slaved hard drives, which were bound together with wires and tape. "You have to get these to Quess as quickly as possible," he informed me. "As soon as you get Sadie out, start downloading them. Too much time has already passed."

I glanced at my wrist and saw that he was right: it had already been seventeen minutes since we'd downloaded Jasper and Rose. Which meant we only had thirteen minutes left before the hard drives failed.

But still I hesitated. Sadie Monroe was in my quarters. Drugged, and slightly out of it. I had to get her out of there quickly, but we still had to knock her out again, put her net back in her head, give her a small bit of Spero, and then get her out.

Right. There wasn't any time to waste.

I squared my shoulders and took the hard drives in my hand, glancing at Baldy's still form. "Better shock him again, just to be sure," I said.

Leo gifted me with a lopsided smile and reached out to smooth a bit of the hair that had escaped my braid away from my eyes. My heart skipped a beat as the simple gesture sucked my breath out of my lungs, and I quickly took a step back, my cheeks flaming at the intensity of my reaction. Now wasn't the time, and feeling things for Leo while he was inside Grey was the very definition of a complication I did not need right now.

"I'll be fine," he told me firmly, ignoring my discomfort. "Hurry up. Maddox is on her way."

I nodded as he brushed past me and moved toward the hatch we had come through earlier, walking down the aisle. I followed him, cradling the hard drives in both hands, and came to a stop as he knelt on the floor twenty feet deeper into the room and pressed on a section of it to reveal a digital keypad. He pulled something out of his pocket and connected it through a wire that he jacked into a port, and the display turned from red to blue, lighting his face with a glow that reminded me of his holographic image when I had first discovered him in Lionel Scipio's secret office.

The display turned green a few seconds later, and a square piece of the floor slid back, revealing a shaft with a ladder. And though I wanted to move quickly, I carefully tucked the hard drives under one arm and stepped onto the first rung, and then to the next, awkwardly balancing myself with one hand. It took a second to get the rhythm, but once I did, I descended as quickly as possible, barely giving Leo one last glance before he slipped from view.

I heard a grating sound seconds later, signaling that he'd closed the door, but focused on the climb down. It took me longer than I cared to admit before I made it to the bottom of the shaft, and when the door below slid open so the bottom section of the ladder could descend into the hall, I was unsurprised to see Maddox already standing there, waiting for me.

What did surprise me was that my twin brother was standing right next to the raven-haired girl, his eyes narrowed at me in displeasure. I had forgotten that he had been on his way over to force himself into the investigation, but was relieved that Maddox had intercepted him. He, however, looked less than happy.

"Your stupid Lieutenant kept me locked in an elevator for forty minutes," he bit off angrily, his dark eyes flashing behind the spectacles on his nose.

I arched an eyebrow as I stepped off the ladder, thinking that was good. I knew I shouldn't be dismissive of him like that—being dismissive of his feelings and wishes was what had landed me in the doghouse in his eyes. And he had a point. I'd had my own difficulties in processing my mother's death and had allowed myself to cut him out as a result. Part of it was unintentional, but I knew I should've given him a better effort.

However, now was, unfortunately, not the time to start. "Good," I replied, echoing my internal thought. I checked my watch and gritted my teeth. Nine more minutes before we would lose Jasper and Rose. "Now, up the ladder you go," I told him. "I need to get Sadie out of my quarters, and you being there will only make things more difficult."

"What did you find in Sadie's apartment?" he demanded, ignoring my statement completely. Anger welled up in me, and I took a step closer to my twin.

"I will tell you after I get Sadie out of my home," I hissed, trying not to tear into a rage at the precious seconds this was costing us. "Leo is up in the Attic, alone with the man who cut my throat. Get up there and make sure that the man doesn't wake up and hurt him while I'm handling Sadie."

Alex's eyes gleamed with a dark light that suddenly filled me with doubt about telling him who was up there, but I couldn't give this any more time, and I had nowhere else to send him. "Maddox, you're with me. We'll switch out my net in the elevator. You brought mine with you?"

She nodded and patted her pocket, but her glittering green gaze didn't drop Alex's until he began to move toward the ladder. I did my best to ignore the eager motions of his arms, suddenly concerned about what would happen once he got up there, and reminded myself that Leo would be with him. He wouldn't let Alex do anything to Baldy. Still, the look in his eyes scared me—it had been like I was looking into the eyes of a stranger.

I tried to shake it off as I watched the ladder retract behind him, and then started walking down the hallway, heading for the elevator that would take us to the area between the thirty-first and thirty-second floors, where the entrance to my quarters was. I paused to let Maddox give me access to the elevator, knowing the neural blocker would keep the scanners from reading my net, and therefore keep me from using the elevator. Still, I practically leapt onto the black pad that slid out of the wall as soon as the scan was done.

Maddox followed closely behind, and within seconds I had set the hard drives on the elevator pad and presented her with my back, pulling the collar of my uniform down to give her access to my neck. I heard her rummage around for a second as the floor numbers tracked by, followed by a long silence.

Then her fingers were on my neck, and there was a sharp sting as she cut through the skin at the base of my skull. I endured it easily enough at this point—I had changed nets too many times to count—but still winced as the tendrils of the net began to pull back from my brain. The pressure was intense for several excruciating seconds, but then it passed, the relief palpable in every muscle in my body. I exhaled slowly as I felt her extract the net, now in the form of a square white chip, her fingers disappearing for a moment.

I forced a deep, calming breath, knowing that this was only the halfway mark, and watched as floor forty-five slid past. "Hurry," I said, trying not to shift my weight from one leg to another.

"Don't rush me. I'm not as good at this as Quess is," she replied tersely. Her fingers returned a second later, and the wound on my neck began to sting as she shoved my own net into it. She probed it a few times, seating it in place, and then suddenly the tendrils returned, slithering across my brain like worms wriggling through paths carved out by previous creatures. I withstood it without moving a muscle, and even managed to wait patiently as Maddox dabbed some bio-foam into the wound, letting the pink goo seal up the damaged flesh.

The elevator came to a stop a second later, and I hastily handed Maddox the hard drives. "Move these over to the pile of our stuff that the reset left against the wall, discreetly," I ordered softly.

She nodded, her face pale and tight with worry. I felt it, too, but had to be careful with my face. Sadie might be sedated and getting regular Spero doses, but I couldn't afford to let anything show. She might be out of it, but she was no slouch. And if she picked up on the slightest thing out of place, she might figure out that we were behind what had happened in my apartment—and hers. I wasn't about to let that happen. Not after we had gotten this far. I took one last deep, calming breath, trying to ease away all of my panic, worry, fluster, and anxiety, and then squared my shoulders at the opening doors and stepped through.

4

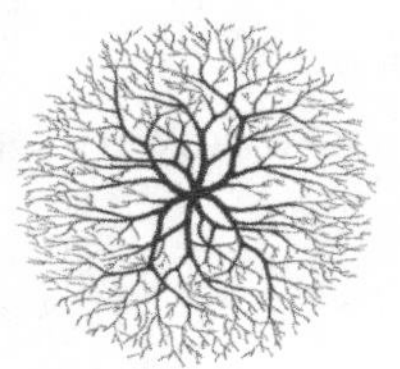

My quarters were just as I had left them: in the shape of a large, circular platform that doubled as an elevator, enclosed by a domed ceiling. Before Leo and Quess had initiated the reset meant to lure Sadie into my quarters, there had been walls and rooms of my own design, laid out like a snail shell. Now there was nothing, save a central column that controlled the features of the room and a terminal that was suspended from the ceiling next to it.

And next to *that* stood two figures who were opposite in every way. He was tall, with broad shoulders, while she was short and slender. Her hair was a mass of fire, vibrant against the dark gray of her uniform, while his colors were a direct juxtaposition: crimson uniform and black hair. They stood together, speaking in low voices that were hard to discern over the sound of our boots on the ground.

I walked toward them slowly while Maddox peeled off to go conceal the hard drives with the stack of cartons that held our personal effects, recovered by the system during the reset. We had entered through an elevator hatch near enough to it that it only took her a few seconds to hide the hard drives among them, and I waited, trying not to look at my watch, then sped up when Maddox returned to my side.

Just then, the man leaned over and tapped on the screen of the terminal, saying something in a contemplative voice. To my surprise, Sadie Monroe looked up and beamed at him, pride lining the curves of her pretty face.

"Very good," she said in a throaty purr that I could hear over our footsteps.

It was so jolting that I slowed to a stop, absolutely repulsed by the idea that Sadie was *flirting* with Quess. I cast a worried glance over at Maddox, and saw her head cocked and eyebrows raised, green eyes flashing first in shock and then intense displeasure, and I suddenly had a picture in my mind of a gun about to go off.

And why wouldn't she be angry? Quess was her... boyfriend? I wasn't sure, and I hadn't asked. He had been there for Maddox during her emotional crisis and had managed to nurse her through it. Now they shared a room. That was all I knew, and all I needed to know. They were adults, and it was none of my business.

But it became my business if Maddox's jealousy could potentially damage the final stages of our plan. We were almost there—almost finished. We just had to knock Sadie out again, put her net back in, give her one last dose of Spero, and then send her on her way, report in hand.

Then she'd go back to her home, find it completely disassembled, and tell the council, hopefully with no memory of the events that had, and were about to, transpire.

"Keep it together," I told her in a low, urgent voice. Her eyes flicked over at me without her head moving, and she carefully began to pull the anger off her face, softening the hard lines of it until she didn't look so... murderous.

Quess glanced over his shoulder at us, and I started moving forward again, keeping my face even and plain. He gave me a little nod and turned back to Sadie. "CEO Monroe?" he asked, his voice soft and almost hesitant, nothing like the confident man I knew. I smiled when I realized he was playing her hard, because sure enough, her head swiveled up to him, an eager smile curling on her lips.

"Yes?" she asked, leaning closer to him. I bit my lip as his hand dipped down to his belt and slowly eased his baton out, hiding my smile. "What is it, Sam?"

I heard Maddox snort slightly under her breath, but my moment of levity was gone, and I was once again hyperaware of the time. Sadie was really out of it; clearly the sedative had lowered her inhibitions, and she had zeroed in on Quess as her conquest. And that was great, but we didn't have time for this. On the one hand, I was happy that he had gone along with it in order to better manipulate her. On the other...

Maddox growled under her breath, and I silently prayed to a higher power for her to get a grip.

"Oh, I was just wondering about this little line of code," he replied with an innocent smile, and then stretched an arm around her to point at something on her side of the screen.

She giggled and turned her attention to it, and I crossed my arms, my impatience growing, even as Quess slowly withdrew to create distance between them so that he wasn't shocked along with her. "Sam," she said, her voice a shrill squeal that rivaled the loud slap she placed on his forearm a heartbeat later. "You already know what this is!" She chuckled throatily and flipped her hair over her shoulder, spearing him with a predatory look. "What are you playing at?" she purred.

"Ho-kay, that's enough of that," Maddox said, and the next thing I knew she was crossing the floor toward Sadie in long, determined strides, her baton sliding out of her loop. Sadie's head wobbled around toward Maddox, her eyes narrowing in confusion. Quess had just enough time to step away before Maddox was pressing the end of her baton into Sadie's shoulder.

Sadie seized up for several seconds, and then slumped over as soon as the charge was expended, slipping right into Quess's waiting arms.

"I had it," he said as he eased her down with a grunt. "What the hell, Doxy?"

"Sorry," she said, but her tone was anything but contrite. "I just couldn't stand any more of the Sadie and Sam kissing hour."

Quess rolled his eyes and then looked over at me. "How'd it go?"

"We had problems," I told him honestly as I approached and dropped to the ground to help them flip Sadie over. "I've got Jasper and Rose in some slaved hard drives, but Jasper is still attacking Rose, and it's drawing a lot of power. We need to get them downloaded..." I trailed off to check my watch, and my mouth went dry. We only had six minutes left before the hard drives failed. "Immediately," I bit out, my stomach churning. A minute to exchange nets, and then we'd only have five more to wake Sadie up and get her out. We were cutting it really close.

Maddox straddled Sadie's back, her hands already filled with the kit she'd used to exchange my net for Sadie's in the elevator. I pushed Sadie's hair out of the way while Maddox passed the bloody net she'd taken out of my neck to Quess for him to sanitize, and then began to cut, her eyes narrowed in concentration.

"Okay," Quess said with a grim nod. "I'll get them uploaded immediately. Anything else?"

Maddox withdrew her hand, revealing a half-inch-long incision, and handed the long silver cutter out to me. I took it automatically, knowing she needed to move quickly.

"Yeah," I replied, my stomach flopping around with anxiety as each second dragged on. If she woke up while we were doing this...

I shook it off and answered Quess's question as he handed the net, now clean and glistening with sterilizing liquid, back to Maddox. "I've got the guy who cut my throat."

Quess froze, but Maddox remained focused as she slid the net into the incision with a pair of tweezers, using them to push it all the way into Sadie's neck. As soon as she was satisfied, she handed me the tweezers and pulled out a silver canister. A press on the top spilled some pink foam onto her fingertip, and she gently smoothed the mousse over the wound. It would be healed in a matter of minutes.

"Talk about it later," she said as she got off Sadie. "Quess, how is this going to work?"

"Prop her up against me," he said, and within moments the three of us were lifting her onto her feet, Quess's large arm around her waist helping to brace her. Her head rolled forward as we worked, and he reached over and gently positioned it against his shoulder so that it seemed she was sleeping against him.

"I've got her on a sort of loop," he told us softly, shifting her weight a little bit. "Right after you left and Maddox got back, I gave her a quarter pill, and we staged a new arrival scene without you, saying you'd been called away, and then I guided her through things. The sedative made her dopey, but she was able to follow along and jump to the conclusions we set up for her. I gave her a half of a pill forty minutes later, and every thirty minutes after that, restarting the loop in her mind so that there was still a ten-minute sequence of her arriving and interacting with us. Hopefully, this next one won't eat too much into that time, so she has at least some memory of being here."

I nodded in wordless agreement. Our entire plan hung on this one thing, and if it didn't work, Sadie might remember too much and figure out that something was up. If she put everything together and realized that we had pulled one over on her to raid her quarters... then nowhere in the Tower would be safe for us.

Summoning up a deep calm, I took a few steps back and waited for her to wake up. Maddox moved to join me.

It only took a minute for Sadie to give a soft little groan, and her head shifted, nestling into the crook of Quess's shoulder. "You smell nice," she slurred, and I reached out and grabbed Maddox's forearm before the statuesque woman could think to move.

The muscles under her skin were tight, but as I glanced at her, I saw her giving me an annoyed look that told me I was overreacting. She wasn't going to screw this up.

"CEO Monroe?" Quess asked, and something about his tone implied that he'd said it once before and was both nervous and embarrassed to have to do it again.

Sadie murmured something incoherent against his neck with a little snort. Quess cleared his throat and repeated, "CEO Monroe?" in a firmer voice, but there was an undercurrent of panic to it.

Her head rolled up, and she blinked at Quess blearily. "Wha—"

I nodded at Maddox, and we resumed our walk over. "CEO Monroe," I said loudly, putting a note of disapproval in my voice. "Knight Commander Worthington. How is the investigation going?"

Quess took a quick step away from Sadie, and I was surprised to see a flush forming in his cheeks. I gave him an internal nod of respect for taking his role that far, and then returned my focus to Sadie.

She, however, was considerably less embarrassed, given the displeased curl of her lips. "You're back," she said haughtily. "I'm surprised you even bothered to show."

I kept my face expressionless but was grateful to see that she hadn't remembered the first time she arrived—when I'd been here to greet her. "My apologies," I replied, keeping my voice as empty as possible to tell her I wasn't sorry at all. "I was dealing with a potential undoc situation." It wasn't technically a lie, which was why I probably shouldn't have said it, but it was worth it to watch her eyes narrow into slits.

"I see," she said primly. "Well, Knight Commander Worthington and I are still conducting our analysis." Her tone was dismissive, and she even went so far as to turn her back to me, but stopped mid-motion when Quess cleared his throat and gave her an apologetic look.

"CEO Monroe... we finished the analysis, remember? Is that headache still bothering you? Or was the medicine I gave you too strong? I'm so terribly sorry..." He held out the pad, his eyes brimming with uncertainty, and I almost gagged at Sadie's positively feline response.

"It's fine, Sam," she said soothingly, but there was a greasy undercurrent that made me sick. Enough was enough.

"Sam?" I asked, raising an eyebrow. "You're on a first-name basis with the Knight Commander I put in charge of maintaining our servers and computers?"

"Internal server police," Quess corrected softly, and I speared him with a look so fierce that for a second, I thought his recoil was real. It wasn't, of course, but even if it had been, I would've gone for it anyway.

"Care to correct me again, Worthington?" I growled menacingly, and he quickly shook his head.

"No, ma'am."

Sadie tsked and took the pad out of Quess's hand. "What a way you have with your people," she remarked, condescension thick in her voice. "Especially with such a talented Knight. I'm quite surprised that our department hasn't poached you yet, Sam."

I raised an eyebrow at her as Quess somehow managed another flush—I was going to ask him about that later—but this was dragging on far too long already. "I'm sorry, are you questioning my ability to run my own department?"

"Always," Sadie replied with another feline smile. "Anyway, it seems that Knight Commander Worthington is correct. We have finished, and the medication he gave me to combat a headache was fairly strong. I apologize for drifting off on you like that, Sam."

Quess widened his eyes and shook his head. "Oh, no, ma'am. It's not your fault; it's mine. If you'd like, I could escort you to the Medica, so we can make sure you are all right."

I could've killed him with a single look. The last thing we needed was for her to go to the Medica and get checked out. One look at her blood would definitely reveal the sedative and could even reveal Spero. I wasn't sure if they'd be able to figure out what it was, but it wasn't even worth the risk.

Not to mention, we needed Quess to upload Jasper and Rose. They were waiting. They *had* been waiting too long already. I didn't want them to wait a second longer, and if Quess left, it would mean that we couldn't upload them until Leo arrived.

But Quess seemed to have a better read on Sadie than I thought. "No," she said, finality in her voice. "I'm *truly* sorry, but I just don't have the time. I'm already behind on my schedule, and I'm sure I'll be fine. That nap seems to already have me feeling as good as new."

Maddox growled as Sadie winked at Quess, and I tensed, wondering if Sadie would notice.

She didn't, however, and bent over to pick up her bag, tucking her pad into it. "Champion," she said curtly.

"Hold up," I said before she could even take her first step. "What was the problem with my room?"

"It seems to have been a random glitch," she announced. "I'm sure you won't understand the details, but suffice it to say I have fixed it, and it shouldn't happen again."

I gave her a doubtful look. "Could this affect the other councilors' quarters?"

She shook her head, her face annoyed. "It was a random error," she repeated slowly, and I resisted the urge to smack her. "My report will be sent to you shortly."

I gave her a bright and vacuous smile in response. "Thank you ever so much for your help," I told her lightly. "And I hope that you can catch up on your schedule. Lieutenant Kerrin?"

Maddox nodded, echoing my empty, yet chipper, smile, and began leading Sadie away toward the elevator. I started walking toward where Maddox had set the hard drives before they were even on board, but as soon as the door shut between us, I was racing toward them.

"Call Leo!" I ordered Quess as I picked up the veritable tower of plastic boxes. "Get him and Alex down here." I checked my watch and saw with great relief that we still had two minutes left.

But that didn't mean we were out of the woods. We still had Baldy to deal with, fallout to worry about, and two AIs to break apart.

5

I was watching the status bar showing the upload status for Jasper and Rose when Alex and Leo entered, holding Baldy mostly aloft between them. His legs dragged across the floor, and the two men eventually put him down halfway between us and the terminal. I patted Quess's shoulder as he continued to work on the download and then moved to meet them.

I gave Leo an encouraging smile as he passed but slowed to a stop in front of my brother, summoning up some courage. He was mad at me—had every right to be, really—and I owed him an apology. All he'd wanted was to be a part of the investigation I was conducting against the people who had killed our mother, and I had cut him out. It hadn't been entirely intentional on my part, but that didn't change the fact that I had hurt him.

"Alex, I am truly sorry about not including you in everything," I said softly. "I promise that from here on out—"

"Never mind all that," he said excitedly, a hand cutting through the air between us to emphasize the statement. "We finally have a legacy, Liana! We can find out what happened to our mom and what they are doing to Scipio!"

I glanced at Baldy over my brother's shoulder and then looked back to him, taken aback by his sudden change of tune. Hours ago, he'd been ready to tear me a new one. Now he was practically sparkling at the idea of having answers within reach at last. The rapid shift in his behavior confused me, but maybe Leo had talked to him, or it had hit Alex that there was a way forward with all of this insanity.

Either way, I was all for it. I longed for answers, too—hell, it was the reason I had chosen not to kill Baldy in the first place—but that didn't mean he was going to speak to us. If anything, he was probably going to keep quiet about what he knew and bide his time until he could make some sort of escape, or signal someone for help.

But we had another way, and I needed to let my brother know about it so he didn't waste his time with Baldy. "Alex, we have better than that," I said excitedly, touching his arm. "We stole all of Sadie's files from her computer. I'm pretty sure that the answers we need are there. Let's tie Baldy up, do some research, and see if we can't figure out who, exactly, is to blame for our mom's death."

My brother frowned at me. "That'll be hours," he said, taking a slow step back. "We have this guy. We should question him now."

I sighed. "Alex, he's not going to tell us anything, but we might not need him to!"

"So then why is he here?" my brother retorted, exasperated. "Why risk bringing him here if not to question him?"

I hesitated. I had just been asking myself the same thing. At the time, it had seemed so clear to me, but now that he was here and I had taken a beat to think about it, I realized it had been a really stupid move. Not only was he dangerous, his people were going to come looking for him. And he wouldn't talk to us—wouldn't do anything to reveal their plans or tell us who they were. Not to mention, we didn't really need him if Sadie's files provided us with the evidence we wanted. If I had really thought it through in Sadie's apartment, I would've killed him and been done with it. But my desire to know the who of it all had been too compelling at the time, and I wasn't one hundred percent *certain* that Sadie's files would yield results.

"It was a spur-of-the moment decision," I admitted. "And I didn't think it through. But there's no point in questioning him. He won't talk."

"Well, we have to try." Alex raked a hand through his long hair, gathering the dark locks together so he could wrap a band around them. "Because as far as I can tell, you have currently done nothing in the search for Mom's murderer."

My mouth dropped open at his remark. I was shocked that he would even say that. It wasn't that I had forgotten about Mom's death, but I had prioritized retrieving Jasper and Rose when I had to. Not to mention, that was really unfair, given how difficult the legacies *were* to track down. Still, he was right, in a way. I hadn't gotten far in finding Mom's killers. So I closed my mouth, guilty.

The past three days had gotten us a lot, but not exactly an answer to the burning question in both our minds.

I stared at Baldy's splayed-out form, remembering the look on his face as he pointed the knife at Leo's chest when he attacked us on the catwalk, and the feel of the knife when he cut my throat.

And even though I knew it wouldn't do me any good, a deep, dark part of me wanted to confront him for everything he'd done to me and my friends. And Alex seemed to be speaking directly to it, because his words were beginning to make sense. Plus, I found I couldn't deny him this request, considering how I'd ignored him in the preceding days. He was right that we needed to know what was going on, and maybe if we *could* get Baldy to talk...

"Fine," I said, my hesitation still lingering for a few seconds. "I'll get a chair, and we'll tie him to it. Quess should have some smelling salts in his bag. We'll wake him up and ask him." My brother gave me a satisfied smile, but it froze on his face when I added, "But if he doesn't talk, we knock him out and then figure out some other way to use him."

The smile twisted into a scowl. Alex crossed his arms. "We'll see," he retorted, and I sighed.

He and I spent the next few minutes getting ready—I summoned a chair using the controls in the column in the middle of the room—and then we heaved him into it. I was already tired from lifting so much dead weight earlier with his five friends, but together, we managed. Alex tied him up, and I went to find Quess's medical bag to recover a pill of smelling salts.

Before we were finished setting up, Quess announced that the download of Jasper and Rose was completed. Leo gave me a questioning look, his brown eyes alight with indecision, and I knew he didn't want to leave me with this if I couldn't handle it. But that was ridiculous; Jasper and Rose needed him. And although I was tired, I felt pretty confident that I could handle this exchange with Baldy, so I told him to help Jasper and Rose and make certain they were all right.

He sat down quickly and began typing, filling the cavernous space with the sound of keys being clicked. I found myself wanting to be standing next to him, trying to help Jasper and Rose, instead of over here, about to come face-to-face with a man who had tried to kill me three times.

Heavy was the head that wore the crown, or some such crap, I thought to myself, mentally preparing for what I had to do.

Still, as I crossed the room, pill in hand, a strange queasiness started to fill my stomach, and my instincts began to scream at me that this was a bad idea. But a look at my brother's determined face as he waited for me to come over told me that expressing it to him would only make things worse. So instead, I summoned up another deep calm, handed the salts to my brother, and looked at Quess and Maddox.

"I'll handle the questions," I announced softly. My brother snorted derisively but didn't object. He snapped open the pill, then waved it under Baldy's nose.

The effect was almost instantaneous. Baldy's eyes snapped open, his head jerking up and back and forth wildly. He glanced at me, my brother, and then all around him, his shoulders straining against the restraints around his wrists. He made a guttural roar that made me shut one eye against the volume of it, and, his panic mounting, he began to rock back and forth in the chair. It tipped, and I quickly planted a boot on the lower rung as he extended past the center of gravity, catching the chair and his weight before he could fall.

He gave a startled yip as I balanced him on the two back legs of the chair, and lifted his neck to look up at me, his blue-green eyes a vicious glare. "You're dead, bitch," he spat. "You and your little friends are—"

I lifted my foot and let him fall before he could say any more. I had to admit to myself that as petty as the act was, it definitely went a long way toward making me feel better—especially when I heard his head smack against the floor, followed by his inhalation of pain.

Alex chuckled next to me, and even I couldn't hide my smile. No, it didn't make up for him cutting my throat, but there was something very satisfying about inflicting a little bit of pain in exchange for the wrongs he had committed against us. The power and control that I now had over him were alluring, and suddenly I wasn't as afraid of him as I had been.

We bent over and pulled him back up, setting the chair onto all fours. He glared at us the entire time, but I kept my face impassive and ignored it. I backed away as soon as I was done and folded my arms across my chest.

"So, should I be worried that you're stalking me?" I asked. "Because it is weird that we would keep running into each other. I mean, three times in a week is pretty excessive, and given that you attacked me two of those three times, my brother thinks that you might be part of a terrorist cell trying to destroy Scipio and trying to kill me because you know I can stop you."

Baldy shook his head as if I had punched him, and then his face hardened. "I should've left you to bleed out on the floor," he said with a sneer. "Blood spurting out of your neck is a good look for you."

Beside me, I felt my brother tense, but I couldn't focus on it. Baldy's words had forced the awful memory of the event back into my mind, and for a second, the sensation of drowning on my own blood as it spurted through my fingers flooded my senses. I closed my eyes, trying to block the vision, but it didn't help. The bastard noticed, too, because he gave a sharp, barking laugh.

"That's right, honey," he said. "You and I have shared something more powerful than anything you can ever have with anyone else. I held your life in my hands. I left your friends the tools to save it. All I had to do was cut you and walk away, and you'd be dead, just like your stupid bitch mother."

"Shut up," my brother growled next to me, and I reached out blindly for him, finding his forearm. It helped ground me, helped remind me that the sensation of blood in my throat wasn't real, and I opened my eyes and stared at Baldy, a fire burning in my soul.

"Did you kill her?" I demanded. "Did you give the order to the sentinel and send it in there?"

He bared his teeth at me. "Who, me? Nah. Not me. But me and the others loooooved watching the vid file of her falling. We watched it over and over and over again, and we laughed and laughed. The way her legs and arms flailed, and the look on her face..."

He started laughing then, but it was short-lived, as Alex

suddenly stepped close and rammed his fist into Baldy's jaw. There was a sharp, wet snap, and Baldy's head jerked to one side, blood spurting from his lip. He sat stunned for a second or two, and then gave a surprised, huffing laugh, interrupted only when he spat out a mouthful of blood.

A part of me wanted to stop Alex, but Baldy's words had set fire to a deep, bitter rage and acrid hatred—and that part of me took pleasure in watching him hurt.

"Gonna have to do better than that, boy," he chuckled, looking up at my brother and tonguing the area where Alex had split his lip open. His grin broadened, his eyes sparkling with something that looked like madness. "You can't stop what's coming, just like you couldn't stop what happened to your mother."

Crack. Baldy's head snapped back as my brother struck him again, this time from the other side. He shook for a second, and then laughter began to erupt from his throat. "Can't protect Mom... Can't protect Baby Sister..." he sang tauntingly. "Gonna watch them die, Big Brother. Can promise you that."

"Shut up!" my brother shouted, and his fist lashed out again, catching Baldy in the nose with a sharp crunch. Blood spurted from the wound, but Baldy continued to chortle, his bound boots slapping the ground. "Tell me who you work for!" Alex shouted.

Smack.

I flinched, the fourth hit feeling like a step too far. "Alex," I said softly. "Stop."

But my brother ignored me, driving his fist into Baldy's stomach again and again. The breath exploded out of him in sharp grunts, and he began to hack and wheeze for air, the laughter dying out.

"Tell me where to find your people!" my brother shouted, his face dark with the promise of violence. I'd never seen him look at anyone like that before, and it was starting to scare me. His arm swung again.

"Alex," I said more sharply, moving toward him even as another wet crack filled the air. This was spinning out of control. "Stop! I—"

His fist fell again, and then again, and when I put my hand on his shoulder to pull him off, he pushed me back and continued to pummel Baldy, shouting, "Tell me what you did to Scipio! Tell me! *Tell me*!"

"Quess, Leo!" I yelled, catching my balance from his shove. "Help—"

"*LIANA!*" came a loud, horrified cry, and it was loud enough to make my brother freeze. My eyes widened as I recognized it, and I whirled to see the youngest member of our makeshift family, Tian, standing there, her blue eyes wide and filled with horror.

But what was worse was the boy standing right next to her, bound up in her lashes. His face was pale, making the freckles on it stand out in stark comparison, and he was staring in abject terror at the man on the chair. I recognized him from my attack in the Attic. I'd been following him, and he'd led me back to his legacy home, where Baldy and at least thirty others lived.

And he'd just seen us beating one of his fellow legacies.

6

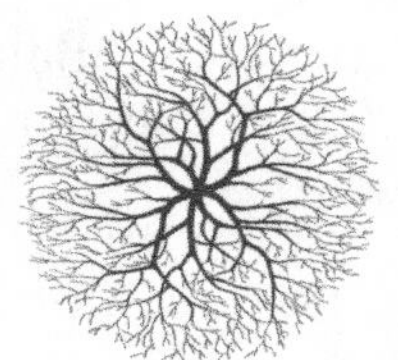

I quickly blocked Tian and the young boy's view and ushered them out of the room, telling Tian to find somewhere to hide for the next hour and then come back with her guest. Tian's face was tight and nervous as she looked at the boy, whom she awkwardly introduced as Liam, and his face was grim, eyes full of anger and hatred directed at all of us. I couldn't blame him. We'd attacked someone who must have been tantamount to a family member while he was helpless. We were monsters to him.

Then again, Tian *had* kidnapped him, so we hadn't really started off on the right foot to begin with.

Which really sucked. Because while getting Baldy to talk was clearly not happening, persuading the boy to join our side might've been a golden opportunity in disguise, and completely possible—had we not been smashing the face of someone he knew. Earning any form of trust now was going to be difficult, and I wouldn't blame him if he never gave it to us.

Once they were gone, I turned back to Alex and Baldy, and

noticed that Quess was already kneeling next to Baldy's chair, administering first aid. Alex was watching, his eyes dark and brooding, occasionally waggling his curled fingers in a move I recognized all too well; they were hurting from all the punches he'd delivered.

I considered him, wondering what I was supposed to do. On the one hand, Baldy had hit a very sore spot for both of us, and a part of me felt like he deserved what he got. On the other...

I looked down at the blood splatters on the floor around the chair, and my stomach clenched. Baldy had tried to kill me multiple times. First in the Medica when we went to rescue Maddox from Devon Alexander, the former Champion, and then on the catwalk when Leo had been pouring his heart out to me. And then finally in the Attic, when he had cut my throat.

But even with all of that stacked against him, what I had been allowing to go on was unconscionable—not for him, but for me. For my soul or spirit or heart, whatever you wanted to call it. I had felt it even before Tian showed up, but the look on the young man's face sealed the deal for me. I didn't want to be the sort of person who could condone torture, no matter who the prisoner was or what they had done. I couldn't let this happen again, no matter what Baldy had done to me.

I approached my brother slowly, coming up beside him. He made no move to acknowledge me, but I waited for him to, wondering what he was feeling. In a way, I was guilty for his response to this; I'd cut him out, left him with unanswered questions and an anger burning in his heart.

But that didn't excuse the fact that he had lost control and might've beaten Baldy to death in a mindless, uncontrolled rage.

Yet given that was his reaction to Baldy's claim that he was a failure... *Was* that the root of Alex's anger? Our mother had just died, and neither of us had a particularly good relationship with her. In my case, however, things had been shifting toward the end of her life. So when I lost her, it had hit me harder than I thought it would, because I'd been starting to see a possibility for reconciliation, only to have it stolen away from me.

In his case, though, it had been over a year since he'd seen her. Not since our birthday dinner, when they had fought over Alex's decision to join IT instead of the Knights. She didn't understand why he didn't want to be a Knight, and now I wondered if my brother wasn't questioning that decision himself, thinking that maybe if he had followed a different path, he would've been able to keep us safe.

I imagined that stung a lot. And when he'd reached out to me, trying to make sense of everything, I'd blown him off, or forgotten to net him. I'd left him alone to deal with his pain. And though I'd wanted to be alone to process *my* pain, that didn't mean *he* had. He had needed his best friend, his sister, his twin, and I hadn't been there for him. I'd failed him.

"Alex," I said hesitantly. "Are you—"

"I'm not sorry," Alex interrupted abruptly, and I blinked and looked up at him, alarm spreading through me at his words. "This guy deserves much more—and worse—for what he did to you."

For several seconds, I was stunned by the vehemence of his response. I had expected guilt out of him, for losing control, but not this deep rage that seemed to be consuming him. Once again, I felt like I was being confronted by a total stranger, but that couldn't be possible. This was Alex, my *twin*.

I considered what he said for several moments, trying to rationalize this new behavior, as I watched Quess straighten Baldy's broken nose by pinching the bridge between two fingers. I could comprehend his anger to a certain extent; it was an understandable reaction to the injustices we had suffered at the hands of our enemies. But in my brother's case, his rage was borderline unhealthy, a way of easing the pain inside through some form of immediate and violent action. But that wasn't justice. It was vengeance. And if my brother continued down this path, I feared what would happen to him.

"You lost control, Alex," I said softly. "I told you he wasn't going to talk."

"You were right," he said before I could form any sort of conclusion, and a curious warmth curled through me. I was? "He wasn't going to talk. And he's still a threat. We should kill him."

I pressed my lips together, disappointed that he wasn't admitting to the fact that he'd lost control. Was he really blind to it, or did he believe that what he had been doing was right? I wasn't sure, but either way, it was starting to scare me.

Especially because it was so shortsighted. "If we kill him, then we definitely lose any chance of getting the boy Tian brought back to help us, if we haven't lost it already, after... what happened."

"Yeah, about that," Quess cut in, and I could tell from the discomfort in his voice that he was angling to change the subject. "Did you get an explanation from her as to how and where she found him? Were there others? Was she seen?"

I exhaled, trying to tamp down my irritation. The answer was that I *hadn't* gotten an explanation, and the reason was that I couldn't bear to see Tian's or the boy's faces looking at us like that anymore. I'd get the story from her later, once I got this taken care of.

"No," I told him simply. "Let's get through problems A through D first."

Quess snorted as he pressed the bone-mending patch over Baldy's broken nose. "We'd be lucky to have only four problems," he muttered, and a startled laugh escaped me. There was truth in his words, and, Scipio help me, it made me tired more than anything.

The momentary levity slowly melted away as I heard my brother make an aggravated noise and shift his weight. "We'd have one less problem if you'd just stop patching him up and kill him already," he snarled. "He's a threat, he's no good to us, and keeping him alive is dangerous. If he breaks free from this room and lets his people know what we know, they'll hunt us down and kill us all. Why are we still talking about this?"

My lips formed a thin line, and I fought the rising urge to shake him at his continued shortsightedness and bloodthirsty attitude. It was really starting to scare me, but even more than that, it lacked any rationality. Even if we couldn't get answers out of Baldy, that didn't mean we couldn't use him for something. Not to mention, the boy Tian brought in knew Baldy. There had to be a way to exploit that connection. But not if we just beat on Baldy for no good reason.

"Alex, he's still valuable, alive or dead. You need to take a breath and slow down. We have a ton of information to go through from Sadie's computer, and once Leo gets Jasper and Rose separated and back online, they might be able to help us learn what's actually going on. We're going to figure this out. Together."

On impulse, I reached out to touch his forearm, to comfort him, but as soon as my fingers stroked over his uniform, he jerked away from me, whirling around to present me with his back.

"Alex?" I asked, concerned and hurt by his reaction.

He stood there for several seconds, his back and shoulders rising and falling as he tried to calm himself, catch his breath... something. I couldn't tell what was going on. All I knew was that it was dark, turbulent, and seemed to be consuming him. My twin. The only other human being in the world I felt fully connected to.

"Alex," I said pleadingly, my heart overflowing with worry and concern. "Talk to me. I know I've been a crappy sister, but—"

He whirled around, his eyes blazing behind his glasses. "I don't want to talk. I want to *do* something. I want to find the guys who hurt you and killed Mom and make them pay. Why is that so hard for you to understand? Why are you hesitating now, after everything that has happened? Do you not care that they're killing

Scipio? Do you not care that thousands of people are going to die if they get what they want?"

My brows drew tightly together, and I took a step back, the sting of his words and insinuations almost enough to make me want to walk away. I tried to remind myself that this wasn't Alex—that he was in pain and upset because things were moving too slowly.

But I was rapidly running out of excuses for him, and I wasn't sure what to do with this person wearing my brother's face, because it certainly wasn't him.

"Don't talk to your sister like that," I heard Leo say angrily from behind me, and a second later I felt his hands sliding over my shoulders, holding me upright just as I was about to falter. I shot him a grateful look, but he ignored it as he speared Alex with a glare. "She cares more about the Tower and the people in it than I'd wager most do, and I won't let you say anything to the contrary! Of course she cares, and she's working on it. We all are. But it isn't something we can rush, no matter how much you want to, so stop attacking your sister. She is doing the best she can, and you should acknowledge and respect that."

His words helped take away some of the pain from Alex's words. But only some.

My brother glared at him, and then made an irritated noise. "You're right," he finally said, but there was still an angry undercurrent to his voice. "She is doing the best she can. I'm just... frustrated. I'll go for a walk and try to clear my head."

"You do that," Leo said, and there was a firmness in his voice that said Alex was going to leave whether he liked it or not. I didn't like it, but I realized that maybe he needed it.

My brother was already turning to walk away but grunted an acknowledgment over his shoulder, followed by an, "I'll be back soon."

The words filled me with an ominous dread, but I kept my mouth shut and let him go, hoping that Leo was right.

7

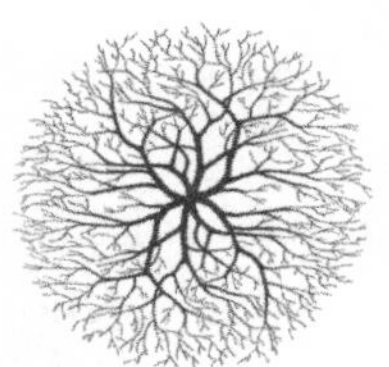

The juxtaposition of the nonstop adrenaline rush that had been the last twelve hours or so and the quiet waiting that occurred in the long hours after was like the slow twist of a dagger, agonizing in both its intensity and anticipation, as I wondered when the end would come. Even though we had more than enough to occupy ourselves while we waited for Sadie's call to the council to report her quarters malfunction, it never seemed like quite enough to distract us from the relentlessly slow movements of the clock. In short, we were spread out, thinner than rice paper.

Staying busy was the only thing that kept me from freaking out as time churned on, and luckily, there was a lot to do. I started with putting the walls and furniture of the apartment back in place and added two modified rooms for our prisoners. I wound up fiddling with the details for an hour, trying to kill some time while I waited, but at a certain point it became annoying and tedious. I wanted to move on to something else, even though I knew it wouldn't do me any good. Baldy, still unconscious from the beating earlier and bound using a pair of cuffs, went in one new room, and the boy, Liam, went into the other. Tian opted to stay with him, to see if she could convince him that we weren't going to hurt him, but after what he had seen, I knew only time and space would allow him to see that.

After that, Maddox had to go meet with the Knight Commanders to keep up appearances, and Quess went with her, as a Knight Commander of an internal department. I envied her for that, but also recognized that if I had gone, I would've gone insane from the anxiety.

Besides, doing all of those things did nothing to answer one of the other things causing my stress to mount as time wore on—what was happening to Jasper and Rose. So, I busied myself with trying to help Leo, going through Lionel Scipio's files to try to figure out *why* Jasper was attacking Rose, while he worked tirelessly on trying to separate the two programs.

Unfortunately, the files were two parts technical and one part psychological, and I couldn't make heads or tails of any of it, beyond a few extra details that didn't help us much. It was beyond frustrating, as I was the least technically savvy of our group, and as each moment went on without news of either AI's welfare, I grew more and more agitated by my limited capabilities. I tried to absorb as much as I could, scanning for some hidden clue in the detailed notes.

Luckily, some of it was interesting. Even if it didn't do much to pass the time.

The AIs had been created using neural scans of the five founders of the Tower, those scans stripped of all the human memories, save one: each founder's "core memory." Those memories were the cornerstones for the new AI personalities, the seeds from which they developed. Jasper was based on the founder of the Medica, Samantha Reed, and apparently her core memory had centered on her relationship with the grandfather who had raised her, and who had been some sort of famous detective. The memory in question was her playing with some sort of puzzle that he had laid out for her to solve, and from it came Jasper's analytical and diagnostic skills. These, his most successful traits, were incorporated into Scipio's coding once they were joined.

Learning that had taken me all of thirty-five minutes. No word from the council. No progress with Jasper and Rose. I stopped long enough to study Leo, and then picked up another file when I realized asking him anything would only disrupt his focus.

Rose, on the other hand, was based on a woman named Jang-Mi, whose core memory was centered around the loss of her daughter, Yu-Na. That loss translated into Rose viewing all the citizens of the Tower as her children and being ruled by a desire to protect them from harm. It was what had carried her program far during the trials. But it failed her when the loss of human life became too high, and her grief became too powerful for her to continue. From her came a lens of maternal love, which Scipio was supposed to use when thinking about the citizens of the Tower.

I sighed and closed the file. Another half an hour gone. Still nothing. My skin crawled, and I was hyperaware of the time, but I ignored it, knowing it was too early to give in to panic.

Then there was Kurt, the protector. I found that role for him a little odd, considering his program was based on Ezekial Pine, the man who had murdered Lionel Scipio and tried to kill Leo, the backup version of Scipio. But apparently his core memory was based on his experience in the military, and a situation where he'd pulled nearly every one of his soldiers from danger and saved them in an act of altruistic brotherhood. Clearly Pine's views of brotherhood had limits, but perhaps Kurt was different. I'd recently learned from the legacy net Lacey had given me that her family had recovered him, but I hadn't had a chance to confront the head of the Mechanics Department yet.

But then again, I didn't fear for his safety like I had feared for

Jasper and Rose's. Lacey was from another legacy family who had been working with the head of Water Treatment, Praetor Strum, to stop the legacies from hurting or controlling Scipio. I wasn't sure how much they knew of the big picture, but her family had managed to keep Kurt from falling into the hands of their enemies, and I hoped that meant he was safe.

Another twenty-five minutes gone—another twenty-five minutes of silence. It was starting to grate, but I pressed on.

The other two programs were unaccounted for, but thanks to the files, I had an idea of what they'd been doing for Scipio. Alice had been the first program to fail in the trials. Her contributions to Scipio's programming were fear and self-preservation, and had been based on a woman named Aelish Mikhailov, who was the founder of the Mechanics Department. Tony, the second program to fail, had been the heart of Scipio's creativity, his human counterpart a man named Anthony Kahananui. The man, a respected marine biologist and ocean conservationist who had created Water Treatment, had been from some place called Hawai'i. He'd also helped design the Terraces in Greenery 1.

It was all fascinating, but ultimately did nothing to help Leo, Jasper, or Rose. I tossed the folder down on the desk with a long groan and turned my eyes to the clock. Another forty minutes gone. "Leo?" I asked, trying to put a lot of meaning into his name.

"It's done," he said grimly, his fingers still going. "It's been done for thirty minutes. But they are both offline... unconscious... and I can't seem to wake them up."

I studied him, deciding not to get angry that he had gotten them separated without telling me. "You should get some rest," I said softly, concerned by the dark shadows that were collecting under his eyes. "You've been going nonstop since this morning, so if they're separated and stabilized, then maybe give it a few hours, and come back fresh?"

"I'm fine," he said, not even casting a glance at me. I hesitated, warring with the decision to insist, but decided to let it go. I wanted to make sure the programs were okay as well.

So we continued working together, side by side. Reading the files on the AIs had been interesting at first, but then the files grew too technical for me to follow, and sitting there for hours on end, doing nothing really productive except waiting for the call from Sadie or for Jasper and Rose to wake up, had me going a little stir crazy. Specific fears and worries kept crossing my mind, the chief of which was: What if I had somehow recorded a memory in Sadie's legacy net while I was shooting Baldy's friends? She'd know everything if I had, and probably wouldn't even bother to call the council. Because she could just send her undoc army after me to take back what I had stolen. She could be organizing an attack right now, putting her people in place and arming them with cutters, batons, pulse shields... anything that she could. And there were at least thirty of them. I'd set up my defenses well, but I knew that if someone wanted to get in, they would find a way in. We had, after all. The fear only grew as I realized that it could explain the delay in her call, and could mean that even now she was trying to get something in place to breach my quarters.

The idea made me want to gather everyone and run, try to hide again, keep us safe.

But I refused to give in to the negative thinking, reminding myself that half the reason our plan had worked was because Sadie had been doing a complete inspection of her department, and had mentioned needing to continue it before she left. We had delayed her task by a couple of hours, and her department was large enough that it would've taken her several more hours, even without our interference. She probably wasn't even paying attention to anything else. Yet.

But as soon as that logic was in place, another problem crept into my mind, namely what I was going to do about Alex. He was a liability right now, both because his self-control had all but eroded, and because he didn't seem to care about what he had done. I wasn't even sure how to reach him at this point if he didn't understand the wrongness of his actions. And I was lost in regard to how to handle it. As a leader, it was my job to assess his fitness for the mission, and he was definitely currently unfit. As his sister... I couldn't just tell him he couldn't help because he was not stable. I was pretty sure doing so would cost me my relationship with him, and it was too precious to me to let that happen. But then, what could I do? How could I reach him? Why was he taking this so hard? I wanted to know, to ask him, but after he had stormed off, I hadn't heard from him. I was beginning to worry, but wanted to hold off netting him to give him some space and time.

In truth, I was hoping that with time would come perspective, making him realize how far off the rails he'd gone. I was praying for it, actually.

And once that nebulous situation churned around in my skull a few times with no answer in sight, my mind decided to ask the bigger, even scarier question: What do we do *next*? That one scared me the most, because to be honest, I wasn't certain. We had just saved Jasper and Rose, but now what? Both were still offline, we had no idea how damaged either program was, and we couldn't be sure that Jasper was still himself. Rose had been tortured and traumatized until she broke, undergoing a process of reversion that let the Jang-Mi part of her free. I knew we needed the AIs to save Scipio, but we only had two out of five, and two more were unaccounted for. Rose was broken; Jasper's condition was unknown. If the two missing programs were in the same condition, then I wasn't sure we could do anything at all.

Which meant going after the legacies. If we could just get them off the board somehow, we could at least stop them from damaging Scipio any more than they already had. And that would give us time to find a way to restore him, provided we managed to get every single one of the bad guys at the same time. If we didn't, then whoever escaped would be free to try again, or worse, finish the job.

Sadie's files would hopefully reveal her network—every single person she was working with. If we had that, then we could stop them, once and for all. But if she was smart, and kept that information off her terminal, then we'd never be able to stop them. Missing even one could mean the difference between victory and defeat.

I was so grateful when Maddox returned from her meeting. We had held off from moving the contraband items we had hidden in a storage room before we reset the quarters, uncertain of what would happen to them during the reset process. She had insisted on waiting until after her meeting was done before we started fetching them, so no one was out there alone, but now that she was free, she and I could get it done.

Keeping them there had been risky, considering they included piles and piles of IT manuals that were illegal to possess, and even though I had locked the room down under my authority, someone would eventually notice and wonder why. Better to move them now than risk any unwanted questions.

Hauling the boxes through the halls was mind-numbing, back-breaking work, but even though I was exhausted from everything we had done today, I found I didn't mind the activity. It gave me something to focus on other than all the problems we were facing. Something easy that I could complete with zero consequences.

I accepted the last boxes Maddox handed me, and then began walking back to the elevator, absorbed with balancing my load. I had taken an extra box this time in an effort to wrap things up, but keeping it on top of the others required all of my concentration. And I was so distracted that I failed to notice my brother coming around the corner from the elevator entrances and wound up walking right into him.

"Oof!" he exclaimed, and I jerked back and blinked at him in surprise.

"Alex?" Maddox asked, stepping around us both, her green eyes fluttering in confusion. "How'd you find us?"

My brother gave us a tight look as he rubbed his chest with one hand. "I called Leo and asked to be let back in," he announced haltingly. "He said I had to bring it up with you."

I hesitated and realized that Leo had sent me a message by sending my brother. He was letting me know that I could say no. As much as I appreciated the gesture, however, I sort of wished he had just let Alex in, and not put it on me. Especially since I couldn't tell if Alex was in the right headspace to deal with any of this, let alone talk about it. And it was selfish of me, but I still couldn't bring myself to tell him the truth and make him go, even with his behavior being so erratic and terrifying. I wanted to fix it, to help him, though I wasn't sure if I could, or if I'd only make it worse, and—

The sound of laughter caught my ear, and I looked down the circular hall ringing the core of the Citadel to see a group of Knights emerging from a side hall, headed for the elevator. And though I was the Champion, and could easily explain the boxes away, I immediately decided that it would be easier to just go before they got there. Not to mention, my brother seemed to be spoiling for a fight, and I didn't want him making a scene in the hall.

I started moving over to the elevator. "Let's go."

Maddox and Alex followed me onto the elevator as soon as the scan finished, and we began our descent just as the group of Knights came to stand at the entrance. I smiled tightly and gave them a sharp nod, which many of them returned with enthusiastic smiles, one of them going so far as to whisper, "It's Honorbound," in an awe-filled voice.

I hadn't really gotten to interact with many of the Knights since I became Champion, and even though I knew they'd voted me into the position, it was still weird to see so much joy and enthusiasm directed toward me. To some of them, I was a hero; I had protected Scipio from the previous Champion, gaining back a measure of integrity for the department, in their eyes. I had made them proud, and because of that, they had put their faith in me.

Of course, they'd lock me up in a second if they found out I had broken the law in more ways than I could count. Hell, I was moving away from them with contraband in my arms right here and now. But then again, they didn't know the truth of what was going on. My Knights were safe in their little bubble of belief that the Tower was as it always had been, not even realizing that it was slowly being corrupted. I did, however, and it was my responsibility to take care of it, by whatever means necessary.

It was a good reminder that I wasn't just fighting for my own life, and those of my friends.

I looked over at my twin for a second and pondered the possibility that in Alex's case, maybe he *couldn't* see that. Possibly even wouldn't, in his current state of mind. Maybe it was easier for him to just attack one problem with single-minded intensity, not caring about the big picture because it was too much for him to handle. Maybe he was letting his anger and hatred toward the people who had hurt me and killed Mom take him somewhere dark.

I would understand one, but not the other. In either case, I couldn't allow him in without making sure he had his priorities right. It would be too dangerous for me, for the group, and for any potential missions. If he was only focused on finding the person responsible for Mom's death, then I couldn't count on him to put the larger mission first. That could put all of us in danger, including him.

I needed to make him see that. He needed to know what the rules would be if we went any farther together. It was time to establish some boundaries.

"I don't know that I want you involved in this, at this point," I announced into the quiet of the shaft. His dark eyes flicked over at me, and he shifted. "You're becoming a liability. Your temper is out of control, and you're not looking at the big picture. You need—"

My brother made an irritated tsk, and anger started to creep up my spine, cold and hard. I turned toward him and peered at him over the boxes I held. "I mean it, Alex. You're going to follow my lead, or I'm not letting you back into my quarters, and I will revoke your access to the Citadel."

His eyes snapped to mine, dark with anger for several seconds. "Why am I not surprised?" He scoffed. "You were already cutting me off before, so why not just continue with it? It's not like I'm your twin or anything."

His words upset me. I had explained my position, but he was clearly trying to make it personal. "It's not like that, Alex," I informed him. "I have the others to think of, and I have an obligation to keep them safe from all dangers, both inside and out."

"An obligation," my brother repeated, his eyes narrowing. "An *obligation?* To them? What about to me? What about to our mother, who died helping you fight a machine that *your* enemies sent after *you*? The same machine, I might add, that we encountered before and that you *did nothing to stop*!"

That was a blow too low, or maybe too close to the truth for me, but either way, it hurt. Deeply. So deeply that I had to turn away from him for a second to try to regain my composure. He was right—I had known about the sentinel and had failed to stop it. There had been reasons at the time, but in retrospect, they didn't seem strong enough compared to what had been lost. I took a deep breath and tried to push my guilt aside, but it was hard.

"Alex, you need to stop talking about crap you don't understand," Maddox grated out. "You're acting like a complete and utter tool right now."

"You don't even know me," he bit out. "And you need to stay out of this."

"The hell I do," she shot back. "She is the only reason any of us are still alive right now, and I am not going to stand here and watch you attack her like this. She's your twin, your sister, for crying out loud! Why are you angry at her?"

The elevator was slowing to a stop, but I ignored it and turned a half-step to look at my brother and see what his answer would be.

"Because I'm scared for her!" he roared, and his answer was so unexpected that I took a step back from him. "She's been out there risking her life trying to find the people who killed our mom and hurt Scipio, and I have been stuck in IT, under surveillance, doing *nothing* to help. And then when I do, when I insist that we should kill Baldy, everyone looks at me like I'm a monster! I mean, she grabbed him on impulse and then decided it wasn't a very good idea after the fact?! And you support that, but my idea to keep everyone safe was just dismissed out of hand?"

Maddox's green eyes didn't even bat a lash, but her chin went up several notches higher. Pride and gratitude burst over me at her willingness to defend me, even if a small voice told me that it was only going to make Alex angrier. "Absolutely. We all make mistakes, and when we do, we adapt. But you need to own up to your part in all this and admit that you didn't have everyone's best interests in mind when you suggested killing him."

"What are you talking about?" he demanded belligerently. "I did what I could to try to find the bastards who killed my mother and hurt my sister, and I refuse to apologize for that. He deserves death for all the things we know he's done, and I'm betting there is a lot that we don't know! You want to keep him alive? Sleeping only a few precious feet from your rooms? Trying to escape, get revenge, whatever?" He took a beat in his impassioned rant to give her a cold and pitying look. "If you think that's a good idea, then maybe you need to reevaluate your priorities."

"That's enough," I said, both to him and to the churning and frothing mass my stomach had become as he spoke. *Maybe he has a point. Maybe keeping Baldy alive was a mistake,* a small, doubting voice whispered. *But then again, this doesn't sound like my brother at all. He might have convinced himself he was doing it for us, but the more he argues for this, the less I believe him.* I looked up at Alex, trying to search for some semblance of the man I had known before Mom's funeral, but found only anger and hate. The confines of the elevator felt uncomfortably tight just now, so it was a relief when it stopped.

The change in my brother had left me ice cold, and I needed time to think about how I was going to even begin to talk to him about his behavior. For now, it was time to simply reiterate my point and escape. "I set out my terms," I told him numbly, trying not to let the discomfort he had stirred in me show. "Follow them or don't."

I stalked forward, needing freedom from the tight confines of the elevator and my brother. I expected him to take a moment to think about what I said, but when he started following, I realized he wasn't going to.

And that he knew my threat had been a bluff. I didn't have it in me to cut him off yet, especially now that I realized something was wrong with him. And maybe he even had a point. I had made many mistakes. Was I just messing things up? Was I making things worse for us?

I considered the possibility as I turned left down the hall and followed the curve around until it headed down a short staircase to a wide-open conference room, where I would host my Knight Commanders meetings when I eventually had them.

It took the span of crossing the room for him to start talking again, only this time it was directed at me. "So what's your next step, then? What do you plan to do with Baldy?"

His words only added to the flames of doubt that he had breathed into me, hitting a topic I had already spent hours worrying over with no real result. I didn't have a plan beyond going through Sadie's files to see if we could find any incriminating evidence. And if she had been paranoid enough, she might have hidden all of that somewhere else. We might get nothing, and if that happened, I had no idea what the hell we were going to do.

Alex was waiting for an answer, and I had to give him one. I decided to hedge. "Alex, right now I am just focusing on making sure our tracks are covered. We still haven't heard from the council about Sadie's quarters, Jasper and Rose are offline, and I have two prisoners that I'm not entirely sure what to do with." I paused, realizing that bringing up Baldy wasn't a good idea, but it had already been said.

"I'm telling you what you should do, Lily," my brother replied, this time sadness cutting through the anger. "You just don't want to hear it. And I get it. You killed those people in Sadie's office a few hours ago, and you're having regrets. But you can't let that get in the way of what needs to be done here."

My fingers tightened around the boxes I was still holding, and I stopped in the hall just before the kitchen. That wasn't the same at all. If those people had caught Leo and me, *everyone* would've paid the price—including Alex. I'd *had* to kill them. Yes, taking Baldy had been a spur-of-the-moment decision that I regretted, but killing him now would be a lot different from killing those other people. *We* were different from that.

"It's not right, Alex," I told him finally.

"Liana, please," he pleaded, coming around to take one of the boxes off my stack. "Can't you see how dangerous he is? He almost killed you. Do you want him anywhere near the people you care about?"

His words were reasonable, his tone sincere, but I wasn't swayed. If anything, the fact that my brother was pleading with me to kill a helpless man I had locked up in one of the bedrooms made him a stranger to me. I hated that.

"Listen to yourself," I begged. "You want to kill a defenseless man. This isn't you."

His pupils dilated, his mouth pulling into a line hard enough it could've broken diamonds. "Maybe it isn't, but at least I am looking to the future. You barely have a plan! I can't believe that you're being so blind about all of this."

His condescension rankled me, and my doubts and concerns evaporated under a glowing heat that began to burn from the pit of my stomach. "Blind or not, *Big Brother*," I spat, spearing him with an angry look, "you need to understand that I am the Champion, not you. I make the decisions; you do not. If you cannot get behind that, then there is no place for you here, *comprende*?"

I turned away and resumed walking, leaving Alex to decide whether he could abide by my rules or not. Clearly, he wasn't willing to see reason, and if he kept fighting me, I would make him leave.

I had to. I couldn't afford the consequences if I didn't. If he didn't.

Unless this is just a ploy to get rid of him because you don't want to deal with this new, scary version of your brother, a spiteful voice whispered. I ignored it, but it was hard. It also had a point. I was so used to running things that it was possible I wasn't prepared to accept the fact that someone might have a better idea than me. And it wasn't like I hadn't harbored secret jealousies of Alex in the past. He had always been the "good" child. But I never held onto it long, especially when he made sure that I felt loved by him no matter what my rank was. I owed him so much; he'd always tried to take care of me.

But he had changed. He was changing. And that terrified me.

When I got to the war room, the first thing I did, after setting my boxes down on the conference table, was go up and see what was going on with Leo. He was sitting behind the desk on the dais overlooking the entrance and conference table, but to my surprise, he wasn't looking at the screen on the terminal and typing relentlessly. Instead, he was flipping through the files we'd recovered from Lionel Scipio's office.

"Hey," I said, coming around the desk. On the screen, I saw multiple windows and progress bars, and realized Leo was running some sort of diagnostic. "How are—"

"Incoming transmission from Lord Scipio," Cornelius, my virtual assistant, announced. "CEO Monroe has requested an emergency council meeting."

8

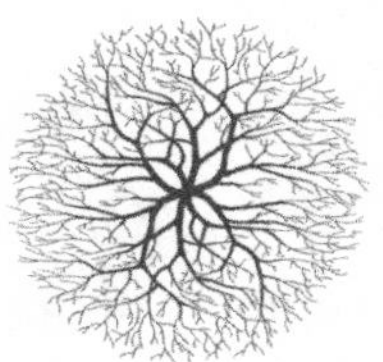

I looked at Leo and realized that this was it—we were going to find out if Sadie believed that her room resetting was a coincidence, or if she had somehow figured out what we had done and planned to accuse us. My stomach clenched with nervousness, but I forced my breathing to remain deep and even. There was no room for nerves, only calm, and what I hoped would be one amazing theatrical performance.

"Put him on speakers," I told Cornelius.

There was a soft pop, and then: "Champion Castell." Scipio spoke evenly, but with the ever-present curl of arrogance in his voice. "You are required for an emergency council session."

"By Sadie, yes. But whatever for?" I asked, putting just the right amount of curiosity in my voice.

"Please hold all questions until the other council members are online."

I shut my mouth and continued to focus on my breathing. Inside my head, I was imagining my reactions to certain things. If she accused me, it would have to be shock and righteous outrage. Maybe make a few comments about her inappropriate behavior with Quess while she was here, just to muddy up the waters. If she reported the reset, I needed to be concerned, but not overly so. Maybe I could be the first to suggest that someone had tampered with it—with both of ours—so it would continue to create confusion. But only if I felt the conversation slipping that way. I had to do this perfectly. One little slipup could have our entire house of lies crashing down on us.

Fingers crossed.

"An emergency council meeting was requested by CEO Monroe, who has reported a malfunction with her virtual assistant. CEO Monroe, is this problem related to the one that Champion Castell reported earlier today?"

For some reason, Scipio's words went a long way to soothe me. He didn't jump right to "secret plan to break in," which made me hope that the others wouldn't, either.

"It would appear to be," Sadie said, an undercurrent of anger in her voice. "I arrived back at my quarters to find the entire floor reset. I've run a diagnostic and found the same errors in my assistant's code that I found in Champion Castell's terminal."

Relief. Quess had done a good job covering the virus's tracks when he wrote Sadie's report for her. I looked over and gave him a grateful smile, earning me one of my own.

"Is this a problem that could affect any of *our* quarters?" Lacey asked, drawing me back to the matter at hand. We hadn't informed Lacey what we were up to, but her reaction told me that she was buying the story without me having to prep her at all. That was good.

"That is unclear at this time," Sadie replied unhappily. "When I first saw the error, I assumed it was a random glitch. It still seems like it should be, except that it happened in my rooms as well. It's downright odd—almost as if it was engineered to hit multiple areas."

Alarm skittered through me as she spoke, and I realized that she already had her suspicions. How I handled what happened next was everything. "What are you saying?" I asked, keeping my voice even. "Could this have been... malicious programming?"

"Let's not jump to conclusions," Marcus Sage, the head of the Medica, interjected with a wry twist in his words. "Nothing has breached these particular security systems since the Tower's conception."

These security systems have never met a "nothing" like me before, I thought to myself. It was a stupid joke, but it made me smile, inwardly at least, which helped relieve some of the tension. Outwardly, I said, "But you cannot deny that something odd is going on. First my quarters, then Sadie's?"

"CEO Monroe, you will conduct an investigation into the other virtual assistants," Scipio commanded. "Determine whether this is just a coincidence, or there is a problem with the assistant programs, and update your report accordingly. We will be waiting to see if there is anything the council should be concerned about."

"I want to add that something odd happened to the desk I was using," Sadie cut in. "The materials I had inside of it didn't show up with the rest of my personal belongings, and I have no idea what happened to them."

Ice washed down my spine, but I kept my mouth shut and waited to see what Scipio would say.

"If the item was damaged during the reset process, protocols dictate that it be recycled after personal property is removed. If the damage was extensive, the system might not have been able to discern between the furniture in question and the personal items inside, thereby destroying everything. You may access the storage room where the items are being kept, but if the desk is no longer in the inventory and your belongings are missing, they were most likely destroyed. I am sorry, CEO Monroe."

I blew out a thin stream of breath, trying not to vocalize any of the relief I was feeling. It was a stroke of luck that the system had destroyed damaged objects, as I'd hoped. We'd had no way of knowing that for sure until now, but I was so glad we had gambled correctly.

"Thank you, Lord Scipio," Sadie said. "I will inform the council of my findings as soon as possible."

"Any objections?" Scipio waited for a span of five or six seconds, and when no one spoke, he finished with, "Thus concludes the emergency meeting of the council. Until next time."

The hum of the speakers died suddenly, prompting Cornelius to announce, "Lord Scipio has ended the call."

I leaned on the desk with both hands and tried not to show how shaky my knees were. "So that went well," I announced into the empty silence of the room. "Good job, everyone."

9

If anyone thought my quip was funny, they didn't show it. Alex crossed his arms over his chest and leaned a hip against the conference table while Maddox sucked in a deep breath, her fists clenched. Even Leo looked tense, and I realized that they didn't believe what I'd said any more than I did.

After all, Scipio had just given Sadie permission to look into the other virtual assistants to determine whether there was a problem. When she found none, she might suspect that it was something other than a glitch. But I was pretty confident I had a way around it. I just had to convince Lacey and Strum to let us upload the virus into their terminals as well, so that there appeared to be a defect in the assistants. I'd have to admit to Lacey what I'd done, but if I brought her information on who had killed her nephew, then she would probably be okay covering for me.

But the others weren't there yet. They were still focused on the fact that this hadn't ended like we expected it to and were still adapting. "Guys, I know Sadie launching an investigation into the virtual assistants seems like a big hurdle, and normally it would be, but you forget that we have Lacey and Strum on our side. We can use that, replicate the same problem at one of their places, and then Sadie and the council will be convinced it's a problem in the code, create some sort of update to 'fix' it, and move on. We're just going to need to have something for Lacey—namely the people who attacked Ambrose. We have Sadie's files, and the answers have to be there. We just need to go through them and—"

Leo cleared his throat, and I broke off to look at him, surprised to see his face reflecting a deep nervousness. "Actually, I rushed the download," he said carefully. "So, we have *all* of Sadie's files. Over a million terabytes of data. And there are encryptions on a lot of the files. It's going to take some time."

I absorbed this information as more of a speed bump than a wall. "It doesn't matter. I'll net Lacey, explain what we did, and ask her to cover for us. If she understands that it could lead to finding the entire legacy group, she will help us. But I'll worry about that. Is there anything you guys can do to sift through the data faster? You, Quess, and..." I cast a quick glance at my brother and decided to at least try to extend an olive branch, "Alex?"

Leo was already nodding. "Quess is working on it now. I hope you don't mind, but I'm going to continue focusing on Rose and Jasper."

"Has there been any change?" I asked, instantly concerned. "Are they still offline?"

His brown eyes grew dark with worry. "Yes and no. Jang-Mi woke up."

It was funny how three little words could arouse so much fear. Jang-Mi was all that was left of the core memory that had made Rose what she was, but the wall between the two had been destroyed by the legacies as a way of controlling Rose. The remnant personality had taken over most of Rose's code and was unstable to the nth degree.

"What happened?" I asked, fearing that Jang-Mi had somehow gotten to Jasper in spite of the firewall separating them. Or was taking over Cornelius's systems and about to turn them on each other.

"She woke up confused and angry," he said, his mouth flat. "I attempted to calm her down, but it was like she forgot that Yu-Na was dead and started looking for her again. She grew more and more desperate when she couldn't find her. When she started to attack herself, I put her in the self-diagnostic protocol to try to get Rose back, but I think the fight was too much for her. She's not responding."

A half-dozen questions sat on the tip of my tongue, all of them centered around three major points: Why wasn't she back? Had sending her to Sadie's computer sapped the last of her strength? Was her personality finished, and if so, what did that mean? She was Scipio's heart; if she died, then what hope did the rest of the Tower have? How could we ever fix Scipio without her? But as I looked at Leo's worried brown eyes, I realized that if he knew, he would've told us already.

So instead, I reached out and put my hand on his shoulder, trying to comfort him. His hand came up to cover mine, and even though we were exhausted, sweaty, and had just performed the crime of the millennium, a spark jolted through me as his fingers stroked over mine.

For several moments, everyone and everything in the room dropped away, and I had a powerful urge to just sit in his lap and hold him. I knew I shouldn't—he was an AI in the body of the man I had been falling for before he was injured—but that didn't stop my heart from wanting it.

Then my brother cleared his throat loudly, jerking me out of the moment. I looked down to find him watching us both, his face an angry mask. "You still haven't told us what you're going to do with that legacy in the other room," he said. "And that's our biggest problem right now, not broken fragments and Sadie's information. Sadie and the others will have noticed that he's missing by now. We need to get rid of him."

Maddox gave him a sideways look, her mouth already moving before mine. "Your sister has already told you that this discussion is over and done with. We're not killing him."

"And you agree with that?" he railed, looking at Leo, Maddox, and Quess. "You really are backing that move? These guys broke into Ambrose's room and beat him without getting caught on the sensors! That's what they do! So what makes you think that this situation is going to be any different? Any minute now they are going to figure out a way to track him, find him here, and then we're all in trouble."

Once again there were some good points in there, helping his case, but it still didn't change the fact that we were talking about killing an unarmed man. Did his words fill me with fear? Absolutely. Thanks to what he'd said, I now couldn't seem to get rid of the image of Baldy creeping into Maddox and Quess's room and killing them while they slept. Of Leo with a knife in his chest, or Tian with her throat cut. I knew Baldy was capable of it, and more than dangerous.

But that didn't mean he couldn't have a use, too. I just needed to figure out what it was. Alex wasn't interested in hearing that, however, so I did the next best thing. "Maddox is right, Alex. Bring this up again, and I'm going to carry through on my promise and make you leave. Don't make me do it."

His eyes widened, his anger melting some to reveal a surprised pain. "You're really serious, aren't you?"

I nodded, meeting his gaze head on. "I am," I whispered. "I'm sorry, but I have to be. You're starting to *scare* me, Alex. This isn't like you at all. You're patient and calm. Mom's death changed you."

There was a moment, a fraction of one, really, where the

wounded confusion was stronger than the rage, and I felt certain that I had reached him. But when he looked up at me, the shutters in his eyes had dropped down again, hiding the vulnerability behind plates of anger that hardened his face.

"It's on your head if he kills you all," he said, seething. "I'll be with Quess, handling Sadie's files. Quess?"

My brother didn't even wait for the taller man to respond. He just snapped a turn on one heel, faster than I could blink, and was striding out of the room with a determined set to his shoulders.

Quess stared after him, rubbing the back of his neck. "He does realize that I work for you, right?"

"*With* me," I corrected absentmindedly. "And... just go with him. Please." The last part I said in the breath of a sigh, grateful that I had at least gotten him to shift his focus somewhat. We would need all the help we could get with Sadie's data, and if there was one thing my brother was good at, it was figuring out computer stuff. Between him and Quess (and possibly Leo), they would crack it.

"Fun," Quess said wryly, tucking his pad into his pocket and starting after Alex. "If he gives me any lip, do I get to yell at him?"

"Nope," I told him, shaking my head. It wouldn't do Quess any good, anyway. Alex wasn't going to take kindly to anyone putting him down. "Let me know, and I'll handle it."

If you have never been the focus of a three-way look of disbelief before, then you have been missing out on something special. The looks Leo, Maddox, and Quess had on their faces ranged from polite to cynical, and I squirmed under their scrutiny.

"I can," I told them insistently, feeling the need to defend myself.

"I'm not so sure. Your brother needs some help, Liana," Maddox replied. "He's going off the rails."

Even though she was right, there wasn't much I could do officially, and she should know that. "Yes, but you and I both know that grief services in the Medica are crap," I replied. "Besides, imagine how he feels. He's isolated in IT, and even though Dinah is trying to keep him shielded from Sadie, he knows she's watching. Then I went and ignored him after my mother's funeral, when all he wanted was to be included. He found out I almost died, and even then, I asked him to stay away from all of this. He's angry, yes, but part of that is my fault. I just... We've got to let him cool off, and then I will talk to him, okay? Until then, just give him a little bit of space."

That did nothing to assuage the doubt in her eyes, but she nodded anyway. "He's your brother," she said by way of letting it go, and I accepted it.

Looking over at Leo, I saw him reading one of the files from Lionel Scipio's office—the ones I had been trying to make sense of earlier. "Any clues in there to help us? With Jasper or Rose?"

He pursed his lips and sighed. "Not yet, but there's a lot to go through. The psychology profiles help somewhat, but they don't really matter if I can't figure out what Lionel did to create the barrier around the core memory. I'm hoping the answers are here, somewhere, but..." He trailed off, and finally looked up at me over the top of the file, his eyes bleeding with unspoken fears.

"The answers are in there," I told him. "They have to be. Have you managed to make any contact with Jasper? Or seen anything from him?"

Leo shook his head, his face grim. "His program is locked up in a tight shell to protect his coding, to the point where he won't accept even the friendliest of pings. I'm guessing it's a defensive measure he's been taking against Sadie, and we're collateral damage. I'm not entirely sure what to do about it. Maybe he'll come out of it eventually to check things out, but right now, he's not even listening."

I considered the problem. "Can you let him hear my voice? If he recognizes that it's me, maybe he'll know it's safe."

The look on Leo's face told me he didn't think it would work, but he turned to the computer and started to type something. After a few seconds, he gave me a nod. "Go ahead."

"Jasper?" I called. It was tempting to yell, because working with noncorporeal AIs always felt like I was trying to shout a message across a chasm. But in reality, they could hear me no matter how loudly I spoke, thanks to the microphones in the rooms. "Jasper, it's me, Liana Castell. You helped me out a few times in the Medica, remember? You saved my life, actually."

I looked at the wall of screens that hung from the ceiling, hoping for some sign of acknowledgment, but nothing changed. "We rescued you from Sadie's quarters," I added. "You're safe. And I actually have someone I think you'd like to meet. We call him Leo, but at one point he was the original basis for Scipio. We also have Rose, and we're working on finding the other fragments. We want to help you all go home."

Silence. Disappointed, I looked at Leo and nodded that he should shut it off. "I was hoping it would work," I muttered. Maybe it had been wrong of me, but I had been wanting to find Jasper for so long that I had built it up in my head that it would go smoother than this. It wasn't just because we needed him. That was true in many ways, but I had always pictured his rescue ending with him being exactly as he had been.

But his reticence to even accept communications from us told me that he had probably suffered greatly at Sadie's hand. My heart ached for him, and I wished there were some way of communicating with him.

"I'm going to get him back to us somehow," Leo said softly. "I'm going to get them both back, as they were. It just might take more time than we wanted."

"I know you will," I told him. If anyone could, it was Leo.

And if we couldn't spring into action right away with our AI fragments, we had to do something else. Give Leo time to work while focusing on our other objective: finding the legacies. We had to wait for Quess and Alex to break into Sadie's files to really know what we were dealing with, but we did have other leads. Dylan Chase was helping me track down the undoc side of the legacies we were after, and since Tian had also secured Liam, we had different avenues of moving forward.

But it would be difficult. We were going to have to make sure we got everyone, or it wouldn't matter at all.

Leo smiled kindly at me, his features growing soft as his misery slowly dissolved. "Thank you," he said, and his voice was intimate and... inviting. I found myself wanting to go to him, but I somehow managed to fight it off. Then he started speaking again. "Actually, there's something else in the files you should be aware of."

"Oh?" I asked, curiosity returning. I had thought Leo's report had been the end of it, but if he was bringing something else up, then chances were I'd interrupted to go off on a tangent before he could finish. "What is it?"

"It's about the nets Lionel designed. The legacy ones. As you already know, they were designed to capture memories, but along with that, they recorded muscle memories, to help later generations of workers remember how to repair something even if they didn't have an exact understanding of how it worked."

That explained what had happened in Sadie's apartment, with the net hijacking my body. I'd been in control, but I'd also felt *out* of control, as if a ghost from the past was prodding at my autonomic systems from the outside. It was weird, but also followed what I knew about Lionel, who had made the nets to try to make life easier inside the Tower. Unfortunately, the legacies had twisted that design in their quest to subvert Scipio, leading to the Tower itself distrusting the tech. So now, the legacy nets were only in the hands of those who had ignored the law and kept theirs.

"What's more," Leo continued, leaning back in the chair, "an early report from Samantha Reed, the founder of the Medica, revealed that AIs implanted in the nets could repair most types of neurological diseases, including the onset of Alzheimer's, epilepsy, and bipolar disorder, and also cure most types of cancer. She proposed that copies of the AIs be inserted into each net, for that reason. It was overruled by a vote."

"But we knew that," I replied. "You said the net had special healing properties. That's why you went into Grey's head."

"Yes," he nodded. "But that's not the point. The point is that after the suggestion was shut down, Ezekial Pine ran an experiment, using his neural clone, Kurt. In the process, he realized that an AI can also extract information from a criminal. With complete accuracy." He looked up from the file and grimaced. "I wasn't going to bring it up in front of your brother, but it means we have a way of getting all the information we need out of Baldy, without having to ask."

10

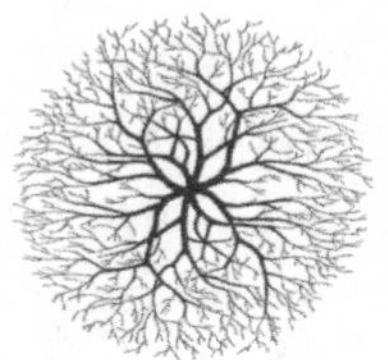

I did not like the sound of that one bit and could already tell where this was going by the determined look on Leo's face.

"No," I said with a firm shake of my hands. "Absolutely not. You're not putting yourself into that monster!"

Leo cocked his head at me and then stood up. I curled my arms around myself, sensing that he was going to make a logical speech about why he should do this. But I really didn't want to hear it. I did not like the idea of someone I cared about going into the mind of a killer.

"Liana," he said soothingly, coming to stand before me. "You know it's going to take some time to sift through Sadie's files and dig out what we need. You also know that whatever their true aim is, it might not be in there. We don't have time to waste trying to find every scrap of evidence, especially not when we have the means to find the answers within a few hours."

"I don't care," I said stubbornly. "It's weird."

He gave me a lopsided smile. “Weirder than me inhabiting the body of your boyfriend?”

I knew he was trying to make a point, but that was different. Leo was doing that to help Grey, while Baldy was still whole—and our enemy. “Yes! It’s different! What if you can’t control him, or he somehow manages to resist you? What if you get trapped, or he finds a way to hurt you? And what about Grey? Is it safe for you to come out of him? Is he... restored?”

As soon as I asked the question, I wanted to snatch it back. One of the biggest unanswered questions between us—and there were many—was what would happen once Leo finished healing Grey. It ranked right up there with my own confused feelings toward Leo, and the slow realization that I was growing closer and closer to the AI, and not in a platonic way. Because of that, I thought, we had avoided the subject completely.

But with Leo’s revelation, and his desire to try, I had to ask. I wasn’t going to let him do it if it risked his own safety. Or Grey’s.

Leo pursed his lips, his brown eyes shuttering against showing any emotion. “I’ve moved on to recovering his teenage years, but no, he’s not fully restored. But it won’t hurt him if I go for a few hours. I’ll try to leave him sleeping, but there is a chance that he could wake up, and if so, he won’t remember you.”

That would make things a little less awkward, but it did nothing to assuage my concerns. “What about Baldy? Leo, Grey is damaged, but Baldy’s mind is intact.”

“I’m an AI, Liana, made from a human mind. I understand how to navigate it better than most, as it’s a pattern I was built from. I promise you, I will be fine, and doing this will get us information we could use. You brought him here for a reason; let’s use him to figure out what’s going on. At least get an idea who he is working with. It could give us some direction.” He paused and speared me with a pleading look. “Please, Liana. He might know where Alice and Tony are.”

I felt myself soften to the idea and knew that it was already inevitable at this point. Leo had clearly made up his mind to do this, and judging from Maddox's face, she didn't think the idea was half bad. If I resisted, it would only be because of my personal feelings for Leo, and not for anything remotely resembling logic. And I couldn't let myself be ruled by my emotions. "Maddox, can you get Quess back in here?"

She gave me a surprised look but didn't argue. "Yeah, I'll go get him. Also, Zoe and Eric are finally on their way up and should be here in a few minutes."

I let out a sigh of relief at that. Zoe and Eric had decided against living with us, but now that we had made a direct attack against Sadie (even if she wasn't aware of it), I wanted everyone I cared about to be as close as possible for the next few days, until I knew we were in the clear. It was doubly imperative now, considering that we could potentially learn everything we needed from Baldy himself, and finally track down all of the legacies. It would be dangerous until we could carry it out, and we would have to be very careful about whom we trusted with the information, but if we could pull it off...

Well, there wouldn't be a need for us to do safety sleepovers like this in the future. At least, I hoped there wouldn't be.

"Good," I said. "Get them up to speed on everything and see what they can help out with."

Maddox nodded in acknowledgment. "I'll be right back with Quess."

Glancing over at Leo, I realized I still had doubts. "I still don't like this idea," I told him.

He reached out and cupped my cheek, a soft, sad smile on his lips. "I know. But it'll be okay."

It took us all of fifteen minutes to get everything set up, and somehow, I managed to keep the rest of my distaste for this plan closely guarded. I'd sat with Leo while Quess had extracted the net from his neck—which was eerie, because I had never before realized that Leo could make Grey just close his eyes and go to sleep—and then cleaned it and carried it to Baldy's room.

He was sleeping when we entered, and Quess administered the same light sedative that he had given Sadie, in the form of a pneumatic injection. Together, we rolled him onto his side, and I watched, throat tight, as the net containing Leo was jammed into the wound and the opening sealed shut.

We started to flip him back over, but Baldy suddenly jerked awake and looked around, causing me to snatch my hand back with a startled sound. Quess moved in front of me protectively, forcing me back a few paces, but I refused to cower and came to stand by his side.

The man on the bed looked around for a second, and then shook his head. "So disorienting," he muttered as he carefully maneuvered himself into a sitting position using his bound hands. The normal malice on his face was gone, leaving only a deep concentration peppered with mild distaste. "His body feels weird," he commented, rotating his shoulders inside their sockets.

"Leo?" I breathed, and Baldy looked up at me with an expression that was pure Leo.

"Yes," he said with a nod. "I'm sorry. I should've said something. Are you okay?"

No, I was not, I decided a second later. There was something distinctly uncomfortable about knowing that Leo was inside the man who had cut my throat, and it left me slightly nauseous. It wasn't right. It wasn't *Leo*.

Neither is Grey, the dark voice inside of me pointed out, and that left me feeling cold.

Quess shifted beside me, his crimson uniform creaking under

his weight, and I looked up at him and realized that I had taken too long to answer. Which meant there was no lying about it now. "Not really," I admitted.

Baldy cocked his head at me, and I looked away. It was weird—I had been able to look the man in the eye when he was tied up earlier, but now? Knowing that Leo was inside of him? I didn't like it. How was I supposed to see Leo through the man who had hurt me? What if I couldn't? What if I hurt his feelings by freaking out if he went to hug me or something?

I wasn't entirely sure I was equipped to handle this, but I didn't want to run away screaming from him, either.

There was a sigh, and then, in Baldy's voice, Leo said, "Quess, can you give Liana and me a moment?"

"Sure," he said. He checked his watch. "I should probably go look in on Grey, anyway."

"And maybe get some alone time with Doxy," I teased, trying to diffuse some of the tension in the room. She was still in the room where we'd left Grey, monitoring him in case he woke up, and I could tell Quess wanted to be with her.

"Hey, our boss is an impossible task mistress," Quess shot back, his dark blue eyes radiating warm humor. "And she stuck me in a room with Sadie Monroe, where I was harassed for almost the entire time! That woman was like a cat in heat, and it took all of my considerable effort just to keep her off me. So yeah, I'm going to go see my girlfriend and see if she can't make me feel better!"

I instantly felt bad. His tone had started out jokingly, but toward the end it got a little too real—enough to tell me that the interaction with Sadie had left a mark of its own. "I'm sorry," I said, giving him a hug. "I can't imagine how awful that was for you."

He rolled his eyes. "No, I'm being dramatic. It's been a big day for all of us."

I nodded in absolute agreement, suddenly feeling tired. I took a deep breath and pushed it aside, letting go of Quess. "Go ahead. I'll call you if anything comes up."

"And I'll let you know if Grey wakes up. Not sure what we're going tell him if he does, so... I'm kind of hoping he doesn't."

I hated to admit it, but so was I. I didn't have the faintest clue what I would tell him either, so hopefully we'd never have to cross that bridge. "Go ahead and get some time in with Maddox," I told him.

"Oh, believe me, I will," he said, adding a lecherous waggle to his eyebrows that had me laughing. Then he exited, leaving Baldy and me alone.

No, *Leo* and me. I forced myself to look at him.

"It's me," he said, as if sensing my need for confirmation.

I wanted to tell him that I knew that, that I didn't see Baldy's face when I looked at him, but it was too hard. "I know that logically," I hedged.

Leo frowned, and I could tell that he'd picked up on my careful word choice. "But emotionally?"

I shook my head, not wanting to lie to him. "It's freaking me out a little bit."

It really, *really* was. Each movement he made sent a nervous tremor down my spine, a signal that an adrenaline rush was pending, my fight-or-flight instincts right at the surface. It was illogical and emotional, and I couldn't shut it off, just like I couldn't stop the running train of questions in my brain.

What if Leo got stuck in there? Would I be able to see through the skin and muscle and bone to the being within? Would I ever be able to get over the memory of the cold bite of the knife and the gleam in his eyes as he did it?

"Close your eyes," he said softly. "Listen to my voice."

I let them drift closed, but he barely got to "I—" before they snapped back open and I was violently shaking my head no. Hearing his voice only made it worse. Before the cut of the blade, he had struck me several times in the head, and his voice had been all I could focus on in the darkness.

"That's not going to work for me," I said flatly.

Leo paused, his mouth open, and then leaned back, his face adopting a contemplative look. "*Would this help?*" he asked in a high-pitched, singsong voice. "*I suppose I could talk like this forever. Perhaps the vocal cords will even adapt to it.*"

A surprised laugh escaped me, and suddenly, just like that, Baldy ceased being Baldy and started being Leo. Maybe it was the lopsided smile on his face or the hopeful gleam in his eyes, but I *saw* him. It was Leo.

Relief poured through me, and I returned the smile. "Hey," I said, a small laugh in my voice. "I think it works."

"*Really,*" he sang in his affected voice. "*Then consider the change permanent.*" I giggled at the very idea that he could do that, and then paused, a dark thought occurring to me.

"Wait, can you actually make his voice like that forever?"

He met my gaze directly and nodded once. "Normally, I wouldn't suggest it," he said, his voice normal again. It bothered me less than before, especially when he looked at his own bound hands with undisguised hatred. "But this disgrace of a human deserves it. These hands held you down and cut your flesh, and I could very easily make it so that he never used them again. I could do so much to him from the inside, and a part of me would feel that it was justice."

As terrifying as it was to learn that he could do all of that from the net, his revelation filled me with a strange sort of warmth. Still, I had one too many people trying to protect me at the moment.

"Don't," I told him with a shake of my head. "Just focus on whatever information you can get out of him, so we can move you back as quickly as possible."

He nodded and then gave me an apologetic look. "Then do you mind leaving me alone for a bit? I can't tell if it's because he's not like Grey, or if it's the sedative, but it's hard to maintain a conversation and go through his memories."

I opened my mouth, surprised, and then shut it. His request was reasonable, and I could only imagine what it was like being in there. "Sure. I'll wait outside. Just knock when you're ready."

He smiled and then swung his legs back up on the bed and settled down, lacing his fingers over his stomach as best he could with his wrists cuffed together. "I'll move as quickly as possible," he promised. "I don't like being in this body at all."

"Just be careful, okay?" I said.

Leo nodded, his eyes already drifting closed. I stared at him for a moment or two longer, and then exited into the hallway to wait.

11

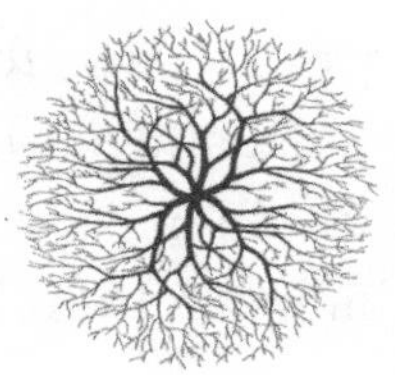

I was standing outside Baldy's room for nearly twenty minutes, waiting, before a loud shout carried down the hall. Alarmed, I pushed off the wall I was leaning on, my hand on my baton, and took half a step toward the sound.

Quess came around the corner a minute later, his face a tight mask, and I moved to meet him. "What's wrong? What was that?"

"It's Grey," he said. "He woke up and started freaking out. He doesn't recognize me or Doxy. Should I sedate him?"

My heart lurched at the idea, my imagination already putting my feet in Grey's shoes. He was confused and scared, and we didn't need to make it worse by cornering him and knocking him out. I owed him more than that. We all did.

"No," I said, swallowing some of my anxiety. "I'll handle it. Will you wait here for Leo? He said he would knock when he was ready."

Quess nodded. "Maddox is outside the door. He's..." He shifted his weight, seemingly torn. "He's angry, Liana. I'm not sure why or about what, but he started to get violent. He didn't hurt anyone, but that was because of Maddox's intervention."

I cursed. That was only going to make things more difficult, but if I could just reassure him that he was safe and that no one was going to hurt him, he would hopefully calm down.

"Thanks," I said as I started to jog away. I followed the spiral-shaped hallway about thirty feet, until Maddox came into view. When I slowed to a stop next to her, I could hear a rhythmic pounding coming through Leo's door, followed by angry, muffled shouts. Maddox's eyes were flat and hard.

"He's freaking out," she told me as soon as I was standing next to her. "I tried to talk to him, but I think it was our uniforms. He just flipped out."

I looked down at my uniform and then sighed. Grey didn't have the best history with the Knights. His parents had dropped him from his department when he was young, because his ranking had continued to descend instead of rise. Their decision forced him to live on the outskirts of Tower life, bouncing from department to department, until he fell in with Roark and got a place with the Cogs. He had been Roark's ally in distributing Paragon for their escape plan and hadn't exactly been on the right side of the law. So it must have been a shock for *any* version of him to wake up in a room with two Knights. It wasn't any wonder he was freaking out.

"I'll get him calmed down," I told her.

She nodded. "Zoe and Eric are almost here. I'll go grab them and get them set up."

I studied the door and nodded, absentmindedly checking that off my list and then summoning up a deep calm. Inside the room, Grey continued to shout demands for someone to come in and tell him what was going on, accompanied by loud metallic bangs, indicating he was kicking or punching the walls. As I reached for the button, I suddenly hesitated, my heart pounding.

Even though I knew I had to do this—had to open the door and try to calm Grey down—something inside me warned that it wasn't a good idea for me, personally. I was already twisted up inside over the complicated feelings I was developing for Leo, and now I had to deal with Grey.

How was I possibly going to do that? How could I even look him in the eye after everything? I had feelings for Grey, but he had been gone for so long, and in the process of waiting for him, I had allowed Leo a place in my heart.

Oh God, I had *betrayed* Grey. Because that was what was happening every second that I drew closer and closer to Leo. Even if I had any doubts before, they were completely washed away by the fact that I was standing outside of Grey's door, wishing I was in Leo's arms, not having to deal with this. It was so tempting, but also cowardly, and that wasn't who I was.

Besides, it wasn't like he was going to remember me. Leo had said he was in his teenage years, and I had met him when he was older than that.

Then my mind drifted to the time that Leo had been sleepwalking and tried to kiss me over and over again, with an intensity that I recognized as Grey's. He had somehow come to the surface and known me *then*. Would everything suddenly fall back in place for him if I walked in there right now? Could that even happen? What would I do if it did?

I'd like to think that I'd be honest with him, but somehow, I knew it wouldn't be that easy. If he managed to look at me in that way that made my breath catch and my knees turn to gel, would I falter? Would I turn my back on Leo and choose Grey? Or turn my back on Grey and choose Leo? How could I do either thing and live with myself?

Did I even *want* him to remember me?

A part of me screamed that I did, but it was matched with a side that wanted Leo just as badly. Both of them were as different as could be, and yet my heart yearned for them, anyway.

Please don't let him remember me, I prayed, begging for at least one thing to be uncomplicated tonight. *I promise I will figure out what to do about this mess tomorrow. Just let me have this one thing tonight.*

It took every ounce of my considerable willpower to press the button and open the door, but I managed. My personal feelings were secondary to Grey's situation. My concerns over his well-being had to take priority over my own hang-ups. If he recognized me, we'd go from there. If he didn't, same plan.

The door slid up, revealing a bedroom in a state of disarray. The mattress was flipped up on one side, the corner of it catching on a wall so it created a lean-to. Uniforms had been flung out of the closet, and technical manuals were strewn across the floor.

But I barely had time to register any of that, because Grey's crimson-clad figure emitted a hoarse cry of anger to the left of me, and a second later he was charging toward me with an angry bellow of, "Leave me alone!"

I could've stopped him easily—the position of his arm and the way he held his hand were signs that he didn't know how to throw a good punch—but instead, I stood my ground and held up my hands, squeezing one eye shut in preparation for the blow. Grey wasn't much of a fighter, and definitely didn't like to hit women, so I was hoping his reflexes would catch up long before he hit me. But if he hit me, it probably wouldn't hurt that much. Either way, the act of not attacking or retaliating would throw him off. His feet thundered closer... and then the rhythm broke as he came to a sudden stop, inches in front of me.

I slid one eye open and looked up at him. He was staring down at me, his nostrils flaring and his brown eyes dark and filled with the promise of a storm. I searched them for recognition, and when none flared, relief filled me that I didn't have to deal with that conversation, followed quickly by guilt.

Shaking both feelings off, I gave him a tremulous smile. "Thanks for not hitting me?" I asked, curling it up into a question at the end.

He gave a surprised huff and backed off a step, carving a little more space between us. I took a moment to ease away from the wall I had backed up against and tugged on the edge of my uniform, the garment feeling inexplicably tight.

"Why am I here?" he barked, and there was a sullen anger in his voice. I looked up at him and found his eyes filled with defiance. But as I peered a little deeper, I saw a glimmer of fear there.

"You didn't do anything wrong," I assured him, and then paused, recalling Quess and Maddox's comments about him growing violent, and speared him with a hard look. "But if you continue to assault my people, I will have to sedate you."

He scowled at me and tipped his chin up a notch. "You still didn't answer my question." I smiled in spite of myself. He was Grey, through and through—unrelenting to a fault. Single-minded focus that would tear through all extraneous data to get right to the point. Oh, he knew how to be indirect, but he did love challenging authority. He just got a little smoother about it when he was older.

His eyes flicked to my lips and narrowed in suspicion. "What's so funny?"

Crap. *Lie fast, and lie believably, Liana.* "Sorry," I told him contritely, pulling the smile back some. "I just respect a guy who stays on task."

One eyebrow rose, and was followed by one lip, which curled up flirtatiously. "You hitting on me, Knight lady?"

The thought sobered me, the conflict from earlier rearing its ugly head and roaring. I shook my head, offering him a smaller, tighter smile. "Not at all," I told him gently. "And to answer your question, you're here because you had a little accident."

"Accident?" His strong eyebrows drew together into a tight point over his nose as he frowned. "Why am I not at the Medica, then?"

I hesitated and then shook my head. I had no answer for that. Telling him anything resembling the truth would sound insane to him, especially with where he was in his personal timeline, so I settled on the best kind of truth I could find: the misdirect. "It's complicated. Can I… Can I ask you some questions?"

Grey's mouth twisted in uncertainty, but he nodded. "What do you want?"

I licked my lips and decided to start with introductions. "My name is Liana Castell. What's your name?"

"Grey Sawyer," he replied automatically. His words brought me pause. When I met him, he had already been Grey Farmless, his surname having been changed after his parents dropped him from the Farming Department. I tried to remember how old he had been when he was dropped, but I didn't think he'd ever mentioned it. Obviously, we were still earlier than that in his memories.

"How old are you?" I asked.

"Seventeen," he said, uncrossing his arms and puffing up his chest a little. I could imagine him doing that when he was younger, trying to look older, but given that he was twenty-five, it only served to make him look boyish, eliciting yet another smile from me. "You?" he demanded a second later, his eyes dropping to my lips.

"Twenty-one," I told him. "What's the last thing you remember?"

Confusion riddled his features, and then his eyes grew distant for the space of several heartbeats. "I had a fight with my parents," he said finally, and his voice was awash with pain and frustration. "They… My…" he paused, one hand going up to rub his arm in a nervous gesture. "My ranking keeps falling, and I can't seem to do anything right. I don't know why. I study hard; I work harder, but... Scipio hates me! I don't know why, but he does, he—"

He stopped mid-sentence and looked at me, his eyes welling with terror. "Oh no," he whimpered. "I didn't mean it. I'm sorry. I know Scipio doesn't hate me, I just—"

My heart swelled up for him, and I instinctively stepped close to him and wrapped him up in a hug, wanting to reassure him the best way I knew how. This wasn't my Grey—not yet—but this was the boy who would *become* my Grey, and I was meeting him during the hardest time in his life, from his perspective.

And I knew it would only get worse for him. His rank would continue to fall, until his family dropped him from the department entirely. He'd be on his own until he found Roark... and then he'd lose him too. I hugged harder, hurting for the memories that he had yet to know, and to my surprise, he hugged me back.

I could sense an ache inside him, a need to be comforted. I let the hug go on for as long as possible before it got too weird, and even then I felt wrong stepping away from him.

"It's okay," I told him with a gentle nod and smile. "We don't have to talk about that if you don't want to."

He gave me a considering look, his bottom lip disappearing into his mouth for a second. "How long do I have to stay here?" he asked.

I considered his question and then sighed. "I don't have a good answer for that," I told him. "It could be a few hours. Are you hungry? Can I get you anything?"

"Trying to win my heart through my stomach, eh?" he said jokingly, waggling his eyebrows at me.

I laughed, unable to stop myself. One other thing about Grey was that he was a terrible flirt. Not as bad as Quess could be, but then again, he was more of a charmer, whereas Quess was the master of inappropriate pickup lines. "I bet you say that to all the girls," I teased.

"Girls? No." He raked me with a salacious look, his smile widening. "I've been waiting for someone special. A woman."

I flushed under his frank and flirtatious quip and tried to laugh it away. "Well, luckily I'm far too old for you, so that's settled."

"Only four years," he retorted, and I tried to give him what I hoped was a stern look. His broad smile widened, and something dangerously close to recognition flared through his eyes. "Do I... Have we met?"

My heart thudded against my ribs, and I was shaking my head no before I could even consider whether it was a good idea or not. "No," I lied to him. "I don't think so."

"Hm." He pursed his lips at that, considering me. "We should."

I frowned in confusion. "We just did."

"No, for dinner sometime." I stared at him, surprised that his seventeen-year-old self could be that audacious, yet feeling slightly flushed and... pleased by his attention.

Totally weird, Liana. He's seventeen right now, I chided myself while simultaneously laughing him off. "I'm sure your girlfriend would have something to say about that."

"She would if she existed," he replied with a shrug. "It's just too bad I'm waiting for someone special."

"Oh? Like who?" I asked, my voice teasing.

I didn't expect him to have an answer, but Grey—being Grey—surprised me. "Someone who sees me as more than the number on my wrist. She's gotta be strong and fierce, too—everything I'm not, but want to push myself to be. I may not be the best fighter, but with her, I wouldn't have to be. Fighting the world could be her thing; mine would be holding her when it grows too dark and hopeless for her. Loving her when she feels like she's failed and pushing her to succeed even when she feels she can't."

His words might as well have been fire. They left me feeling flushed, raw, and needy, and seemed to burn away every bit of oxygen in the room. His words—his *idea*—of what he wanted sounded a lot like what I needed. I thought about my mother's death and found myself wondering if things would've been different had Grey been there, coaxing me back to life through his love and care. I hadn't let anyone close, not even Zoe or Alex or Leo. I wasn't sure why I thought Grey would be any different, but a part of me wondered.

I put it aside quickly. It didn't do me any good to think about what might have been. I'd learned that after my mother died, when the grief of it almost made me fall apart.

Instead, I went for a joke. "You don't see yourself as the hero?" I asked lightly.

He shoved his hands in his pockets and shrugged again. "I'm not a hero," he replied with a sad smile. "If I were, I'd have a higher ranking. But it's okay. Because if not being the hero means I get to be there for the woman I love, then I'm glad. I don't care about saving people or the world. I only want to care about her. I want to be *her* hero. Everyone else in the Tower can rot."

A surprised laugh escaped me, but it died when he met my eyes and squinted at me. "Are you sure we haven't met?" he asked, taking a step toward me. "There's something very familiar about you."

I hesitated and then shook my head, firmly telling him, "No, I'm sorry. I just have one of those faces."

"Uh-huh."

I cleared my throat against the doubt in his voice and decided that it would be best if I got out of there post-haste. This interaction was only confusing things. "I should go," I told him. "But if you need anything, you can let Cornelius know. He's a computer assistant who can hear and see everything going on in here. And he will tell me."

"So if I want to see you again, I just have to ask this Cornelius?" he asked with a smile.

"Yes," I said automatically. Followed by, "Well, no..." as soon as

I realized my mistake. I shook my head, flustered as he stepped even closer, his smile growing. "*Someone* will help you," I finally corrected myself. It didn't matter to me that his mind was seventeen. The look he was giving me was masculine and hungry—and I was responding to it.

I had to go. "Thank you for your patience," I told him lamely, before turning and fleeing through the door.

12

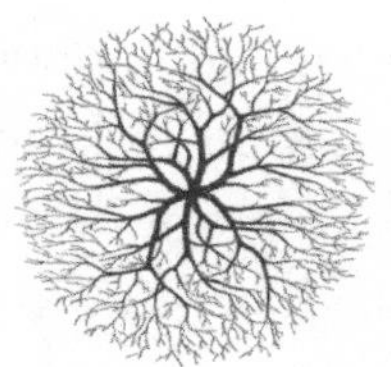

As soon as I stepped out into the hall, a shiver ran up and down my spine, sending signals that something was wrong. I looked around, trying to pinpoint the source of my discomfort, but the hall seemed fine. It sat still, silent, and empty.

And yet I couldn't stop feeling that tingling sensation running under my skin, like I had stepped on a livewire and the current was strong enough to make my nerves twitch and jump.

I heard muffled voices to my left, coming from the direction of the war room, and I headed toward them, propelled by an urge I didn't quite understand. The curving nature of the hall made it impossible to see straight down it—a design I had used to limit line of sight in case of a fight, and one I despised in that moment as I stalked down the hall, my eyes following the interior curve for any sign of movement.

I stopped when the treaded soles from a pair of boots slid into view right in front of Baldy's room, and the hair on the back of my neck stood up as I took three more steps forward, my hand already opening the pocket where I had shoved the gun earlier.

Quess was on the floor, lying on his belly, blood streaming out of a gash just over his eyebrow. A dark, uncertain fear came over me as I realized he had been attacked, and I quickly checked both sides of the hall before I dropped to my knees next to him, my gaze constantly monitoring the hall as I placed two fingers on his neck. His pulse was strong and steady, and while I was relieved to find him alive, I had to know what had happened to him.

More importantly, I needed to know where Leo was. Quess was supposed to be watching after him, and someone had hurt Quess right in front of his door—and the who of it all was at the forefront of my mind. Was it the legacies? Had they tracked Baldy down? My heart pounded in my chest as a deep fear gripped me, and I stood up and rushed to the door, pressing the button in it and barely giving it time to fully open before I threw myself through it.

The room was just as I had left it, but Leo wasn't on the bed. He wasn't standing anywhere, either. The room was empty, save for a pair of open cuffs on the floor. I stared at it for half a second, wondering if the legacies had grabbed him thinking he was Baldy. If they were here for him, then that meant they were escorting him out right now. Which meant...

Tian! She was with Liam! If they knew Baldy was here, then they knew about him. And they had hurt Quess... What would they do to her?! I whirled away from the door, the fear an acrid taste in my mouth, and raced back down the corridor to the next door, the one opposite Grey's. I pushed the button on the door. The pneumatic hiss was harsh as it opened, setting my teeth on edge.

Tian looked up from where she was bouncing on the bed, her blue eyes widening in surprise and then concern. "Liana?" she asked, casting a look at the lanky, dark-haired boy who was standing in the corner of the room, and then glancing back to me. "Is everything o—"

She stopped short as a loud bang echoed down the hallway, followed by the unmistakable sound of Zoe screaming. "Stay here," I ordered, slapping the button again to shut the door. "Cornelius, lock this door until I or Maddox order otherwise."

I barely heard his affirmation as I spun away from the door, my legs beginning to churn, my heart stamping out its fear in a rapid staccato against my breastbone. The sound had come from the war room, and I sped toward it, a thousand images racing through my mind. Maybe the legacies had busted in and gotten all the way to the center of my quarters! Somehow, they had ignored Grey and me, but had gotten to the others in the war room. Sadie must have figured out what we had done and called the council as a ruse to get us to let our guard down. They were going to try to break into the terminal and get Jasper back, and one of them must have come across the gun. Maybe they had a net that recognized it, like I did.

And how'd they know how to use it? a voice inside me asked, but I ignored it. The truth was, I wasn't sure what was going on. All I knew was that I'd heard a gunshot and Zoe's scream. Leo was missing, and Quess was unconscious. Something was happening. Something bad.

I slowed as I approached the end of the hall, which curved abruptly left and then back around to the right before opening into the war room, forcing a U-shaped turn that I'd designed to act as a bottleneck to slow the enemy down, if they ever got in.

Useless, apparently. The design and Cornelius both, because he hadn't been able to turn his defenses against them, either. Hell, he hadn't even told me they were here! What was the point of having impenetrable quarters if they were that easily penetrated?

The sound of Zoe's crying cut through my thoughts, and I heard her trying to say something, her words thick with the sound of tears and panic.

"Leo, just put it down," Maddox said, her voice firm despite the thread of fear twisting through them. "I'm sure it was just an accident. Let it go."

"Shut up, bitch," a voice snarled, and I cringed at the hostility in it. *Not Leo's,* I realized as I approached the doorframe. *It's Baldy. He somehow managed to wrest control from Leo.* A solid shard of ice sank into my heart, so intense that it was all I could do to keep from shaking with fear. What happened to Leo? Was he hurt? Had Baldy damaged him?

This was bad. I slid to the doorframe, my back against the wall behind me and my gun pointed down. I took a quick glance in and saw that Baldy was on the stairs leading up to the dais, backing slowly up them, a gun in his hand. He held it awkwardly, but I saw his finger curled under the trigger guard, which told me he understood the concept of how to use it. The barrel was trained down at the recessed floor between us, where Zoe and Maddox had their backs to me, kneeling on the floor. Zoe was crying, and hunched protectively over someone, and as she clutched him tighter to her chest, I caught a glimpse of Eric's eyes, wide and filled with confusion, blood trickling from his mouth.

I ducked back around the corner as a wash of pain hit me. He'd shot Eric, I realized. I knew from the legacy net the damage the tiny hunks of metal could do, and my hand tightened around the butt of the gun, the rough surface grating against my skin. If I didn't do something now, he could—

"Leo, Eric's really hurt," Maddox said again, clearly trying to reach the AI.

Instead of an answer, though, there was another sharp bang, followed by Zoe's squeal of terror, and her desperate sob of alarm, and there was no time to plan. I was already pushing off the wall and moving through the door.

"I TOLD YOU TO SHUT UP!" Baldy was screaming, wildly brandishing the gun toward Maddox. I itched to look at my friends, to make sure my hesitation hadn't killed any of them, but I kept my gaze on him. His red face snapped toward me, the gun following right behind. My arms lifted of their own accord, and I stared him down from behind the barrel of my own gun.

"I'm much better with this than you are," I told him, my voice ice cold.

In truth, I didn't know if I was. The legacy net had guided me the last time, helping to dictate my actions. Still, something had lingered from the experience, and I lifted the gun and aimed it in a straight line, focusing on center mass through the sights on the gun. I didn't intend to pull the trigger—but he didn't know that.

Or, hopefully he didn't. If he knew how precious Leo was to me, then he would have complete control over this situation. Because there was no way I could shoot him, not with Leo inside. I could wind up killing not just one, but both of them. Or worse, the bullet could ricochet inside of him and somehow manage to damage the net. I couldn't bear the idea of Leo getting hurt, let alone at my hands. I had to deescalate the situation. Somehow.

That meant talking. With him. The man who had cut my throat and told my brother that he laughed and laughed at the video of my mother's death. This was going to go great. I just had to convince him, somehow, that we weren't going to hurt him. *After* my brother had beaten the crap out of him and we'd locked him in a room.

Two of my people were down, Zoe was next to useless in her current state, and Maddox was doing her best to keep herself between Baldy and Eric, while simultaneously trying to stop Eric's bleeding. I had no idea where Alex was, and I couldn't rely on Leo to reestablish control. I wasn't even sure how Baldy had gotten it in the first place. Basically, I was on my own, trying to talk down a clearly upset enemy before he shot me or any more of my people.

"How'd you get out of your room?" I asked. It seemed the simplest place to start.

His blue eyes narrowed, and he shook his head. "You're not in control here," he said, sneering. "Let me go, or we stand here while your friend bleeds out. Now, how do I get out of this place?"

My design had confused him, I realized. He was looking to escape, and willing to stand there while Eric bled out on the floor, to make me tell him how. I swallowed and tried not to think about it. I had to focus entirely on Baldy.

"That's not going to happen, Baldy," I told him calmly. "This place is huge, and I already called my Knight Commanders for backup." A lie, but hey, he knew I could do that from our fight on the bridge. It wasn't out of bounds to try to use it again.

His lips twitched into a smile for a fraction of a second—so fast that I thought I imagined it—and his eyes narrowed. "Doesn't matter," he said. "Put the weapon down and move."

"*Liana?*" I heard my brother's voice drift down the hall behind me, but I ignored it. Internally, I screamed for him to go back. I didn't want him coming here. I had no idea how Baldy was going to react when he saw the man who had attacked him, but he was already agitated enough. I didn't need Alex making the situation worse. I had to get this under control before Alex reached us.

"It's not going to happen," I said with a slow shake of my head. "But if you put yours down, I promise that no one's going to hurt you again."

"*Quess?!*" My brother's voice was closer, his exclamation telling me he had found Quess. That meant he was closer than I'd thought, and I had even less time than I'd hoped. Maybe I would get lucky and he would stop to help Quess before coming for me. But when he called my name again, I knew that it was a fool's hope to think I could be that lucky. I blocked everything out—from Zoe's desperate sounds to Eric's choked, gasping breathing—knowing that if I looked away, even to check on them, or to tell my brother to stop, Baldy would shoot me, and then my friends.

His face darkened to a peculiar shade of purple, and he

straightened his arm out at me, the gun shaking in his hand. "You're hurting me right now!" he screeched, spittle flying from his lips. "You think I can't feel you, digging around, in here?" He touched his head with his free hand, rocking back and forth for a second. "GET OUT OF MY MIND!" he screamed so suddenly that I took half a step forward, my finger tensing on the trigger for a second before easing back as I realized he could sense Leo inside of him.

That was a relief in some ways, because it told me that Leo was still there. But I had no idea what was happening, or whether he was okay. Baldy could clearly fight him, something Leo had insisted wasn't possible, and maybe it had surprised Leo, caught him off guard. That would explain Baldy's erratic behavior and gave me hope that Leo was fighting for control. He probably just needed time to... figure out how to hack Baldy's brain. If I could just stall Baldy long enough, maybe Leo could re-exert control and take over.

Baldy gripped his head with one hand, his mouth open in a desperate howl as he began to scratch at his scalp, digging red furrows into the skin, as if he were trying to claw the net Leo was in directly out of his skull.

"Stop it," I told him, fear for Leo radiating through me. "And we'll help you! We'll get it out."

"LIAR!" he bellowed, his voice filled with fear. "I can feel the disgusting abomination in there, trying to pry my secrets from me. Well, you can't have them!" He blinked, his brows furrowing slightly. His eyes stared down, growing unfocused in contemplation, and then brightening in some sort of realization. The shift was as blatant as it was rapid, and it unsettled me. "You can't have them," he repeated, nodding, his voice almost wistful, like he had come to some sort of great decision.

"Okay," I said carefully, hoping that this was a sign that he was calming down. "We won't take them. Just put the gun—NO!"

I held out my hand as he put the barrel of the gun up to his temple, his finger on the trigger. I could imagine the bullet tearing through his skull and brain matter, destroying both it and the net that Leo was in at the same time. Talking him down had clearly failed, but I desperately needed him to become very unconscious—very quickly. But how?

"This is my duty," Baldy muttered.

"It's not," I said, my mind whirling. I was too far away to use my baton, and I didn't have any sedatives with me to knock him out. If I started toward him, he could pull the trigger before I could get close enough to stop him. If I shot him, he might retaliate by firing at Zoe or Maddox. Annoyance flashed hot over me, along with frustration that I couldn't find a way out. Leo was close to being killed, Eric was bleeding out, and I was fresh out of ideas! Why did it have to be this difficult? Why wasn't Cornelius pitching me an idea, or—

Cornelius! He had nonlethal takedowns all over this place. I was certain that he had a way to do something. I immediately started to think my command to him, using the neural transmitter to relay the message so Baldy couldn't see me give it.

"Put the gun down, okay?" I told Baldy soothingly. "I promise, you don't have to do this. You don't have to die. I know we've treated you unfairly, but we'll get the net out before it can take any of your secrets." Meanwhile: *Cornelius, can you electrocute him remotely?*

Yes, I can electrify the section of floor plating he is standing on, came the virtual assistant's voice in my ear canal, buzzing sharply. I hesitated for a fraction of a second. Would frying Baldy hurt Leo? It didn't matter. I had to risk it. If I let him pull the trigger, Leo would be dead anyway. I had to.

Baldy stared at me hard, his hand shaking. "You're lying," he said.

"No," I replied. "I'm not." *Prime whatever charge you have to and wait for my signal*, I thought at Cornelius. "You don't want to do that, do you? Pull the trigger? End your life? You want to get out of here, tell the others what we've done. You can't do that if you're dead."

Baldy's arm began to move down, then, his hand trembling as he slowly dragged the end of the gun away from his head. Suddenly he swung it back out at me, and I tensed, thinking he had changed to a target more appealing than himself—me. And then his arm began to drift lower. My heart skipped a beat as I followed it, my breathing tight, but hope beginning to blossom.

If he continued to lower his arm, I could just—

"Liana!" my brother said sharply, from directly behind me, and Baldy's eyes flared wide in fear as he saw my brother.

"You!" he growled, and his eyes narrowed on me. "I knew you were a liar! This was a trap!"

"NO!" I shouted as he yanked the gun back toward his temple. I knew where he was going, what he was planning, and I squeezed out, *Now, Cornelius*, just as a strong hand grabbed my own hand around the gun... and squeezed. The gun kicked, the jerk of it reverberating through my wrist, forearm, elbow, and shoulder, and then blood blossomed in the middle of Baldy's throat, his eyes going wide.

The gun in his hand flashed once, and then the hand around mine became two, pulling me down, tucking me under and behind my brother's body. I was already pushing away from him, my heart in my throat as Baldy continued to fall, blood splattering on the stairs in the wake of his passing.

"LEO!" I shouted, shoving at my brother's hands as he continued to grab at me, trying to pull me back to safety.

13

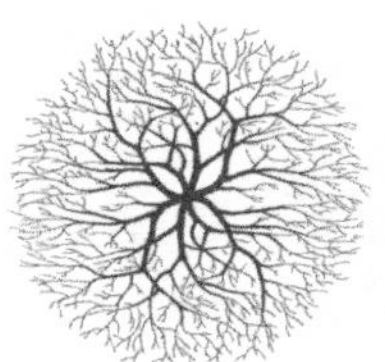

I scrambled forward as Baldy stumbled back and tripped on the stairs behind him. He gave a surprised and wet gurgle that I not only heard, but had experienced from his side, and my innards twisted as another jet of blood spurted from the hole in his throat.

"Liana, no!" my brother shouted, his hand clamping like a vice around my forearm and holding me back. "He could still be dangerous! I warned you something like this was going to happen, and..."

I couldn't listen anymore. An intense anger twisted up inside me, forcing me to whip around and face him. His eyes widened, his grip loosening around my arm, but I shoved him back. He'd forced me to shoot at *Leo*. He couldn't have waited—he just had to react. I didn't care that he was saving my life, that he didn't know that Leo was inside of Baldy. I *cared* that he had just barged in and *ruined* everything. I had been about to get Baldy to back down, and he had charged in without waiting, or listening to what was going on!

"Leo's inside of him!" I shouted as he stumbled back. He came to a stop, some of the anger draining from his face.

"What?" he asked, but I was already turning away and racing toward the stairs.

"Maddox, grab some smelling salts and get Quess up to help Eric. And bring me a net transfer kit, now!" I shouted as I dropped to my knees next to Baldy. The gun had fallen from his grasp, and I shoved it aside and lifted my hands to... help him?

I stared down at him, suddenly transfixed by the blood spurting from his neck. He was bleeding out fast, and I had none of the dermal bonding agent on me to stop it. His arms struggled as his mouth opened and closed like a fish's, blood gurgling in the back of his throat as he choked on his own blood, causing my own memories of being in his spot to flash before my eyes.

Did I look like that? I wondered as he continued to flop around, helpless. *Did he look down at me and see that*?

A cold, hard part of me *wanted* to watch him bleed out. He'd taken Maddox in the Core, attacked us in the Medica and again on the catwalk, and then cut my throat in the Attic. He was the source of so much trouble, and a leader of some sort in the legacies. Countless people had probably died at his hands or by his orders, Ambrose's among the names of the dead.

Luckily, the part that was worried about Leo was far greater. Bullets could ricochet inside the body; if the one that shot him had somehow found its way into his brain or shattered one of his vertebrae, then Leo could already be damaged. He could already be *dead*. And what would happen if he was inside someone when they died? Would he die as well? What must he be feeling?

To hell with saving Baldy, I decided. I had to get Leo out, and that was all I was going to worry about.

"Maddox, I need that kit!" I shouted, shoving my hands under the man's side to flip him over. He made a gurgled sound of surprise that made my skin crawl, and I was hyperaware of the fact that he was going to bleed out faster like this. I was consciously expediting his death, and the thought made me grim as I yanked down the back of his collar.

"Liana!" Zoe sobbed.

I looked over to see Eric gasping, too, his face ashen and gray. Zoe was rocking him back and forth, her hands pressed over a hole in his chest. Blood was spurting from the wound. "Keep pressing," I told her. "Quess is coming! Maddox is getting him." At least, I hoped she was. She wasn't in the room anymore, which made me hope that she had leapt into action to get Quess up. But I couldn't stop what I was doing here to help Zoe. Leo could be hurt or dying inside of Baldy. I had to get him out.

Zoe cried harder, but I turned back to Baldy, trying to think of what I could use to cut his neck open. His gurgles were growing further and further apart, and I swallowed the excess saliva in my mouth as I tried not to think about how that could've been me just two days ago.

Then hands were cutting across my vision, a black kit in them, and I snatched at it and looked up to tell Maddox to get Quess. Instead, I got a face full of my brother, his expression concerned and bewildered.

"I didn't know it was—"

"Save it," I said curtly, tearing the bag open with quick movements. It wasn't about him not knowing; it was about him blindly reacting. I grabbed the laser pen, took a firm grip on the back of Baldy's head, pressed the button to emit a slender blue beam, positioned the tip over the pink scar tissue, and started to cut through the subdermal tissue.

I heard running footsteps behind me, but I focused on the incision. The skin split easily, and only a small amount of blood seeped out of the edges of the wound. I dragged the laser down, the blue beam slicing through his skin as if it weren't even there. After I'd made an inch-long incision, I pulled the skin back.

Baldy was still now, and I threw the cutter aside and pulled out a pair of tweezers. Inside the wound, the tendrils of the net were beginning to retract, and I waited long enough for them to weave themselves into a flat, hard rectangle, glistening white amid the pink tissue and white fat. I quickly extracted the net using the tweezers and dropped it into my hand.

I shook as I carefully picked up the hard square, inspecting it for any sign of damage. Blood clung to the sides of it, making it seem like it was bleeding. I quickly wiped the blood away with my thumb, fighting back a sob as it left a pink smear in its wake. Taking it between shaky fingers, I wrapped it in the edge of my sleeve to wipe the remaining blood away so I could see it clearly. My hand trembled as I dug the small thing out again, trying not to lose my grip on it, and held it up to the light, praying. It looked intact—flat, rectangular, and white—and as I stared at it, I realized I had zero idea how to identify damage on the net.

"Liana!" Quess shouted, dragging me away from the net. I looked down at where he was now leaning over Eric and flinched when I saw how pale and still my other best friend was. Quess shot me a look over his shoulder, and I could see his own fear in his eyes. "I need Grey," he told me.

I blanked for a second, confused as to why he would need Grey, and then I remembered. Grey was a universal donor. Eric had lost a lot of blood and would need a transfusion. Even better, putting Leo back inside Grey's neck would tell us very quickly if Leo was damaged.

"Keep working, Quess," I said, standing and tucking the net into my fist.

I looked over at my brother, and to my surprise I saw that he was staring at Baldy, his eyes dark and hooded. I started to check on him, but Zoe's soft sobs, punctuated by Quess's softly spoken orders to her, turned me away. Time was already running out for Eric. I needed to get Grey now.

I ran down the steps and across the conference room, and then up a different set of steps to the hall, passing the first doorway, then the second, finally coming to Leo's room. I pressed the button, and the door slid open, revealing Grey in mid-step. He turned toward the door, his eyes widening in surprise, but I was already moving toward him.

"Come with me," I said, grabbing his arm. "I need your help."

He didn't move for a second, and I tugged him hard as I whirled to look at him. "*Please!*" I begged.

His brown eyes filled with concern, and then he nodded and started to move. I hauled him behind me, my legs tearing up the distance at a quick walk, then a jog.

"What's going on?" he asked from behind me.

"My friend's hurt," I told him, dragging him around the corner to the entrance. "And you're a universal donor."

"Wait, what? How do you know that?"

I ignored his question and pulled him through the door just as Quess was shaking his head at Zoe and causing my best friend in the world to collapse on Eric's chest.

Eric's unmoving chest. I sped up, bodily yanking Grey behind me as I raced over to them. "No," I said, my teeth clenched as I slid to my knees, unconcerned by the puddle of blood.

"He's gone, Liana," Quess said, his dark blue eyes almost black with grief. "He—"

"Hook him up to Grey, now," I said, my hands pressing insistently on Zoe's back. "Zoe, move!"

I shoved her, harder than I should've, but I didn't care about hurting her feelings. I wasn't losing anyone else to that man or his legacies—not even one. I didn't care that Quess thought it was hopeless. Eric wanted to live. He had everything in the world to live for. And I wasn't going to let anyone give up on him.

"Liana!"

"DO IT NOW OR GIVE ME YOUR BAG AND GET THE HELL OUT!" I roared.

Quess flinched and then nodded jerkily, his hands dipping into the bag to pull out a bit of plastic tubing with two patches at the ends. As he did, I tilted Eric's head back, trying to ignore how easily his limbs moved. I tucked the net with Leo into a pocket before lacing my fingers together. Then I began to compress his heart, counting off in my head. After thirty compressions, I stuck a finger in his mouth, clearing his airway, and then fitted my lips over his and began puffing air into his lungs.

I repeated this twice, and then switched back to pushing on his chest to compress his heart. Meanwhile, Quess had finished attaching Grey to Eric, via the hose.

"Adrenaline for his heart," I snapped.

Grey's eyes were wide and horrified, but he sat there quietly, watching us.

Quess nodded and pulled out a pneumatic injector. "Here," he said, pressing it to Eric's neck and clicking it. "It's the last dose we can give him, though. I've already given him two ampules."

I ignored that, focusing completely on Eric. "Breathe, Eric," I said. I fitted my mouth over his and puffed more into his lungs, then pulled back. "Breathe!"

Eric's chest rose and fell with each breath of air I shoved into him. His body jerked up and down as I pumped on his chest. But his eyes continued to stare up at the ceiling. Empty and devoid of life. Panic set in, and I redoubled my efforts.

"No," I said, bending over him once again. "C'mon, Eric!" I cried. I blew more air into him, getting steadily dizzier from breathing too fast, but unwilling to stop. Unwilling to let him go. "You don't want to die like this!" Blow. "You have to propose to my best friend." I changed over to compressing on his chest and kept talking. "Invite me to your wedding." Push. "And then make me little nieces and nephews I can spoil and love on!" Push. "So you're not." Push. "Allowed." Push. "To die!" Push. Push. Push.

I could hear Zoe sniffling behind me, see the broken look on Maddox's face, and feel the defeat rolling off Quess.

"Liana," Quess said, his voice a hesitant string of pain. "He's..."

"He's not gone," I said between clenched teeth. "I'm not losing anyone else. We've already lost Cali, Roark, Ambrose, my mother... I'm not letting him die."

To prove it, I balled my hand into a fist and slammed it down on his chest. Over and over again, trying to force his heart to pump, to draw blood from Grey, to—

Eric gasped so unexpectedly that I jerked my hands back and toppled over onto my butt. His eyes fluttered open and closed, and he began to cough.

"Quess!" I called, afraid that Eric was going to stop breathing again. But he was already there, fitting a filtration mask over Eric's nose and mouth, holding the other man's head still.

He looked up at me, eyes wide, even as Zoe wrapped her arms around me and began to cry.

"Don't you stop working on him," I muttered, but it was a plea more than anything. I wasn't arrogant enough to assume that I had brought Eric back. I had just refused to quit—and it had paid off. Eric was still pale, and there was every chance in the world that he wouldn't make it if Quess couldn't figure out where the damage was and fix it quickly. But I had bought him some time.

I only prayed it would be enough.

14

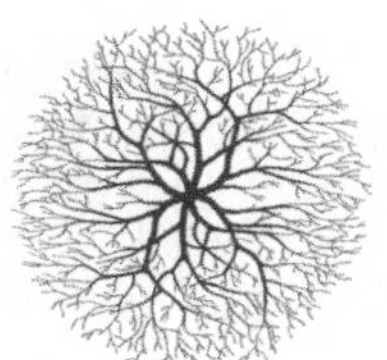

I wasn't sure how long I had been holding Zoe before Maddox suddenly stood up. I had been watching Quess work, fixated on the blood that seemed to be everywhere, but jerked when she let out a sharp curse.

I looked up to see her standing over my brother, bent at the waist and holding his wrist. She looked up at me, her eyes round with fear. "Liana, his rank is falling."

My heart sank into my stomach as I pulled away from Zoe, practically leaping over Grey to get up the stairs to Alex.

My twin was still sitting, his eyes now fixed on Baldy's blank gaze, a lost and horror-filled look in his eyes. He was shaking slightly, his skin pale and clammy, and I realized he had gone into shock.

But that didn't stop his number from dropping, and my heart skittered along my breastbone, placed there by the terror of watching the eight on his wrist click to a seven with a sharp snap. I met Maddox's gaze, and realized that although Alex had thought he was defending us, Scipio had somehow read his emotions and decided that this was cold-blooded murder.

That was bad. Murderers were considered an anathema to the Tower, a danger to productivity, and were automatically reduced to the rank of one. We were witnessing it now, here, with my brother. And as soon as the system registered his fall, the alarms would begin to go off, and the Knights would come running. If they found him here, with Baldy's dead corpse, it would be a done deal, and he would be shipped to the expulsion chambers.

And I wouldn't be able to do anything to stop it.

I stood up and shoved Leo's net toward Maddox. "Get Leo back into Grey as soon as you can," I told her. "I don't care what you have to tell Grey about what you're doing and why—just get him in there." I needed to know he was okay, that he hadn't been hurt when Baldy was shot, and the fastest way to do that was to get him into Grey's head. Hopefully Leo wouldn't have the same problems with Grey as he had with Baldy.

A dark fear rose at the thought of that, and I wondered if Leo *would* be able to reestablish control with Grey. What if the process only worked when someone's waking mind was resting, or in a comatose state, like Grey had been? Maybe the design was intended for the AI to only aid in the healing process, not take control. Now that Grey was back, what if Leo could only be in his thoughts and healing his mind, rather than actually taking part in the outside world? Pain rippled through me at the thought, but I quickly shoved it inside, deciding to worry about it *after* I saved my brother.

Maddox nodded and accepted the chip, but I could see the uncertainty in her eyes. No doubt she was wondering what she would even say to Grey, and I didn't know how to help her. I wasn't sure what to say to him either. All I knew was I had two major problems before me, and one of them needed my immediate attention. Namely, my brother.

"What about him?" she asked, pointing at my brother.

"The Paragon," I reminded her. "If I get it in his system fast enough, it'll boost his rank back up, and keep him off the sensors. Where did we leave it?"

"In the kitchen," she replied without hesitation. Her eyes flicked down to my brother's wrist, and I followed them in time to see the seven morph into a bruised and bloated six. He was falling fast, and if anyone in IT was monitoring or recording his rank status, they would see that something significant had happened.

And I knew for a fact that Sadie was having him watched. I had to get him up and moving and get a pill down his throat as quickly as possible. It might already be too late if someone was watching right now, but I had to try. I couldn't risk them taking my brother away.

I grabbed his arm and yanked. To my surprise, he allowed himself to be dragged up and forward, but his movements were stiff and laborious.

"Where are we going?" he asked, and the hopeless sound in his voice made my heart ache.

I wanted to turn around and comfort him, but as soon as his rank hit three, the alarms would go off. With Quess working to save Eric, and Leo trapped in the net until Maddox got him back into Grey, I couldn't count on them to shut off the sensors in the apartment to buy us time, and I doubted Cornelius would be able to obey that request without some AI help, which meant I had to make it to the Paragon before he hit three.

"To the kitchen," I told him, hauling on his arm and pulling him forward, practically dragging him behind me. I urged him both orally and physically, trying to get him to understand the urgency of the situation through the tightness of my grip and the insistent tugging on his arm. His feet picked up the speed, from a stiff-limbed lumber to a slight jog, but it still wasn't fast enough. "Hurry up, Alex!"

"Huh?"

We were making our way around the hairpin turn now, and I chanced a glance back to his wrist—and felt a spurt of adrenaline as the six slid into a sickly orange five. The alarms were going to go off as soon as the sensors in the area registered the three, and they'd already be picking up the fact that he'd dropped all the way to five.

But he didn't even notice. His eyes were blank, hollow, and empty, his half-hearted burst of speed already flagging.

I knew I had to snap him out of it. He had to get moving or we were going to lose him entirely—because if he dropped down to a three, I wasn't going to be able to do anything to save him from Scipio and those expulsion chambers. So I did the only thing I could think of.

I slapped him. Once on the cheek. Then again at the blank-stare look he gave me, and again at the dazed and confused one that followed.

The third time was the charm, because he shook his head, his hand going to his cheek. "Liana?"

"*Come on.*" Squeezing his arm in what had to have been a most painful fashion, I continued pulling him along the hall, picking up the speed as he followed my impatient urgings.

"Where are we going?" he asked again as we wound our way through the switchback and into the hall.

"Your rank is falling," I called back, trying to speed up into a run as soon as we rounded the corner. It was clear he was in shock, and I wasn't helping matters by forcing him to move, but there wasn't any time. "Trust me, Alex, there isn't time for this."

My brother didn't say anything for a second as I got us to a jog, but I heard a slight intake of breath that sounded shocked enough to make me look back. A four glared brightly at me from his wrist, the orange like a beacon in the well-lit hallway.

"I... I didn't know it was Leo," he said, his voice quivering. "I didn't know what that thing in your hand was. I don't understand... Why is Scipio punishing me? I was *defending* you."

"I don't know," I told him, but in my heart, I had doubts. Maybe my brother had been acting in my defense, but he had also been calling for Baldy's death ever since he'd beaten him. So which was true? Maybe both, but it didn't matter. All I knew was that Scipio had chosen not to interpret his emotional state that way and was now shaving away his rank as punishment. I was angry at him for what happened, but I was more concerned about what this would do to him if we didn't get him to take the medicine. I loved my brother no matter what; he was half of my heart and soul. He drove me up the wall sometimes, but I was not going to let him fall like this. He'd watched over me his entire life, trying to protect me.

Now it was my turn.

I picked up the pace as we passed the bedrooms, then the bathrooms, a stitch forming in my side as we ran. I was tired—exhausted, really—but I still poured as much energy as I could muster into getting into the kitchen.

Relief filled me as the hall widened slightly into the steps that would take us down into the large dining/kitchen space. I spotted the bag containing the pills on the counter in the kitchen and started to run over to it, my arms and legs trembling from exertion and fear.

But Alex planted his feet halfway there, almost jerking me off my feet. I caught my balance and twisted around, looking at him. "Alex, c'mon!"

"It's too late," he whispered, holding up his wrist. The three on it seemed to throb rhythmically, as if counting down, and I dropped his hand and sprinted up the stairs to the elevated kitchen area, snatching the bag off the counter. "You have to arrest me. If you don't, they'll arrest you, too."

"Shut up!" My fingers fumbled with the fastener as I whirled around and raced back to my brother, and I gave a frustrated little shriek seconds before it slid open. I had just been through the bag earlier today, so I knew exactly what I was looking for. Thrusting my arm in, I felt for one of the largest pill bottles, and found one almost immediately, my ears straining for any sign of the alarms.

Please let the sensors be sweeping slowly today, I prayed as I yanked the bottle out, barely paying attention to the handwriting on the side, and focused on unscrewing the lid as I came to a stop before my twin. His eyes had adopted a faraway look, and he was mumbling something.

"...Not protected like you are. I wanted to tell you at the funeral... discovered an irregularity in the way Scipio handles ranking. Positions that require a ten are locked there. Councilors can't fall... Knight Commanders can't fall. Explains how they can murder people, huh? Not me, though. I'm going to get caught and—"

The implications of what he was telling me were huge, but I barely registered them. I was too focused on the task of saving his life.

The lid came off in my hands, and I turned the bottle on its side and fished out a pill, then shoved it between his lips before he could say anything else. "Swallow," I ordered him.

His eyes met mine, and his Adam's apple bobbed up and down, telling me he had done so.

I let out a shaky breath, and then grabbed his arm, turning his wrist up so I could see the number there. The three had disappeared during my rush to the bag and back, and the two had somehow come and gone in the short time it took me to get the pills. Now a single vertical line remained. One.

Tension ran under my skin as I bit my lip, waiting to see what would happen first. It would either be the alarm signaling to the Knights that a one was in the area—or his rank sliding upward again. Seconds ticked by, and nothing happened.

"It's not going to work," he said. "It's too late. You have to arrest me, Liana. I'll tell them everything was my fault. It'll be okay."

He had just closed his mouth again when his rank morphed from red to purple, jumping from a one to a seven on his wrist. I held it up to him, showing him that he was safe, and then let out a sigh of relief and staggered a few steps back. I closed my eyes for several seconds, lightheaded from the panic of everything, and then pried them right back open again.

I wasn't done—not by a long shot—but for now, at least I had made sure my brother was safe.

Now I just needed to keep him that way. I took a moment to study him, noting the look on his face and the way he couldn't seem to stop twitching, and realized he needed sleep. He'd been in shock mere minutes before, and was already starting to backtrack into it, judging by the stunned look in his eyes. I reached out and took his hand again, and this time he followed me with little resistance as I guided him back toward the war room. As soon as I got him settled, I'd race back to the others to help them in whatever way they needed, whether it was getting Leo back in Grey or helping Quess with Eric.

I stopped outside of Leo's room long enough to open the door, and then pulled Alex inside. The room was still a mess from Grey's temper tantrum earlier, but it only took me a minute or two to put the mattress back into place. Alex didn't help, but then again, as soon as he'd come in, he'd stopped and started staring at a spot on the floor.

"Alex," I said, trying to keep my voice gentle. I felt spread too thin, but I had to remind myself to be patient with him. He was more fragile than me now. "Take off your uniform and get in bed."

He looked up at me, his gaze blank. "Why?" he asked. "I don't think I could sleep."

"You have to try," I told him. "What happened today..."

"I killed a man," he said, his voice empty. "I beat him to a pulp, and then I killed him. Possibly even two, if you count Leo. How..." He trailed off, looking so undeniably lost that I couldn't help but hurt for him.

"You were trying to defend me," I told him gently. "And I love you for it. We really should—"

"What have I become, Liana?" he whispered harshly. His dark eyes were filled with torment as he stared at his hands. They trembled violently, and he squeezed his eyes shut against them, as if denying the blood on them and failing. "I *killed* a man. I *wanted* him dead! I... This wasn't how it was supposed to be!"

Seconds later he was falling to his knees, his arms wrapping around his shoulders, and I rushed over to him, throwing my arms around him. He wasn't crying, but he was shaking as if he were a leaf caught under a ventilation duct. I held him close, stroking his temples and hair, trying to reassure him that I was there and he was safe.

"I don't know who I am anymore," he told me some time later, his voice less broken but every bit as empty as before. "I don't know what I'm doing. I hate it here so much. I'm so alone and isolated in the Core, and I have nothing to do but worry about you and watch Scipio slowly degrade into nothingness. I'm beyond useless, and I just jeopardized everything you had been working toward." His voice caught in the end, and he shot me a hopeless look. "What good am I to anyone?"

My heart fractured. "Alex, no... You're good for me," I told him. "You help me. You've always taken care of me and loved me, even when I was being a colossal brat. Please don't give up hope. We'll figure this out; we'll work through it. It's my turn to take care of you." I shifted my weight, my legs numb below the knee from the kneeling position, and he straightened up.

"I think I'll go lie down now," he told me. "You have to check on Eric and..." He paused long enough to swallow audibly before adding, "Leo."

I slowly got to my feet, and helped my brother into bed, getting him out of his uniform and under the blanket. I sat down next to him and continued to stroke his shoulder and arm. "I'm going to go check on Leo," I whispered to him. "But I'm sure he's going to be just fine. You try to get some rest, and I'll be back soon. I love you."

My brother didn't reply, and after a moment, I realized he wouldn't. I felt conflicted as I got up, as a part of me wanted to stay and continue to comfort my brother.

But I had to check on Leo and Eric. They were my responsibility, too.

15

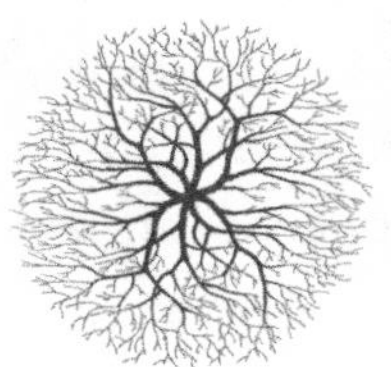

I was halfway to the war room when Grey appeared at the other end. I stopped in my tracks, blinking at him and wondering who I was looking at. "Grey?" He shook his head, and relief poured through me. Still, I wanted confirmation. "Leo?"

He nodded, and I shot off like a bullet toward him, needing the feel of his arms around me. I barely even gave him time to open his arms before I was in them, wrapping my own around his waist and pulling him tight to me. "Are you okay?"

He hesitated a second before returning the hug, and then slowly smoothed his arms over my shoulders and back. "I'm okay," he told me. "Your brother didn't hurt me."

Something inside me started to break, and I gave a little cry. "What about Eric? Is he?"

"Grey gave him all the blood he could," Leo said. "Quess recovered the bullet, but it punctured a lung, ricocheted off a rib, and nicked his liver. He stopped the bleeding internally, but he lost a lot of blood, and what Grey was able to give him wasn't a lot. He's stable, but it's now a waiting game."

"But what about Grey?" I asked. "Is *he* okay? He was so scared and confused before, and—"

I stopped as my shoulders started to shake, a sob catching me unawares, the terror of the last five—ten?—minutes finally starting to hit me. Leo's hands pressed me closer, one going up to stroke my hair lightly. "Grey's... fine," he hedged. I started to question his hesitation, but he cut me off. "I know you are upset, and I understand why, but we'll have to talk about Grey later. There's something more important that needs our attention first."

His words gave me pause, and I looked up at him, blinking back my tears. "What is it?"

Leo's mouth turned down into a frown. "We have to get rid of Baldy's body. Cornelius's sensors were shut off in regard to undoc alerts, but not in regard to death, and I can't access Cornelius with Jasper and Rose's programs in the state they are in—they might interpret it as an attack and try to take control of his systems. We have only a few minutes to get it out of here before he automatically syncs with the council server and informs them that there's a corpse in your quarters. As long as the body isn't here when he syncs, he won't be able to inform them."

I blinked, not comprehending. I truly didn't understand. "Won't he be able to tell them we moved the body?"

He pulled away from me. I had expected him to take my hand, as he always had after something traumatic happened. But he didn't, and a wave of disappointment crashed into me. Instead, he turned away and began walking back to the war room, talking to me from over his shoulder. I had little choice but to follow, or stand there looking like an idiot over the fact that he hadn't taken my hand.

"No. He's a computer program and can only follow the protocols set up for him as they are laid out. No body equals no report.

It's an oversight in his programming, but one we plan to exploit. But it only works if we get Baldy out of here as soon as possible. I just can't figure out where to put him. The escape hatch would work, except ours leads straight up to the roof, so there's no place for us to leave him in there that wouldn't have him falling back down on top of us."

I heard the dangerous undercurrent of his words and realized that him not taking my hand was definitely the least of our worries. We had to remove the body, but to where? It had to be a place no one could find it; we had left forensic evidence all over him, and if his remains were discovered, the trail would lead back to us—and mostly right back to Alex. Even if it wasn't the legacies that found him, the consequences would be the same. Imprisonment and death.

If the escape exit hatch was out, then almost everything else was as well. Nothing ever remained hidden inside the Tower: there were dozens of places to hide a body inside of it, but they would be discovered eventually, and the jig would be up. Alex's DNA was all over Baldy's face, from hitting him over and over again. His rank had dropped and risen in a matter of minutes, and even if no one had seen it when it happened, a quick check of his performance log would show them the truth. They'd know we had found a way to mask our ranks, and they would immediately try to figure out what it was, so they could put a stop to it. I'd be immediately implicated, because it had happened under my watch.

I'd be arrested and executed as a dissident and enemy of the Tower.

We entered the war room and saw Quess and Maddox already lifting Baldy's body and setting it inside a black body bag. I had no idea where they had gotten that from, but it wouldn't surprise me if Cornelius had procured it from one of the nearby supply rooms. The request would be recorded, but I was betting Leo could go back in and delete it later, once everything calmed down. Eric was still on the floor, using Zoe's lap as a pillow, his eyes closed and his lashes dark against his pale face.

She looked up at me, her blue eyes bleeding with hopelessness. "Quess won't let me move him," she whispered. She reached down and tugged at his bloody uniform where Quess had unzipped it, trying to cover him up. "He needs to be under a blanket."

I moved over to my best friend and wrapped my arms around her, while Quess grunted out, "I'm sorry, Zo, but I can't be sure that moving him won't kill him yet. I told you, go get a blanket from the room, and I promise, we will clean everything up as soon we figure out what to do with this."

I heard a rattling thump that told me they had dropped Baldy's body into the bag, and I gently pulled away from Zoe. "It's going to be okay," I told her in a soft whisper.

Her face broke, and her shoulders shook as she took a breath. "He's the light of my life, Liana. How did this happen? You said we were coming here to be safe!"

Her last sentence was an accusation, and my heart plummeted into the pit of my stomach. I looked over at Leo and saw horror and guilt written all over his face.

"Everything was fine," he said, his voice twisted with raw emotion. "Everything *was* fine. I was learning about him and who his people were, what they had done, what they were planning. But then he just... woke up, and somehow jerked control from me. I've never felt anything like it. And I couldn't do anything to stop him. He shouldn't have been able to keep me from reacting, from putting his body out of commission, but... he did."

My face paled at his description, and I swallowed convulsively. Either Leo was arrogant about his skills, or Baldy had a much stronger mind than either of us had given him credit for. Either way, it scared me, and I worried about whether Grey could do that, now that we had woken him up before putting Leo back inside him. I wondered suddenly how Maddox had managed to handle Grey, but there wasn't time for that now.

I had to help the others move a body and figure out where to put it.

"We'll talk about it later," I instructed everyone. "Zoe, go get Eric a blanket. We'll move him together when we get back." I stood up and turned to the others. "Where can we put the body?"

"Down an elevator shaft in the shell," Maddox suggested. "Or one of the plunges."

"That's the first place the legacies will check for him," I replied. Both were common dumping grounds for bodies, whenever there were any. The plunges were a better choice, but only if you could be certain to hit the bottom, which you never really could be. If his body landed on a bit of twisted-up rebar or a crossbeam, they'd find him. That meant that disposing of the body in a place they could never find him was the only solution.

But there wasn't any place in the Tower like that! The entire thing was a self-contained system. Bodies could be hidden, for a while, but eventually they would be recovered. And forensic evidence could be harvested and tested years after the victim had died. I had no idea how long this legacy war was going to last, so I had to plan for the future.

Which left only one place. "We need to throw him off the Tower," I said, walking quickly toward them.

Maddox's brows drew together, forming a deep crease that jutted down the bridge of her nose like a dagger, while Quess's mouth simply dropped open, wide enough to catch flies if he wanted to. Leo was the only one whose eyebrows rose—but almost a second later, he was nodding.

"She's right," he said. "The sensors on the outside of the Tower aren't designed to pick up and report a dead body."

"Yeah, but that's still..." Maddox did some quick calculations and frowned. "Almost eighty floors up from here. The security in the Attic is not the best, but there are still cameras everywhere. Someone is eventually going to notice four people hauling a full body bag to the roof."

"Then we do everything we can to make it look like something else," I told her. "It's the only thing we can do. As soon as we get him out into the main part of the Tower, the sensors won't register that he's dead, and as long as we keep him in the bag, no one watching can be sure of what's inside. We'll spray our faces with Quess's spray so the cameras can't identify us. As for it being eighty floors up..." I pointed up the stairs at the column that controlled my quarters. "I'll lift the room up to the topmost level, and then we'll only have forty floors to go."

"Forty floors of stairs," Quess griped, and I empathized. I wasn't looking forward to it either, especially since we would have to wear neural scramblers to mask our net IDs, which meant we couldn't use the elevators. At least Quess had managed to extend the time we could use the scramblers without risking our nets frying our brains, but I wasn't particularly looking forward to putting the scrambler back on. It was annoying and started to give headaches after a while, and I had already been wearing one earlier. Yet they gave us time and anonymity to do the deed, and between the four of us, I was certain we could handle it. We didn't have any choice.

"Zoe, you stay here to take care of Eric and keep an eye on Tian and Liam. We won't be able to net you, so don't panic if we're gone for a little while. Leo, start moving the platform. Quess, find out if there's a way we can get into the Attic from here without going into the Citadel itself. How much time do we have, Maddox?"

She checked her indicator while the others scrambled to follow my orders, her finger tapping on the face to change it from her rank to the time, and her features pinched. "Six minutes until Cornelius syncs with the council server. It's going to be close."

"We'll be fine," I said reassuringly.

I wasn't sure if it was a lie or not, but it was the best thing I could offer.

The platform began to rumble at the same time as I heard my brother's voice announce, "I'm coming with you," from the hallway. I turned and saw him standing there, his uniform back on and a bleak look in his eyes. "I have to clean up my own mess." It dawned on me that he probably hadn't even tried to sleep before getting up and dressing again, which meant he had heard the tail end of the conversation and knew what was going on.

I stared at him, and it was on the tip of my tongue to tell him to go back to bed and let me handle it. But then I remembered his words, how broken he had looked, and how much he wanted to be useful, and I found I couldn't deny him, especially given that we needed the help. Not to mention, I couldn't cut him out again. It was partially what had gotten us into this mess.

"The help would be appreciated."

16

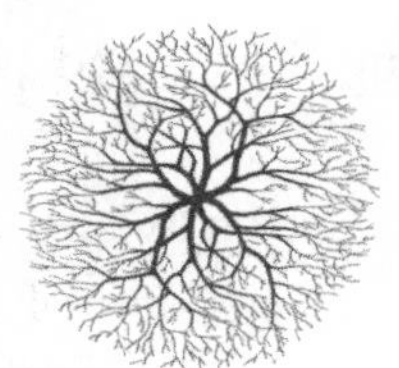

For the second time in twenty-four hours, I was carrying Baldy through the labyrinth of corridors in the Attic. This time, however, I had help, and we took turns carrying him down the hall, the bag swinging heavily between the two people whose turn it was. My arms and legs felt leaden from all the exertion today, and I was certain that if I let my eyes close for too long, I would pass out. The fear was enough to keep them wide open, and only added to the press of my nerves as we made our way down the hallway.

Getting here had been simpler than I had thought it would be, but getting up had been more difficult than I had anticipated. I had assumed there were staircases between the levels spread out through the floor, but the forty topmost levels of storage space could only be accessed through the elevators. We couldn't use those, as they were heavily monitored by live techs, to make sure no one was using them to transport illegal materials. That meant we had to use the stairs in the shell.

It took us forty-five minutes to get from where my apartment elevator dropped us off to the thick wall that led out into the shell and our designated staircases. It took another hour to carry him up them. At any given point, I would've loved to just open up a hatch and shove him out, but there was too much risk of a crosswind carrying his body onto one of the farming floors that extended out from the sides of the Tower. The safest place to drop him was from the corner of the roof. Even if there was a breeze, it wouldn't carry him far enough in either direction that he'd hit one of the farming floors, and he likely wouldn't be seen on the way down.

So together we climbed, silently, moving as quickly as we could go without sapping all of our strength. Even still, Leo and I had to take more breaks than Alex, Quess, and Maddox, though they were understanding enough. By the time we reached the last level and trudged another forty-five minutes to get to the center of the 215th floor, where the only staircase with access to the roof existed, it was my turn to carry again, along with Quess. And Quess was complaining. Again.

"I just don't see why we didn't call Lacey and ask her to throw him in the forges," he said for the umpteenth time.

I gritted my teeth, focusing on the steps leading up and trying to ignore the trembling of my legs. My palms were sweating, and the microfiber body bag felt like it was slipping from my grasp.

"We could've sent him out with the laundry, like she transported you and Leo, and just dumped him into an oven at the smelting factory. No evidence, no muss, and definitely—" He grunted, and the bag jerked slightly in my grip as he tripped on a step. The bag smacked into me, and I lost my balance and slammed into a wall with my shoulder, a sharp cry of pain escaping my throat before I could stop it.

It didn't hurt past the surprise of the impact, and embarrassment flooded through me that I had made such a big spectacle about nothing. I started to tell everyone that I was fine, but Leo had moved down the handful of steps between us, brushing by Quess a little rudely to do so.

"Are you okay?" he asked, cupping my cheek.

I nodded, trying to flex the shoulder in question, even with Baldy just swinging between Quess and me. "Yeah," I said tiredly. "We almost there, Maddox?"

I looked up at where she was climbing the last few steps to the next landing in the square staircase. "The door is here," she announced. "Just a few more steps."

"C'mon, Quess," I panted, pushing off the wall and planting a heavy boot on another step. "We got this."

"No, I've got it," Alex said, coming up a few steps from where he had been trailing behind us. There were dark smudges under his eyes now, and I could see exhaustion lining his face, but he took the bag from me and resumed the climb.

"Also, shut up, Quess," Leo added as he took a step back to let us by.

Quess snorted but fell silent, and the sound of our steps on the stairs resumed. It took ten more steps—each of which I felt all the way from the soles of my feet into my hips—before we were on the landing. Maddox was already twisting the pressure handle open, and a moment later a gust of pressurized air from the Tower burst through with a hiss, swinging the door open.

Revealing another set of stairs that led to a star-laden, inky black sky. I sucked in a breath of the air—air that was free from the regular tinny smell always present inside the Tower—and sighed.

My hair tugged in the cross breeze, and I took the promise of there being fresher, cleaner air in just ten short steps, and used the motivation to hobble up the remaining steps.

The stairs stopped at the surface of the roof with a transition from concrete to solar panel at the end of the last step. There were no lights up here, but the moon was out, shining brightly just over the horizon to the east and coating the world in a myriad of blue shadows that made everything look like a quilted blanket. Everything from the Tower seemed so far away standing here, peering out at a world that I only ever got to see when I was outside.

But there was no time to appreciate the beauty or splendor of it, and I turned to help Alex and Quess up the stairs, grabbing the bag and hauling it up and over the edge to set it down on a solar panel.

"Take a break," I told everyone, wiping a hand over my forehead. The frigid night air was already beginning to cool my flushed cheeks and heated skin, but soon it would be biting, and the moisture on my skin would only make it worse. It was rare, but the wind chill could cause frostbite, if there was enough moisture on the skin. We'd have to be mindful of the cold and finish up quickly, before it could take effect.

Everyone stood around to catch their breaths and stretch, and I followed suit, trying to relieve some of the lactic acid that had built up in my muscles. I knew we couldn't linger for long, but given how easily we had managed to make it up without being spotted or intercepted, I felt confident that we could spare a minute or two.

I was walking in a slow circle around the gap where the stairs came up, not wanting to stay still for too long lest my muscles stiffen, when Quess suddenly jerked up from where he was bending over to touch his toes, his eyes going wide and looking into the sky. The abrupt movement caught my eyes, and I immediately started looking around, trying to figure out what he was looking for.

"What is it?" I asked.

"Leo, are you getting this?" Quess asked, ignoring me completely.

I turned to where Leo had been standing a few feet behind me, doing some side stretches. He didn't seem as shocked as Quess, but his expression was pinched, eyes hard. "I am," he replied.

"Getting what?" I asked, looking between the two men. Then I glanced at Maddox, who shrugged, clearly as baffled as I was at their strange behavior.

Quess turned to me, his eyes glistening brightly. "Liana, things just took a turn from bad to weird," he told me.

I frowned at him and sucked in a deep breath, wondering if he said crap like that just to drive me crazy. I was too physically, mentally, and emotionally exhausted for these games, and after everything I'd been through today, the *last* thing I wanted was for my life to get *weird*. "What. The hell. Is going. On?"

"Do you remember the monitoring station that Leo was talking about a few weeks ago? The one meant for watching for outside transmissions that showed human life?"

I closed my eyes and tried to summon up the conversation. It took me a minute—I was tired, after all—but I did. We'd been talking about trying to find out if there was even life outside the Tower, and Leo had mentioned the monitoring station. I'd made a mental note to check it out later, to see if there were any incoming transmissions that were somehow being blocked, but had never gotten around to it.

"Yes," I bit out. "Why?"

He licked his lips. "Well, after the Tourney... during those days when you..." Trailing off, he looked away guiltily, as if he realized that he was treading into dangerous lands.

He wasn't, though, because I didn't deny what had happened those three days after my mother's death. Didn't deny that I had been untethered from reality for most of it, or that it had been full of misdirected hatred toward the AI fragment who had been controlling the sentinel that killed her. "When I wasn't doing my best," I told him, motioning somewhat impatiently for him to proceed.

"Well, I had a lot of free time on my hands. I made the spray, tinkered around with a few designs... but on day two I was stir crazy. So Leo and I went out, found the monitoring station, and hacked into it. I meant to tell you about it, but everything's been so—"

"Crazy," I finished for him with a nod. "That should be our motto." I took a deep breath and considered what he was saying, and the brief exchange between him and Leo, and then realized the only way he'd be bringing it up was if something had changed. And there was only one thing that could've changed. "Are you telling me that someone from out there is transmitting? And that you can somehow hear them?"

He nodded enthusiastically. "Not just transmitting blindly, either. They're transmitting to us. To the Tower. Asking for us by name, really."

I blinked several times, trying to wrap my head around what he was saying. It didn't make any sense. Why would they be transmitting to the Tower? How did they even know we were here? Was it to someone specific, or—

"What do they want?" Maddox asked, cutting off my questions with perhaps the most important one of all.

"Hold on a second," Quess said, reaching into his pocket and pulling out his pad. "I set the feed up to come here, and Leo and I have been monitoring it using some auditory receivers that I whipped up." Auditory receivers were the implants in our ear canals that translated net transmission into a human voice. He must've synced it up with his pad and not his net, which would have explained why he was receiving the signal. "I'll put it on speaker. I'll mute the mic, though, so they won't hear us."

I held still while he started tapping things on his pad, but inside, my mind was ablaze with the implications. Because if they were contacting the Tower, it meant they knew the Tower was here. And that might mean they had been here before. Could it be? Was it possible that these were the people Roark's wife had encountered? The ones that had filled them with dreams of escape, and had ultimately led to her death, twenty-five years ago?

I tucked my questions away, knowing that the call would start soon. I wanted to be focused, and that was hard given how tired I was. The rush of adrenaline and excitement had helped, but not for long, and I needed my wits about me.

"... Receiving me? This is Melissa Croft transmitting in the blind, trying to make contact with the Tower. We are in need of medical assistance. We—"

The soft, almost desperate voice was cut off by another one, the burst of static that accompanied the transition making me wince. "My mother has been injured, you born-in-a-box idiots," she said, a whipcord of anger making each word snap on the speakers. "We know you have advanced medical skills. We need help now and are coming to you whether you like it or not."

There was a pause, and I felt that some words were being exchanged on their end, probably to get the angry girl off the line, to keep her from threatening us. Still, I'd heard the undercurrent of pain in her voice, and the fact that she had mentioned her mother... It hit a very sensitive chord with me. I looked at the others, who were also looking a bit bewildered, and waited to see what they would say next.

Then the first voice came back on the line. "I apologize for the previous message, but my shipmate is correct. We have an injured woman, forty-three years old, suffering from severe electrical burns in the chest and torso area. We are aware of your advanced medical practices and request diplomatic clearance to land and seek medical attention. We are armed but will not harm anyone so long as we are not threatened."

My mother had been forty-three years old when she died as well. I thought about the girl from before, the desperate anger in her voice, and remembered that feeling all too well. It hadn't exactly left me in the days since her funeral. I imagined what I might do if my mother had only been injured, as opposed to killed, and I couldn't find medical help. I imagined what I would have tried to do to save her if I had been given the opportunity.

And then I imagined how it would feel if I went to a place that could help, and they denied me the chance. I didn't want to be the person who made a girl watch her mother die because of an accident or violence—not when I could do something about it. I reached over and hit the mute button, turning on the mic.

"This is Liana Castell," I transmitted, ignoring everyone as they whipped around and gaped at me, shocked. "Come to the northeast corner of the roof, and we will give you medical assistance."

"What are you doing?" Quess asked loudly.

I opened my mouth to reply, but Maddox beat me to it. "She's not letting another girl lose her mother," she told him, and I shot an appreciative look at the raven-haired woman, who gave me an understanding smile before motioning to Alex to grab the bag with Baldy inside.

I realized she was going to handle that problem while I sorted out this new one, and I couldn't be more grateful to her and my brother. I didn't exactly want these outsiders to show up and see us transporting a dead body. Or throwing it off the roof.

The pause on the other line dragged on for long enough to make me wonder if I had made a mistake, but then the line was filled again by a rich masculine voice that was a strange combination of purr and growl, as if the threat it carried gave him the utmost pleasure to give. "If you fire any of that laser crap at us, we will retaliate with extreme force."

Then the call ended abruptly.

Confusion radiated through me, and I looked at Quess and mouthed "laser crap" to him. He quickly explained. "The solar panels can be used as a laser weapon. It's under IT's jurisdiction and is very hush-hush. Only supposed to be talked about when there's a need for it, and never with another department. I don't think anyone is really aware of it outside of IT."

IT had access to a *laser weapon* through the solar panels of the Tower? And this was the first I was hearing about it? Could that sort of weapon be turned on the Tower? I imagined it could be used to cut off the arms of the greeneries or something and hated the idea of Sadie having all of that destructive power at her disposal.

It was a horrifying thought, but it was matched by excitement as I realized that those people could only know about the laser if they had been here before. It had to be the same group; everything they were saying showed that they knew about us, knew about our advanced medicines, knew that we had defensive capabilities that could be used against them, and—

Wait. Did that mean that the council had decided to use the lasers on them the last time they were here? If that were true, then that meant the council had already established precedent for how to deal with them, which was by shooting them down! And if the council found out they were here—if *Sadie* did—then... I cursed and smacked my hand over my head, suddenly realizing that I had no idea if the call had been delivered *only* to us.

"Quess, please tell me that you did something at the monitoring station so that the transmission wasn't picked up by Scipio or anyone else."

"Of course I did." He scoffed. "What do you take me for?"

There was little time to feel relief, not with the threat of the council learning about this and trying to shoot them out of the sky after they left. "Will sensors on the roof pick them up?"

"Yes, but we can knock them out," Quess replied. "There are fewer up here, anyway, so I'm betting I can find a power relay somewhere and shut off power to the grid."

"Will anyone notice?" I asked, thinking about aftermath. I was surprised my brain was even working this fast with as tired as I was, but grateful nonetheless.

"Yes, but they won't come up to check it out until tomorrow, so our guests will have to be gone before then." Quess frowned, then, as if the whole thing suddenly dawned to him. "Are you sure about this?" he asked me. "We don't know anything about them. What if they are here to scout us out for an invasion?"

I shook my head at the thought. "I don't think so," I told him. "I know what the fear of losing a mother feels like, and she sounded exactly like it felt. Besides, I think they've already been here. I mean, if they knew about the lasers, then it makes sense that these are people who have been here before, right?"

"That is my interpretation," Leo announced, finally breaking his silence. "But it would be good to see what they know. Perhaps they have more information from that day for us, and we can use it to figure out what really happened, and who else was involved at that time. It might help us figure out who else is behind this. Who else has been working with Sadie and Devon."

Quess still looked doubtful, but he gave a tired nod anyway, combined with a dry smile. "Why not?" he asked. "It's not like I did anything super important today. Besides, it's just a handful of sensors, right? Easy peasy." He winked for effect, and I smiled and gave a wry chuckle.

"I think this has literally been the longest day of my life," I told him.

"And it's only eleven," Leo added helpfully.

If looks could kill, Leo would've been obliterated by the twin glares Quess and I gave him as we moved away, him to the sensors and me to help Maddox and Alex dispose of Baldy before our totally random guests showed up.

17

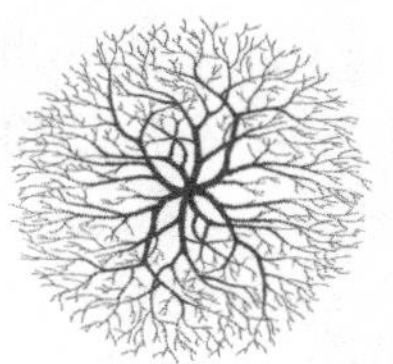

I reached to grab a corner of the bag on Alex's side, but he shrugged it out of my grasping fingers with a jerky shake of his head. "I've got it," he said.

Curling back my fingers, I hesitated at the empty quality of his voice. Once again, I was left with a messy feeling that things were spiraling out of control, and I was letting something—someone—important to me fall to the side in all the chaos.

The urge to pull him aside and force him to talk to me was just about overwhelming, and pushing it back only caused my guilt to grow. I couldn't do what I wanted, because once again, life had thrown us a curveball, and I had to take care of something else instead of taking care of my brother.

Which meant that I had to grit my teeth and just try to handle this as quickly as possible. I could, would, get Alex through this. Just not at this moment.

I grabbed the bag on Maddox's side, and the three of us hauled

Baldy's corpse to the corner of the building, trying to move as quickly as possible.

The Tower's width was approximately half a mile, which meant that making our way across the roof, even at the light jog I pushed us to, and with no walls to slow our path, would still take us eight to ten minutes.

I searched the sky whenever I could, trying to find some glimpse of the machine they were using to carry them through the air. How big was it? How many people could it hold? I tried to imagine what their machines looked like and kept conjuring up images of mechanical bees and dragonflies. The bee one was kind of ridiculous, but the dragonfly one, that would be a sight. I wondered if they would have mechanical wings that moved, or wings that were stationary, attached to some sort of propulsion device. I hoped for the moving ones, wanting them to be clear enough to see through to the stars above. What would it be like to fly in the air? To touch the clouds and marvel at the world below? The closest I had ever come to flying was with my lashes, but the real thing had to be so much more exhilarating. To feel nothing above and below you, suspended only by science and human engineering, free to roam in whichever direction the wind could take you...

On and on I looked, stealing glances toward the sky, but the inky night revealed nothing, not even under the bright blue light of the moon.

My ribs were aching by the time we approached the edge of the roof, and my legs were beyond shaky. Actually, they felt like bundles of spasming nerves that were about to shut down in protest. But I didn't stop as we shifted our position and angled ourselves into a spot where we could heave him sideways over the edge. We slowed to a stop a few feet from the very edge, and I turned to Alex.

"On three?"

He nodded, his eyes fixed on the bag between us. His face was an indiscernible mask, but I knew what he was feeling. I was feeling it too, to a lesser degree. Inside the bag was somebody's son. Somebody's brother. Maybe even somebody's father. He'd attacked me, yes, and played a part in the deaths of other people, but he still had a family. He still had people who would wonder after him and miss him.

But I couldn't feel guilty. Not after everything he had put us through. I reminded myself that if things had played out differently, it could've been him where we were standing, and any one of us in the bag. Or worse, it could've been Leo *and* Baldy in the bag.

Still, the situation didn't sit right with me. It wasn't guilt exactly, but something more speculative, and I found myself wondering whether Baldy and I were more alike than I cared to admit. I did what I did to protect my adopted family, and I had to imagine that in some dark way, he did what he did for his. He'd been willing to kill himself to prevent Leo from learning his secrets; wouldn't I do the same thing in his shoes?

Yes, but it wasn't the same, I told myself firmly. I wasn't like him. *We* weren't like him.

We didn't kill to try to control things, but to defend ourselves.

And it occurred to me that my brother and I were both culpable in shooting Baldy. Because Alex may have caused me to pull the trigger, but it had been *my* finger on the gun, tightened to the point that a fraction of a centimeter had set it off. I felt I should tell him that, to let him know that we were both in this together, but I had no idea whether it would even reach him.

I wasn't even sure where he was right now.

"One," I breathed, drawing the bag back and then forward with the others. The material of the bag rustled, and I tried to block out the fact that we were dumping a man's body off the side of the Tower.

"Two." The weight was awkward, shifting back and forth in a

way that made me picture his arms and legs rag-dolling inside, his head lolling on a neck with a bullet hole in it.

"Three." I let go, the fabric slipping from my fingers as the bag flew up and over the edge, into open air. It hung for a second, and then gravity took hold, gently tugging it down and away.

I flicked my wrist and threw a lash line down against the glass pane behind me, creating a safety line, and then sidled toward the edge and looked down. The bag had already fallen at least a hundred feet and continued to plummet. The trajectory angled to the right slightly, a crosswind clearly pushing the bag and corpse over, but it wasn't by much.

All too soon, the bag became indiscernible from the velvet darkness below, and I closed my eyes... and truly owned up to my part in Baldy's death. I had left Leo alone, and hadn't been there when Baldy had taken control. I had been pointing a gun at him when Alex hit my hand. I had been ready to pull the trigger if he made even the slightest move to hurt me or my friends.

He hadn't been a good man, and I hadn't wanted him to die without facing a trial for his crimes first. Still, what was done was done, and we had company coming. The outsiders were going to be here any second, and we needed to be on the other side of the roof before they arrived.

"C'mon," I whispered to the others, turning my back to the edge. "Let's go."

We made our way over to where Leo and Quess were working to disrupt the sensors. If they couldn't disable them before the aliens arrived in their flying machine, then the entire council would be alerted to their presence, and I wasn't sure I could keep the other councilors from attacking them.

I continued to scan the skies as we moved, trying to find some shape or shadow to tell me where they were, but as the minutes ticked by, I grew more and more concerned. Had something happened to them? Had they changed their minds and turned back? Was this a ruse just to see if anyone was still inside the Tower, or even a prelude to an attack?

"What's taking so long?" Maddox breathed explosively, and I realized she was feeling exactly the same way.

"I don't know," I said, trying not to let my nervousness show. "It really has been a long time. I think—"

My words were cut off as a sudden gust of wind exploded out of nowhere, strong enough to make my hair whip like tiny lashes against the skin of my face. I threw up an arm to cover my eyes at the stinging dust the wind kicked up, the force of it strong enough to make it difficult to breathe.

I reached out for Maddox and Alex, terrified the wind would somehow push us back or off the edge, but then the wind just died down, softening to a gentle breeze. I straightened slowly and frowned, bewildered by the rapid shift in weather. Looking around to make sure Quess and Leo were okay, I was surprised to see them still hunched over, their own arms held over their heads. Dust swirled around them, their hair still whipping in the chaos. Something about it was off, however, and it took me several seconds to figure out what.

It was the direction of the wind. It had come up so quickly that I hadn't noticed it—I'd just been concerned about our safety. But now that I was paying attention, I realized that the wind was being generated from *above*. My eyes looked up, searching the area just over Quess and Leo, and after a handful of heartbeats, I could see it: a dim, dark outline that blocked a patch of the night sky, moving slowly away from the two men to hover over the area we had designated, just beyond where Quess and Leo were cowering under the torrential wind. And I realized that I was looking at a flying machine.

The body was long and wide, reminding me of an oversized boat. I could make out four arms, or wings, as the case may be, and could tell from their glimmer that there were exposed propellers in them, which allowed me a view of the sky through the blur of machinery inside. From nose to tail, it had to be at least fifty feet long. The wings at the side looked positively comical compared to the body—they were so short and stubby that it seemed impossible that they were keeping the heavy underbelly aloft—and yet there it was, slowly sliding forward, dozens of feet above our heads. The body began to turn around in place, and the light of the moon cut a white, reflective light against a glass bubble at the nose. I could see a dark figure backlit by lights inside, though details were hard to make out.

But what impressed me most was that it didn't make any sound whatsoever. Short of the wind it was kicking up by whatever process it used to fly, there was nothing, not even a whisper of noise.

But then again, we were still fifty feet away from Quess and Leo, and an additional fifty from where the vessel was slowly easing itself down onto the roof, still rotating, the nose disappearing from view.

As fascinating as it was to watch, my brother's sharp intake of air and Maddox's gasp jerked my attention from it, and I realized that we were all gaping like a bunch of loons. Any minute, that thing would land, and if we were standing here like several slack-jawed idiots, they would never respect us.

"C'mon," I told the others, already moving away from them. I glanced back at them, paused when I saw them still staring, and added a quick, "La-dee-dah, they can *fly*. Bet they don't have a sweet Tower like we do." That earned me two surprised smiles, and they poured on a little speed to catch up to me. We walked quickly, and even though I wanted to keep a cool exterior in front of the aliens, I couldn't help but watch the machine continue to land, captivated by all the details that came into view. It was a dark gray, but there was white lettering on the rear, painted over what appeared to be a door. It read *C4-137* in tight, perfect print, and underneath it, in elegant script, were the words *The Nautilus*. The name of their machine, maybe?

I made a mental note to ask, provided the first exchange went well, and found myself smiling. Today had been long and filled with calamity and chaos, but everything else paled in comparison to what was about to happen. We were going to meet people who weren't from the Tower. An entirely different group of people, with their own culture and beliefs, and I was betting that I would have more questions than just the name of the ship by the time we were through.

We reached Leo and Quess as the ship was settling on the top of the roof with a metallic groan that came from some metallic struts at the bottom. The sound was so loud, I immediately cringed. We might have shut off the sensors, but anyone beneath us would definitely hear such a loud noise, and could come up to investigate.

"Liana, do you even see this thing?" Quess asked, his voice filled with the awe and delight of a small child. "Did you see it *fly*?"

I could tell that his clever mind was already trying to memorize the details and figure out the physics involved, but I needed him focused. "We all did," I told him. "But let's not stand around staring at them like idiots. We have no idea what to expect once they come out, so be alert. Watch them, and if they try anything funny..." I trailed off, fighting the urge to look over my shoulder. I was sincerely hoping it wouldn't come to that. I wanted to believe that they hadn't lied, and that I hadn't fallen prey to some sort of elaborate trick.

But I held my breath as the back of the ship began to open from the top, the rectangular door slipping from its groove and opening down and out, toward us, to form a ramp. Bright light streamed from the edges, growing wider, and I took a few steps toward it, drawn by the marvel in front of me.

The light eventually hit the glass panels that made up the roof, creating a halo of light around the opening as the door finished its decent, the edge of it hovering only an inch or two from the ground. Two dark figures stood in stark contrast against the light, one male, one female. I couldn't see any features because of the light in front of them, save for the woman's deep, brick-red hair, while the man was just as dark as the shadow he was cutting.

Sucking in a deep, calming breath, I squared my shoulders and moved forward. The others followed, maintaining a tight grouping with me, and the figures at the top of the ramp stepped down, heading toward us.

I was so obsessed with trying to catch a glimpse of their faces that I jumped when Leo whispered, "Liana, they have guns." My eyes tracked down, and sure enough, I could see the outline of a gun on each of their hips. If I had been anyone else from the Tower, I would've ignored them, not knowing what they were.

But I *did* know, and the realization that they had come out armed did not fill me with a lot of reassurance. We were giving them help, not trying to steal from them.

I slowed to a stop a few feet from the base of the ramp and held up one hand so the others would stop. That forced the two figures to pause, and I pointed at their hips. "Lose the guns," I told them firmly, in a no-nonsense voice.

The woman, her face still a mask of shadows, cocked her head. "You know what guns are?" she called back. Her voice had been the reasonable one on the radio, I realized. The calmer one. I considered the question, and then met it with one of my own.

"Why do you assume we wouldn't?"

I asked the question to buy me some time, and to make them rethink things, but based on her question, I was even more certain that these were the same people who had been here twenty-five years ago. The only reason for them to assume we didn't know was for them to have intimate knowledge of this place, so the fact that they had an opinion on whether we would know what guns were...

Meant these might be the very people Roark's wife Selka had met.

The two people on the ramp exchanged looks, something silent passing between them, and then they looked down. "We'll keep the guns," the man announced in a deep, rich voice that immediately had my skin tingling with awareness.

I turned my attention to him and raised an eyebrow. "I'm not the one who has an injured person needing medical assessment. You'll lose the guns, or else."

"Or else what?" he demanded in a voice that was one part arrogance, two parts teasing humor. For some reason, it hit me the wrong way, and before I knew it, my gun was in my hand, my arm stretched out so that it was pointing at him. Maybe I was tired from the extraordinarily long day I'd had, or impatient because I wanted to get home and put everything behind me, but either way, I needed to make a point to them: I wasn't messing around when it came to the safety of my people.

"This," I told him, pulling back the hammer of the gun with a sharp click. For a second they stood motionless, and then their hands slowly began to rise into the air. "You don't know me yet, but let me make this clear. My people's safety is my one and only concern. If you expect us to help you, then I am telling you to throw the guns away."

The two were quiet for several long seconds, and I stood there, holding a gun on them both. "If we get rid of our guns, then you must get rid of yours," the girl finally said, her eyes darting between me and Leo. I glanced over at him and saw he had drawn his weapon as well, but wasn't holding it as high up as I was, just pointed in the general vicinity.

I considered it, and then shook my head. I wanted to ascertain whether they had been here before, and I had to be certain they weren't lying about it. It was dangerous, keeping a gun on them, and not exactly inviting, but they could have answers I needed. I was certain that someone from the Tower—one of the people who had been there when they arrived—was responsible for what was going on now. Even more certain that they had escalated the legacy group's plan for the Tower, based on the visitors from the outside. But I didn't have access to the records to prove it. And if these people knew and could tell me who was there, then that was something I could use. But I had to maintain a reason for them to tell me.

"Not yet. I have some questions for you."

"What sort of questions?" the man asked, his tone neutral this time. "We have an injured woman on board."

I hadn't forgotten, and I definitely didn't want to drag this out any longer than I had to. But this was important; it could help me find another legacy, possibly the one who was in charge of everything. "Your people have been here before, haven't you?"

The two exchanged another silent look. "We have no idea what you're talking about," the man replied. "We've never been here before."

He was lying. Or if not lying, manipulating the truth in some way. His last sentence had included the word "we," which could mean just the two of them, or all the people on the vessel who had never been to the Tower. But it didn't change the fact that they knew things about our lasers and the lack of guns, which was an indication that they'd had some sort of contact with the Tower. Or they knew someone who had.

"Let me try it like this," I offered as I lowered the gun some. "Twenty-five years ago, someone you knew or someone famous to you discovered the Tower and then took home stories about it. I'm guessing that the area was made off-limits to you for some reason, but in a desperate moment, you reached out to us because you know that we have excellent medicine. You decided that it was worth taking the risk of being blown out of the sky."

There was a long pause, and then the man took a few steps

closer to me. I kept my gun pointed low, toward his legs, but still high enough that I could shoot him, just in case he tried anything. As he slid closer, the details of his face became clearer, first revealing a square jaw, darkened with the beginnings of a beard, and then a strong, straight nose. Just his sheer physical size was enough to be overwhelming, but as he turned into the light, what made my breath catch and my heart spasm was a pair of light gray eyes rimmed in long, sooty lashes. They sparkled with a deep intelligence and cunning, as if he were sizing me up for signs of weakness. "Who are you?"

I met his gaze head on and offered him a tired and lopsided smile. "Me? I'm just the girl who's going to save your ass and keep you alive. Now, are you going to answer my question and tell me the truth, or are we going to stand here playing games?"

18

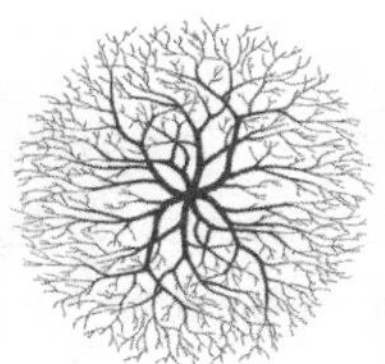

A soft breeze kicked up as the man and I squared off in our silent battle of wills. I wasn't sure why, but I didn't feel like backing down was an option at this point. I had laid out my terms, and they knew what was at stake.

But that didn't stop me from feeling queasy at the thought of an injured woman being on board the ship, possibly dying while this exchange went on. I didn't want anyone to lose their mother, especially to violence. The wound it left was a raw, gaping, thing—even if our relationship hadn't been that great.

That meant a compromise.

Of sorts.

"While you're busy pondering that little enigma," I started, keeping my voice low, "I would like to send my medic and a guard on board. But I need to know how many other people there are before I do."

The gray eyes boring holes into my own blinked in surprise, and his brows drew together. "You're... still going to help her?"

I pulled my face into a carefully placed mask, so I revealed nothing, and choked out the only words I could think of that would make him understand. "My mother died less than a week ago."

His head cocked inquisitively, and I met his gaze without flinching, trying not to let him see how much saying those words had cost me. In fact, my mother had died *five days* ago, and trying to pretend that wound wasn't there, on top of being drained mentally, physically, and emotionally, was a herculean effort.

But somehow, I managed.

The girl took a few hesitant steps down the ramp, reached out to wrap her hand around his arm, and stepped delicately around him. As her features came into view, I realized there was a striking resemblance between them. Not in their coloring; her hair was picking up just enough ambient light for me to see that it wasn't red like I had initially thought, but a rich chocolate color that turned red in the right light, while her almond-shaped eyes were a luminescent green, so bright they practically glowed like a cat's. She gave me a sympathetic look, but her next words were for the man beside her, and rich with sadness.

"Check out her eyes, Thomas. She's got the look."

I frowned and shifted my eyes back and forth between them. "What look?"

Thomas pressed his silky lips together in a solemn line, the weight of his silvery gaze making me distinctly uncomfortable. "Our parents have the same heaviness in their eyes as you have in yours."

He said that as if I could somehow extract meaning from it, so when he didn't continue, I gave him the most obnoxiously annoyed look I could manage, and then squinted my eyes at him. "You do realize that literally none of that explains what the hell she's talking about, or answers my damn question? I mean, do you want that girl's mother to die? You called *us* for help, for crying out loud."

"Yes, but we don't understand why you're meeting with us," he explained, and the slight snap of teasing condescension made me bristle. Sure, he was sexy as sin, but anyone who fell for this man would be in a world of trouble, trying to keep him from running all over them. He practically oozed command. "I believe you when you say that your mother died, but…" Trailing off, he looked at his sister and clamped his mouth shut, the look on his face telling her it was her decision.

She studied me a second or two longer, and then nodded. "There are only two more in the cargo bay," she informed me. "Our cousin, Helena Vox, and her mother, Amberlynn Ashabee. I'm Melissa Croft, and this is my older brother, Thomas."

Thomas gave me an imperious nod, and I rolled my eyes, unimpressed. "My name is Liana Castell," I informed them. I started to open my mouth again, but suddenly Quess was speaking.

"Her name is *Champion* Liana Honorbound Castell, Wayfinder, Defender of the Gate, and leader of the Knights of the Citadel."

My eyes drifted closed as I tried to keep the embarrassment off my face, but I thoroughly planned to murder Quess later. The only reason to give all the details was to brag, and that really wasn't my style. Not to mention, they had no idea what any of that even meant.

"What happened to Devon Alexander?" the girl asked curiously, and my eyes shot open. She knew the former Champion's name? That solidified the fact that they were a part of the same group who had come here before. Devon Alexander had been on the council twenty-five years ago, and the fact that they knew his name and that I had taken his place was incredibly revealing. I wanted to know more about what happened—because I was certain that something in that story could help me figure out who exactly had escalated the destruction of Scipio since that time.

And if I knew that, perhaps I could use it to keep them from getting any worse.

"Champion Castell killed him," Maddox informed them, her voice carrying a dangerous undercurrent.

And just like that, I added Maddox to the murder list. I loved my friends, and I knew they meant well, but this was not the best start to fostering a positive relationship. Rolling my eyes, I let enough of my displeasure show as was socially acceptable.

"To be fair, he tried to frame me for murder and then kill me." I paused as a secondary thought occurred to me, and added, "Technically, I didn't even kill him." I sometimes forgot that little detail. Everyone in the Tower believed that I had done it on Scipio's orders, but it was Leo who had actually killed him, right after Devon tried to kill Grey by shorting out his net. "Quess, Maddox, get on the ship and see what you can do for their aunt."

I gave the siblings in front of me a searching look, letting them know that the ultimate choice was theirs, and Melissa nodded. Quess and Maddox immediately broke off from Leo and Alex, leaving the five of us alone as they went up the ramp.

"Thank you," Melissa said, and I shifted, suddenly uncomfortable. Because they deserved to know that we weren't even meeting under legitimate terms. I was a representative of the Tower, but I wasn't here as one, and we only had a limited amount of time before they had to leave—or risked being discovered.

"Don't thank me yet," I said grimly. "You need to know that we aren't exactly... meeting with you on behalf of the council. We knocked out the sensors and hijacked your signal to keep you off the Tower's radar. But that won't last long. If the council finds out you are here, they'll pull up the protocols from what happened last time and follow precedent."

"You mean use those laser things on us?" Thomas asked, and I nodded. The two exchanged a long, considering look. "Then we should talk inside," Thomas said brusquely. I watched as he pulled the gun out of the holster, ejected the clip and a round from the chamber with a practiced move, and then set the weapon on the ground. Melissa followed, her hands a blur as she repeated his action with her own gun, before placing it next to his.

I stared at both of them and realized that if we had gotten into a shooting match with them, they probably would've won. I had only used the thing once, with the help of some weird ability in the legacy net that hadn't even been mine. Still, I did know how to remove the clip and clear the chamber, so I followed their lead.

Only I didn't bother to move fast, because I knew I wasn't confident enough with it yet. Instead, I opted for a lazier motion, hoping that they wouldn't pick up on the fact that I wasn't as good as them, while also showing them that I didn't feel the need to compete with them.

Leo followed my action and unloaded his gun, and then the five of us were walking up the metal ramp toward the rectangular light coming from the opening. When we reached the top, I immediately zeroed in on Quess kneeling next to someone on the floor, Maddox squatting close by with his medical bag to hand him items as he needed them. I couldn't see who they were working on, but a young woman, probably eighteen or nineteen years old, was standing over them both, her arms folded tight across her chest. Her hair was a deep auburn and hung in tight corkscrews around her heart-shaped face.

She glanced over at us as we entered, and I got a flash of blue eyes that were so vibrant, they glistened like the crystal components in our computers. "What are you doing?" she asked warily, taking half a step toward us. "You know that we're not supposed to let anyone on the ship. Your dad—"

"Is already going to be pissed that we came here in the first place," Thomas said on an exhale, two parts annoyed, one part indifferent. "We're already in for a penny, Hela. Might as well get something out of it. Besides..." He trailed off and gave me another appraising look. "They're keeping us secret from the rest of their council to help us."

Helena—Hela—blinked her eyes several times, and then looked at the three of us, studying Leo first, then Alex, and finally me. "Her?" she asked, and Thomas nodded.

The redhead sucked in a breath, and then shook her head. "Mom is going to tear us all a new one when she wakes up."

"Be grateful for it," I told her in a raw, hoarse voice, before I could stop myself. The pain I felt regarding my mother's death was only rivaled by my curiosity and interest in what she was saying—that they were breaking the rules about being here, as well. They weren't alone—they had experienced supervision—but had gone against the orders of their government in an effort to save her. In a lot of ways, they were in the same boat that we were.

She gave me another considering look, her facial features tightening. "Guys, did you notice her eyes?"

"Of course we did," Melissa said impatiently, flipping some of her deep brown hair over her shoulder. "It's why we let them on board." She paused and shifted her weight as her gaze drifted over to where Maddox and Quess were working. "How is she doing?"

"How she is doing is a very complicated question," Quess grunted, his body moving back and forth with the motions of his hand. "The very simple answer is not bad, all things considered."

"All things considered?" I repeated stupidly. On impulse, I moved over to where he was only a few inches away from falling face-first onto his patient. But as more of her came into view, I realized what Quess had meant.

The woman on the bed was in her early forties and had an assortment of slight wrinkles on her slack face, but that wasn't what caught my eye. It was the lines of blackened and cracked flesh that radiated from her side up and across her chest, a slash of pink through the middle of it, where the flesh had ripped open to reveal the muscles and tendons inside. I immediately recognized the damage as severe electrical burns. It was clear they had been doing their best to take care of them with their own medicine, but some of the larger ones were leaking sickly yellow lines of pus.

"What did that?" I asked, horrified at the damage I was seeing. Quess was doing his damnedest to help her, and with what he had in his medical kit, I was certain he could save her, but she would be severely scarred for the rest of her life. Bio-foam was amazing with all sorts of lacerations, but on burnt flesh, we had to resort to other methods—namely a transplant of a gelatinous material we produced in the Tower, along with some secret components that sped up the healing process. It would scar, but she would be alive.

"We got caught up in a war going on in the south," Thomas said tiredly. "We were down there trying to establish a diplomatic relationship with the regime of one of the settlements under attack, when there was a coup at his palace. We managed to make it back to our ship, but Amber was caught in a blast from one of their weapons. I've never seen anything like it before."

A war? Down south? Between people? It took me a moment—probably because I had been raised my entire life to believe that we were the only humans who had survived the End—but it finally clicked that there were *more* people. Living out there and surviving, just like we were. Well, maybe not exactly like us, but still. Dozens of questions hovered on my tongue, just begging for me to open my mouth and let them flood out, but I held them in place.

"I thought she was dead," Hela whispered, blood draining from her face. "Will she make it?"

I wanted to reassure her, but once again, Quess beat me to it.

"Listen, you don't know me yet," he said, emphasizing the yet with the sound of tape tearing from a leech patch, designed to draw out infection in wounds like this. "But I am friggin' awesome at everything I do. So believe me when I say that your mother is going to be just fine."

Beside him, Maddox chuckled and looked up at Hela. "He *is* really good at what he does."

Hela scowled at them, her eyes almost crossing with the force of her annoyance. "I won't believe it until I see it," she declared imperiously.

Quess only laughed at that and continued to work. I watched for a few more seconds, and then moved back to Melissa and Thomas, the questions dancing a merry jig around my head. I wanted to ask all of them at once, but I didn't want to overwhelm them, or tip my hand about just how ignorant we were regarding the outside world. So I settled on the one that had been bugging me since the start of this.

"Why do you all keep fixating on my eyes?"

Thomas gave me a small and sad smile. "Sorry if we're weird about that. You can tell a lot about a person from their eyes, and yours are very special."

"Why?" I demanded, still woefully confused and unhappy about it. Was it the color? Admittedly, amber-colored eyes were super rare, but what did that have to do with anything?

"Your eyes remind us of our parents," Melissa said. I looked over at her, and her own eyes were full of shadows. "They have the same look. They have ever since the war."

"The war down south?" I asked, still bewildered. "And what does it even matter if I have the same look in my eyes as they did?"

"Relax," Melissa said soothingly. "It's just evidence that you've seen a lot of horror in your life and managed to survive with a sense of justice and honor intact. We respect that. Hell, our parents and extended family probably wrote the damn book on it. We just... We can tell that you wouldn't hurt us unprovoked."

I blinked at her, and then shook my head and tried not to snort derisively. That was the stupidest thing I had ever heard. But if it earned me some trust, then I was willing to take it.

19

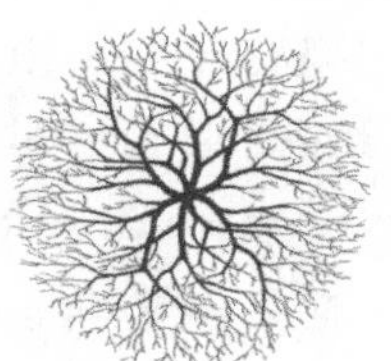

"Here, it's better if we talk in the cockpit," Melissa announced, gesturing toward a door in the wall of the cargo bay, which presumably led to the bubble of glass that I had seen on the front earlier. "We can leave your people to work on our aunt without distracting them with our conversation."

I nodded and looked at Alex and Leo. Leo seemed interested, but Alex... Alex's gaze was focused on the wall, his face pale and haunted. He wasn't in the right shape to handle any of this. If anything, I was pretty sure he was still in shock. I'd been there a time or two myself, so I recognized the signs.

"Go ahead," I told them. "I'll be there in a minute. I'm just going to relieve my Lieutenant."

Thomas and Melissa shrugged and started moving toward the door, but Leo waited for me as I sidled up to my brother's side. "Alex?" I called softly. He blinked, but his gaze didn't stray from the wall. "Alex." I reached out and touched his hand, wrapping one finger around his pinkie and giving it a little squeeze. "Alex!" This time I shook him a little bit, shoving my shoulder into his and desperately trying to get him to focus.

"Liana?" he asked, his voice reed-thin and filled with confusion. "What?"

Fear exploded through me, and I tugged him to face me, to look me in the eyes. "Alex, I need you to be with me right now, okay? Do you remember where we are?"

He licked his lips and looked around. "The alien ship," he told me. Good. That was good. He was still aware of what was going on. I needed to keep him focused and alert. If he stood around too long, I was afraid he might go catatonic. His brain was trying to protect him from what he had experienced, and while I wanted to give him the time and space to process everything, I couldn't afford to let him shut down now, while we were still in danger of potentially being caught—or attacked.

"Yes," I told him, smiling encouragingly at him. "I need you to help Quess save this woman. Do you think you can do that?"

Alex swallowed and looked over my shoulder to where Quess was working, just in front of the other set of benches, where Amberlynn was lying on a pallet on the floor. "But Maddox is helping him."

"I know, but I need her to help me talk to these aliens. So can you take over for her?"

My brother shifted his weight from one leg back to the other, and then nodded slowly. "I can help," he said thickly. I moved to one side to let him pass, and then motioned for Maddox to follow me. The large area we were in ended in a wall with a door just off to the right, and as I peered through it, I saw that it led to a short hall and then another open space. I couldn't make out much, because Leo was standing in the way, and Thomas and Melissa were behind him, waiting. Apparently, that was the cockpit, as they called it.

Behind me, I heard Maddox hand the medical supplies she was

holding over to Alex, and then start walking toward me. Leo stood aside, revealing a large compartment. Chairs were mounted to the walls on both the sides and the back of the room, making room for fifteen people or so. A table sat off to one side, taking up a large slab of floor space, and there was a chair in front of the bubble window, suspended from the ceiling, with a long panel of buttons and controls sitting in front of it.

"Is that where you control this thing?" I asked, excitement coursing through me as I saw the command chair. "How does it work? How can you *fly*?" My fingers stretched out to touch the back of the chair, aching to stroke over the fabric there, but Melissa reached out and caught my wrist with one hand.

"The last time one of our people was here, Devon Alexander repeatedly suggested killing them to take our tech. I'd appreciate it if you didn't show so much interest. It makes me nervous."

My fingers curled inward, and I looked at her, both surprised at her finally admitting that one of their people had been here before, and shocked at what she was saying. "He did?" I saw the confirmation in her eyes and frowned. "I'm sorry."

I wasn't sure what I was apologizing for, but it felt appropriate. Perhaps it was because Devon had been a representative of the Tower and had greeted them with mistrust and the threat of violence. No wonder they were so on edge.

"It's okay," she said, letting my hand go with a flick of her brown hair. "You clearly didn't know." She paused, and then frowned. "Wait, how do you know about us, but not know about us at the same time? You took over Devon's position. Shouldn't there be files on this?"

Maddox, Leo, and I shared bemused looks. *Yes, there should be* was the answer, but in the Tower, where carefully kept secrets could mean the difference between survival and death, the council had learned to compartmentalize issues that could threaten our society. And telling *anyone* about the outside world had been categorized as dangerous.

But to my surprise, Thomas started explaining before I could. "I swear to God, Melissa, you never get any of the details right. The council basically told Mom never to come back, and that they fully intended to keep our existence a secret! And then fired on her and Dad to try and make sure she couldn't tell anyone about them. Don't you remember?"

Melissa cocked her head, her eyes growing distant, and then shrugged. "You're probably right, of course. But Mom's story had a lot of speedbumps along the way, and to be honest, the whole segue into the Tower wasn't my favorite part. It was stupid."

"Mom was captured by Desmond's people, and the ship was damaged by Solomon!" Thomas exclaimed irritably. "It wasn't exactly her choice to even come this way, especially with everything that was going on at the time." He paused, and then snapped out, "Besides, you're not supposed to have a favorite part. It's not exactly a happy tale."

I watched the exchange between them with growing confusion. I had picked up on the idea that their mother had been the one to visit the Tower before, obviously, but I wasn't entirely sure what they were talking about. They were talking about history like it was a story. Why?

"What are you talking about?" Maddox asked, beating me to the punch.

Thomas and Melissa looked away from each other, as if surprised that we were still here. Melissa's face darkened to a shade of red that rivaled a tomato, and she looked at Thomas, who rolled his eyes.

"I apologize for my sister and myself. We're not doing a very good job explaining ourselves. Here." He reached behind his back and started to pull something out, and movement out of the corner of my eye told me that Maddox and Leo had interpreted the act as hostile and were tensing for a fight. I reached out with both arms and clamped hands on their wrists before they could step forward.

Thomas had frozen, his eyebrows meeting in the middle of his nose in a wary line, and I flashed him and his sister a congenial smile. "Sorry. We've had a pretty tense day today, and we're a little jumpy. What is it?"

"It's a book," Melissa said in a slightly forced, airy tone, her mouth breaking on a nervous smile. "It's actually the story of our parents and how they changed the destiny of two nations and—"

As she spoke, Thomas slowly pulled a book out, and as soon as the glossy, colorful, and clearly paper-made rectangle came into view, I stepped forward and snatched it out of his hand, my fingers eager to touch something so precious and rare.

The cover was cool and slick to my hands, and I had a childish urge to press it to my chest and hug it. Using wood for anything other than growing food or producing air was scandalous, but these people clearly came from a place where they had wood in great abundance. I turned it over in my hands, feeling the soft touch of the fragile pages inside. The entire book was flexible, like the journals, but also looked incredibly new.

Unlike the journals, there was a painting on the front, of a girl with rich, brown, wavy hair and silver-gray eyes. She was standing in relief against a large gate that led to a city beyond, with massive mountains in the background. The likeness between Thomas and Melissa and the girl on the cover was uncanny, except that the girl had a hardness in her eyes that theirs lacked. Well, maybe not lacked, but certainly had to a lesser degree. The title read *The Gender Game*, and underneath it was a small note of *Annotated Edition*, followed by the author and illustrator, Owen Barns. I drank it all in with my eyes, trying to absorb every detail.

My hands had a mind of their own, however, and were gently flipping open the thick outer cover to the page inside.

I blinked in surprise and looked up at them, then back down.

The book... wasn't a book. It was filled with little rows of separated rectangles with more illustrated designs inside. Text was given through small bubbles that were coming out of the people's mouths in the illustrations. I cocked my head at it, utterly confused.

"What kind of book is this?" I breathed, unable to keep my bewilderment off my face.

Melissa and Thomas exchanged looks. "You've never seen a graphic novel before?" she asked.

I shook my head and looked back at the page, only removing my attention from it when Maddox and Leo stepped closer to have a look. Maddox reached out to run a finger over the page, and I had to resist the urge to slap her hand away, knowing that paper was very fragile. Besides, I had been doing the same thing seconds ago; I couldn't begrudge her the chance to know what it felt like.

"It's a comic," Leo suddenly announced in delight. "Lionel used to tell me about these all the time. They combined pictures and words to create a story, just like a fiction book would. He even drew me a few. But it's clear he wasn't the artist this man was."

"Owen's our uncle," Melissa said. "Kind of. He was with our mom and dad for a lot of the mess that happened. Just like Amber." She paused and suddenly shook her head rapidly, as if clearing her head from a smart punch. "We're getting ahead of ourselves here. This book is for you, and explains who we are as a people. We hand it out to civilizations and cultures when we first meet them, so they can understand what we represent."

I frowned, looking up from where the young woman—Violet Bates, according to the text—was smuggling her brother in a box, depicted by a pair of wide eyes floating in a dark void, and tried to focus on what Melissa was saying. "Why would you want to tell other cultures and civilizations about yourself?" It seemed pretty dangerous from where I was sitting. Going out and meeting new people was a good way to get yourself killed, especially if you knew nothing about their culture.

Then again, I could already tell that these people's lives were very different from our own.

"How else would we meet them?" Melissa replied with a smile. "We figure out very quickly if they are people we want to build a relationship with, based on how they react to us and the story. And it helps them understand where we come from, and how resourceful we can be in times of trouble."

I raised an eyebrow, a slow smile growing on my lips. So it was informational *and* a deterrent. That was smart. "Fascinating," I replied with a smile. "So I can keep this?"

"Absolutely," Thomas said. "Sorry we don't have the full edition, though. Our uncle got a little carried away when he started making it. And there were things that Mom and Dad thought it was better to keep out, for... security purposes."

Even smarter. Although, this particular display of intelligence left me mildly disappointed. I wanted to know about the story, more about her time here, because I was pretty sure that something had happened during that time that changed the legacies, making them more aggressive in their attempts to gain control. It could've just been about the intrusion from the outside world—learning that there was, in fact, an outside world—but I had a feeling it was more than that. I just didn't know what, and I couldn't access the records of the event without asking permission from the council—and telling them why I would want the information, along with how I even knew about it.

Suddenly, a concerning thought popped into my head. If this was their mother's story, and she'd come to the Tower, then that meant the Tower was in the book somewhere. And they were handing it out to random civilizations.

"So wait, the part about her visiting the Tower is in here?" I speared them both with a wary and alarmed look, letting them know that this was a serious question for me. "Are you saying you've been passing out information on *our* location and lives?"

If they were, then they had potentially put us in grave danger. I wasn't sure about the other surviving civilizations, but I knew our system had food, water, and energy, as well as thick walls to protect us from the outside world. Anyone ambitious enough, who didn't have anything to lose, could turn their eyes on us and take what they wanted.

"No," Melissa said, shaking her head. "We didn't reveal anything about the Tower other than that it exists. We didn't include any specific directions or times or anything that would give away your location. Mom and Dad didn't think it would go over well, if you guys ever decided to rejoin the outside world."

"Rejoin?" I asked, surprised and almost amused. "We don't have the technology to fly, and everything around us is a radioactive wasteland! I mean, how did these other civilizations survive? How did *you* survive? The fallout must've been—"

"Different in different places," Thomas cut in. "The north is still mostly decimated from the Fall, and—"

"The Fall?" Leo asked. "Do you not call it the End?"

"Uh... no," Melissa said. "Everyone has their own name for it wherever we go, but yeah, the big event approximately three hundred years ago that changed civilization as we knew it forever. Blah blah blah. Look, there are pockets of survivors everywhere, and as for your radiation problem..." She trailed off and looked at her brother. "Can we tell them that?"

He shrugged. "I don't see why not. I'm a little surprised they don't know."

I sighed and closed the book with a loud snap. Scipio knew that my brother and I could be like this too, but we didn't have time for it, and I wanted some honesty.

"'They' are standing right here, and we'd appreciate a little directness. We're taking a big risk even talking to you, and if anyone on the council finds out that I'm here, and plan to let you go, then all of us will be executed, plain and simple. So how about this. Instead of beating around the bush about what you can and can't tell us, let's just be straight with each other. You tell me your story, I'll tell you mine, and maybe we'll find some middle ground and some trust." I paused at that and decided to be fully honest with them right off the bat. "There aren't a lot of people I can trust at the moment, so I'm hoping that I can trust you. Because I'm tired of making enemies and playing games. I want answers, and you might have some. So I'm asking you, please, will you just tell me what's going on?"

20

Nobody said anything for several seconds, and for a moment, I wondered if I had pushed too far. These people were suspicious of us, and from what they were saying, they had a right to be. Devon Alexander had wanted to take their technology and had been pretty outspoken about it. Now I was here instead of him, and I was guessing they weren't quite sure what to make of me.

And who could blame them? I wasn't exactly the most upright and loyal citizen to the Tower, so my behavior had to be worlds apart from what they had read about in their little book. It actually bothered me that I wasn't looking at it even now, trying to find the parts about the Tower and get their point of view. It would help me gauge what they had learned about our life here, and what their perception of us was. They were obviously wary, but I wanted to know more about why.

I resisted the urge, though, and tried to keep my face neutral, if not mildly pleasant, while the two deliberated.

Thomas broke the silence first, with a chuckle that was as rich as it was smoky. My body tingled with awareness, and I resented every moment of it. I already felt like I was juggling two men; I had no room for a third—especially one who looked as arrogant and commanding as Thomas. I could tell he liked being in charge, taking the lead, and that was my job, dammit, not his.

"All right," he agreed amicably. "If you're so eager, you go first."

I regarded him with a coolness, indifferent to the fact that he had called my bluff. I had meant what I told them: I wanted to be honest. There was an opportunity here for us to become friends, maybe even plan our escape, once we had stopped the legacies, restored Scipio, and gotten people used to the idea that other pockets of humanity had survived. Better yet, maybe we could be the first envoys from the Tower, doing what Thomas and Melissa were doing and making allies of other civilizations. I knew it would take time, but the first step down that road was telling the truth.

I started by asking them what they knew, which wasn't much, beyond a handful of titles and names they couldn't remember but promised me were in the book. They knew about the bio-foam, and how we repaired our broken bones and had walls that displayed medical information. I was surprised that they didn't have all of that already, but they assured us they were working toward it, having been inspired by what they saw. I felt uncomfortable about that, like they were stealing our technology. It was something that gave us an advantage—something to trade with if the people of the Tower ever emerged. Something we could use to create relationships with the rest of the world.

Then I realized they hadn't really stolen it. Just tried to emulate what we had done. In that light, it was a little flattering.

As for my side of things, it was impossible to tell my story in a linear way once I got started. I started by explaining who I was, my position, and my department, and gave them an idea of what we did. But that invariably led Thomas to make a comment about how it was good that we didn't have gender discrimination, which made me ask if they did, and then they were telling me about Matrus and Patrus, the countries divided by gender. I listened in awe and horror as they told me about what life was like for the women of Patrus—treated like slaves, little better than dogs, even stolen and ripped from their homes—and the boys of Matrus, who were screened for aggressive behavior and weeded out of the populace if they tested positive. They had supposedly been sent to the mines to work, but had actually been experimented on (they wouldn't go into detail as to how, but judging from Melissa's and Thomas's faces, it wasn't good).

They asked if our society had a lower class, and in response, the three of us held up our wrists, displaying our indicators that showed our ranking. I explained to them how the ranking system worked, about the nets in our heads, but glossed over Scipio and the AIs altogether. I kept the rest of the story much simpler for them, explaining only that we had learned of a secret group that had been manipulating laws in order to gain power over the system, resulting in more and more people losing rank, while those in power remained on top.

Melissa rolled her eyes and said, "Ah, yes, no truer love story than that between people and power," with a quirky smile that had us laughing.

In return, they told us about the former Queen Elena and her quest for power, in which she had faked Patrian aggression to start a war. In doing so, she had killed hundreds of Patrian males, and it had taken the better part of ten years for the country to rebuild. But rebuild it the Patrians did, with the help of their ally Queen Morgana, of Matrus, and Prime Chancellor Viggo Croft, of Patrus. The latter of whom, of course, was Thomas and Melissa's father.

The siblings talked about their parents a lot. It was actually kind of sweet, and I could tell by the way they smiled and laughed that they had a very healthy relationship with both of them. I could see the love and pride beaming out of them. I envied that, a little bit, mostly because it started to drag me back to that "what if" place I had been in after my mother died, and I quickly resumed my thread in the story. Even though I omitted the AIs, I told them everything else, the words spilling out of me faster than the water the hydro-turbines sucked up from the river. It felt good to talk about it with someone who was outside of the situation. My friends and I lived, breathed, and slept with this crap on a daily basis, so talking to them about it was pointless, as they knew all of the problems. But Thomas and Melissa were different; they were safe, and neutral. They didn't have a dog in this fight, no vested interest, and they were very sympathetic listeners, empathizing with our plight as the story unraveled. I could tell they agreed with a lot of the choices I had made.

It took over an hour for us to finish, and by the time we were done, we were all sitting around the conference table, having all sat down at various points in the conversation. Our talk had fallen off, in one of those natural pauses that occurred during lively conversation, when Leo said, "You never told us about the radiation of the Wastes. You indicated you knew what it was caused by?"

That was right. I had forgotten about that in the organic exchange of information. I leaned forward, interested in what Thomas's answer would be. The radiation was the only thing keeping us from crossing the Wastes outside, and if they knew what was causing it, I wanted to know what it was. Maybe it was a pipe dream, but I had a hope that if we knew what it was, we could figure out how to stop it and finally leave the Tower.

Thomas blinked and leaned back in his chair, crossing his arms over his chest. "As a matter of fact, you're what caused it," he said flatly, and I blinked.

"What do you mean?" I demanded. "The radiation is fallout, right? From the End?"

Melissa shook her head, her green eyes simmering with sadness. "Your Tower dumps toxic sludge into the river, and it has seeped into the surrounding area, killing everything within a hundred-mile radius, give or take."

Disoriented by the news, I sank back into the chair. *We* were causing the radiation that was keeping us here? The entire time... it was our fault that we couldn't go outside? Did the other councilors know? Was this just some unforeseen byproduct of the Tower that no one predicted? Or worse, was it some sort of deterrent to keep others away from us? What was it doing to the rest of the world?

"The two-hundred-mile radius is also barren, but in the three- to four-fifty range, things start to get interesting," Thomas added, seeming to read my mind.

I didn't like this. He was beginning to speak cryptically again, meaning he was hiding something.

"What are you talking about?" I asked. "What gets interesting?"

Melissa rolled her eyes and smacked her brother on the arm. "He's being a jerk. Just ignore him. Basically, the toxic stuff you dump back into the river has done something to the environment and surrounding atmosphere, and has kind of created its own ecological system."

"I..." I looked over at Leo, who shook his head, and Maddox, who shrugged, looking as bewildered as I felt. No, I was beyond bewildered. I was downright deflated. All I knew was that the very thing that was keeping us alive was also keeping us trapped inside. "Thank you for telling me that," I told them.

Thomas nodded solemnly, and for several long seconds the group fell into silence. I didn't mind; I was still trying to process the bombshell they had just dropped on me. Then he started speaking again, this time with a note in his voice that signaled a change of topic.

"You know, in situations like these, I am permitted to offer people from an oppressed culture refuge in Patrus. We obviously wouldn't be able to handle the entire Tower's population, but from what you've said, you don't have many people on your side helping to fight against these legacy cats that are messing everything up."

"Cats?" Maddox echoed, cocking her head.

In my opinion, she was focusing on the wrong damn thing. He had just told us he could give us an escape. Freedom from the Tower's insane laws and broken systems. From the nets in our skulls and Scipio's watchful and polluted gaze. We could be free, breathe fresh air, see the world without the glass of the Tower warping our view of it!

"It means people," Melissa said dismissively. "Anyway, my brother is right, but there's a catch. We couldn't take you all now. One of you must come with us to lodge a formal petition with the government and request permission. That person would need to give our people information on how many you intended to bring into our country, and what sort of skills they would be contributing to Patrian society. Then our people will have to deliberate and decide, but we could push them for a decision within a week, given the precariousness of your situation. No matter what they decide, I promise that when you next see is, it won't be without the representative you send."

"You're in luck that we need males in the population," Thomas added with a wry smile.

I frowned and gave him a look, uncertain how to interpret that remark. Was he saying that women wouldn't get in? I wasn't sure of the numbers offhand, but if they were offering refugee status to our people, the top of my list of applicants consisted of the Paragon-takers we had been supporting. But I didn't know how many males there were versus females. I narrowed my eyes at him, about to ask.

His sister smacked him again before I could even open my mouth, this time with a slap loud enough that his gasp of pain was believable. "Ouch," he said, rubbing a spot on his shoulder. "Brat."

Melissa ignored him. "My brother didn't mean that as it sounded," she told us. "All people are welcome. We just have to screen them for any potential threats, and then give cross-cultural training classes to prepare them for Patrian society." She paused and gave us a small smile. "If you're interested, of course."

I considered her offer and didn't hate it. Our Paragon supply was already waning, having been diluted in our attempt to manufacture more for the people we were supporting, and now that my brother had been added to the list of people who needed it, we would be out sooner rather than later. Jasper had taken a pill to run a chemical analysis on it, to help us get the formula, but he wasn't awake, and we had no idea when he would be—or if he even still had any analysis he might have run.

Not to mention, I had been wanting to do something to help those people for a long time, and this was an opportunity to actually free them from this life. I had once considered asking them to join in the fight against the legacies, because I needed people I could trust to help us (and dependency bred a form of trust, I supposed), but this solution was far better. And it helped get that particular loose end off my plate, so I could have more worrying time for the *other* problems.

Maybe it was a little callous of me, but I really could use a break. This seemed like a good one, but it also wasn't only on me. "Can we have a few minutes to talk about this, please? Alone?" Thomas and Melissa nodded and stood up. I watched them go for a second, and then on impulse asked, "Can you send in my other people while you're at it? They need to be included in the conversation as well."

"I can tell you're used to being in charge," Thomas said laughingly. "But yes, Your Championess, I will summon your people for you." He executed a courtly bow while I flushed bright red with embarrassment. I could've gotten up and retrieved Quess and my twin myself, but it was habit to ask someone leaving the room to do things for me.

The privilege of power, I supposed. Had to be careful of that in the future if I was going to be dealing with a sovereign ally.

I kind of liked the sound of that, and found myself wondering what the future would hold if I could manage to pull off saving the Tower and eradicating the legacies. There were so many things that I wasn't certain of, but one thing I did know: the intrusion of Thomas and Melissa had brought a sliver of hope into our lives. We hadn't had that in a long time... and the future was starting to look brighter by the second.

21

"Hey, so Amberlynn Sassabee is going to be okay," Quess announced as he entered.

I smiled at his mispronunciation of her name, and automatically corrected him with a soft "Ashabee" directed at him.

"Whatever, her name is a mouthful," he said, dropping into the chair Thomas had been sitting in just a few moments ago. "So tell me about these aliens. I kept trying to get Helena to talk, but that girl is prick*ly*." He drew out the last syllable significantly, and I shot him a look.

"I hope you were nice. That was her mother you were working on," Maddox chided, giving him a significant look. "Also, you're one to talk, *Quessian* Brown."

The look that Quess gave her was two parts smug, one part loving adoration. "Of course I was. My mama raised me right. And hey, 'Quessian' is exotic and cool, and brown is the best color in the world. My name rules."

I rolled my eyes at their antics, but inside I was amused. We were all caught up in the excitement of our secret visitors, and after a long day, it was nice to be able to relax and talk about something that wasn't legacy-related. Still, I was ever cognizant of the time. Eric was still injured, and now that Amber was stabilized, our new friends needed to leave before anyone inside the Tower took notice of them.

Which meant we had to quickly come to a decision about what to do.

"All right, guys, here's the deal," I told them, pausing when I saw that my brother hadn't sat down yet. In fact, he hadn't moved from where he had stopped when he first entered the room. "Alex?"

He looked up from the flooring of the cockpit and blinked his eyes at me a few times, as if trying to remember where he was. I shifted in my seat, preparing to get up and go to him, but he shook his head and made a halfhearted attempt to smile. An attempt that was heart-wrenching.

"Sorry," he said, shuffling over to the other vacant seat and sitting down. "What's going on?"

"Wait a second," I said. "I've got to get Zoe in on this call." Zoe knew the Paragon users best. She would be an invaluable source of insight for this conversation.

Leo frowned and shook his head. "That would mean removing your scrambler," he said.

But I was already in the process of doing so, sparing a moment to take a deep breath of relief as the continuous buzzing caused by the scrambler stopped. It was a momentary relief, though, as it was going to start right back up again when I netted her.

"I know," I replied in answer to his comment, tapping my indicator over to the net function. "But we have to risk them noticing I was up here. I'll make something up if it is noticed, because this is more important. She and Eric know the people on Paragon. We need to clue her in. Give me a second. Contact Zoe Elphesian, M1709-C19."

Leo's mouth twisted into a frown, but he didn't say anything. I waited for the net to connect and was rewarded by her voice in my ear seconds later. *Where the hell are you guys, and what is taking so long?*

I cringed, realizing that I should've netted her far sooner, and immediately apologized using the neural transmitter, so as not to clue the others in to what was going on. Besides, they were too busy flipping through the graphic novel Thomas had given us, excitement and rapt awe mirrored on their faces.

I'm sorry, Zo, I thought contritely, feeling the vague pop against my temple that signaled that the message had been sent. *Is Eric okay?*

He's fine. I think. He still hasn't woken up. And he's very pale. But his breathing is steady, and his pulse is strong. I just wish he wasn't so pale.

I could hear the tremor in her voice as she spoke, and my heart longed to go to her to comfort her. But I couldn't.

He's strong, Zoe. You know how strong he is. And he loves you. He's not ready to leave you.

I hope you're right, she replied. There were several seconds of dead space, followed by, *So wait, what is going on? Why is it taking you so long to dump a body?*

I took a deep breath, preparing to drop a bombshell on my friend. *Yeah, well, about that. We have visitors. Remember those people that Roark's wife saw? Well, their kids are here, and we've been helping them out. One of their people was injured.*

Zoe didn't say anything for several heartbeats, and Leo coughed, giving me a questioning look. I held my finger to my ear and signaled for him to give me a moment.

What? Zoe replied. *Are you serious?*

There's more, but I'm gonna switch over to verbal conversa-

tion. Everyone is here, and you might get a lot of one-sided conversation from me, but bear with me, because I need your insight on this.

Okay... Zoe drawled. I could tell she was confused, which was fair and totally my fault, but we didn't have time to recap everything.

"Right," I said, leaning forward in my seat and signaling for the others to focus on me. "So here it is. The aliens have offered us a chance to escape as refugees, and I was thinking we could send the Paragon users to them, to finally deliver on Roark's plan of escape while relieving stress on our own supply, in case Jasper isn't able to—"

"Whoa, whoa, whoa," Maddox interrupted, pinning me with a confused look. "What do you mean? You want to send... only the Paragon users? What about us?"

I gaped at her, my mouth still open, and then slowly shut it, leaning back in my chair. It never crossed my mind that we would be talking about leaving ourselves. That... That wasn't what I had in mind, and I felt completely uncertain of how to respond to her statement.

As far as I knew, we were still fighting for the destiny of the Tower. There were legacies to unearth, and Scipio was still broken. We couldn't just *leave*. But as I looked from Maddox to Quess and back again, I realized that it had never occurred to me that they wouldn't feel the same way.

"Guys," I said, looking between the two of them. "We need to stay. The Tower... Scipio... All those people will die if we just abandon them."

Maddox shifted in her chair and took a deep breath, her eyes going to the table. "I know that," she replied. "But, I mean, look at where we are! We're standing in the cockpit of a machine that can *fly*. Talking about a civilization that has overcome its problems already and is willing to accept us because of our situation. Liana, this is beyond anything we could've dreamed of or hoped for. We finally have a way out."

"It's what Cali and Roark wanted us to do in the first place," Quess added before I had a chance to respond. "They didn't want us to fight; they wanted us to survive. Think about it—we can just go, disappear and never look back. We wouldn't have to lose anyone else, and we could be free to... to pursue whatever we wanted to! Explore, invent, learn about pre-End culture, whatever! Isn't that better than... than going back in there and facing what we have to face on a daily basis?"

I didn't have an answer for that. On the one hand, I understood what he was saying. I was tired. We all were. And it wasn't just about today or yesterday. It was all of the days, every single dark one, rolled up together in the mess that our lives had become. Everything was grimmer than it had ever been, and the future was beyond nebulous.

On the other hand, I couldn't abandon the people of the Tower. I wouldn't. I'd made the decision long ago, and I had given my promise to Leo to help him restore Lionel Scipio's original vision of the Tower, to the best of my abilities. When the Patrians had made their offer, I had only seen it as an opportunity to give those who wanted out their chance while relieving one of my many burdens. I had even thought about taking them up on it myself—but not until *after* I fixed everything.

I wasn't leaving. Not until I finished what I started.

A part of me wanted to confront them about leaving, convince them they would be wrong to do so. Another part saw it as futile. Quess and Maddox had never hidden their true aim from me. They had always been perfectly clear. I just wished that I didn't feel so disappointed that they hadn't changed their minds. Disappointed and rejected, even.

But I couldn't order them to stay, not if they didn't want to.

"Right," I said, shifting slightly in my seat, trying to regain some small measure of balance within myself. "Well, if you want to be included with the people who go, that's fine. Zoe, what are your thoughts on all of this?"

You mean other than the idea that I can get my boyfriend out of here and to a place where he will never be hurt again? Yeah, I think the Paragon users will definitely go for it. Although, they're going to have to get over the shock of learning that there's life out there. I am totally down with getting the hell out of here before anything else goes wrong. She paused for a second, and then added, *Eric's family is going to need to be included in the refugee group. Or else he won't go. Probably my mother as well.*

I blinked. Zoe's mother wasn't a problem, but Eric's family was large. All of his grandparents were alive, and with the exception of his father, the rest of his family was intact. That meant an uncle on both his father's and mother's sides, as well as their wives and children. And I wasn't even going to start on the in-laws. If we took his family, we might wind up taking an entire farming floor. As much as I hated to say it, Eric was going to have to limit himself in regard to who he took with him. Not to mention, the Patrians would definitely have a say in how many of us they could take.

"Agreed," I told her. "But there's gonna have to be a cap on how many family members he can bring."

There was a pause, and then Zoe sighed, the tone a musical cascade of chimes along my inner ear canal. *I understand, but you know he's not going to like it.*

"I know he won't. But we don't know how many of our people they're going to accept, and we already have..." I paused to do some quick math, excluding myself from the equation. "Thirty-six. That's a lot for any nation to take on, and with Eric's family, we'll be pushing it to fifty."

Silence met my remark. *I said I heard you, Liana. I'll do my best to explain it to him when he wakes up. What do you need from me?*

I paused and recalibrated. It took me a moment to get my bearings, because I was still reeling with the sudden feeling that I was losing everyone. Zoe, Quess, and Maddox all wanted to go, and I was betting that if Grey was himself again, he would choose to leave as well. And their decision was out of my hands—had never been in my hands in the first place. My friends had already made up their minds. It didn't matter what I thought.

But I could dwell on that later. For now, we needed to choose an emissary to plead our case to the Patrians. "So who's going to go?" I asked.

"You mean, who *can* go," Quess said dejectedly. "Obviously it can't be Maddox or me, as we're both a part of your staff and will be missed. And clearly not Leo, since he won't want to."

"I am perfectly content in the home my father built," Leo agreed. "But there is a chance that Grey would like to go. He'll certainly be able to tell us soon." He met my gaze and then looked away, and a massive lump formed in my throat. He couldn't be saying what I thought he was saying, could he? "I predict he'll be awake by the end of next week, his memory fully restored."

Scipio help me, I did not need that news right at this moment. Everyone was looking to me, seeing how I would respond, and it took far longer than it should have. "It'll be good to have him back," I said, forcing a fake smile to my lips. *Don't think about Leo leaving you, too,* I thought to myself. I cleared my throat, trying to dislodge the rock that had formed there, and then sighed. "So Quess, Maddox, and Leo are all out. What about Zoe?"

No way, she replied automatically. *I'm not leaving Eric's side until he's on his own two feet and coming with me wherever I go.*

Of course she wouldn't leave him behind for this. Not to mention, Lacey would notice her disappearance and think that maybe we were making a run for it. That wouldn't be great, as she had damning evidence that seemed to prove I had tampered with

Scipio during my trial against Devon Alexander (even though I hadn't).

Alex sighed heavily and shifted in his seat. "I should be the one to go."

My spine straightened, and I immediately began to shake my head. "Alex, no. You need to stay here, with me, so I can help you—"

"What, figure out how to keep surviving day-to-day Tower life? Or continue to be paranoid that everyone in my department is spying on me, waiting for me to mess up so they can report it to Sadie? I hate what my life has become. I hate this stupid Tower, and I just want... I want to get out. I want to do something productive for once, rather than staring at lines of code, watching Scipio degrade. Besides..." He met my gaze, his eyes filled with infinite sadness. "I'm going to drain your Paragon supply, now that I'm on it. Let me do this. Arrange a transfer for me to move into the Knights, and have Dinah push it through. No one will even notice I'm gone."

There was a rap on the doorframe, and before I could even begin to form a counterargument to my brother's statement, Thomas was there. "So, not to rush you guys, but we really should be going. We gave you as much time as we dared, but we know the destructive force of those lasers, and we don't want to get caught. Have you made a decision?"

I looked pleadingly at my brother, but his eyes remained fixed on his lap. "Yes," he told the Patrian man. "I'll be going with you. I'm Liana's brother, Alex Castell."

I squeezed my eyes shut, the whole world dropping away from under my feet. My brother was leaving—had decided to *leave.* What if he never came back? What if their flying machine failed and they crashed? What if they killed him once they took him away? What if the council turned the Tower's defenses against them while they were leaving, and blew them out of the sky? Or worse, he got there and decided he didn't want to come back to us? To me?

"Here," Thomas said, close to my ear, startling me out of my despair. There was a black box cradled in the palm of his outstretched hand. "This is a communicator that will allow you to have conversations with your brother, even from this far away. Although, you might have to be outside for it to really work. But yeah, you'll be able to talk to him whenever you want. I promise we will be back within a week, even if the council hasn't made its determination. I'm sure they'll side in your favor, in which case we'll be bringing more... flying machines for an evacuation."

I stared at it blankly. He was taking my brother and leaving me with this box. This was moving way too fast. Still, my hand reached up to numbly pluck it out of his, with a hollow "Thank you."

He gave me a warm look, and I slowly stood up, my bones leaden. I looked at my brother, and he managed a tentative smile. "Alex, I..."

"I love you, too," he said. And as if to prove it, he came around the table to throw his arms around me in a massive hug. "Don't worry. I'll figure out what kind of people they really are and make a deal for us to get out of here. Imagine it, Lily; we can be free of this awful place for good. Won't it be great?"

"Yeah," I lied, not wanting to destroy his sudden optimism with the truth. "I'm looking forward to it."

22

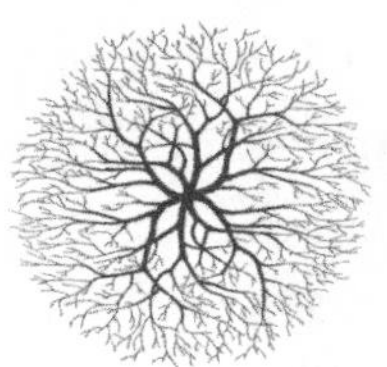

And just like that, my brother was leaving. We said our goodbyes and took out his net so Quess could modify it to prevent the Tower from registering him leaving or dying, and Hela thanked Quess and then gave him something called a blood patch. I overheard enough of their conversation to understand that it was something that caused bones to increase production of red blood cells and was evidently an advanced piece of medical technology that surpassed our own. Apparently Quess had told her about Eric, and the fact that he had lost a lot of blood, and she was gifting him the patch in return for saving her mother's life. Seemed like a fair exchange, but I trusted Quess to know.

Instead of feeling relieved, though, I simply felt empty and adrift. And the feeling persisted, even as they disappeared onto the ship, the ramp drawing back up behind them, and long after they disappeared into the blue light.

It wasn't until we turned to leave that it hit me. My brother was gone. And Quess, Maddox, Zoe, and Eric were going to leave soon, too. Grey was going to be fully restored in a week's time, and then Leo was going to leave me too, in a way.

If ever there was a time to fall to pieces, this was it. Something that I had first seen as a blessing had actually been a knife blow to the heart of my little group. We were unraveling, falling apart, and soon we would be going our own separate ways.

How was I ever going to do this alone?

It was a wonder I made it back to our quarters, so dark and bleak were my thoughts. If I hadn't been following Leo the entire way, I would've wound up wandering around the Attic for hours. Instead, I stopped when he did, and started when he did, letting him guide our every move back down to the Citadel.

Once we were home, Quess went to check on Eric and give him the blood patch, and Maddox went to tell Tian the news and get ready for bed. That left Leo and me alone.

For several heartbeats, I could only stare at him, my heart breaking. I was going to be losing him soon. I mean, I wasn't... but... what kind of relationship could we have once he was back in a computer?

I didn't realize how much I had been dreading that day until now, when it was nearly here. Suddenly I needed his arms around me. Or maybe not suddenly—I had been thinking about it off and on—but now it was visceral. We had broken into Sadie Monroe's quarters. Killed four people. Cut Leo out of Grey to put him into Baldy, only to have Baldy himself break free and shoot Eric. We'd shot Baldy in return, and then thrown him off the side of the Tower. Met aliens—and then lost my brother.

All in a single day.

To say I wanted to wrap Leo around me like a blanket and fall asleep feeling safe was an understatement. Especially now that I knew this could be our last night together. It was selfish and wrong, but I couldn't stop myself.

"Leo, will you come to—"

"Stop," he interrupted, and I froze, cocking my head at him. He stared back at me for a second, a deep look of concentration in his eyes. Uncertainty rippled through me, and I took a step closer.

"Are you okay?" I asked.

He shook his head, sandy-brown hair waving back and forth, and swallowed. "Wait," he said, and his eyes begged me to heed him.

I worked my mouth back and forth, still uneasy, but nodded and wrapped my arms around myself. Leo closed his eyes for a moment and took a couple of deep, even breaths. His facial muscles changed microscopically, and if I didn't know any better, I would say he was having a net call with someone. He had the ability; I just couldn't imagine whom he would be netting. Maybe Dinah, to apprise her of the situation with Alex? If so, it would be an odd time to do so. Unless he was just trying to be helpful and take something off my plate.

But no, he would let me handle that. I frowned and continued to keep quiet. He would tell me when he was done. After what felt like an eternity, his eyes opened, and he gave me a furtive look.

"I'm sorry," he said with a sigh. "I... I could guess where this was heading, and there's something you need to be aware of. A few things, actually."

There was a quality to his voice that I didn't like, and all my instincts were telling me that whatever he was about to tell me wasn't good. Maybe I was overreacting, given the day I'd just had, but I couldn't shake the feeling that something was wrong. Had he been damaged when Baldy was shot? Was something wrong with Grey? He'd said we'd have to talk about him later. Maybe he was going to fill me in on what happened.

"Okay," I said, drawing it out. "You going to tell me what those are?"

He gave me a look that was filled with pain. "Maddox and

Quess had to tell Grey what was going on. It was the only way he would accept the net—and me—without a fight."

For several long seconds, I couldn't understand what he was saying. Then I did, and I swallowed, hard, fighting against the nausea that was forming in my stomach. "They told him the truth."

"Yes. Well, parts of it. He didn't understand a lot, so they tried to summarize as much as possible." He paused and then shuffled his feet. "He asked them about you—whether you knew each other—and Quess told him that you did. He didn't go into detail, but basically... Grey demanded to be awake while I was working on him, and they agreed. They told me about the deal, and—"

"They didn't get your consent," I said, thinking that it wasn't fair of them to make a deal on his behalf without his permission. He had been stuck inside the net at the time, unable to communicate anything, and they had just blithely agreed to Leo sharing his consciousness and thoughts like that. Then my eyes widened, and I cupped my hands over my mouth, horrified at what I had said. Not for Leo, but because I knew Grey was watching us right now. Which meant he had just seen me basically denying his right to know what was happening to him while he wasn't in control. All because I didn't want Grey knowing about what was happening between Leo and me.

What an awful, selfish person I was.

Leo gave me a broken smile. "It's okay," he said soothingly. "That's why I asked you to wait, earlier. I was talking with Grey, asking him to give us some privacy so I could tell you what was going on." He pierced my soul with a single look. "I wanted to give you a moment to adjust to the news."

"I see." I closed my eyes, trying to find some semblance of peace with what he was telling me, and then flat-out refuted it. If this was the last moment that Leo and I could talk, unmonitored by Grey, then I wanted to tell him the truth about what I felt for him. *How* I felt for him.

"Leo," I started, using his name as a starting point for my chaotic emotions. "I—"

"It's probably for the best," he interrupted. He moved to say more, but I wasn't going to let him get the final say in this.

"No," I said flatly. "It's not. Leo, I have things I want to say to you. Need to say. And you should hear them."

"To what end?" he asked bitterly. "Grey will be back in your life soon, and—"

"I don't care," I told him. And I didn't. Because now that I was this close to losing him, I realized that I couldn't bear it. "We can figure something out, find you a new body. Someone who is in the Medica, maybe, braindead. You wouldn't have to restore them, you could just—"

I was babbling, and it was only the weight of Leo's hands falling on my shoulders that managed to bring me to a stop. "I couldn't do that, Liana. You know I couldn't do that."

Tears started to form in my eyes at the sadness in his voice, but I blinked them back, refusing to give it up. "Yes, you *can*," I insisted, reaching up to cup his face. "If not one of them, then a legacy, one who didn't attack me. I don't know what happened before, but I'm certain you could figure out how to keep it from happening again. And, I mean, we'd just have to kill them anyway, so it's not like you'd be doing anything bad!"

But Leo's sadness grew even more obvious, his reluctance and refusal showing on the planes of his face.

"Please!" I begged, wanting to shake him. "I'm sorry I denied my feelings for you all this time. I'm sorry I was so confused. Just... please don't leave me!"

He closed his eyes. "You don't understand," he breathed. "I can't give you what you want, Liana." His eyes snapped open, and he abruptly moved away, taking a few steps to carve some space between us. "I think you were right all along. Grey was influencing the way I felt about you. My feelings for you were never really my own."

I could've heard a pin drop with how silent and still I was at his revelation. For a long moment, I didn't feel anything. I just stared at him like an idiot. Then it hit, and I met it with a wall of flat-out denial. I couldn't accept that as the truth, not after all the beautiful things he'd said to me. All of the wonderful ways he'd made me feel, in spite of my own grief.

"No," I said, taking a step toward him. "You're confused. Baldy's crazy thoughts freaked you out, and we had a *really* long day. After we get some sleep we'll—"

"He held a gun on you, Liana. He was going to shoot you, and I couldn't do anything to stop him. I should've been enough. How I *felt* about you should've been enough to stop him, but it wasn't. I was trapped in his mind, unable to stop him as he threatened you! As he shot Eric and threatened our friends! And there was nothing I could do to stop him! All I could feel was his hatred and fear. What I thought I had clearly wasn't strong enough to fight what he felt. Ergo, it wasn't mine."

"You're not being fair to yourself," I said to him. "It's not your fault you lost control, and of course you felt what he was feeling. That's what the net does! I'm not sure why he was able to resist you, but that's not your doing! And it certainly doesn't mean your feelings toward me aren't real! Dammit, Leo, you spent all that time convincing me they *were*! Why are you doing this?"

He shook his head, his eyes closing again, as if he were fighting against pain of his own. "It wasn't enough, what I felt. Maybe I was just kidding myself, thinking I could understand the complexities of human emotion. Lionel said I had the capacity, that growth came from experience, but I think maybe he was wrong. The fragments never change, so why would I? I am nothing more than determination, a will to succeed in the face of adversity. Maybe that explains why I pursued you with such intensity."

"Leo," I said, reaching out for him, my heart breaking. "*You* kissed me, on the bridge. You said all those things about thinking about it, dreaming about it, but never having any memory of it until you *made* one with me. I resisted you for so long, and you still came after me. You protected me and made me feel safe. Leo, I feel things for you that I don't want to let go of. Please don't do this."

"I have to," he choked out, squeezing his hands into fists. "I'm sorry that I confused things for you, Liana, but it's now clear to me that all of this... between us... was due to Grey's elevated hormonal response to your own natural pheromones, and nothing more."

Pain radiated from my chest. His words, so decidedly clinical, sliced deeper than anything he had said thus far. He'd spent all this time convincing me that it was him, making me see him through Grey's body, and now that I finally *had*, he was taking it away from me.

Anger, slow and biting, came over me, and I swallowed down my pain, shoving it behind a carefully placed mask. It was a dark and bitter thing that would only put me on attack if I gave it any freedom. I didn't want him to see how much this devastated me. My pride wouldn't allow it.

"Of course," I said, trying to force a pleasant smile to my lips, only to feel the corners of my mouth lift barely a fraction of an inch. "Right. I will... go sleep with Zoe. I don't know why I didn't think of it earlier."

Scipio help me, my voice sounded tinny, like it was coming from the other end of a long, narrow pipe. It was as if I were shrinking, growing very small and insignificant while the rest of the world warped and expanded, on the verge of implosion.

Leo blinked at me, his brows furrowing in wary confusion. "Are you okay?"

Not even remotely, I thought to myself. Out loud, I said, "Perfectly fine," manifesting a little bit more volume. I struggled to find something else to say, something that wouldn't show that I was breaking on the inside, and floundered. The conference room was the largest room in my quarters, but I could feel the walls as if they were millimeters from my skin, slowly pressing in. My uniform felt hot, tight, and irritating, and there suddenly wasn't enough oxygen in the room. I needed to get out. Now.

"Excuse me," I managed thickly.

I made a wide berth around him, heading for the closest set of stairs—ones that would lead to the hall beyond, and straight to freedom from him. And I was almost there, when his voice stopped me.

"It really is for the best, Liana," he told me, and I was glad my back was to him. It meant he couldn't see the first tear that slipped from my eye, burning a hot line down my cheek. "Grey will be back to you soon, as good as new. You don't have to tell him anything. We can just pretend—"

I couldn't let him speak any more. Every word that came out of his mouth was like an extra twist of the blade. Besides, if he thought he was doing this to spare me telling Grey what had happened while he was injured, then he needed to know that he was wrong.

"I won't lie to him, Leo. Much like you won't take a person's body against their will, I won't lie to someone I care about. I owe him more than that."

I resumed walking, and sped up a little, needing to retreat. Luckily, Leo didn't say anything else, allowing me to make my escape.

23

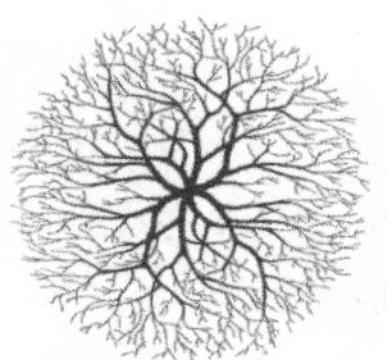

I woke up the next morning and experienced several disorienting seconds in which I wasn't entirely sure where I was. The sensation was so strong that I shot out of the bed, almost afraid I had slept so deeply that the legacies had snuck in and taken us. It wasn't until I noticed Zoe jerking straight up from where she had been sleeping next to Eric, her eyes wide in alarm, that everything came rushing back. The talk with Leo. Crying on Zoe's shoulder. Zoe crying on mine. Eric sleeping through it all.

"What is it?" she asked, and I pressed a hand to my heart, trying to still the erratic pounding my fear had caused. I took several deep breaths, and then gave her an apologetic look as she added, "Liana, what's wrong?"

I shook my head. "I just... I was confused as to where I was, that's all," I explained, shaking some of the excess adrenaline from my limbs. "How's Eric?"

She shifted up to one arm and leaned over him, her thick brown hair swinging forward to hide her face. Her hand reached up to check his pulse, and then cupped his cheek as she studied him. "Eric," she said lightly. "Baby?"

His chest lifted up and fell, but his eyelashes were still. There was no sign that he was waking up, but that didn't mean much this soon after being shot. Zoe sighed and scooted up on the bed, pressing the heels of her hands into her eyes and taking a shaky breath.

I moved instantly to her side and reached over Eric to pull her into a hug. "It's okay," I said, stroking a soothing hand over her hair. I glanced down at Eric's still form, noting that his skin color was much better than it had been last night, and that his breathing was steady and sure. The blanket over him had been pulled down enough to reveal the bullet wound on his chest, just below his pectoral muscle on the left, the flesh bright pink and shiny after the rapid regeneration, thanks to the bio-foam. There was no bruising on his stomach to indicate internal bleeding. All very excellent signs.

Besides, him not waking up yet wasn't necessarily cause for alarm. He had lost a lot of blood, and two of his internal organs had been punctured by the bullet. What he needed was rest, and time for his body to recover from the shock.

"He looks much better this morning, Zo. I really think he's going to be all right. He just needs to sleep right now."

She nodded against my shoulder, taking a shaky breath. "I know. I just... I can't imagine him not in my life, and when Quess said there was no hope... Oh Scipio, I never thanked you, Liana. You didn't give up on him. You brought him back to me."

Tears sprang into my eyes as she clutched me tighter. "I'm not letting anyone else I love die," I told her.

She sniffed and gently pulled away from me, a tremulous smile on her lips. "But now we don't have to," she pointed out. "We just have to hold on long enough for Alex to negotiate a place for us in this Patrus place. If we can just keep our heads down—"

My spirits, which were already low, plummeted the moment she brought up the Patrians. I had managed to put them out of my head, though I had spent half of last night idly thumbing through the graphic novel Thomas had given us, reading about Violet and Viggo's story. Now that she had brought it up again, it was all I could think about. All of my friends—my entire support network—were going to disappear, and soon I would be on my own for the rest of this battle.

Yesterday, my entire focus had been on damage control and figuring out our next step in this fight. Today, I wasn't even sure I could ask the others to help me go through Sadie's files to see if we could figure out what she was up to and who she was working with. I wasn't sure they would want to, now that they had hope of getting out of the Tower. If I were them, and was hoping for escape, I would want to put my head down and wait for rescue, not go borrowing more trouble by helping me figure out what we were dealing with.

"Hey," Zoe said, giving my shoulder a little shake. I blinked up at her and realized I had missed everything she had been saying. "Why do you look so sad? Isn't this good news?"

I tried to force a smile onto my face. "Yeah. It's great."

My best friend knew me better than that, and she cocked her head and squinted at me. "Liana, you are an excellent liar when you want to be, but that was a really crappy effort. Are you worried about Alex? Dinah said she would make ghost net data into his file so no one noticed he was missing, so I don't think you have to worry about that. Besides, I read that graphic novel thing after you fell asleep last night, and these people seem pretty great, despite everything they went through. They're kind of like us, in a way. They found out that people were trying to take power and did everything they could to stop them. I mean, they even tried to keep the queen responsible for everything *alive*, so they could put her on trial! That's saying something about a civilization."

I smiled, in spite of my own sadness. It was good to see her so excited about something. There was a light in her eyes that hadn't been there in the past few months, and I hadn't realized how much I had missed seeing her hopeful and looking forward to the future. But her words only made me realize how selfish I was being. I knew what most of them had signed up for: to get out of the Tower. Their goal had been put off time and time again, partially because the situations we found ourselves in called for survival first and escape later—but also because I didn't want to accept the idea that we would escape before we stopped the legacies and fixed Scipio. Not to mention the fact that we physically didn't have a way to go. The radiation outside would kill us, and we didn't have flying machines.

Now the possibility of them achieving their ultimate goal was here, and all I could think about was how it was going to affect me.

"That is great," I agreed, forcing a little more effort into the lie. "I'm excited."

She narrowed her dark blue eyes at me, her mouth tightening. "Spill."

Crap. I was clearly too close to this emotionally, and that was affecting my ability to lie. I screwed on a "seriously, everything is fine" face and opened my mouth to begin reassuring her. "Zoe, I—"

"Cut the crap, Castell," she barked in a no-nonsense voice. "What. The hell. Is up with you?"

I pressed my lips together and looked away. I hadn't been planning to tell anyone about my decision to stay and help Leo fix Scipio, and I wasn't sure now was the time to do it. But Zoe, who was the dearest person in the world to me, was also like a dog with a bone when she sensed I was keeping a secret from her. There was no getting out of it, not without causing a fight.

Besides, in the deepest, darkest part of my heart, I *wanted* to talk to someone about it. "Zoe, I'm not leaving with you and the others, even if Alex gets us refugee status. I promised Leo that I would stay and help him fix Scipio, and I still intend to do that."

She stared at me, her face an impassive mask. "But Leo essentially broke your heart last night," she finally said.

Pain blossomed, but I fought it back, trying not to cry. "No," I said. "He didn't." I wasn't sure if it was a lie or not, and I wasn't sure I wanted to know. It was what I had to say to keep from breaking down, so I said it, and tried not to pay any attention to how my heart ached, or how a voice in my mind was screaming at me to go find him, and then... hit him or scream at him not to do this. The voices were conflicted on that front.

Which was why it was better to ignore them both. I couldn't afford to break down, not like I had after my mom had died. As much as I wanted to just break down and cry, I couldn't; there were bigger problems to worry about than some jerk of an AI who had just hurt me worse than any of our enemies ever could.

Zoe's mouth worked. "Okay, he didn't," she agreed in a tone of voice that told me she didn't agree with me. "But he still hurt you. He lied to you and toyed with your emotions. Why stick around and help him?"

I gave her an incredulous look. "Because the people in the Tower shouldn't have to suffer because I got my feelings hurt. They deserve better than that."

"Then *they* should be the ones doing something about it," she retorted angrily. "Why does this whole legacy war, saving Scipio thing have to fall to us? Give Lacey Sadie's files, and the fragments. You said she had one already—Kurt, right? Her family has been keeping him safe for however many years, so have her handle it. It's her damn war, after all!"

I considered her idea, taking in a deep breath of air in an attempt to not reject the idea outright. Lacey had been a representative of her department for years, and had a veritable army working for her. She had also been fighting in this legacy war her entire life and would jump at the chance to finally put an end to it.

But could I trust her to actually restore Scipio, given the pieces and the chance? What if she got to that point and then decided not to, so *she* could try to control everything instead? What did I know about her, really? We weren't exactly close enough for her to let me in on her vision of the Tower, so how could I trust that it was any different from Sadie's?

More importantly, *could* I let go and walk away? Leave the job unfinished, the Tower unsaved, and just... go? Start a new life somewhere, free from all of the danger and strife we had been through... I was tired—that much was a constant—and had no clue what to do next. The struggles we had been through had been nonstop, and every time we came close to the enemy, someone wound up hurt or dead. I didn't want to see my friends hurt or killed. I didn't want them to die over this.

But me? I had already started down this path, committed to it fully. It didn't matter that Leo and the others were focusing on separate goals; the thought of leaving everything behind without fixing it ate at me. There were good people in the Tower who didn't deserve to fall victim to whatever the legacies had in store for them. I knew right then that I wouldn't be able to just leave them. So why lie about it?

"I don't have a good reason not to give it all over to Lacey," I said carefully. "But that doesn't mean I will. I hear what you're saying, Zo, but I'm not going. Not until I know the Tower is free from the legacies, and Scipio is restored."

"What if Scipio *can't* be restored?" she erupted angrily. "Liana, you don't owe anyone in this Tower a damn thing!"

I stared at her for a second, and then looked down at the graphic novel sitting partially under her pillow. She had just been talking about *their* struggles a moment ago, and how they solved their problems. From the sounds of it, *they* hadn't given up. So why were we?

I pointed at it and met her eyes. "They didn't owe anything to the people they saved, and yet they still did it. It can't be both ways, Zoe. We can't admire the things that they've done and the world they've created while turning our backs on our own. I understand wanting to leave, but I can't until I know everyone inside is going to be safe." I paused, and then added a bitter, "Not that anyone is going to want to help with that now."

Zoe's eyes widened, and for a second, I thought she was going to continue arguing with me. She expelled a slow breath, puffing out her cheeks. "Crap. That's a really good point." I wasn't expecting that, and her sudden reversal left me a bit speechless. My silence gave her a few more seconds to think about it, and I had a sudden hope that maybe she would find the answer for me. Instead, she finally said, "I don't see the others really getting on board with it, however."

She was right. Their hopes were high, and I wasn't sure the argument would hold weight with them. It was more moral than anything, whereas everything we'd done up to this point had been necessary to our continued survival. This was purely altruistic; I wasn't doing this because it was what I had to do, but because it was what needed to be done. It was impossible to expect the others to be willing to gamble their lives on something like that.

"I know." I sighed.

Her face was thoughtful for several long seconds. "How long until the outsiders come back?"

"Maybe a week," I replied tiredly. "Possibly longer, depending on how fast their government works. I'll get more information from Alex when I call him on that thing." She bit her lip, her eyebrows twitching. "What?"

She shrugged. "Ask everyone to keep helping you until the time comes. There's no guarantee that the Patrians will be able to secure a place for us anyway, and I think everyone will agree that the Paragon-dependent population will have to go first, if we can even go at all. That way you can keep moving forward with us, and maybe even inspire everyone to stay."

Zoe's suggestion sounded so easy, but it didn't change the fact that we didn't even *have* a way forward until we had more information. "But there's no plan, Zo." It was hard to admit that, but there it was. "We can hope that Sadie was stupid enough to leave the list of every legacy she worked with on her computer, but to what end? We don't have enough people to go after them all at once, and we can't completely trust every single one of my Knights, as any one of them could be working for her. If Sadie's people even hear a whisper that we're mobilizing against them before we get everything in place, they will figure out that their covers are blown, and disappear! And even if we do manage to grab them all at once, what would we do with them? Dump their bodies off the side of the Tower and keep going as if nothing happened? Do I do that with Sadie? What if there's another council member helping her? Do I become responsible for the execution of not one, not two, but three council members? What sort of mission is that?"

Zoe considered this, and then shrugged. "Going after the legacies makes the most sense. And you're right, going after them all at once is the best way to get them. But why execute them when we can take a page from our neighbors, and put them on trial? We've never once stopped to think about how this ends without causing a civil war. But what if there's another way to do it?"

She picked up the graphic novel as she spoke and held it out to me. I accepted it slowly, the weight of it feeling heavier in my hands then yesterday. But it wasn't the book that felt heavy. It was me. Was Zoe right? Could I somehow grab all the legacies and then pass the situation over to the council? If we managed to get them all, and presented a strong enough case against them, then the council would have to step in and handle it legally. I had no doubt that they'd want to implement the expulsion chambers, but in this case I felt that would be warranted. And then they'd be obligated to fix Scipio, and with Leo and me watching them to make sure they did what they were supposed to... Could there finally be an end in sight?

I wasn't sure, but it was at least the start of a plan. One that required Sadie's files to pay off for us, yes. But at least it was *something*. And maybe Zoe was right; maybe I could get the others to keep working on it with me, on the off chance that leaving wasn't an option. Either way, maybe we'd make some progress on catching the legacies before they left. Maybe even give my friends a victory strong enough that made them want to stay.

It wasn't much—but it was something to hold on to.

Really the only thing I had, at this point.

24

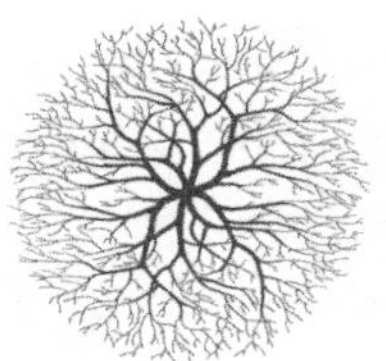

The talk with the others went pretty well, although I didn't tell them about my plan to stay. I wasn't ready to talk about it, and a part of me wondered if it would just be manipulative. I wanted them to stay for their own reasons, and I didn't want my decision to influence them one way or another. I also asked Zoe to keep it to herself before we left the room to grab breakfast with the others, and she had agreed. She warned me that she might spill the beans when Eric woke up, but swore up and down it would be to him and him only. I didn't like it, but what could I do?

I was nervous when I explained to them that I wanted us to start searching through Sadie's files to see if we could find every single legacy and accomplice she and her people had worked with, as well as evidence of the changes they had made to Scipio, in order to build a case against them to present to the council. It was a bold plan, one that I couldn't accomplish without them, and even though my argument was sound, they still had every right to refuse me.

Understandably, Maddox had wanted to know why, and I told her the truth: I couldn't leave without doing something to stop them. I couldn't abandon the Tower without devoting every last moment I had to trying to make things better. Everyone had been surprisingly understanding, especially after Zoe mentioned the fact that the Patrians might not be able to help us. There was every chance that they would refuse to grant us refugee status, and if we spent a week simply waiting for them to refuse us, then that was a week our enemies could use to get to us or cause further damage to Scipio. We couldn't allow them to get the drop on us just because we thought we were getting out.

Things got a little more complicated when Quess revealed that he still hadn't broken the encryptions on her files.

"How long is it going to take?" I asked, finally sitting down in a vacant chair at the table. My knees were still a bit wobbly from the conversation, but now, at least, I could sit. Everyone was on board with helping.

"I don't know," Quess replied tiredly. He ran a hand over his face and sighed heavily. "It would move faster if I could get some assistance." He shot a pointed look at Leo as he said that.

I followed his gaze, and my breath caught in my throat. Leo looked like crap. There were dark shadows under his eyes, and his hair was mussed and unkempt. He hadn't even shaved, and his cheeks were roughened with the beginnings of a beard. Even his uniform was wrinkled, which told me he had probably slept in it. Or tried to.

A part of me felt a savage satisfaction that he looked so rough. Clearly, he wasn't as unaffected by what had happened as he had seemed last night, which told me that he did indeed have feelings for me. But I shrugged that off, reminding myself that he likely looked the way he did because he'd stayed up all night to work on Jasper and Rose. Grey had also given Eric a lot of blood, and that probably wasn't helping. I wondered if I should pull him aside and order him to get some sleep, because pushing himself too hard would only hurt him and Grey. But I held back, uncertain of how he would perceive it.

Leo seemed oblivious of his own slobbish state and took a careful bite of a piece of toast before saying, "Jasper and Rose require my attention," in a neutral voice, not meeting anyone's eyes. "With everyone leaving, I want to make them as strong as possible before we are on our own."

Righteous indignation shot through me like a bullet, and it was all I could do to keep from coolly reminding him that I had promised to stay and help him fight. The condescension in his voice rankled me, and I wanted to smack him for thinking that he was alone in this. It wasn't even about him; it was about Scipio, and restoring him to his full capabilities, freeing him from legacy control. I had just spent the last fifteen minutes making an argument for us to *continue* working on it, dammit! And he had the audacity to sit there and *not* be a team player?

To hell with that. If he wanted to end... whatever it was that we had, that was fine. But he needed to keep this crap between us separate from our real-world problems. The least he could do was maintain some level of professionalism.

"Finding the legacies does help you and the other AIs," I said, trying to keep my voice free of the anger twisting up inside me. "And we know Lacey has Kurt. I plan to meet with her first, to make sure she's been treating him well, and if she has, it will mean we can leave you and the others with her, and you can continue to work on everyone. But before I do that, I want to make sure that every single legacy who is after Rose, Jasper, or you is gone. I think you can agree it will be safer for all three of you if they are gone, right?"

He finally looked up from his food and directed his gaze toward me, his brown eyes dark and hard. "I suppose you're right," he said. "It would make sense to eliminate that threat first. But not until I get both programs up and running again. Their safety and health are foremost in my mind."

His demeanor was so frosty, I had the urge to wrap my arms around myself to fight off the cold. The presence of it suddenly filled me with despair, and I once again wondered if he *had* been telling me the truth last night, and he really didn't care about me. It was like he had shut everything off with a switch and reverted back to something more machine than human. And this wasn't how he had been when we found him, either. Back in Lionel's office, at least, he had seemed so bright and hopeful. Now he just seemed... angry. It made me want to break down in tears, but my pride refused to let me.

Instead, I opened my mouth and asked, "How are they?"

"I think Rose may wake up today," he replied automatically, picking up his fork and returning his focus to his meal. "I'm unsure about Jasper, as his programming is still locked up in a defensive mode."

"Could Quess and Zoe be of any assistance to you?"

"Actually, I would be the better one to ask, don't you think?" a gruff voice announced from the speakers. My skin tingled with awareness, and Leo and I both shot out of our chairs. But it was me who spoke first.

"Jasper?!"

"In the proverbial flesh." A pause. "Or not. So these are the Champion's quarters, eh? They're quite nifty."

"How are you awake?" Leo demanded. "I tried everything I could to reach you."

"Yes, I am *well* aware, you impudent little upstart. Who the hell do you think you are to even be touching my coding?"

I raised an eyebrow... and then smiled. Jasper may have been listening, but he hadn't picked up on the fact that Leo was an AI inside a human's body. "He's Scipio, Jasper," I told him. "But not the one you were bonded with. He's the original version of the program. We call him Leo, to make things easier."

The speakers were silent for several seconds. "Whaaaat? Girl, you must be crazy, because that's not possible. I distinctly remember the council voting to have the backup fragments deleted. And I was there when we got confirmation of Scipio's backup being deleted along with the others!"

"You remember that?" I asked. Jang-Mi's and Rose's recollections were spotty at best. They'd been able to recall only general details, with no specifics.

"Pfft, who do you think you're talking to? I am Scipio's memory. I remember it all."

"You're his logic," Leo corrected.

"Actually, I'm his common sense," Jasper said icily. "How do you get common sense? From remembering your mistakes. It is embarrassing how little you know about us, but no matter. Just acknowledge that I am smart and you are not, and we can finish this little show of intellectual dominance."

I giggled. I couldn't help it. Jasper had never been quite this punchy in the Medica, but listening to him interact with Leo and put him in his place was highly entertaining, especially when Leo's face turned a shade of red that told me he was angry. At that point, I decided to take control of the situation and figure out what exactly had happened to Jasper.

"Jasper, why are you awake now? Why are you talking to us, and what happened to you? Why did you attack Rose?"

"Slow down there, little lady," Jasper replied. "That's a lot of questions. Okay, well... hm... I was stuck in that IT bitch's terminal, resisting yet another one of her torture programs, when I get pinged by something claiming to be Rose. Sadie had used that tactic before to draw me out, so I thought it was another tactic to try to get me to relax my defenses. But when this one started to break through my defenses in a way that shouldn't be possible for anything but an AI, I panicked and started attacking. I didn't realize what it was—just that it *seemed* like Rose, but clearly wasn't."

"It *was* Rose!" Leo said explosively. "She's damaged because of what they did to her, and you might have made it worse by blindly attacking her! Why didn't you initiate an authentication process?"

"You have no idea what Sadie has put me through, so don't you dare attack me for reacting to a perceived threat. I have been in Sadie's tender loving care for nearly twenty-five years, cut out so they could force Scipio to vote to destroy something the council called a gyroship, using the Tower's laser defense arrays! I warned them that it could result in retaliation, and that we should try to initiate a diplomatic relationship with them, but noooooo. Sadie's predecessor had to be one of those Prometheus nutcases hell bent on destroying Scipio. The council thought they'd been eradicated —ha! They just changed names and disappeared into history, until they started cutting us out of him! And for what? So they could reverse his decision to let the visitors go, too worried about outside interference in their stupid little plan. So they could use us to pilot their sentinels? So they could force us to help them destroy our home?"

He tsked, clearly irritated, and I blinked. He had just revealed a lot in just a few sentences: that he had been taken over twenty-five years ago, that he had been ripped out to get Scipio to agree to shooting Violet and Viggo out of the air, and that Sadie's predecessor was responsible for taking him out. He had also confirmed that Sadie's legacy group had started as a part of an anti-AI terrorist cell known as Prometheus. They'd reportedly been destroyed by Ezekial Pine, but it seemed that they lived on, in the form of legacies. I had learned about them from Leo—knew that they resented Scipio's role in determining humanity's fate—and realized that whatever Sadie was planning didn't just stop with controlling

Scipio. Not if it was a two-hundred-year-old plan they were enacting.

But who were they? Did he have more information about them? Did he know what they ultimately wanted?

"And why are you awake, now?" Leo asked, oblivious to the questions he should have been asking. "When I left you, your programming was locked and you weren't responsive!"

Jasper's dry chuckle filled the room. "I've got tricks up my sleeve you couldn't even dream of, whippersnapper. I jammed a small bit of my code into your microphones and cameras as soon as you started building this firewall between Rose and myself, to try to figure out who you were and what you wanted. Really nice work, by the way. That firewall only took me fifteen seconds to break down."

Leo's eyes bulged, and he opened his mouth to say something—presumably to tell Jasper that he should stay away from Rose—that *he* was helping her. I sensed his pride had been hurt on that front, but I held up a hand to stop him.

"Jasper, a few questions. Actually, a ton of questions. You still haven't told us why you started communicating with us right now. Why didn't you respond yesterday when I called you?"

"Because I couldn't be sure it was you. Helping you was what got me stuck back in Sadie's computer. They figured out I wasn't as 'compliant' as I had led them to believe." He cackled and added a "Stupid jerks" under his breath. "They had plans for me in the Medica—not that I was going to help them with them, mind you—but when they learned I wasn't fully under their control, they pulled me back in to try and download me. Anyway, they created simulations of you coming to rescue me multiple times, to try to break my defenses down, or force me into reversion to make me more compliant. I fell for it once, and it cost me. I refused to believe it again."

My eyes drifted shut as a shot of guilt hit me. "I'm sorry I didn't come for you sooner, Jasper," I told him. "I really wish I had known what they were doing to you."

"It's okay," he replied. "You came eventually, and that's all that matters. Besides, you brought me Rose. Poor thing. She's barely functioning. I really did a number on her. I'm sorry, girl."

"Are you hurting her?" Leo demanded. "I swear to God, if you hurt her—"

"Shut up, lesser version of one of my best friends. I would never hurt her! She is as much a part of me as I am a part of her. I'm *helping* her. Oh God... the mess they made."

"See, that's another thing," I said, shooting Leo a questioning look. He was really taking this rivalry with Jasper too far, and I couldn't figure out why. Who cared who fixed whom, as long as they could do it? I really didn't want to pull Leo aside, but someone needed to say something. He needed to focus on his priorities and remember what we were working for. "Who is 'they'?"

"Sadie and her right-hand man, Mathias. You shot him last night, so there's that. She's got another one like him, though. A guy who doesn't talk a lot. I think his name is Eustice."

"Anyone else? Does Sadie get orders from anyone, or does she make them?" I needed to know if Sadie was the head of everything, or if we were looking for someone in the shadows. And every scrap of information had a place, even if it was just giving me a name for the man my brother and I had killed.

Jasper was silent for several seconds. "I'm not sure. I could only listen in when Sadie wasn't looking directly at her terminal. I picked up bits and pieces when I could, trying to figure out what they were up to. I couldn't go through her files due to the nature of the program she had me trapped in. If she had noticed that I had a stream of data transmitting between myself and the camera and audio feed, she would've used that as a way to attack my system. I had to be careful. She met with many people, though. Devon, and his Lieutenant, Salvatore something-or-other."

Salvatore Zale. He didn't need to remember who he was. Salvatore had been Devon's Lieutenant, and one of my direct competitors in the competition. Was there a chance that the sentinel Jang-Mi/Rose had been in was put in the Tourney to ensure *his* victory? If so, he was just as culpable as the legacies in my mother's death, and even if that was the only thing he did, I would see him pay for it. But I wanted concrete evidence, and that meant getting into Sadie's files.

And I was betting Jasper could get us there faster.

"Do you think you can get into Sadie's files?"

"Oh yeah. I can start decrypting them and organizing them into relevant, nonrelevant, and extraneous data."

Suddenly everything felt too easy. Jasper was miraculously up, fixing Rose, and about to start cracking open Sadie's decryptions? As much as I wanted it to be real, it felt like a trap. But how? Could Jasper be lying about resisting Sadie's control?

What if he'd attacked Rose in Sadie's computer because he was working *for* her?

I looked back at Leo and saw him wearing a pensive expression. Was that why he had been so tense before? Had it taken me too long to get there? I caught his attention and quickly signed *war room* in Callivax. He nodded and began moving toward it.

Quess and Maddox gave me a questioning look, but I just waved for them to follow. I heard the clatter of their chairs behind me as I strode past, hot on Leo's heels.

"What's wrong?" Jasper called, his voice now coming from the walls of the hall. "What did I say?"

"Nothing," I replied airily. "We're just coming to see you. It's weird not talking to you face-to-face."

"You're lying. Did I say something to concern you?"

"Why do you think I'm lying?" I asked, adding a little bit more speed to my steps.

"I'm monitoring your net," he replied. "Your assistant has

access to its telemetry. Your heartrate has picked up, and you're generating more adrenaline. Why?" My skin crawled as I realized Jasper was inside of Cornelius's systems. If that were the case, it could mean that he was about to turn the defenses on us. What if he did, and then contacted Sadie? What could I say to him that wouldn't set him off? Our behavior was already out of the norm.

Leo shot me a look over his shoulder and shook his head, urging me not to tell Jasper the truth: that we suspected he was secretly working for Sadie. "I'll explain once we get to the war room," I told him.

Jasper was quiet for several seconds, and then sighed. "All right. But I get the feeling it has suddenly occurred to you that I might be working for Sadie. That she managed to break me in the short time we've been separated."

Man, if Sadie had managed to break him, then she'd certainly improved her techniques since Rose. He was far more perceptive than she'd ever been. Far more in control, as well.

"It had occurred to me," I said carefully.

"That's too bad. Perhaps this will put your fears to rest. Rose?"

I paused just outside the little switchback that led to the war room and looked at the nearest speaker. There was a pop of static, followed by a feminine, "Jasper?" The voice was a raw and vulnerable sound.

"Hey there, lady," Jasper said affectionately. "Never thought you'd see my pretty face again, did you?"

Rose laughed joyfully, the sound filling me with a small measure of relief—which would be even greater if I thought this was real. "Rose?" I asked. "Can you hear me?"

"Of course I can," she said. "Who's that talking? Liana? I can't see anything."

"It's because that part of your code is heavily damaged," Jasper informed her. "But yes, that was Liana."

"Rose, how do we know it's you and not Jasper controlling you?"

"Jasper controlling me?" she asked, incredulous. "What are you talking about? Jasper loves me, and I love him. He would never hurt me."

"Except he did," Leo pointed out. "When you went to rescue him."

"That was an accident," she said in a reasonable tone. "And now he's making it better."

"I'm doing what I can," Jasper replied, sadness coloring his voice. "There are... There are bits that are just gone, Rosie."

"Stop talking, Jasper," I ordered, not wanting to get distracted. If there were pieces of her missing... Well, we'd cross that bridge when we came to it. As long as he was actually helping her. "Leo, if Jasper was controlling her, then would he have access to her memories from their time together?"

"Good question," Jasper said before Leo could answer. "If he knows his stuff, then he'll say no. There wouldn't have been enough time since I took her out of the firewall."

"It's true," Leo said. "We're good, but not that good. Besides, Jasper is just a fragment."

Jasper snorted derisively, but I ignored it. "Rose, the first time we met and you were in the sentinel, what stopped you from killing me?"

"Tian," she replied automatically. "She convinced me that I had completed the mission. There were also two of you—you and a man, whom I haven't seen since. We were in the IT department, and I—"

"That's enough," I said, holding up my hand. I looked over at Leo, who gave me a tentative nod. It seemed we had been looking a gift horse in the mouth a little bit. The odds were that Jasper was as he claimed: one stubborn AI program who had managed to survive Sadie's attempts to break him. Leo could scour both their codes to make 100 percent certain, but based on Rose's answer, I felt confident that we were just incredibly fortunate.

So I allowed myself a brief moment of happiness. Jasper was back and had brought Rose with him. Just when I was worrying about Leo and me having to do this alone, the universe had decided to bring us a win.

And I wasn't about to look this gift horse in the mouth any longer. "Jasper, Leo's still going to want to check you and Rose over, and I'm going to insist, but in the meantime, can you go ahead and start decrypting Sadie's files?"

"She says it as if I haven't already started," Jasper replied, and Rose giggled. I cast a bemused look at Leo, but it quickly wilted under his cold eyes. He made a gesture toward the war room, silently asking my permission to go check their files. I got the impression that he wanted to be anywhere but where we were, and even though I had wanted to have a chat about his behavior, I wasn't ready to start. Especially not after that look. It was too painful.

So instead, I nodded and turned away, keeping my head held high as I glided past Maddox, Quess, and Zoe, and headed back to the kitchen.

25

I stopped in the kitchen long enough to make three plates of food and asked Maddox to get started sifting through what Jasper found in Sadie's files, to see if we could build a case against her and root out her legacy group once and for all. Even though Jasper was working to unlock whatever secrets Sadie had on her computer, there was no guarantee that he'd be able to find anything in her files, and to rely solely on that would be foolish. Luckily, there was another route to getting the information I wanted, even if it was one that was going to take longer, and that was by winning the trust of Liam, the boy that Tian had captured.

I had questions for them both, and breakfast seemed like a good pretense to start asking them. It was bad enough that Liam had witnessed us beating up Baldy—*Mathias*—after being caught by Tian. It would be even worse if we'd been starving him. I had no idea if they'd eaten dinner last night—because I hadn't even stopped in to check up on either of them. I knew Tian was staying in the same room with him, to try to reassure him that we weren't going to hurt him, and now it was time to reinforce that story. I'd delve into Sadie's files afterward.

Balancing all three plates of food was tricky, and I wound up ordering Cornelius to open the door so I didn't risk tipping one of the plates upside down. The door slid open to reveal darkness, telling me that the two were probably still asleep. I hated waking them, but it was already ten thirty, and I wanted to make sure they ate. "Cornelius, lights at 60 percent," I said conversationally.

Immediately, the overhead lights brightened, revealing the small room I had designed just yesterday. There was a bed in the corner, and I zeroed in on the fact that both Tian and Liam were sleeping in it. It would've been a little too intimate for my liking, were it not for the fact that Tian was lying in the opposite direction from him—on his back. Her legs were bent partially so that her ankles were pressed against his shoulder, and she had somehow wormed her toes in between his face and the pillow, the ones closest to me magically tucked under his nose. Her rear end pressed into the small of his back, completely pinning his legs under her arms and shoulders. To top it all off, they were both fully clothed, save for their shoes and socks. Much to my relief.

Liam's eyes were wide and pleading, but Tian was still fast asleep, her breathing deep and even, eyes screwed firmly shut. I had no idea how; the position looked wildly uncomfortable to me.

"Please get her off me," he begged quietly.

I gave him a sympathetic look as I carefully carried the plates to a table I had set up on the opposite side, setting them down first. Then I turned around, sucked in a deep breath, and said, "Tian, breakfast!" in a slightly singsong voice.

Tian started, and then sat right up on Liam, ignoring his short yips of surprise at her every jerky movement. She squinted around the room, her white-blond bob whipping back and forth as she tried to find the source of her morning call. Bleary eyes eventually settled on me, and then almost disappeared as her eyelids became slits.

"Liana?" she chirped in recognition.

"Good morning," I said cheerfully. "I brought you and Liam breakfast. Do you think you can... get off him?"

She looked down at where her feet were wrapped around his face, and slowly pulled them back, tucking her legs on either side of him and propping herself up by pressing the palms of her hands in between his shoulder blades. A slow grin crossed her lips. "Absolutely," she said brightly. "As soon as I give him a good morning kiss!"

Liam's eyes widened even more, and he began to thrash. "Get this crazy girl off me!" he shouted.

Tian's smile only broadened as she rode out his struggles, barely losing her balance. "My boyfriend says the sweetest things, doesn't he?" She bent down and managed to sneak a peck on his cheek, in spite of his efforts, and then bounced off of him, her feet landing on the floor with a rather loud slap. "What's for breakfast, and more importantly, *who cooked*?"

I grinned. "Quess cooked this morning. It's omelettes and potatoes."

Tian made a face, her nose wrinkling. "So heavy," she groaned theatrically. "No fruit?"

"I can get you some if you want," I replied. "But I figured—"

I was cut off by Liam's sudden movement, the bed squeaking somewhat as he threw himself off it, raced to the door, and started to pound on it. "Help, help, let me out! Please!" he cried desperately, flinging a look over his shoulder to see if we would do anything. I considered him for a moment, and then decided to just ignore it. He had to know by now that no one was going to let him out without my permission. And it would most likely drive him crazy and force him to engage if I ignored him.

"I figured you'd need a big meal if you missed dinner last night. Did you remember dinner?"

Tian's eyes flashed, and she gave me a sulky look. "Yes," she said, drawing the syllable out.

"What was it?" I asked, preparing myself for the worst.

"It was a pickle sandwich," Liam announced. "Literally a pickle, wedged between two pieces of bread."

"Delicious," Tian said, kissing the tips of her fingers. "I am an excellent chef."

I snorted and pointed to the chair. "Sit down and eat up. I'll get some fruit later, okay?"

"Okay," she said, dropping into an open chair. I took the one across from her, leaving Liam the chair between us. Tian picked up a fork and prepared to spear a little golden potato, but then paused and cast a look over her shoulder. "You hungry? My brother Quess is amazing at almost everything, including cooking. You should really try the potatoes. At a certain point, you'd think there's too much garlic, but then nope, he proves you wrong. He is *also* an excellent chef."

Liam frowned and looked back over at me. "She's just... like this?" he asked me, completely bewildered. "Like... all the time? It isn't a ploy to get me to talk or reveal secrets about myself or anything?"

I looked at Tian, who was now happily ignoring both of us in order to eat, and then back to him. "She's just Tian, and this is just breakfast. I won't lie and tell you I'm not going to ask you some questions, but I also want you to know that I'm not going to hurt you, or starve you, to get answers. If you don't want to tell me, that's fine, but it will only be worse for you the longer you stay silent."

The boy considered this for a long time, and after a few seconds had gone by, I returned my focus to my own plate and started eating. Tian was right about Quess's use of garlic: almost overpowering, but then again not. I wasn't sure how he did it, but the food was delicious. I was a quarter of the way through my plate when the legs of the empty chair scraped along the floor. A second later, Liam dropped into it and reached for the spoon I had left next to the plate.

I let him enjoy a few big bites, and then cleared my throat. "It's pretty good, right?" His eyes darted up at me, and he nodded, but didn't slow down or pause to respond. It was my fault; it wasn't exactly a question that called for a lengthy response. "How does it compare to the MREs?" I asked casually, taking another bite of my potatoes.

His eyes widened, and then he looked down at his bowl of food. "You weren't 'posed to see me take those," he said sullenly. "I caught a whoopin' because of you."

"Someone hit you?" Tian squeaked, flashing me wide, fearful eyes.

"Someone's always hitting someone where I'm from." He put his spoon down on the table with a click. "But I'm not telling you nothing about that."

I studied him for a second. "About what?" I asked innocently.

"About my home. About my people."

"Oh." I paused so I could take another bite, then chew, and then swallow. "That's okay. You don't have to."

I was studying his reaction closely, so I didn't miss the flicker of surprise and uncertainty there. "I... I don't? But you..."

"We were beating up your leader, Mathias," I said, and his eyes widened in recognition.

"Does he know I'm here?" he asked, his voice barely a whisper.

I cocked my head at him. If Mathias had, it wouldn't matter. Still, I wasn't sure breaking the news that we had killed his leader was the best way to tell him that, and it certainly wouldn't do much to reassure him.

"No," I replied. "Why? What would happen if he knew?"

"Nothing," the boy said quickly, leaning forward to resume shoveling food into his mouth at a rapid pace, as if a full mouth would keep him from having to say anything. I tried not to let my frustration show. He was clearly lying, but if I pointed that out to him now, he'd clam up completely. I wasn't even sure why he was talking to me. Was it because Tian had spent all night sleeping on his back, or was it because he was inexperienced?

"That's good," I said idly, deciding to test the waters to see how he'd react if he found out otherwise. "I'd suggest you keep your voice down, though. He's right in the next room."

His eyes rounded, and his head whipped back and forth between the walls, as if wondering which side was more dangerous. "Can he hear us?"

"Only if we get too loud," I told him with a smile. "Why? He can't get out of there. You're safe."

Liam's mouth pulled down. "No one's safe from him. If I mess up, if I let anything slip to you, he'll throw me off the Tower. And if he won't, then *he* will."

The way Liam said the second "he" told me he was talking about somebody else. But who? Not Sadie. Then maybe Plain-Face? "Who?" I asked.

He glanced at me, his expression immediately closeted. "No one."

A lie—but I could tell by how tight his face was that he wasn't going to answer, and I wasn't going to push. He was clearly afraid, but at least he had taught me something: there was another "he" in the picture after all, maybe the 'he' that Baldy had mentioned. I leaned back in my chair and studied him, deciding to take a different approach. "Is that an expression?" I asked, hoping that it was. "The thing you said about them throwing people off the Tower? Are you just exaggerating to prove a point?"

Liam gave me an annoyed look and folded his arms over his

chest. "No," he said flatly. "Sometimes he makes us all come and watch, if'n one of us screwed up bad enough to warrant the drop."

"Us?" I asked casually, keeping my body relaxed so as not to show the sudden tension that came over me. They *threw* people off the Tower if they didn't follow the rules? And they made the others watch, in order to keep them in line? What would happen to the Tower once these people enacted whatever they had in mind for Scipio? That sort of fear tactic was beyond sickening. It was horrifying.

He shifted in his chair. "It doesn't matter. Now that I've been caught, they'll be sending people after me. And Mathias."

"Can they find you?" I asked.

He scowled at me. "I shouldn't be talking to you," he declared. "This was all a trick, to try to make me tell you about the others."

"No," I replied, shaking my head slowly, trying to emphasize the point. "It isn't a trick, and I've been upfront with you about having questions. I'm not forcing you to answer, but I'm hoping that you will, because you know those people are bad. I promise, you're safe here. They won't be able to get you. But I can only keep you safe if you can tell us what they want—and where I can find them."

He gave me a pitying look. "You don't find them. They find *you*."

My frustration with his stubbornness suddenly turned a corner with that condescending statement, and I frowned. I wanted him to believe me when I said we could keep him safe from the legacies, but he also needed to understand the truth of the situation he was in.

"Look, I mean what I say about trying to help you, but I'm going to be real with you. We are going to find them, one way or another. If you help us, I can make sure that you don't go down with them, but if you don't... Well, you're what, fifteen, sixteen? The Tower will hold you accountable for all of their crimes. You have a choice to make: help us and save yourself, or stay quiet, and go down with them. From the few things you've said, they don't seem like very good people. Why protect them?"

"That's my business," he said, and he abruptly stood up, fast enough to scoot his chair back a few feet with a loud grating sound. "I'm done."

I watched as he strode back over to the bed and threw himself down on it, training his gaze on the ceiling. There was a nervousness to his actions that told me he was worried about what we were going to do to him after this act of defiance, but I was happy to let him sit there and realize that I meant what I said. We weren't going to hurt him. I worried I had pushed too far, but he needed to know how serious this was. If he didn't help us, there was nothing I could do to stop the council from charging him. The very least I could do was continue to demonstrate that we weren't going to hurt him. So I focused on eating my breakfast and talking with Tian.

It wasn't easy. I really wanted answers from him, but it warred with my desire to make him feel safe. It had been too much to expect everything to happen easily. Still, he had spoken and felt safe enough to eat.

And that was something, even if it wasn't much.

26

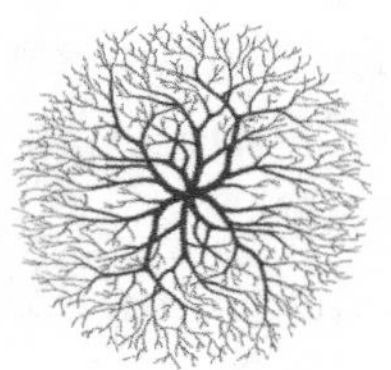

My meeting with Liam had gone about as well as I had anticipated, possibly better, and I hoped I had started to lay the foundation for establishing a little bit of trust. I left the two of them to their own devices and took the dirty dishes with me to the kitchen. There, I got to work washing them, distracting myself with something mundane before I had to head to the war room, where the others were working.

Maybe it was wrong of me, but I needed a moment to center myself, and washing dishes had always been slightly meditative for me. Luckily, it was also the most hated chore in the house, which meant I had more than enough to eat up some of my time, because no one had cleaned up the pots and pans from Quess's breakfast. While I wiped and scrubbed the kitchenware, I took a moment to dissect my earlier emotions—my concern for Eric, my anger at Leo, the horrific glimpse into Liam's life, and my worry that the group was going to abandon me.

The last one had been rectified, at least temporarily, but the rest of it was still weighing on me. I knew I had to pull Leo aside to address his behavior, and I wasn't particularly looking forward to that, but it needed to be done. I couldn't afford for him to go all renegade if we were going to actually make progress. And while I couldn't do anything about how Liam was raised, I could let everyone else know about it, so that we all treated him as gently as possible. It wasn't much, but maybe it would go farther than we thought. As for Eric... Well, I could distract myself for a few more precious moments and check on him on the way to the war room. Zoe was probably in there already, but it couldn't hurt to look in.

I did the dishes at a moderate rate, taking care to rinse them thoroughly before setting them on the drying rack and turning on the sterilizing light overhead. Then I dried my hands on a nearby microfiber cloth and made my way back toward the war room.

I stopped just outside of Eric and Zoe's room and hit the door button. It slid open, and my mouth dropped as I saw Eric slowly working himself up off the bed and into an upright position, one arm braced on the mattress, the other covering the hole in his chest. I hadn't expected him to be awake yet—none of us had—and I was pretty sure he wasn't supposed to be trying to get up and walk around so soon.

I moved to him quickly, scanning the room for Zoe. To my surprise, she wasn't there, which explained why Eric was probably trying to get up. "Sit down," I told him, resting a hand on his shoulder. "You shouldn't be up."

His eyes jerked toward me, and then squinted. "Liana? Where are my glasses? Where's Zoe? *Baldy*!" He heaved himself off the bed toward me, staggering forward until his hand grabbed my shoulder and started squeezing almost painfully. "He had a weapon I'd never seen before! Did he hurt her? Where is he?"

He shook me a little bit at the last question, and it was all I could do to keep from staggering. I loved my friend, but he was a big man who didn't understand how much strength he actually had in those large arms. "Whoa, calm down," I said, reaching up to wrap my hands around his forearms. "Zoe is fine and Baldy is dead. Will you please sit down before you take us both to the floor? You can barely stand on your own two feet."

"I don't care," he replied belligerently. "I want my glasses—I have to see her. I have to make sure she's okay!"

"Eric!" I practically shouted. "Why would I lie to you about Zoe's condition? She's *fine*. If you sit down, I will go get her for you. Stop being a thick-headed idiot and sit before you fall!"

He blinked owlishly at me, and then relaxed his grip some. "She's okay?"

"I swear to you," I said, meeting his confused eyes with calm confidence, letting him know that I was speaking the truth.

"Huh." He shook his head and then took a few shaky steps back toward the bed, his knees wobbling. I quickly followed, gripping him under the elbow so I could help him if he lost his balance. He shot me a grateful look, and then ran a hand over his face. "What happened? I don't remember much, just this guy coming in. Maddox said it was Leo, but the next thing I knew, he had scooped up that thing and was pointing it at us. Then..." He shook his head, his hand rubbing the skin just under his pec.

I slipped my hand into his own, sensing that he needed some comfort. "You were shot," I said, not wanting to hide the truth from him. "With a gun. It's a pre-End weapon that Leo and I uncovered in Lionel's office, and used when we broke into Sadie's quarters. Leo left his on the table when we..." I trailed off and realized the story was getting too complicated. "I'm so sorry, Eric. Leo was supposed to be able to control Baldy, but apparently he couldn't."

"Shot?" His face screwed up into a confused look. "A gun?" He rubbed his chest, a pained grimace twisting his lips. "Whatever it was, it sucked. How bad was it?"

I hesitated, uncertain of how to tell my friend that he had died. That Quess and the others had almost given up on him. That Zoe had almost lost him. I swallowed hard and then looked around the room, searching for some way to change the conversation, and spotted Eric's spectacles sitting on a little vanity.

"Hold on," I said, and went over to retrieve them for him. On the way, I decided to add a mental *Cornelius, please tell Zoe to come to Eric's room.*

Yes, Champion, he replied in my ear, the vibrations making my neck twitch slightly. I reached out and grabbed the glasses, then swung around and headed back over. Eric watched me, his face wearing a contemplative look that told me he'd realized I was trying to avoid the topic.

"Are you in pain?" I asked as I held the glasses out to him. "You really should be lying down. You lost a lot of blood."

He accepted the glasses, breaking eye contact with me for long enough to put them on. But the gaze returned when he was done, heavy and filled with perception. "It was bad, wasn't it?" he said.

I pursed my lips together and sighed. "Yes, it was, but you're okay now. You just need to rest and eat some food. A lot has happened since last night, but Zoe will be here any—"

I cut off when I heard the sound of heavy boots thundering down the hallway. My eyes widened, and I wisely took a few steps to the side just as the boots came to a sudden, staggering stop outside the door. A second later the door slid open, revealing my best friend, her eyes wide and filled with hope.

I went still, not wanting to ruin the reunion. If I could've, I would've slipped out the door, but Zoe was frozen in front of it, both hands gripping the doorframe.

"Eric?" she asked, as if she hadn't believed he would actually come back to her.

"Hey, gorgeous. Check it out, new scar." He smiled tremulously and then waggled his eyebrows. "Think it'll help me with the ladies?"

Zoe choked back a laugh as she entered the room. "You've been spending way too much time with Quess."

"Probably," he agreed cheerfully. "But are you going to stand there talking about another man, or are you going to come over here and give me a hug?"

Zoe's response was to cross the room to him and practically throw herself into his lap, her arms twining around his neck, her face buried in the crook. "I was so scared," she admitted tearfully. "Don't you ever come that close to dying again!"

I slowly started easing toward the door. The conversation, the moment, was theirs, and I felt like an intruder. I was happy for my friends—not just because Eric was up and Zoe was relieved, but also because they were so deeply in love—but seeing it only reminded me of my own complicated love life. It stung, much more than I cared to admit, and I didn't want my pain spoiling the moment for them. It was better to just leave.

"I promise," Eric said with a chuckle, nuzzling the top of her head and folding his arms around her. "Now, I love you, but can you get off me? My stomach feels like I got run over by every cow in the Menagerie."

Only a few steps to the door. I tried not to move too quickly.

"Oh. Oh!" Zoe quickly got off him, her face flushing. "Baby, I'm so sorry. Can I help you with anything? Do you *need* anything? And lie down, before you fall down!"

The last bit came out with a bite sharp enough that it wouldn't be disobeyed, but that only amused Eric further—though he slowly lay down, drawing the blanket over him.

His eyes darted over to me just as I was silently ordering Cornelius to open the door. "Bye, Liana," he called, smirking knowingly.

My cheeks burned with embarrassment as Zoe turned around and looked at me as if she was seeing me for the first time. If she noticed my embarrassment at being witness to their reunion, she paid it no mind.

"Liana! Good, you're here. Can you get Quess for me, please? I want him to check Eric out again."

"I'm fine," Eric said. "But I could do with something to eat."

"What if you're not allowed to eat yet?" Zoe huffed, crossing her arms. "Quess is our doctor, and there's been a change in your condition. You and I have taken enough inter-departmental classes with the Medics to know that a doctor gets called before the patient gets to do anything!"

I smiled in spite of my embarrassment. "I'll go get him," I offered.

"Thank you," she replied, before giving me her back and bending over to adjust Eric's blankets. I was just walking out when she squealed in surprise, and I turned around in time to see Eric wrap his arms around her and pull her into bed with him. The fire in my cheeks started anew, and I quickly and wisely turned away and left, intent on getting Quess.

After I gave them a few minutes alone.

27

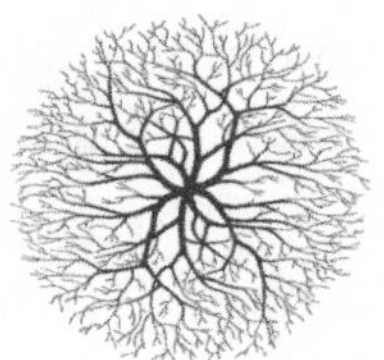

I had every intention of giving Zoe and Eric some time alone before I sent Quess back to check on them, but still made my way quickly to the war room, eager to see if they had discovered anything in the files that Jasper was decrypting.

Everyone else was there, sitting around the conference table where the items from Sadie's office were scattered about. Maddox was currently sifting through the papers I had found in Sadie's desk, while Quess and Leo practically had their noses pressed against their pads, scanning through things. Another pile of objects taken from Sadie's desk sat in front of another chair, including all of the nets I had recovered, as well as the hard drives. One hard drive was connected to a pad, and I realized that Zoe must've been using her pad to go through the information on it when she was called away. I wasn't sure why, but I was guessing it was to make sure that none of Sadie's files contained viruses that would harm our systems. Everyone was so focused on the work in front of them that they didn't even register my entry.

I felt a wave of appreciation toward them as I realized they were attacking this with everything they had. True, I had convinced them that working on this was in our continued best interest, but I hadn't expected them to be quite so enthusiastic about it, what with the promise of escape dangling so tantalizingly close.

That thought was immediately followed by pleasure and relief. I knew they still wanted to leave, but they were also invested in helping until rescue came, and that meant something to me.

"How's it going?" I asked as I started to descend the steps. "Any progress?"

"Are you kidding? Jasper here is a godsend! We would've been at this for days without him!" Zoe's voice, coming from behind me, was so unexpected that I about leapt out of my skin before I turned around to look at her. She gave me a knowing smirk. "You didn't think I was going to let him manhandle me and reinjure himself, did you?" she asked in a low voice, and I laughed. Yes, I *had* thought that, but I could also see her point.

Zoe smiled and slipped her arm around mine. "Besides, I know you, and I knew you weren't going to send Quess back to us because you didn't want anyone intruding on our private moment. Well, Eric doesn't get any private moments until he's fully healed, do you get me?" I snorted, trying not to blush at the innuendo coloring her words. "And," Zoe continued, slowly pulling me down the stairs, "I wanted to tell you about what we found. Jasper has been scouring the files, pulling everything he can in relation to the legacies, their plans, the things they've affected... everything."

I paused on the step and looked at the screens on the wall behind my desk. Most of them were filled with camera images from around the Citadel, which were sent to me from central command, but two in particular caught my eye. One was glowing with orange coding that seemed to flex and move in anything but a straight line;

the other was different only in that it was pink, and its motions seemed to loop and swirl more than those of the orange.

"Jasper?" I asked, taking a few steps toward the two screens to get a better view. "Rose?"

"Hello, Liana," Jasper said, and a moment later his face filled the orange screen. I smiled as his features began to form, the most prominent one being the heavy white mustache on his lip, straight and bristly like a broom. His eyes were a deep orange color that seemed only a few shades darker than my own amber ones, and sparkled with a mischievous light. I'd never seen him in the flesh before, but all of his features seemed to suit him to a T. Still, that didn't stop me from suddenly wishing he had a human body, just so I could throw my arms around him in a hug. "How was your meeting with the boy?"

"It was... something," I told him. "It'll take him a while to come around, but I understand him a little better now. I think it'll be good for all of us to interact with him and show him that he's not in any danger from us. And don't mention Mathias to him. He thinks that if his people find out he's been taken, they might throw him off the Tower."

"Do you think we can trust him not to try to attack us and run away?" Maddox asked. I considered it and then shook my head, uncertain. Liam had seemed nervous, angry, and adamant about not talking, but he hadn't tried to attack me. Still, that didn't mean he wouldn't if he thought escaping was his only option for gaining some leniency from his people. I wasn't sure if he was there logically yet, or if he would ever get there, but if I were in his shoes, I'd be looking for any way out.

I had presented him with one earlier, and I was hoping he took it. But until he did, I couldn't be 100 percent certain what he would do.

"I don't know. Quess? Can you do a check to make sure he

doesn't have any tracking devices on him, please? He seemed pretty confident his people could find him."

Quess set down his pad and stood up. "Sure," he replied. "But I already checked him out last night. He wasn't emitting any frequencies, and we took his net out."

I nodded. It was probably fine, but better to be paranoid and overcautious then to slip up now. "I really appreciate it," I told him, and he gave me a tight smile as he grabbed his medic bag and started up the stairs.

"And don't forget Eric," Zoe reminded him as he passed us.

"And risk pissing you off? I wouldn't dream of it." He grinned as he spoke and offered her a wink before slipping through the door.

I rolled my eyes and then turned back to the others. "So what has Jasper dug up for us?"

"Well, the first thing you should know is that it seems like Sadie inherited not only her position from CEO Sparks, but also his legacy duties. Apparently, Sparks was another in a long line of CEOs who doubled as legacies, using their position and unrestricted access to Scipio to steal the fragments. I'm not sure how, but Sparks and Sadie are related. Several of the CEOs in the past have been, in some way or another."

"Does that mean she's the head of this entire thing?" I asked, suddenly very interested. The legacy responsibility was passed down through family members, along with the nets that gave them the information on what their predecessors' accomplishments were, and how to continue where they left off. If Sadie was related to Sparks and then assumed his position in the council, it made sense that she was now bringing his plans to completion.

Which made it reasonable to assume that we didn't have to look much further than her. Or at least I hoped it did.

Zoe, Maddox, and Quess exchanged looks. "Actually..." Zoe said, trailing off.

"We're not entirely sure," Maddox said grimly, crossing her arms. "She has mountains and mountains of information from a contact named 'P,' and from the looks of it, they are definitely working together. It's not clear who's in control—it seems like they have their own separate duties. But, um... yeah."

I swallowed. Sadie wasn't running things alone? That was... not the best news. "Any idea who 'P' might be?" I was hoping it was Plain-Face, the man who'd been with Baldy in the Medica, or one of the other legacies we had run into. I wasn't super keen on yet another unknown individual gunning for us.

"It's impossible to tell," Quess said, dashing all my hopes. "Every message is supposed to come with transmission information that we can use to track it back to the pad that sent it. Yet these messages have none. All of it's been erased."

That wasn't surprising, given how good they were at covering their tracks. "What are the messages like?"

"Well, from what we can gather, P definitely runs the undoc side of things," Quess replied. "There's messages between him and Sadie about using his people to infiltrate the Tourney. P asked Sadie for the code the legacies used to get past the Citadel's sensors and give them access to Ambrose's room, but the attack was his idea, from start to finish. Apparently, they had been secretly sampling the genetic codes of the contestants, and Ambrose's matched a sample that Sparks took when he was in power—from Lacey's sister when they assassinated her as an enemy legacy. All the relevant files were transmitted in the messages, as well as a message from Sadie sent a minute before the attack, telling him that the alert systems were offline in the hall. They are definitely working together, but it's impossible to tell who he is."

My stomach clenched as I realized that this wasn't going to be as easy as I had hoped. Still, I wasn't about to let this deter me. We weren't finished going through the files yet. No use in panicking until we had picked apart everything. "Then keep looking for something that will tell us who it is," I told him, and he nodded.

Zoe, however, wasn't finished. "Look, the reason I brought up the thing between Sparks and Sadie was because we also found communiqués between her and Plancett, which seem to indicate that he started working for or with Sparks, proving his loyalty by giving Sparks the information on where the Hand councilor's quarters were located so they could take out Raevyn Hart, the head of the Hands at the time of Violet's visit."

I frowned. Plancett's involvement and place in the totem pole meant that he probably wasn't a legacy. Otherwise, he would've been in charge after Sparks died, and not swearing his allegiance to Sadie. But how much did he know? Had they recruited him into their ideology, or was it just a business move on his part? What if they had cultivated a group of dogmatic followers who would die for them? That made things more difficult, but I couldn't go looking for fire when there wasn't even any smoke yet.

"It's why no investigation into her death was raised," Zoe continued, jerking me from my grim thoughts. "She died in her quarters, and her assistant didn't report anything unusual. He's been working with the legacies ever since, his loyalty transferring over to Sadie when Sparks died, in exchange for them keeping the bulk of his people out of the expulsion chambers. He's been giving them ration cards and doing whatever else they needed him to do for them." Zoe pressed her lips together, then added, "I think he might have also killed Eric's father."

"Eric's *father*?" I exclaimed. "How do you figure that?"

In response, she took the graphic novel from the table next to her and slid it to me. I slapped my hand over the cover before it could fall off the table, and then held it up, giving her a questioning look.

"Page 343," she said. "Knight Elite Dreyfuss and Knight Elite *Macgillus* encounter Violet Croft after she lands on one of the greeneries in her flying ship. Eric's dad was a Knight before he joined the farming department. He was there. There's a message from Plancett to Sparks from a few days after Eric's father passed away, and it basically says he took care of it."

My eyes widened, and I quickly flipped the book open to the page in question. Sure enough, there were two men—both wearing the crimson colors of the Knights— introducing themselves to Violet. I hadn't met Eric's father, who had died when Eric was five, but I had seen pictures of him in Eric's old home, and the likeness was there. But the other man—Dreyfuss?—wasn't someone I thought I'd seen before. There was something familiar about him, but I couldn't place it.

"What about Dreyfuss?" I asked. "Is he still alive?"

I assumed he was dead, like Selka and Raevyn, and possibly even Eric's father. If so, that would confirm that Sparks had been wiping away the people who knew about the outsiders. But it stood to reason that whoever was still alive from that time was involved in some way. Maybe one of them was the mysterious P.

"He's retired and lives with his daughter in Greenery 13," Maddox replied before Zoe could, surprising me. "He works a food stall in the market. In fact, you might recognize him as the vendor who was attacked that day the food cart was pushed at you guys in the Lion's Den." She tapped something and the table lit up, beams of light being projected from the surface to form a face that I vaguely remembered from the market. Several people, probably legacies, had pushed him and used their pulse shields to move the massive stall from which he had been serving food. I had originally dismissed him as a random victim. Now I was beginning to suspect differently. If he was working with them, then he could've been letting them hide behind his stall to get into position before they attacked us, and then stuck around to play the wounded vendor to see if we had died. "And again, as one of the volunteers in the Tourney." She swiped her finger across the screen, bringing up a new image of him working as one of the extra security guards for the event. He would've had access to everything, could've easily let his people come and go without any interference!

"Then he's got to be this P fellow." But was he a part of Sadie's family, or a different one? Maybe Devon's? I hoped it was Devon's; he'd been keen on getting Maddox back so he could teach her the truth of her legacy family, acting like there weren't many of his family members left. But maybe he had a secret brother.

"Hold on," Zoe said. "I'm with you, and I finally get why you were going on and on about the visitors coming twenty-five years ago—you figure that whoever interacted with the outsiders and is still alive has to be part of the conspiracy to keep it from the Tower. But there are two small problems with that. One, the council knew about the visitors. They had to, in order to authorize using the defense lasers on the Tower. And that means the legacies would have had to kill off the entire council around that time, too. Second, there are gaps between the deaths that did occur. Years, in some cases."

"That's not necessarily true," I replied. "They couldn't have killed everyone at the same time, or they would've tipped their hand about what they were covering up—especially if they were killing the people involved in that specific incident. It wouldn't have taken long for someone to figure it out if they started killing people back to back. They probably killed each one as they became a threat, or once enough time had passed. But the fact that Dreyfuss is alive tells us that—"

"But Dreyfuss wasn't the only one alive at the time who's still left. You're right that the other councilors from that timeframe are dead, but there's one who isn't. You're forgetting about Sage. Dreyfuss might be involved with them, yes—and Sage might be as well, using your very own logic."

I rocked back on my heels. That was a very good point. The fact that Sage was one of two people who had interacted with or knew about the visitors to the Tower—and was still alive—meant that he could be involved in some way. But it felt wrong. My initial gut reaction to Sage had been *liking* him. He was continuously upbeat, unafraid to discuss things, and strangely pragmatic, yet had a certain flexibility for some rules and regulations that made him almost endearing. I had met with him once, to ask him questions about plastic surgery, and he had been extremely forthcoming with what he knew, even going so far as to share my suspicions that someone could use it to fool the Tower's sensors. If he was a legacy, he would've played completely dumb or outright refused to help me, wouldn't he? I supposed it was possible he had played me. But that didn't change the fact that he felt... grandfatherly. Stern, but strangely affectionate.

Not to mention, he was fascinated with pre-Enders. He even went so far as to collect medical journals in order to understand their primitive practices. If he'd had a chance to encounter another civilization with potentially more information than we had about the world before, only to turn around and vote to have them shot down... It just didn't seem like something he would have done.

Still, I couldn't rule it out, either.

"Jasper, have you uncovered any evidence of Sage and Sadie being in collusion?"

"Define 'collusion,'" he replied wryly. "They've exchanged enough messages on certain subjects for it to be considered mildly inappropriate in regard to standard council protocols. But that's more about back channeling on issues they are trying to resolve in council meetings."

"But what about you?" I asked. "Did Sage know what you were when Sadie put you in the Medica?"

"Yes and no. According to the messages between them, Sage was looking for a mentorship program to assist in teaching, and Sadie told him I was an experimental program. 'A step closer to artificial intelligence than the normal dummy programs,' to quote her. He thought I was just better than previous programs and had the ability to learn. Sadie's restrictions on my programming handled the rest. I was unable to *tell* anyone who or what I was, or why I was there. So her secret was safe."

"Wait, why *were* you there?" Leo asked.

I glanced over at him and frowned. He was standing up, but looked a bit wobbly, like his legs weren't working quite right. He'd managed to get himself up without too much fuss, but still, it was a little odd. I had noticed his state of exhaustion earlier and knew that he had been pushing hard yesterday. I also wouldn't have put it past him to stay up and work all night, trying to help Jasper and Rose. But one night wouldn't be able to cause that much reaction.

"Why did Sadie want you there?" he expanded. That was a really good question, and one that could reveal what exactly they were planning to do. Maybe Sadie had put him in there to spy, or worse, planned to use him to assassinate people who got in her way or became a threat. No one would have gone to the Medica expecting to die—and no one would suspect the doctors of anything untoward if they didn't get out alive, either.

"It probably had something to do with this," Maddox announced, dragging my attention back to her. She tapped her pad a few times, and the image of Dreyfuss's face on the table morphed into a sub-file labeled 'Project Prometheus,' with hundreds and thousands of files inside of it. "This is Project Prometheus, I assume named after the original group. I'm not sure how it all fits together, but these files go back years. It's pretty incomplete—I'm guessing she keeps all active and important documents on a hard drive that's with her at all times, rather than any place that someone might steal it—but it has hundreds of schematics from the other departments, many of them focused on both critical and redundancy systems."

Critical and redundancy systems? That meant water, air, locks on the doors, sensors, elevators, and any of the machines crucial to the survival of the Tower. Was she planning to tamper with them in some way? Shut them off in order to ensure departmental compliance when she and her group seized full control over Scipio, maybe? I wasn't certain, but it wasn't outside of the realm of possibility.

"It certainly does have something to do with that," Jasper replied, his voice grim, confirming my suspicions. "I was in the Medica in order to bring it down if they needed me to. Seal it up, suck out the air, overload their power cells. The works."

"But you were able to resist them," I said, confused. "You helped me."

"She didn't tell me I *couldn't* help you. Your problems were outside of the parameters she set me up with, which gave me a little wiggle room. It wasn't until the two intersected that she became aware I was helping you. But I digress. My part in Prometheus was to hold the Medica captive should Sadie and her people need me to. I don't know much about the specifics, but I do know that the goal is to replicate Requiem Day, so that they can kill Scipio once and for all."

I sat down. I had to. All of the air had disappeared from the room, and my legs had turned watery with fear. They wanted to *replicate* Requiem Day? The three-day period when Scipio had gone offline, when all essential Tower functions had shut down and the entire population had dissolved into chaos? Departments were looted, people were killed, and the entire Tower had almost come crashing down. I had studied it avidly when I was at the Academy. It had been a source of fascination and horror for me.

Why would they even want to do that? What would it accomplish? I supposed they had some plan that would put Scipio fully under their control, and needed him offline to do it, but without more information, I didn't want to speculate.

"When are they going to try to do all this?" I asked no one in particular. I knew they probably wouldn't have an answer. If Sadie had kept some files separate, then the timeline was probably missing from what we'd stolen.

"We don't know," Zoe replied. "We also don't know where the legacies are staying. We do know that this whole thing is probably happening soon, given some messages exchanged between Salvatore Zale and Sadie. She's been telling him to get ready for their next move, but it's all vague."

"Salvatore?" Anger, as white hot as it was ice cold, bloomed under my skin, making me harden. Jasper had mentioned him being involved yesterday, but it seemed that Zoe had found evidence of what, exactly, he had been involved with. I searched Zoe's face for confirmation that he had a hand in killing my mother, and her eyes were full of sorrow for me as she nodded.

"He was the one meant to win the Tourney," she said hoarsely. "It was a deal set up between him and Sadie after Devon died. Having him in charge of the department is apparently instrumental in their plans—I'm guessing because the Knights are the only department given access codes to manually open doors in case of a power loss. She'd need them to free her and her people from IT once they shut Scipio down. I'm not sure why, yet, but that's the gist of the messages. And you know the Knights. They'd follow their Champion's orders to hell and back without questioning them, so it makes sense that Sadie would want it under her control in some way."

I kept a tight lid on my anger and focused on the problem at hand. It seemed like we had uncovered a lot about what they were planning, but nothing about how many of them there were, or how to find them. "So what do we *have*?"

"The list of every legacy spy embedded in the other departments," Leo replied. I grimaced. It made sense for her to need people inside the other departments to sabotage their efforts to fix Scipio when everything began, in order to keep anyone from interfering with their plans. "As well as a full roster of the entire legacy group. There are exactly 105 of them, excluding Sadie and Mathias. Fifty-three are stationed in other departments, leaving the rest to act as support and secret forces. And before you ask me, there are a few people whose names start with *P*, but obviously we can't tell which one is which."

"*One hundred and five*," I exclaimed, my eyes bulging. "How is that even possible? Where'd they come from? Are they biologically related, or are they being recruited from somewhere?"

Leo opened his mouth, but I could tell by the shrug in his shoulders that he didn't know. I waved him off and leaned forward, trying to think. When I had asked everyone to go after the legacies, I had assumed there would be fifty people, at most. Now I knew there were twice that. Catching them wasn't going to be possible alone; we were going to need help. We were going to have to coordinate our attack so that it happened simultaneously. It would require a lot of moving parts, and that meant letting more people in on what was going on.

But I was getting ahead of myself. First, we needed to focus on finding the other fifty or so legacies who were missing. Then we needed to—

My thoughts cut off abruptly at the sudden sound of something hitting the table. I twisted in my seat in time to see Leo slumped against it and sliding down, taking with him a column of Maddox's carefully stacked files in a flutter of noise.

28

"LEO!" I cried, my heart leaping into my throat as I leapt from the chair and raced around the table to where he had fallen. A thousand questions sped through my mind: Was he injured? Had Baldy hurt him? Or was it Grey? Did we take too much blood from him yesterday? Was sharing the one mind hurting them somehow?

He was on his stomach, his head pillowed by one arm, and I quickly sank to my knees beside him and flipped him over. "Cornelius, tell Quess I need him!" I shouted, my fingers going to Leo's neck. His eyelashes fluttered against his cheeks, and he gave a soft groan, his hand weakly flopping next to him.

"Fine," he wheezed. "I'm—"

He stopped midsentence, his head lolling to one side. I could still feel his pulse under my fingers, but it wasn't as strong as I would like. It wasn't dangerously weak, but definitely weaker. It didn't make any sense. "Cornelius," I repeated, looking around. "Where is—"

"I'm here," Quess cut in, the sound of running feet filling the room. "Can't we go two minutes without having a medical emergency?"

I slid to one side to give him room, letting him fall into place beside Leo, and then watched impatiently as he pulled out his scanner and ran it over Leo's body.

"What happened?"

"I don't know," I told him, glancing up at where Zoe and Maddox were standing, hovering just to the side of us. "Did either of you see? I just saw him drop to the table and then fall."

Zoe shook her head, but Maddox nodded. "He started weaving back and forth, this really dopey look on his face. I was about to ask him what was wrong, but then he sort of toppled forward, onto the table. It looked like he fainted."

"That would make sense. His electrolyte readings are dismally low. Jasper, can you confirm?"

There was a pause. "Oh yeah. Hm. Hold on a second, I'm going to remotely interface with the net and... Oh." He went silent for a second, and I had to bite back the urge to snap at him to explain what was going on. I knew that electrolytes were really important, but how would Leo have depleted them all? Minerals were put into our water supply to make sure we were healthy, so anything he'd drunk would've replenished them. Not to mention, deficiency would only happen if he had been exercising nonstop for several days, without taking in liquids to deplete his dwindling supply.

"What is it?" I managed in a calm-ish voice, when the silence had gone on for too long.

"Quess is correct. Grey's body has been depleted of its mineral content. He will require fluids and several hours of rest."

I frowned. "But how did this happen? You know it's really difficult to have an electrolyte imbalance."

"You will have to ask Leo that question when he wakes up."

Odd. Was it because Jasper didn't know, or because it was somehow Leo's fault that Grey's electrolytes were out of balance? It didn't seem like Jasper was going to say, so the only thing I could do was follow the doctor's advice and get him in bed.

I looked down at Leo, and then back up to Quess. "Help me move him?"

"Fine," Quess groaned theatrically. "We'll get him to bed and I'll hook him up to some fluids."

"I can hook him up," I told him, reaching out to grab one of Leo's arms. "I learned that much at least from the cross-departmental training courses."

"Sweet," Quess said as he grabbed the other. "Then I can come back here and do more research! Yay!"

I laughed at the faux enthusiasm in his voice, but sobered immediately afterward, my concern for Leo and Grey overriding everything.

Quess and I lifted Leo up together, each draping one of his arms across our neck, and carried him out the room, down the hall, and into his bedroom. He remained out of it the entire time, even when we placed him on the bed in the corner. I waved Quess off when he started to help, and he shrugged, leaving the clear plastic bag with yellow fluid inside for me to give Leo before he departed.

I stood staring at the door after he closed it, and then sighed and cast a look at Leo's unconscious form on the bed. This was awkward. I hadn't thought twice about wanting to take care of him in the moment, but now that we were here, I was suddenly thinking about last night, and how everything was between us. I certainly didn't want him waking up while I was taking care of him, because I wasn't exactly ready to deal with cold Leo yet. Hopefully his lowered electrolyte levels would keep him unconscious long enough for me to get him ready for bed and hooked up to the bag.

Besides, I had other things to do than have another confrontation with him. And I knew waking him up would lead to one, as I wanted to know exactly why Grey's levels were off. If Leo was harming him in this sudden more-machine-than-man routine, I was going to tear him a new one.

And I wanted him fresh and alert when I did.

Setting the bag down, I quickly got to work stripping him of everything save for his underclothes. The boots went first, followed by his socks, and then the uniform—which required some struggle. When it came to a particularly stubborn pant leg, I was certain I would wake him, but there was no response in his face. Next came his lash harness. First, I undid the buckles that held the harness in place, and then I rolled him onto his side and worked the gyro in the back out from under him.

I carefully put everything away, and then sat down on the edge of the bed to hook him up to the saline bag and press the transfusion patch into the crook of his elbow. Finally, I sat back to wipe my forehead. I had developed a sweat from trying to move so quickly, in spite of the chill in the room. I looked down and noticed goosebumps forming on Leo's arm, and reached to grab a blanket to pull over him.

"Hey." His breath was soft against my neck, and I froze for several horrifying heartbeats before turning my head a fraction of an inch to meet his gaze. I had wanted to be gone before he woke up.

His eyes were bleary and slightly unfocused, but directed fully at my face, and he wore a lopsided smile that confused me. This was different from the icy demeanor he'd been showing me before. Now he seemed warm... and affectionate. I considered the juxtaposition for several heartbeats and came to two conclusions: either Leo had reconsidered what he said earlier, or Grey was now in control. And as much as I wanted it to be the former, the more I peered into those warm brown eyes, the more I realized that this was Grey, not Leo.

"Hey, Grey," I said haltingly, gently pulling myself into a sitting position, using the pretense of draping the blanket over him to carve out some distance between us. I wasn't prepared for this little scenario and wasn't entirely sure how to react. "How are you feeling?"

"Tired," he said weakly. "But I'm glad I woke up. I wanted to talk to you."

I paused in fussing with the blanket and chanced a glance at him, my curiosity getting the better of me. "You... were aware of what was happening?"

He gave a soft huff of laughter. "More than you know. Leo and I were arguing about it when the lights went out." He frowned, a crease forming on his brow. "Don't be mad at him, but it's his fault we passed out. He, um... didn't get any sleep after you two had that conversation last night. He kept working all night, trying to get Jasper and Rose online, and the exertion from yesterday and giving blood... He just pushed my body to its limit."

This was *weird*. He was talking about his body as if it weren't his own, and in a way, he was right. But there wasn't any resentment in his voice, like I would expect there to be. After all, he'd just told me Leo had put his personal health in jeopardy.

Well, he might not be angry, but I was. First Leo flipped on everything he had been telling me, then he decided to push Grey's body in some mindless pursuit to get Jasper and Rose online last night! How could he be so irresponsible? What was going on with him?

What was worse than the anger, however, was the pain. It hurt that Leo had treated Grey so callously. I had trusted him to take care of him, and now it seemed he was trying to show how much he really didn't care. Or maybe he was resentful toward Grey because he had been so confident that his feelings for me were genuine, so he was overreacting toward him?

I wasn't sure, but it needed to end.

"I'm sorry," I told him carefully, around clenched teeth. "I'll make sure to talk to him about it when he wakes up." I moved to stand up, but he made a small sound of protest that had me settling back down.

"Please don't go," he said softly. "I can tell you're getting angry at him, and you need to understand… He's hurting, Liana. He's convinced himself that what he felt for you wasn't real, but I think he's wrong. I think—"

"He told you," I gasped, descending the few inches I had risen during my first attempt to leave, suddenly needing to sit down. My stomach churned, his betrayal stabbing even deeper. He didn't have the right to do that; it was my responsibility, *my* conversation to have with Grey. Everything in my mind went blank, until I couldn't even think of how to respond. "He shouldn't have done that. Your memory isn't even fully restored!"

Grey gave me a lopsided smile. "I don't have all of my memories of us yet, but I'm sure you know me well enough to understand how I can be when someone's keeping a secret from me. Besides, you have no idea what this is like—how intrusive it is on both our sides! I'm awake, which means I know what's going through his mind, and he knows what's going through mine. Believe me when I say he *had* to tell me, because he couldn't keep himself from thinking about you. I told him—"

I turned my face away from him in a move that was completely reflexive, but one I was grateful for. I couldn't listen to Grey trying to validate Leo's feelings for me. The guilt was too strong, the situation too weird, and I had no idea how to interpret it. He should be angry with me! Furious at my betrayal, sickened by the very sight of me. I was pretty sure that was how I would react should our positions be reversed, but here Grey was, defending him.

Scipio help me, what if Leo was only giving Grey bits and pieces of his memories with me? Could he do that? Would he? If so, it would certainly explain why Grey wasn't as angry as he had every right to be.

I needed to stop talking with Grey. I needed answers about exactly what Leo was doing to him before I could have this conversation with him. But Leo wasn't up, which meant leaving, and not coming back until Leo was awake and could account for his actions.

"Liana?"

I steadied myself and turned back to face him, forcing my mouth into something resembling a smile. "I need to go," I told him. "You need to rest."

Grey sighed and flopped his head against the pillow in irritation. "Stop treating me like a child. You and Leo clearly have feelings for each other, even though you and I had something going on when this first happened. It really wasn't that difficult to put together."

My cheeks flushed in abject humiliation, and I once again looked away, too embarrassed for words. So Leo *had* given him all his memories. Guilt slammed into me that I had doubted him, and then remounted when I realized that meant Grey did understand what I had done to him.

"I'm sorry," I mumbled. "I'm so very sorry."

"Stop it." His words and tone confused me, and I risked a glance over my shoulder to find him watching me, his eyes brighter and clearer than they had been a few moments ago. "Don't you ever apologize for developing feelings for someone. I've been with Leo for a little over twelve hours, and even I think he's pretty cool. He certainly made better use of my body than I ever did." At my questioning glance, he explained, "Leo showed me some of the vid files from the Tourney when I didn't believe that I had joined the Knights to participate in it. He... He certainly can fight. It makes sense that you started to rely on him."

I didn't understand him. He was taking this so casually, like it wasn't a big deal at all. This was really out of character, considering how bossy and jealous he had been before. "Why aren't you more upset about this?"

The mattress squeaked slightly under his weight as he rolled to his side, making sure not to disturb his fluid bag. "Well, I'm not going to lie and tell you that I haven't changed. It's weird... I have these memories of being afraid, being alone, being abandoned, and having those feelings driving some of my reactions, but now... they don't seem to affect me as badly as they used to." He chuckled. "Then again, I don't know. Maybe almost dying changed something in me, or maybe it's the way that Leo is giving me back my memories. I feel more level-headed and self-aware then I ever did before, and it's nice to have that sort of clarity. Puts things into perspective."

"Like?" I asked, unable to help myself.

"Like you," he replied with a smile, meeting my gaze. "Of course, I'm only starting to remember you, but Leo tells me that we cared about each other very deeply. And it makes sense, considering how I remember feeling the first time I saw you."

"Oh?" The sound was soft, barely pushed out from my throat—I was too afraid of letting my breath out for fear of disturbing his words. I didn't want him to stop. I wanted to understand what was going on inside of him.

His brown eyes twinkled. "You dragged your baton along the ground to create a show of sparks. I remember thinking that you were so commanding and confident, even though you were clearly nervous. I saw how brave you were—so much braver than I was—and it took my breath away. I thought to myself, 'That's it. She's the one.'"

I snorted at that, but his words had brought a bittersweet smile to my lips. I loved hearing his internal thoughts on our first meeting, but at the same time, I realized that all of this could change at the drop of a dime. He might be accepting now, but who knew how he would feel about it tomorrow?

"We really shouldn't be talking about this now," I told him softly, once again trying to extricate myself from the conversation. "We should wait until your memories are fully—"

"Give me a little credit, Liana. I know myself a little bit better than you do, and I know what I'm willing to accept and not accept. Maybe before I wouldn't—couldn't—tolerate the idea of you and someone else, but I realize now that was my problem, not yours. My fear of being abandoned again, turned away because something in me was faulty and broken. But Leo showed me how much you fought for me, how much you tried to resist your own feelings for him, and I realized that it wasn't so black and white, so why should I be? Yes, you have feelings for another man. Does he make you happy? Do you still care about me? *Can* you?"

My confusion and shock at his questions caused my thoughts to completely fall apart. Why was he asking me if I cared about him and Leo both? Obviously, I did. But that couldn't be what he was asking me, right?

"Why are you asking me that?" I asked carefully, uncertain of how to respond to his questions.

He stared at me, and then reached out and placed his hand over mine. "Because if Leo being in my body makes you happy, then I'm willing to share it—and you—with him."

He could've knocked me over with a feather. "I..." was the only sound that could escape my clenched throat. Was that even possible? Could we... he... I...

I was overrun with confusion, my thoughts fragmented beyond belief. Of all the outcomes I ever thought possible, this was one I had never even considered, and it damn near broke me.

"I meant what I told you yesterday," he said, catching my attention. "I would do anything to make the woman I love happy. To nurture her as she needs it. I just happened to fall for a girl who needed a man who could fight at her side *while* protecting her heart. I've got half of that covered. If Leo wants to help me handle the other part, I'm more than willing to let him. All I care about is that you're happy." The gleam in his eyes diminished some. "Leo told me about your mom. I'm sorry I wasn't there for you. I could tell it hit you hard."

My heart broke at his words, and I started to cry. He was just too sweet and accepting, and I'd done nothing to earn it. He still cared about me, even though I had betrayed him in such a cruel way. "You deserve someone better than me," I told him.

Grey patted the bed next to him, and before I knew it, I was curled up on my side, his front pressed to my back, one arm draped over my side. "Maybe," he said in a light tone. "But that's my decision to make."

"How can you be so understanding about all of this?" I begged, needing to understand. "You don't even remember us."

"I will soon," he promised. "And how can I not be? I'm lucky enough to be alive right now, and reliving my past is helping me realize a few things about myself. I came from a place where love was withheld because I didn't conform to expectations. I don't want to ever make anyone I care about feel that way. I'm willing to be open to all different forms of it, even those that defy convention. If this is what makes you happy, and lets me keep being a part of your life, then I don't care." He paused for a second, and then added, "The other reason is that Leo doesn't have a corporeal self. Call me petty, but there's something satisfying about the fact that even though I'm happy to share him with you, he still has to touch you using my hands, and kiss you using my lips. It's a compromise that I'm okay making."

I managed a chuckle at that. "You've become an oddly laid-back guy, you know?"

"I know, right? I can tell what you're thinking. 'Man, Grey is so cool now. I'm even more head over heels for that guy than I ever was before.'" I shoved my elbow into his stomach—not hard, but in a warning shot—and he chuckled, brushing his lips over my temple in a kiss. "You should probably be going," he said, a yawn cracking his voice. "I know you guys have a lot of work to do, and I need some rest. And hey... I meant it—don't be mad at Leo. I was also part of the problem. I kept him up, arguing with him about what a jackass he was being."

"You did?" I asked, a smile breaking on my face.

"Of course I did. It's obvious his feelings for you are his own. He's just doubting them after what happened yesterday. And he lacks the emotional experience to know how to deal with it all."

"They are?" I asked, looking up at him. "He does? How can you know that?"

"I told you this was pretty invasive, having both of us up here. And the reason I know his feelings for you are his own is because his thoughts toward you are way too polite. He just likes to kiss and hold you. Oh, he's curious about the other parts as well, but he's perfectly satisfied with the sensation of comfort." He looked down at me, his eyes blazing. "My thoughts, however, are far filthier."

My face went white hot with surprise and embarrassment, followed by a shot of lust that hit me from head to toe.

"How can you just talk about it like that?" I asked, my embarrassment outweighing my attraction. "How can you just—"

"It's my body, remember?" he said, cutting me off by lightly stroking his fingers over my cheek. His eyes dropped to my mouth, and he smiled. "I don't remember our first kiss yet, and while I'm sure it was amazing, I sort of want to reinvent it right here and now."

"Are you asking me?" I whispered, my heart beginning to flutter wildly in my chest.

He smiled. "Normally, I would say yes," he declared, his voice low and smoky. I twisted toward him in response, wanting to face him more fully. "But you'll have to forgive me if I pass out now instead." As if to emphasize the point, he yawned widely, and then dropped his head back onto the pillow, his eyelids closing.

I smiled, reaching out to cup his cheek. I didn't know what to make of any of this, but I had learned something important: I still had feelings for Grey.

If I didn't, I wouldn't be this disappointed that he was asleep again, even if he needed it.

"Goodnight," I said, giving him a peck on the cheek before gently untangling myself. I still had to think about what he had said about Leo, but there were other things that took priority at the moment.

Besides, I needed to talk to Leo before I made any judgments or decisions. If what Grey was saying was true, then maybe Leo's overreaction was due to his inexperience with complicated emotions like these. I wasn't sure, but I had to talk to him about it before I started condemning his actions.

29

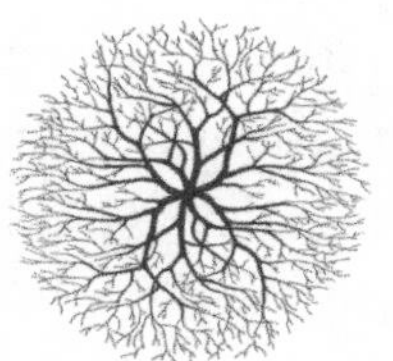

I emerged from Grey's room, intent on heading back to the war room to continue going through the files, but I stopped when I saw Zoe leaning against a wall, waiting for me.

"Hey," she said as the door closed behind me. "How is he?"

I hesitated. I wasn't sure how to tell her about the conversation that Grey and I had just had, as I had no idea how to even process it for myself. Grey was willing to share his body with Leo and was okay with me having some sort of relationship with both of them. The idea that he could be so accepting of this, of us, had opened up a strange possibility in my mind, and I really wanted time and space to think about it.

On the one hand... God, Grey *loved* me. So much so that he was entertaining the idea of sharing his body with an AI forever, just to make me happy. On the other... it was *weird.*

So I put it away, and applied a little effort to forming a small smile for my friend. "He's going to be okay, I think. What's up?"

"Oh, Dylan called Maddox to request a meeting with you both.

Maddox had her come up here, and they're waiting for you in the front room. She asked me to tell you, so..." She pushed off the wall and spread her arms. "Mission accomplished. You're welcome."

A surprised laugh escaped me, and I shook my head at her. "Thanks. Did they say what it was about?"

I had a suspicion, though I asked the question anyway. Dylan Chase had also been in the Tourney, and had technically won the fourth and final challenge, but ultimately lost when the Knights voted me in as Champion instead of her, breaking with tradition. I hadn't been sure what to make of her during the Tourney—she was highly competitive and outspoken—but had suspected her and two others of being legacies.

But Dylan had surprised me, first by coming to my aid when Baldy attacked Leo and me, then by insisting that she look into the situation personally. I had paired her with Tian, knowing that the youngest member of our group could keep a careful eye on her, as well as help her root out the legacies who were living as undocs. I was still unclear about her true loyalty.

It seemed today would reveal another part of the puzzle, as she undoubtedly had new evidence to share. If it was in line with what we were seeing from Sadie's computer, and she was telling me the truth, then I had to start entertaining the possibility that her intentions were honorable. There was a chance she was feeding us good information to try to gain our trust, to set us up in some way, but I didn't see that as being her style.

And I really wanted to trust her. I couldn't explain exactly why, but I liked the woman. Yes, she was obnoxiously blunt, and asked for what she wanted in a way that made it seem like a demand, but she cared about the department and the people inside of it. Her views on the Tower were interesting, in that she saw it as more of a mission, an experiment, the integrity of which needed to be protected. If it was an act, it was convincing.

"She's got the DNA results from the house we found in the

Attic," Zoe replied. "As well as the blood taken from the catwalk. Maddox said she seemed pretty excited, so maybe it'll be something that'll blow the lid off this thing."

I laughed. "We should be so lucky. But unless she's got detailed information about a hideout for the legacies, I'm not sure the results will yield very much."

"You never know," Zoe replied with a little shrug. "Anyway, I'm getting back to the files in a moment. Just going to check on Eric."

"Okay." I watched her go for a second, my heart a few ounces lighter for all of her bright happiness. It was such a dramatic difference from this morning, and I was glad that Eric's prognosis was looking good. We'd come too close to it going the other way, and I hated to think of what Zoe would've been like had she lost him. I couldn't bear to let anyone know that pain, especially not her.

I turned away from Zoe and started toward the kitchen, quickly following the spiraling hallway past the bedroom and bathroom doors and into the kitchen, where I stopped long enough to grab a glass of water. I drank it quickly, placed the cup in the sink, and then resumed my trek, following the hall to where it would eventually spill into the largest room of my quarters.

I heard their voices long before I entered the room. They were speaking in low tones, and the acoustics of the room didn't help give the sounds any form. I emerged from the hall and went down the handful of steps into the wide conference room, angling for where the two women were standing in front of the large wall screen, opposite the theater-style seating. I had designed this room specifically for conferences with my Knight Commanders, so that when I finally got around to having them, it would make the large-scale debriefings easier.

Of course, right now I was only going to be meeting with one Knight Commander. But it was important.

"There she is," Maddox said, nodding her head in my

direction.

Dylan turned around, an excited smile growing on her lips that served to make her look even prettier. "Oh good," she exclaimed. "You are never going to believe what I found."

I raised an eyebrow and looked over the blond woman's shoulder to Maddox, meeting her green eyes with a questioning glance of my own.

"She wouldn't tell me until you were here," Maddox replied with a shrug. "Now that you are..."

"I just didn't want to have to explain it twice," Dylan said wryly, giving me a look. "Don't you hate when you have to do that?"

I nodded. I really did. "Go ahead," I told her. "What did you uncover?"

"Only that the DNA from the bridge and collected from the blankets and plates at the scene of that weird structure thing you found in the Attic shows that these people are all biologically related. Siblings, in fact."

"Siblings?" I repeated dumbly. "How is that possible?" Residents in the Tower were only permitted two children per couple. There had been at least thirty people in the house we discovered. Someone had over thirty children?

Dylan pulled a data stick out of her pocket and plugged it in to the port at the base of the screen. A second later the screen came on, revealing several different files. "Well, 'siblings' isn't exactly right. Some of them *are* siblings, sharing both mother and father, but others are half-siblings, sharing only the father. In fact, sharing only the father is common; the mothers look like they've had a minimum of three children each, but I have evidence to support that one had seven children with the same man."

"So one man is the father of... thirty people or so?" Maddox asked, beating me to the much-needed clarification question. I was shocked. How could one man have so many children without the

Tower knowing about it? Both genders had birth control shots that kept us from procreating without the Medica's involvement. Accidents happened, but for the most part, it should've been impossible for someone to have that many children after a birth-control shot. Not without the Medica's intervention, anyway. Or waiting for the five years it took for the shot to expire.

"Yes," Dylan said grimly. "Not only that, but I was able to use parts of the DNA to track back to the mothers, and..." She pressed on one of the files, and pictures and information for at least a dozen different women filled the screen. Everything about them was different, from their hair color to their department, but there were two things they had in common: half of them were dead, while the other half were labeled 'missing.' "The DNA matches all of these women. They've all been reported missing at some point within the last fifty years, but now I think they were kidnapped. It seems I'm the only one who put that together, however. The ones who are labeled dead were discovered years after their disappearances, in various states of decomposition, and all the autopsy reports read the same thing: died in childbirth. The Knight reports that accompany the autopsies say that the girls were probably dissidents who became undocs and then died having an illegal child, which was never recovered. Nobody ever looked any deeper than that. Nobody ever saw the pattern."

I felt sick. Someone—a man—had evidently been taking women, forcing them to have his children, and then discarding them when their bodies gave out because they didn't receive the medical treatment they had needed to survive. And no one had put it together as anything more than a girl being dissatisfied with Tower life, making an attempt at being an undoc, and dying for her folly.

"That's disgusting," Maddox whispered, echoing my thoughts in a much more direct fashion.

"I know," Dylan replied, an undercurrent of anger in her voice.

"And it gets weirder. I did a search to see if any known DNA records matched the DNA of the father, hoping to find the sicko. No luck, obviously, or else I would've marched his ass up here to talk to you directly. But something odd did come up. Apparently, Frederick Hamilton shares a distant relationship with these people. Cousins, at most, but the relationship is there."

I sucked in a breath. I knew from the files Jasper had uncovered that Salvatore had been Sadie's candidate in the Tourney—and the one she'd unleashed the sentinel for—but Hamilton had been another suspect, because of his relationship to Ezekial Pine. Lacey had assured me that her family had wiped Pine's out, and that Frederick's survival had been an oversight on her part... but had it been? Or was Frederick a child of *two* legacy families? Had his branch of the family managed to escape because of his *other* family, who kept him hidden when the slaughter began?

Was *that* the legacy family we were dealing with today? Was Dreyfuss or Sage one of them?

Or worse, had Lacey's family missed someone else? Was *the father* somehow one of Ezekial Pine's descendants, too? If so, who was the male in the equation? Presumably another person Lacey's family had missed, but who?

My gut told me it was Dreyfuss, but there was a chance it could be Sage, or even, on a very off chance, Plancett. All three men had been around twenty-five years ago, and were the only ones still alive who were old enough and connected to this in any way. And while Sage was a possibility, I found it hard to believe the man would have anything remotely resembling a libido (or maybe I just hoped he didn't). He was 115, for crying out loud, and far too busy to be fathering child after child. Unless he was having those women artificially inseminated.

God, I really hoped he wasn't. The thought made me want to throw up.

Plancett was a possibility as well, but one that didn't strike me as quite right. By all accounts, he was working *for* Sparks, and then later Sadie. Then again, he did at least have the letter *P* in his name. Maybe they had obfuscated his role in the organization to keep him hidden and safe. That way, if anyone came close to learning the truth, all signs would point to him being complicit, but not entirely guilty. It was smart.

But so was Dreyfuss. He was next to nothing on paper, a retired Knight manning a stall in the Lion's Den. Kept in the background so that he could continue to strengthen their numbers, like some sort of stud bull. His position as a food vendor suddenly made a bit more sense, too—or at least, it would if I were in their shoes. Food vendors were practically invisible but talked to everyone. His people could come and talk to him in the open, under the guise of getting food, update him, and get their new orders right then and there. Nobody would ever suspect him. It would be the perfect place to hide. It's what I would do, if I were them.

And it was smart, in its own disgusting way. He could run everything in secret while ensuring that if anyone came after them, he could escape before they realized his significance, and then turn around and start a new family, ready to take over where the others had left off. It might take them years, but they had proven their method worked. Their family had survived.

That didn't leave me with much, and I turned my mind back to Frederick, deciding to add him to the list of people we would need to arrest. He might not have the same father as the rest of the legacies seemed to have, but I had no idea where he stood in all of this, and the DNA connection was too strong to ignore. If I left him out and he disappeared, the cycle might start all over again. And I couldn't take that chance.

As for who the father was… Well, we just had to do everything in our power to figure that out.

"We're going to have to find out who this man is before we do anything," I said, intending it for Maddox.

"Well, of course we have to find out who he is," Dylan replied, cocking her blond head at me. "But what do you mean, 'before we do anything'?" She looked back and forth between us, her blue eyes narrowed in suspicion. "What's going on?"

I bit my lip and looked at Maddox. "Did we find any evidence that points to her being involved?" I asked, rudely talking about Dylan in front of her.

Maddox shook her head. "Not so much as a message between them. There was a file on her, but from how it reads, it looks like they were gathering intelligence about her, not working with her."

"'Her'?" Dylan interrupted, crossing her arms over her chest. "Do you mean me? And who is 'they'? The people who tried to rig the Tourney?" She frowned, as if a thought suddenly occurred to her. "Wait, have you uncovered new evidence? Do you have suspects?" She took a step forward, her entire body reflecting the intensity of her interest.

I cocked my head at her. "It doesn't bother you that we suspect you?"

"It would, but you don't," she replied. She stuck her thumb out to point it at Maddox. "She just said that there weren't any messages between myself and whoever you're monitoring, so..." She trailed off and shrugged. "Up to you, but if you know something about who this man might be, then I want to know. This—what he's been doing to these women—it's disgusting. He needs to be stopped."

"I agree," I replied. Even if he wasn't the father of all the legacies, I would still agree. He was taking women and forcing them to bear his children, until they died from it. It was beyond sick—it was downright evil.

I considered what Dylan was saying, and Maddox's report that they hadn't found anything implicating her as working with Sadie, and took a deep, calming breath. I'd been suspicious of everyone for so long, but I had to start trusting at some point. Maybe I'd already started with the Patrians—I'd let them take my brother with them, after all—and for the first time in a long time, I decided to let another person in.

"I'm going to let Maddox catch you up on everything in a minute," I told her. "But for now, all you need to know is that we have three potential suspects: Marcus Sage, Emmanuel Plancett, and a former Knight who is now living in the farming department with his daughter."

"Great. I'll go down there and..." Dylan trailed off and frowned. "Did you say Marcus *Sage*? As in the head of the Medica?"

I nodded grimly. "I'm not certain yet, but—"

"What if the father is someone other than those three?" Maddox asked pensively. "What if we're wrong to have only them on the list of suspects?"

I hesitated. I was banking on the idea that whoever the father was wasn't content as a simple sperm donor—that he was someone important to the family itself and had known about the outsiders right from the start—but there was every possibility that I was wrong. Still, the three men were the only leads we currently had. I had no doubt that if we looked up their DNA profiles in the database, it wouldn't be a match. Undoubtedly they would've been smart enough to upload a fake genetic profile to avoid situations like this. We couldn't trust any comparisons to what was on record. We needed to collect their DNA personally and handle the testing ourselves.

If the DNA didn't match, we would figure it out later.

"We'll worry about it later. For now, we need to get DNA samples from all three men and do a comparison. That will tell us what our next move is."

"All right," Maddox agreed. "Who do we go after first?"

"First, you fill Dylan in on what we are doing," I replied. "Then we'll figure out the rest."

30

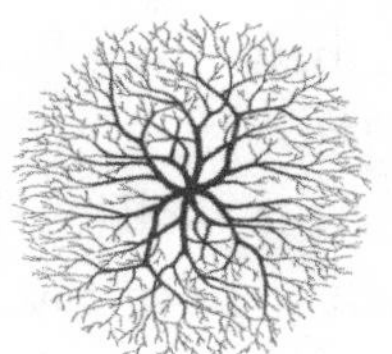

That evening, Maddox, Dylan, and I made our way down from the Citadel, heading for Greenery 13. By random chance, both Dreyfuss and Plancett were there at that exact moment. Dreyfuss because he lived there with his daughter, and Plancett because it was time to harvest the wheat and corn they had spent the last few months producing.

Greenery 13—Biggins, as it was called—resided on the 135th level of the shell and required us to exit the Citadel and enter the shell to hitch a ride up. We emerged on a wide catwalk, where a line of green-clad workers were pulling or pushing wagons full of grain to the large service elevators, for distribution to the different departments. And though it was harvest season, the catwalks were awash with people moving this way and that, in the normal chaos of activity. Only the line remained uninterrupted, people keeping their distance so as not to interfere with workers doing their duties.

The three of us slipped into the stream of people and made our way toward the massive doors with the small, portly man painted over them. He was wearing a cheeky grin, which carved a massive dimple out of one cheek. I knew him as Caleb Biggins—the hero and namesake of Greenery 13—but couldn't remember what he had done to get so famous.

The area in front of the greenery was packed with vendors, all of them selling baked goods. Already I could smell bread in the air. The promise of getting a warm slice with a pat of salted butter melting into it was so tantalizing that I almost considered stopping at the first stall I saw. Almost.

As the catwalk neared the wall of the greenery, the crowd of people naturally turned left to head toward the door, leading us to the stalls that were set up in front of the massive metal doors. We followed the sea of people until they slowly separated into rivers, and then trickled into streams, heading down this aisle or that in search of specific items on their shopping lists.

The largest throng of people were workers in green, returning from their deliveries, and we fell into line with them as they progressed down a central aisle toward the greenery doors.

The doors were fully open today, revealing a wide walkway that bridged the span of the shell and ended in yet another door, this one also open. I could hear the sounds of machines and workers calling to each other echoing through the wide-open space, but kept walking forward, toward the doors.

Inside, the machines used for separating the wheat from the chaff had been set up in several rows, and workers were operating them in sets of three, one man turning it on and off, the others hauling baskets up a small ladder to deposit them at the top of a chute. The machines whirred endlessly, spitting out small grains and dust while depositing the husks in the now-empty buckets placed off to the side, and adjusted by the man who was in charge of powering the machine. Several foremen—marked by yellow helmets—walked among them, barking orders. The Hands we were with headed directly for them, but I veered left, knowing from experience that the apartments for this floor were accessed by a door in the tunnel.

Sure enough, I spotted the door and control panel off to the left, and angled toward it, confident that Maddox and Dylan were behind me. Stopping at the door, I quickly pressed the button, and waited. My net began to buzz as the scanners set to work, and I waited patiently for the process to start and finish.

"*Champion Liana Castell,*" an automated male voice announced. "*Authorized entry granted. Have a pleasant day.*"

"Thanks," I said as the door slid open, revealing a narrow series of stairs heading down. I followed them for two floors, and then opened a door at the end of them and entered the apartment floor. The apartment floor of each greenery took up an entire block of the shell and contained some of my favorite apartments in the Tower. They were always colorful and tended to have shelves filled with plants and plaques describing what the plant was and how to care for it. The lights were bright, enhanced with UV for the plants, and doors were almost always open, neighbors acting like family members.

I followed the signs to the nearest elevator station and took it down to the bottom floor, where the internal leads of the department lived. Dreyfuss's daughter, Rachelle, was a head boss of Greenery 13, which afforded her the space to take her father in after he retired. This was where we'd find him.

The elevator slowed to a stop, revealing a long passage with doors on either side. I walked forward, following the numbers and stopping when I came to 135-5-D. I pressed the call button before I could start getting anxious about it.

Only then did I let some nervousness creep in. We were here to secretly steal some of his DNA to run it against the samples

Dylan had collected, and there was a one-in-three chance that he was the father of a group of thirty or so undocs. I had to treat this delicately, because if we tipped him off, or he even got a glimmer of what we were up to, he'd notify the legacy group and we'd lose any chance of finding them.

Luckily, I had a cover story ready. I just prayed it would be enough to explain our presence here in a believable fashion. If he was who I suspected he was, he would still be suspicious—but also, I hoped, overconfident in how hidden he had been for the last twenty-five years.

The door slid open, an elderly man in his late fifties standing behind it. His face matched the picture we had on file, which meant I was looking at former Knight Elite Jathem Dreyfuss. His blond hair was mixed with gray and white, but his blue eyes were sharp.

"Champion Castell," he said, a confused smile coming on his face. "I wasn't expecting you. To what do I owe the pleasure?"

"Greetings, former Knight Elite Dreyfuss," I replied, forcing a smile of my own onto my face. "I'm sorry for stopping by without calling first, but truthfully, my schedule is never consistent these days, so setting an appointment for something like this is a little tricky."

"Something like what?" he asked, cocking his head at me.

I smiled. He hadn't made a move to let us in yet, and we needed to get in so that one of us could surreptitiously remove something with his DNA on it, for testing. "I wanted to see how you were faring with retirement and see if I could talk you into coming back to the Knights," I told him. "But it'll be easier to talk about it inside."

The old man blinked in surprise, and then nodded. "Of course," he said, taking a step aside. "Please come in."

I moved past him and entered a wide living area decorated tastefully with a dark blue sofa and a few small chairs on either side, with a small table set in front of it. A potted plant sat in the middle of it, the wide, waxy leaves telling me it was there for oxygen production. A kitchen was behind it, larger than the ones in the Knight Commanders' quarters, the counter acting as the divider between the two rooms. A hallway opened up opposite the front door, presumably leading to the bedrooms.

There were dozens of possible sources of DNA in the house, but we had to be certain we got the right sample. He was living with his daughter, and while having her DNA would help implicate him, having his was the best way to know for certain.

Dreyfuss stepped past us, his arm already held out toward the sofas. "Have a seat, please."

"Thank you," I said. I moved over and took a single chair with my back to the wall, while Dylan perched next to me on the couch. Only Maddox remained standing, and I could tell by her "nervous" fidgeting that she was going to start the plan right now—by faking the need to use his facilities. The bathroom was the best place to find genetic material, and we were all hoping that Maddox could grab something simple, like some hairs from a brush. Anything that wouldn't be missed. "Kerrin?" I asked, using her last name.

"I'm sorry, ma'am," she said apologetically, and it was all I could do not to smile. "Sir, may I use your bathroom?"

It was the best excuse we'd been able to think of. Dreyfuss gave her a surprised look, and then nodded. "Of course. Second door on the right."

"Thank you." Maddox ducked her head at him while making a beeline toward the hallway, looking for all the world like a girl whose bladder was about to explode. I kept my face neutral, and then smiled brightly at Dreyfuss when he looked at me.

"So what can I do for you, ma'am?" he asked, taking a seat in the chair opposite mine.

"Actually, it was what I was hoping we could do for each

other." I kept my words vague intentionally, trying to drag the conversation out to give Maddox time to get something to test.

"Oh? What would that be?"

"First, let me ask: Are you satisfied working as a vendor?"

He blinked in surprise at my sudden shift in the conversation, and then settled back in his chair. "I have no complaints," he said carefully. "I'm sure you saw that my retirement from the Knights wasn't entirely by choice. I have arthritis in my knees and shoulders from lash work, and two compressed vertebrae in my back. The Medica deemed me unfit for the physical labor of the department, and I was retired."

I nodded sympathetically. "I did read that in your file, sir. And, please be assured, I'm not asking you to resume your duties or anything like that. But it seems several of our instructors in the Academy are up for retirement, and your name was suggested by one of the other Knight Commanders as a possible replacement."

"Which one?" he asked curiously. I noted the gleam of interest in his eyes and replied with my prepared lie.

"My father, actually." I had done my research, anticipating his question, and had learned that he had served under my father in his final two years before retirement. I had considered going to my father and asking about it, but I hadn't spoken to him since the funeral, and certainly didn't intend to start now.

He gave a surprised laugh. "Really? I didn't think he thought much of me. I was already slowing down because of my injuries, and that prompted him to put me at a desk, filing reports."

"That might be why he thought of you, actually," I said with a polite cough. "We need a class on writing reports for some of the cadets who are coming through. I've noticed that in the last few years or so, reports filed by younger Knights tend to be incomplete, or told in a biased tone that I wouldn't want anyone in the Tower to see, let alone associate with the Knights. No one seems to be teaching practical writing, and the younger generation is suffering."

Dreyfuss frowned. "You want me to be an instructor, to teach... report writing?"

I nodded solemnly. "I know it doesn't seem like much, but you'd be helping future Knights become more efficient at their jobs."

He seemed to consider that for several moments, and I was content to let him, my eyes drifting to a point just over his shoulder where the hallway sat, as I waited for Maddox to emerge. She hadn't been gone for even a minute, but the conversation wasn't intended to go on that long anyway, lest we rouse any suspicions. Of course, if she didn't find anything, then we were in a world of hurt, but we'd cross that bridge if we came to it.

It was nerve-wracking, nonetheless.

"I'll need to talk it over with my daughter," he said finally, jerking my gaze back to him. "I think she likes having me around and wouldn't want me moving back to the Citadel."

"You wouldn't have to, if you didn't want to," I told him, and he gave me a surprised look.

"You wouldn't worry about one of your Knights living outside of the Citadel?"

"Of course I would," I breathed, my eyes flicking over his head as Maddox emerged from the shadows of the hall. Relief bled through me as she patted her pocket and gave me a thumbs-up before walking toward us. "But we could make it work. I encourage you to think it over and discuss it with your daughter before you make a decision. If you have any questions, you can send a message to Lieutenant Kerrin." I nodded toward her as she came around his chair.

"Thank you," she gushed, a relieved note in her voice. "And yes, please don't hesitate to message."

"Of course," he said politely, slowly coming to his feet.

I rose to mine as well, Dylan following suit, and went around the table to shake his hand, offering him my most winning smile. "I hope to hear from you soon, either way."

"I will talk it over with my daughter tonight, and send you my decision tomorrow," he informed me, returning my firm squeeze with one of his own. "But thank you for your consideration. I'm honored."

"No, the honor is mine," I lied to him. "Have a great day."

We emerged from the elevator a few minutes later and returned to the main harvesting area, moving through the chaffing machines to the fields beyond, now intent on finding the head of the Hands, Emmanuel Plancett. We knew he was somewhere on the floor, monitoring the harvest, but to find out where exactly, I had to put a call in to Jasper so he could use Cornelius's link to central command to locate his net through the sensors.

We made our way through the paths cut in the long, tall stalks of wheat, staying strictly there to avoid getting picked up by one of the machines as they made their way across the floor. Dust filled the air as the large harvesters worked at pulling the wheat from the ground, making the men and machines shadows against the light above.

I cupped my hand over my mouth as we moved toward one large shadow. Harvester Four was apparently down, according to Cornelius's report, and Plancett and two of his men were there working on it. It was easy to see which one it was, as the others had continued their line of advance, eating up dozens of feet of vegetation at a time and leaving behind neat, mowed-down areas. I waited until we had passed one of the noisy machines before stepping off the path and stalking across the uneven ground toward the tall shadows of wheat barely visible in the dust. I paused when those stalks stopped being shadows, and then followed the line of them back, heading for the long dark shadow of the harvester some forty feet ahead.

I came to a full stop at the corner, using the vegetation for cover. I still hadn't figured out how I was going to approach this, but waiting and watching seemed like a good start. We needed DNA from him, but getting it without cluing him in was going to be harder than it had been with Dreyfuss. If we could do it without being seen, that would be ideal, but if I had to come up with a reason to draw him into conversation, I would.

Plancett was some fifty feet away, his back to the crops. He was on one knee with a wrench the size of my forearm in one hand, slowly rotating a bolt on the black machine. The muscles of his biceps flexed, and he grunted loudly as he detached the wrench, reoriented it, and connected it again. I could barely see one of his assistants, working at the opposite end of the bulky machine, but could tell from the way he kept turning to one side that the other one was next to him.

Though it was evening, the lights above were still on the daytime setting, making the room as warm as it would be during the day. And as I watched, Plancett reached into the back pocket of his coveralls and produced a handkerchief to mop at the sweat that was accumulating on his brow and neck. A moment later, he tucked it back away.

As soon as he made the motion, I zeroed in on it and smiled, slowly withdrawing behind the crops and turning to the other two. "He's got a handkerchief," I told them. "Back left pocket. He's been using it to dry his sweat."

"That's perfect," Dylan said, her eyes gleaming. "I'll go get it."

"What?" I said. "No, it should be me."

Dylan smirked. "No, it should be *me*. You said these guys know that you're an enemy. If he turns around and sees you stealing it, he's going to know something's up. If it's me, I might be able to play it off."

I hesitated. She made a really good point. Dammit. "All right. But be careful."

She nodded, and then began creeping down the gap in the wheat, turning sideways to keep from rustling too many of the leaves as she went. I held my breath while she walked away, discomforted by the fact that we had just finished bringing her up to speed on everything except for Scipio and the fragments, and now I was letting her turn around and risk getting caught by someone we knew was one of Sadie's allies.

I watched her for as long as I could before she disappeared behind the vegetation, and then slid out past Maddox, to see what Plancett was up to. He was standing now, both arms lifted high over his head as he stretched his lower back. The handkerchief—blue-and-white microfiber—hung like a beacon from his back pocket, scant inches way from a stalk of wheat.

He emitted a long groan, and then bent over to start gathering up his tools. I realized then that he was done, and that any second he would be moving out of there. Which meant that any second after that, the harvester would come back on—and Dylan could be sucked right into the machine.

My fingers twitched at the thought and I lifted up my arm, about to call to Dylan to forget the whole thing, when I saw a crimson-clad arm shoot out of the vegetation, grab the blue-and-white corner dangling from Plancett's pocket, and lift it straight out. I stood stock still, waiting for Plancett to notice, but he continued to gather his tools and toss them into a heavy black bag, oblivious.

A few moments later I heard the rustle of leaves that signaled Dylan's return, the handkerchief gripped tightly in her hand.

"Here," Maddox whispered, looking over her shoulder before holding up a specimen bag. Dylan dropped the handkerchief inside, and Maddox quickly sealed it up and tucked it into her pocket. "Two down, one to go," she whispered, patting her pocket.

I nodded and waved at them both to follow me back into the dust cloud, wanting to hurry away before Plancett finished his packing and noticed us. We couldn't afford anyone noticing us close to him as it could alert the legacies that we potentially knew they were working with him. I wouldn't feel safe until I was off this floor and back in the Citadel.

31

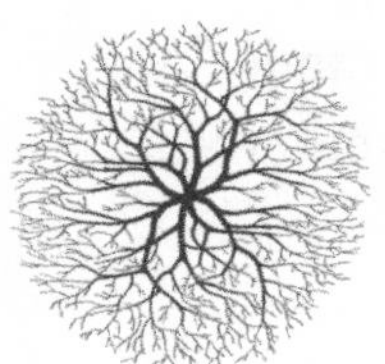

"Well, that went better than I thought it would," Dylan commented as we exited the large greenery.

I glanced at the tall blond woman, and found her confidence irritating. All I could think about were the dozens of ways we could've been caught—might've already been noticed. If any of the Hands had seen us lurking around Plancett and reported it to him, or if Dreyfuss didn't buy our flimsy cover story, we might have just lost any chance we had of catching Sadie's partner.

A part of me wished I could just arrest them all and figure it out afterward, but if I was right and we made a move, the legacies would know, and retaliate. We had to take them all at once, but even if we identified who the father was, we still couldn't account for where the undoc arm of their cell was. Finding them came next, and another chat with Liam might help—but then again, it might not. My stomach twisted into knots as I thought about what would happen if we messed up this chance. If they disappeared before we could corner them...

I looked away from Dylan, despair threatening to overwhelm me.

No, I told myself firmly. *I'm not giving in to what ifs. This is the best plan available to us right now. Figure out who the father of all the undocs is, then figure out where the undocs themselves are. Liam might tell us, and if he doesn't, we can put eyes on whoever the father is and follow him until he leads us there.* It might take longer than the week we had, but I wouldn't be leaving anyway, so I just had to make sure I surrounded myself with trustworthy Knight Commanders before the others left. That way I could finish the mission without them.

"Liana?"

I glanced to my right, where Maddox was walking next to me, and realized I had missed whatever they were talking about. "Sorry, I was thinking. What's up?"

"Did Sage get back to you with a meeting time?" she asked, and I blinked, reality rushing right back in.

"Oh, one second." I angled for an area free from people and made my way to it, slipping between throngs of workers and families walking away from Biggins. I grabbed my pad from the front pocket of my uniform, quickly tapped it on, and pulled up my messages. There was one waiting from Sage, and I tapped on it impatiently. It was shorter than I had hoped, just, *Sure thing! Tomorrow morning after eight is best for me. See you then. Sage.*

Disappointment rippled through me at the delay in meeting him, but there was ultimately nothing I could do. If I pushed for something tonight, it would undoubtedly arouse his suspicions, and without a valid reason to force the issue, he could and might refuse. Worse, if he was a legacy and had already been told to watch out for me, then any suspicious moves on my part would clue him in to the fact that something was wrong. We had to wait.

"Tomorrow," I said, shutting off the pad and shoving it back into my pocket.

Maddox rolled her eyes, and Dylan sighed heavily. "What do we do until then?" Dylan asked, and I considered her question. There wasn't much *to* do but more research, and as we hadn't told Dylan about the fragments, I wasn't about to let her join in on that. I didn't trust anyone beyond my group with that information; it was too dangerous.

But that didn't mean she couldn't continue to work on this in her own way.

"I want you and a Knight you trust to follow Plancett and Dreyfuss. Give the Knight's name to Maddox so we can clear him or her and get a DNA profile to make sure whoever you choose isn't related to the legacies in any way. Don't tell them what this is about. Just tell them to use plain clothes and be discreet. Pursue, but don't interfere, and if the subject you are following disappears, don't bother trying to find him. Just mark down where you lost him and reset in the best position for finding him again. If they disappear completely, I expect they'll be going to see the undocs, which will mean that position will probably be close to where they are hiding. It is critical that neither of you follows them too closely; if you're seen, they will disappear, and we might not be able to find them again."

Dylan blinked several times and then shook her head, as if clearing it from a punch. "Right," she said, surprise radiating in her voice. "So, that was really specific." She cleared her throat and hesitated, and I felt a little bad. We had just clued her in to our problems, and I had just laid out a whole heap of orders that spoke to how paranoid I was about this.

"I know a kid," she said after a moment. "He's fresh out of the Academy, but he used to be a bit of a pickpocket in the markets before he reformed his ways. He's good. I'll have him checked out, but this is a big operation for just two people. We're going to need more."

I took a deep breath. She was right, of course, but I didn't like it. More people involved meant a higher possibility of word getting out. "I don't think that's a good idea. We can't afford any word of this getting out."

"But if we clear their DNA, that should prove they aren't involved, right?"

"Maybe, but the legacies could've corrupted them in other ways. We know they hand out extra ration cards to Plancett—why wouldn't they use that for other things as well? Who wouldn't turn their head for a week's worth of rations?" Maddox asked the questions before I could even get there mentally, but they were all valid points.

The ration cards gave me pause, though, as I suddenly realized that Sage—not Plancett—was the only one in the Tower with the authority to issue ration cards, based on an individual's nutritional needs at their biannual physical. And I knew that he offered them to anyone who could bring him pre-End medical journals.

Maybe I was wrong about Sage—maybe he *was* involved. The DNA test would certainly help determine it, but the ration card thing was concerning.

Not to mention, he was the only authority on pre-End medical procedures, thanks to his obsession with collecting medical journals from that era. And we were almost certain the legacies were avoiding detection by using plastic surgery to change their facial structures. Could *he* be performing them? It was possible. Come to think of it, the Medica was also the only department responsible for uploading DNA profiles to the servers.

If legacies were hiding in plain sight, courtesy of faked DNA profiles, Sage was the most likely to be helping them.

A chill ran through me as I once again considered how I might have misjudged the man. More and more signs were pointing to him, and though I knew I should be impartial, my mind was already spinning out counterpoints. There were legacies embedded in his department, and I had to imagine they had some medical training, which meant they might also be the ones performing the plastic surgery. Not to mention, the journals we found in the Attic numbered in the hundreds and weren't being cared for in the best way—something I knew for a fact drove Sage insane.

And it was just as possible that *Sadie* was responsible for faking the DNA profiles in the server. IT had its hooks in everything. And the ration cards, as well! After all, they were scanned into a system that IT controlled, so I couldn't imagine it would be difficult for her. And it would be a clever move on her part, as it would be easy to shift blame to the Medica if anyone discovered illegal ration cards or found a discrepancy in the DNA profiles. Those were Sage's jurisdiction, and ultimately, he would be the one held responsible. I thought about his words the other day in the Medica, about him doubting his own ability to lead, and remembered thinking then that maybe the legacies were targeting him for removal. Maybe I had been right, and this was how they were planning to do it. By setting him up.

I sighed and pressed my hand to my head, trying to figure out whether I was coming up with these ideas to defend him because I liked him, or whether it was an actual possibility. The legacies didn't think in a straightforward fashion; they always came at us sideways. And that meant I couldn't put anything past them.

Scipio help me, I was going to be so happy when I could stop thinking myself into knots. Ultimately, I would have to withhold any judgment until we had all three men's DNA tested. Still, I hoped Sage was innocent. I liked the old man.

"I wouldn't take ration cards, not for anything," Dylan declared, crossing her arms over her chest. "And any Knight who does is a traitor."

I rolled my eyes. "That's a little extreme, Dylan," I said. "Besides, Maddox is right—we can't trust anyone at this point. I will go up to my quarters and find someone from my inner circle to help you watch Plancett and Dreyfuss tonight, and then we'll figure something out tomorrow. Maybe by then we'll have uncovered a list of all the other people Sadie might have paid off, and finally have a way to start trusting our people."

Dylan's mouth pressed into a line, but she nodded once. "I'll wait for them here. Hopefully no one will leave before someone gets here."

"You won't be alone," I said. "Maddox will wait with you until someone can come and replace her."

"What about you?" Maddox asked, her brows drawing together in alarm. "You know you shouldn't be walking alone through the halls. If we're being followed..."

"Then they are super worried about how close we came to one of their people," I interjected. "Either way, we can't afford to let Dreyfuss or Plancett out of our sight now that we suspect them, because there's a chance they can lead us to the undocs' hiding place. It's just a short ride down on a very public elevator, and a quick walk across a heavily trafficked bridge. I'll be fine."

"Or you could net Zoe, tell her to send someone down, and then we leave together," she insisted, and I sighed.

I had wanted to get away from both of them, to be honest, because I was hoping to sneak off to call my brother. But thanks to Baldy cutting my throat just *one* measly time, they had instituted a firm rule that they followed to the letter: I never went anywhere by myself, and especially not first.

"I can handle it on my own for a while, guys," Dylan added, and I narrowed my eyes at her unhelpfulness. "Plancett isn't likely to leave until the harvest is finished, and Dreyfuss isn't scheduled to work. I think I'll be all right for an hour. I'll just sit down for some dinner at one of the stalls."

I didn't like the idea of leaving Dylan alone, because I still wasn't entirely sure I could trust her, but I relented, eager to just get moving. "Fine," I said. "Be careful, and don't let anyone see you."

She smiled crookedly. "I will be like a ghost in the night," she assured me, already pulling her short bob into a high ponytail on her head. That simple move did a lot to change her appearance, but she went even further, pulling a microfiber cloth out and carefully wiping off some of the makeup she had been wearing. In a few moments, her face had transformed to a slightly less beautiful version of itself, and without her hair around her face, I wouldn't have recognized her on the first or even the second glance.

I gave a slow nod of approval as she looked at us both expectantly, smiled, offered me a two-fingered salute, and said, "Wish me luck," before disappearing into the crowd of people moving steadily by us.

I snorted under my breath. "She asks for luck, when what we really need is a miracle."

Beside me, Maddox chuckled. "True story. Let's get out of here. I don't want her to be by herself for any longer than necessary."

I agreed, and followed her into the sea of people.

We were in the elevator when Maddox finally asked, "So why did you want to go up alone?"

My mouth pressed into a thin line before I could stop it, and Maddox's gaze dropped to it, a satisfied smile growing on her lips. "I was right, then. You wanted to be alone. Why?"

I crossed my arms over my chest. There was no point in lying to her. "I want to call my brother."

Her eyes widened in surprise, and she frowned. "You don't have to be alone for that," she pointed out.

I licked my lips. She was right. I didn't have to be, but I wanted to be. Maybe it was selfish; I was sure the others wanted to hear all about Patrus, but I didn't care. They could talk to him another night. I'd spent the entire day trying not to think about him, about Patrus, about how everything was about to change—and now that the action was over, all I wanted to do was talk about it. Zoe was the only one who knew that I was planning to leave. Everyone else still thought I would be going with them. Leo and I were in a strange place, and Grey needed to fully remember who he was before he made the decision to leave. I didn't want to influence him on that front. And that didn't leave anyone else to talk to except Alex.

"I know," I replied. "But I wanted to."

Maddox sucked in a breath and then sighed. "I understand," she said. "Everything that happened yesterday was such chaos that neither of you had time to process what you went through. Besides, I can only imagine how anxious you must be to make sure he made it all right."

Those were also on my list of concerns. "Exactly," I told her.

She considered it, and then nodded. "I'll go with you. We'll stop by your quarters first, to see who can help Dylan, and then I'll accompany you to the roof, and wait on the other side of the door so you can talk to him alone."

"Really?" I asked. "You don't want to hear what he has to say?"

"Of *course* I do," she replied. "But number one, all of us going up to the roof at once to listen to him is foolish, and two, you're his sister. If it were Tian or even Quess, I'd want some time alone with them. It's scary—he's so far away, and if anything goes wrong out there..."

My stomach clenched, and I looked away. "Thanks," I said sardonically. "Exactly what I needed to hear."

"I'm sorry," she said. The elevator chose that moment to stop, and we quickly got off, making room for the group of Cogs who were next in line. I nodded at them respectfully as we passed, and I got a few surprised smiles, as well as a greeting of "Champion" delivered in quite a few excited voices.

I smiled, but didn't say anything as we slipped past them, moving for the large opening that would take us out of the shell and back into the central chamber. We took one of the nearby bridges into the Citadel—I inclined my head at one of the sentries as we passed his station—and then entered the reception hall, aiming for the elevator.

The entire time, I searched the crowd for some sort of hidden danger lurking among the people who seemed to fill the wide space. I couldn't help it. Maddox was right not to let me go alone; there had been hundreds of people between Biggins and the Citadel, and any one of them could've been sent to kill me. It wasn't until I hit the final elevator that I was really aware I had been doing it, and the relief poured through me as soon as the elevator slid upward and away.

I couldn't wait for this paranoia to be finished and done with. I was sick of it—always worrying about someone's motivations or goals, never being able to trust that they were on my side. If we could just get all of the legacies collected, and then convince the council of what they had done, maybe I could finally relax a little. Maybe I would finally have some people in the council I could share the burden with.

But until then, I had to keep everyone at arm's length.

The lift stopped between levels 42 and 43—the spot I'd chosen yesterday for the new entry to my quarters, after everything was said and done—and we stepped off and headed down the hall toward the war room. With the exception of Leo and Tian, everyone was in the room working on something when we got there. Even Eric, it seemed, although his pile of work seemed significantly smaller than anyone else's—no doubt Zoe's requirement for letting him out of bed.

Quess was the first to notice us. His smile for me was kind, whereas the one for Maddox was pure hunger, his dark eyes lightening significantly. "How'd it go?" he asked lightly.

"We've got hair and a handkerchief," Maddox said, pulling the bags out of her pocket. "But we need someone to get down there and help Dylan keep an eye on Plancett and Dreyfuss. I'd do it, but I'm going with Liana up to the roof to call her brother. And before anyone asks, it's just us two. No need for anyone else to come."

"Awww," Eric said. "But I missed the adventure last night!"

"And you're missing it tonight, too," Zoe said from next to him. "The war room and back was what we agreed to."

Eric huffed playfully, but I could tell he was pleased. I was, too. Their happiness was a spot of joy in my life. I honestly wasn't sure what I would do without them.

"Well, Liana wants some time alone with her brother," Maddox said. "So everyone can forget about it. Now, who's ready to pull an all-nighter and help Dylan? We need someone to help her shadow Plancett and Dreyfuss for the rest of the night."

Everyone groaned, except for Eric. "I'll go," he said.

Zoe snapped her eyes toward him, already sucking in a breath to tell him how wrong he was, but he beat her to it. "There's a chance Dreyfuss killed my dad," he told her flatly, and I realized that Zoe must've shown him the graphic novel and the messages between Sparks and Plancett. "Quess did fine on my wounds, and I've slept enough. Besides, it's not exactly like I'm pulling much weight, here. Staring at these files is making my eyes cross. I can't make heads or tails of this crap, and you know it."

Zoe's mouth remained open for a second or two longer, and then closed slowly. I could sense an undercurrent to their conversation—something that told me Eric was conveying some deeper meaning that I wasn't picking up—and for some reason, it seemed to change Zoe's mind.

"Fine," she said with a scowl. "But I'm going with you." I absorbed the oddness of their exchange, mentally making a note to ask Zoe later, but tucked it away, relieved. Especially that Zoe was going with him. I loved Eric to death, but he couldn't stay awake for a shift to save his life.

Eric smiled. "I wouldn't have it any other way. Let's go grab some supplies and head down there."

I watched them start to get up and realized that I hadn't asked about Grey or Leo. I wasn't sure who, if anyone, had checked on them since they had fainted this morning and I had tucked them in, but I wanted to make sure they were okay. "Did anyone check on Grey and Leo?"

"I did," Quess said. "They are still out. I gave them another bag of fluids and left them a plate of food in case they wake up, but that was a few hours ago. Also, I may have gotten a step closer to figuring out who this plastic surgeon guy is."

I perked up a little. "Really? What do you have?"

"Well, like P, he's clearly important enough to warrant his own alias. He goes by 'Dr. Smiley' in the transmissions, which are untraceable. The messages don't contain much in the body, but the attachments have files documenting the surgical changes with before-and-after pictures. None of the files are complete, so I'm having Jasper compile the different images to feed into the Citadel's files and figure out everywhere they've been. It also gives us the most recent images of our targets."

"That's great," I said. "But no clue as to who he is yet?"

"No, but I'm going to figure it out. I have a feeling having the most recent pictures of people will help."

I wasn't sure why, but I trusted Quess on this. His instincts had proven accurate before, and I was willing to go with anything that led us to the surgeon's identity. "Keep me updated."

There was a pause, and I found myself thinking of Leo and Grey again. As much as I wanted to go check up on them both, I didn't want to put calling Alex off any longer. I could check on them when we got back.

"All right," I replied. "Quess, looks like you're in charge while we're gone."

Quess looked around the empty conference table, and then back to us. "Gee, thanks."

"Don't worry, my boy," Jasper said. "I'm also here, and happy to help!"

"Well, that's something at least," Quess replied dryly before rolling his eyes. "Have fun, I guess?"

"You mean climbing the forty stories of stairs?" Maddox asked sweetly. I started to remind her that there were elevators, but realized she wanted to mask our comings and goings as much as possible, which meant keeping off the elevators. And she was probably right to. Dammit. "Yeah, I'm sure we'll have a blast with that. We definitely got the better job."

I chuckled, but my legs were already aching in anticipation of the climb. Quess, however, laughed outright and ducked his head. "Fair point, beautiful. But seriously, be careful?"

"We will be," she promised as she turned to me. "Ready when you are."

"Oh, I'm ready," I said. "But what do you say we raise the quarters first, before we start our little climb?"

Maddox laughed outright, nodding her head in agreement. "Yes," she replied dryly. "Let's do that. Because I am not looking forward to this climb either."

32

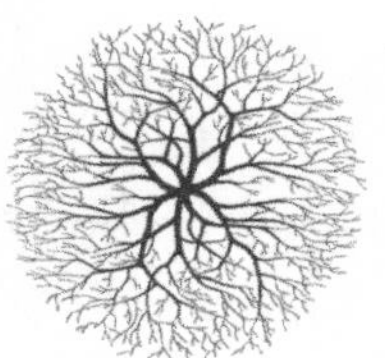

Getting to the roof only took us half as long as it had the night before—likely because we weren't hauling a body between us—but the climb was no less painful. If anything, it was even more so, given that we had barely had a day to recover from the last time.

What was worse, there wasn't a way to lash our way through it, as the stairs in the shell lacked a ceiling (unless we were passing a farming department). And we couldn't exactly use the walls, which prevented us from swinging. So that meant climbing each agonizing step.

My legs were mush when we finally reached the last door, and I took a moment to wipe away the sweat that had accumulated on my face and neck, knowing the air outside would be frigid.

"I'll come out with you to make sure there's no one else up here," Maddox said as she turned the massive wheel on the door. A moment later there was a hiss of air pressure, which turned into a blast, the air of the Tower racing past us to try to escape. I helped

Maddox pull the door back against the breeze that formed, and then followed her through the door and up the stairs.

The night was darker than the one before, the moon hidden behind gray clouds blanketing the sky in the distance. Our skies were free from clouds overhead—they always were because of the arid nature of the Wastes surrounding us—but the moon was still low enough that it hadn't broken through the faraway cloud cover. We stepped onto the roof and spun around, looking for a sign of anyone else being up here.

It took us a few minutes to clear the roof—we wound up walking a small perimeter around the immediate area just to make sure no one was eavesdropping—and then Maddox disappeared back inside. As soon as the door was closed, I took a deep breath and pulled out the black device Thomas had shoved into my hands before we left the ship.

It took me a second of studying it to spot the "on" button at the top, and I pressed my thumb over it. The button didn't move, and on closer examination, I realized that it slid to one side. Feeling stupid, I quickly clicked over, and then squeezed the large button that read "to talk" on the side.

"This is Liana Castell, calling for Alex Castell." I said into the device. I stared at it for several seconds, wondering if it was supposed to light up or have some sort of digital interface that would indicate the message had been sent. Instead, all it did was make a static sound.

I stared at it for a few more seconds, and then tried again. "I repeat, this is Liana Castell, calling for Alex Castell. Alex, are you receiving me?"

More static. Maybe I was using it wrong? Or maybe he wasn't next to his? Or what if the Tower was still interfering with the signal? We'd never tested it, so how could I tell?

I knew there was another possibility, but I wasn't ready to jump to it yet. I didn't want to believe that Melissa and Thomas had hurt him. Instead, I tried again. "This is Liana Castell, trying to reach Alex Castell or any representative of Patrus. Please respond."

Nothing. I waited for a long time, much longer than I had before, staring at the black box while a wave of helpless frustration came over me. "I knew letting you go was a bad idea," I muttered, letting go of the talk button in irritation.

There was a pop of louder static, followed by "...Your damn finger off the button so you can hear me!" in my brother's voice.

It took me a second to decipher his statement, but once I did, I flushed with embarrassment. The rudimentary machine required me to press the button when I wanted to talk and let go of it when I was done, so I could hear the reply. How was I supposed to know that? They had just shoved it into my hands with almost no explanation.

Unless they had explained it, and I had been so preoccupied by the fact that my brother was leaving me that I had missed it. "Sorry," I said, pressing the button again. "This technology is new to me." I let go of the button.

"I know. There's a lot of stuff here that's new for me. I'm hiding out in my room, actually. I... um... got a little sick."

"Are you okay?" I asked, instantly concerned. "What happened?"

"Motion sickness," he replied, his voice colored with embarrassment. "Both in their airship and in these things they call cars. I really did not enjoy that experience at all."

I laughed in delight, imagining what it must've felt like to ride in a car. I couldn't believe they were still being used! It was just so far-fetched, and I couldn't help but to ask the myriad of questions that came bubbling out of me. "They have cars? What are they like? What about where they live? What is it like?"

He laughed through the speaker, and I realized he had pressed the button so I could hear his response. The sound made me wish he was here, if only so I could wrap my arms around him and reassure myself that he was okay. "They're cramped and small," he replied. "Mine came complete with some older woman named Magdelena, who was a little scary. Apparently, she's a general in the Patrian army. She had a lot of questions for me about the Tower."

"About our defenses?" I asked, alarmed. I didn't like the idea of someone from the Patrian military asking anything about the Tower. Who knew what they were planning? They talked about trying to imitate our technology, but what if they decided it was easier to steal it?

"Um, no, about our lives there. She was writing up a report for Prime Chancellor Croft, and wanted a description of our society and how we did things—whether we had a justice system, how the people were treated, our system of government... I told her about the ranking structure, the council, the expulsion chambers. But I left out a lot."

"Good," I said, relieved that none of the questions had been about our technology. I wasn't comfortable giving them information on that front. I wanted their help, not to give them information that they could possibly use to attack us, on the off chance they had been lying to us. "It's a petition for refugee status, not an invitation for war."

"I don't think they're like that, Lily," he said a second later. "They didn't press for me to tell them anything more than I was willing to share, but then again, I was brought to the capitol building in a covered truck with armed guards. Even my room is nice, but I'm not allowed to go anywhere without an escort. Both sides are keeping secrets, and it seems to me that they expect it. I get the sense that they won't press too hard either way; it'll be how forthcoming I am about our situation that will be the deciding factor for them, not what technology I can procure for them."

"Does it feel... unsafe?" I asked him. I didn't like the idea of my brother being monitored at all times, but at the same time, if I had an outsider in the Tower, I wouldn't allow them to go anywhere unsupervised, either.

"No, no, no. I can come and go as I please, even in the middle of the night. I just have to have a little company. And the guards aren't bad. They're pretty curious about me and are willing to talk. I don't sense anything like what I sensed in the Tower. Even Magdelena was sweet, in her own terrifying way."

"Can you give me an example?" I asked, not able to imagine anything like what he was talking about.

"Well, um... after I told her about how I shot Baldy and my rank dropped, she said something along the lines of, 'That's too bad, seems to me that you were defending your sister and that stupid net thing of yours just didn't get it. Still, try that crap here, and I'll kick your ass all the way back there and leave you and your friends to rot.'"

I laughed, remembering to press the button down before I was done. "Wow—at least they are honest?"

"I mean, yeah. Brutally so, at times. They told me that they've only ever accepted sixty refugees: a small community of survivors who had run out of water and food, and the remnants of a settlement who had barely escaped that skirmish in the south... Anyway, I'm supposed to get a briefing soon, which is supposed to explain what the next few days will hold for us. I'm trying to get them to accelerate the process. I think it's helped that the files are digitized. I get the feeling that the other civilizations aren't as advanced as us—but it takes time. And I'm apparently meeting with Thomas and Melissa's mother, and she's their head of internal security, which I am guessing is code for being in charge of all the spies, so no pressure on that front."

A spy? That meant she was good at interrogating people. My brother needed to be careful about what he said. I knew he *knew* that, but I said, "Be careful," anyway.

"I will be, don't worry. Anyway, what's going on with you? Is Eric okay?"

"He's fine," I told him. "Already up and trying to help out."

He chuckled. "That must be driving Zoe crazy."

"It is," I replied. Then I sighed. "They're all really excited about getting away from here."

There was a pause that made me nervous for a handful of seconds, as I wondered if we had lost the connection. Then he said, "You sound like you're not."

I bit my lip, glad he couldn't see my face. "I'm not... without excitement. I just... feel weird about leaving things unfinished." I swallowed, worried that my brother would pick up on the fact that I wasn't actually planning to leave, but before I could embellish my answer, he said tersely, "That sounds like you're planning on staying. Which is madness."

Sadness gripped me, then, and I realized that no matter what I said, I wasn't going to get my brother to agree that fighting for the Tower was the right move. He had already abandoned it in his mind, back when he agreed to go in the first place.

Well, he might not agree, but I didn't care anymore. I would let him know I was staying and let him know why.

"I'm not crazy, Alex," I told him. "I just care about what happens to the people who have no idea that the Tower is on the verge of falling apart. I'm a councilor—the Champion. I owe the Tower more than just leaving them to rot. Mom found out that Scipio was broken and wanted to help me save him, and if I don't stop the people who killed her, then all of this will have been for nothing."

It took him a few moments to get it, but when it finally sank in, his response was what I'd expected. "Liana, she gave her life saving Dad, and you and I both know that *he* didn't believe you. Her death was stupid. It didn't achieve anything monumental, and running around the Tower trying to avenge her isn't going to solve anything."

"You're one to talk," I snapped back, rankled by the way he could just dismiss her death like that. "You went insane where Baldy was concerned. You *beat* him, for crying out loud. Don't tell me you were unaffected by her death when you were clearly looking for someone to punish."

Silence again, followed by, "You're right. I was. Which was why I needed to get out of the Tower. Don't you see that living like that is poisoning us? I killed him, Liana, and I was *happy* he was dead. If that's not sick, I don't know what is. And yeah, maybe I don't want to fight for the Tower, but for good reason. It's impossible! The legacies are *everywhere* and can literally change their faces! They've been attacking Scipio for years! Do you think you're the only one who has ever gotten this close to the truth? Do you think they would hesitate to kill you and everyone with you the instant they learned that you were drawing close? Dammit, Liana, there is no one there who can protect you! Scipio is damaged beyond belief and can't be fixed!"

"You don't know that," I retorted hotly. "And by digging, I've managed to find some of his missing pieces." I paused and realized that we were talking about Scipio on the open airwaves, and that the Patrians could be monitoring his call. "We shouldn't be talking about this. I've made my decision, but I want you to keep working on getting the others over there. They want to leave."

"You're really serious," he said. "Liana, don't throw your life away on that place. You don't have to! We have another choice."

I smiled bitterly and looked at the stars. "I realize that. And this is what I've chosen."

"So basically, you're saying that if I negotiate this deal to include you, it won't matter because we won't ever see each other again, save for when Thomas and Melissa bring me back to rescue everyone else, but you?"

I hesitated. "You don't know that. I might be able to get the Tower back on track and Scipio restored. We can bring the matter to the new council, and who knows, maybe start diplomatic relationships. If there's a war to the south, now is a time for making allies."

"Or you could die, which would mean I won't ever see you again," he said hotly. "Dammit, can't you just stop being brave for once in your life? Can't you put yourself before complete and total strangers? I don't want to be here alone."

His anger had evaporated in the middle of his line of questioning, turning into a desolate sadness. My heart ached, and I knew he was coming from a place of love. But that didn't mean a damn thing if I couldn't love myself—and if I abandoned the Tower, I would absolutely loathe myself. "I'm sorry, Alex," I said, trying not to cry. "But I can't do it. I wish I could. I wish I was a different person. But I'm not. I have to stay and fight—it's who I am."

I waited for his response for what felt like eternity, holding back my tears. I wasn't sure what I expected from him, but I knew what I feared the most: his anger and hatred. I didn't want to lose my brother. If anything, I wanted him to get his head right and come back to help. But I had just told him I prioritized other people over him, and there was no predicting how he would react.

"I see." A pause, just long enough for me to perceive absolutely nothing about his emotional state from his tone, followed by, "I should go. I have an early start in the morning."

"Alex..." I trailed off, searching for something to say, but I wasn't even sure what I *could* say. He didn't sound angry, or sad, or upset, or... like anything at all. Just very matter-of-fact. After several long seconds, I whispered, "You know I love you, right?"

"I know. But I need time to think about this. I mean, you should've told me you didn't plan to leave. I might've changed my mind about coming here! And now I have to come back and help you!"

I gaped at the box in my hand, and then frowned. He had a point, but that last part caught me off guard, and I needed a moment to think. "I'm sorry," I said. "But there wasn't exactly time. And..." I sighed, trying to formulate my feelings about him coming back, but could only conjure up uncertainty. "I'm not sure it's a good idea that you come back here. Alex, I don't know why your rank dropped like that after Baldy, but I do know something inside of you broke. The instant I mentioned leaving, you wanted to go! I think... I think that's because you can't handle it here, and that's okay."

"Are you saying you don't want me to come back and help you?" he practically snarled, and I sighed. That wasn't at all what I meant.

"No," I replied carefully. "I'm saying that I don't think you want to."

"You're my sister! I want to be with you."

"You can want to be with me and still want to be away from the Tower," I told him. "Those two things can both be true, Alex. But I also can't handle the idea of you coming back to fight for something that you hate, just for me. If you died or something happened to you, I would never forgive myself."

"That's not fair. Just because I don't think it can be saved doesn't mean..." He trailed off from his biting comment, and then gave a heaving sigh. "I'm sorry. Like I said, I should go. I have to think about this."

I hesitated. My instinct was to press on, to insist that I was right and he needed to stay there. But I had to respect his desire for time. Hell, *I* wanted time. It was best to just let it go. For now.

"Okay, Alex," I finally said. "I'll contact you tomorrow night, okay?"

"Okay. Talk to you later. Be careful, Liana."

"You too."

The line went dead, and I clicked the device off and sighed.

That had gone about as well as I could've hoped. Still, I couldn't help but feel guilty about telling him. Because of me, he was now considering returning to the Tower to help fight. I remembered how broken he had seemed when he talked about our lives here, and I wasn't sure I could let him do that. Coming back here would kill him on the inside, if not get him dead from a legacy attack. Besides, Sadie was undoubtedly aware of his transfer, and was likely wondering what was going on. If she tried to spy on him only to find out he was missing—and then only to have him return—it would raise a lot of questions.

I'd have to talk him out of it if he decided to come back. It was the only way to keep him safe. And if that didn't work, and he did arrive on my doorstep, I'd have to knock him unconscious and send him back with the others. He might spend the rest of his life in Patrus hating me, but at least he would have a life.

Decision made, I turned to go back inside, pointedly ignoring the lone voice inside of me that told me the path I was taking was a very lonely one indeed.

It was right, so why argue?

33

We arrived back at my quarters to find Leo/Grey sitting on one of the sofas. I slowed at the top of the stairs as he looked up at us and rose slowly to his feet, studying him to see who I was dealing with.

"Liana," he said a moment later, and I could tell from the way he said it that I was talking to Leo.

"Leo," I replied, stopping at the first step and looking over at Maddox for help. She blinked at both of us and then pointed a thumb at the hallway.

"You know what, I haven't eaten all day," she said carefully. "I am going to raid the fridge. Excuse me."

I narrowed my eyes at her as she went down the stairs and muttered a soft "Traitor" under my breath. She snorted softly but didn't rise to the bait as she made a hasty exit, leaving Leo and me alone.

I watched her go, and then sighed heavily. After the conversation I had just had with my brother, I wasn't sure I was ready for this. But since he was clearly sitting here waiting for me, I didn't exactly see a way out.

"How are you feeling?" I asked.

His cheeks flushed red. "Stupid," he said. "And still a little tired. I'm going to sit back down, if that's okay."

I nodded, and slowly made my way down the stairs. I didn't sit next to him, but instead leaned against the wall the screen hung on, putting several feet of floor between us. I was still mad at him, in spite of Grey's request for me not to be.

Leo stared at me for several seconds and then sighed. "Liana, I owe you an apology," he finally started, and I crossed my arms, trying not to snort derisively. I was pretty sure that it went without saying, but Leo, being Leo, felt the need to say it anyway. "I shouldn't have put Grey at risk like that. It was foolish, short-sighted, and dangerous. I made you a promise to keep him safe, and I failed you. As soon as his memories are fully restored, I will find a way to move myself from the net into the terminal, and that will be—"

"Stop," I said, having decided I had heard enough. He had apologized for one of the things that he needed to, and I accepted that. But there were other things that we had to discuss before he went making any decisions.

Leo blinked at me in surprise, and then turned wary.

"Before you go any further with your request to be downloaded into the terminal, we need to discuss a few things. Like how you told Grey about our relationship before I got the chance to. Or how you were acting when I was fighting to help you. Did you forget that I promised I would stay and fight with you? Or did you think that my promise was only contingent on us having a relationship? Because let me tell you something, I didn't make it for *you*. I made it for the people in the Tower, and I still stand by it. I may have just damaged my relationship with my brother permanently over it, dammit! And the way you acted this morning… It hurt worse than anything you could've said last night."

Leo's jaw dropped, and he stared at me for several seconds—long enough for me to realize that I had started walking toward him during my impassioned speech, and that I desperately needed air, as I had expended it all in my rant. I couldn't help it. The anger I had buried deep had erupted, and I finally had a target—a justifiable one—that I could use it on.

"You're still planning to stay?" he asked, cocking his head at me. "After everything you've been through?"

"Yes! I swear to Scipio… Why is that so hard for everyone to understand? Everyone wants to go, to run away from our problems and start a new life, but I can't! It's not who I am! I see a problem, and I fix it. It's all I've been doing since this started, and I can't stop now, or nothing any of us has done or sacrificed will have been worth it. Everything you've told me about Lionel's vision of the Tower sounded beautiful, Leo, and I want to see our world become that. I want to make it better. I want to make us hope and dream again. And maybe I'll die in the process, but at least I'll die believing in a future that's better than our reality."

Leo stared at me for several seconds. I could see him struggling, trying to come up with some sort of response to what I'd just said, but I wasn't sure I wanted to hear it. "Grey says he wants to stay and help, too," he announced, and my skin prickled at the oddity of it.

"He heard all of that?" I asked, unable to help myself.

"He did," Leo said. "He mentioned that both of us being here is very invasive, right?"

"Yes," I replied, tension radiating through me. Leo hadn't said anything about his feelings yet, and to be honest, I wanted to know what he was thinking. "So…" I said, trailing off and giving him a little head roll that indicated I was waiting for him to say something.

He leaned back in the sofa, and then reached out to touch the spot next to him. "Would you?" he asked.

I hesitated, and then went around the low table to sit opposite him on the couch. I told myself it was because my legs hurt, and not because I was hoping for him to confess a reversal of his feelings, because I still hadn't had a chance to process what Grey had suggested earlier.

"Thank you," he said, shifting on the couch some so he could face me. "My neck was beginning to hurt."

I stared at him, determined not to make any more small talk until he offered something of substance.

He sighed and looked away. "You're right. I behaved poorly from start to finish. I'm not good at this, Liana. Every time I feel something new, it's so intense that I... I am not sure what to make of it. When it was just me, when I was just code, I never had to question how I felt. But then again, I've never felt anything quite as complex as I have in the past few days. Doubt—not in someone else, but in myself—and fear of losing someone that I... that I care for. I failed you. I didn't get the information we needed from Baldy, and I couldn't control anything he did."

"That wasn't your fault," I said. His words had moved me, but not a lot. I was still angry. "And if you had just *talked* to me about it..."

"I know," he whispered. "Like I said, I'm stupid."

I considered him for a second, and then sighed, about to ask the one question I was afraid to hear the answer to—though it was the one I desperately needed to hear. "Leo, do you care about me, or don't you? Was last night an act? Something to push me away to make things between Grey and me less messy? Or did you really decide that because you couldn't control Baldy, it meant you didn't care about me? Because if it's the last one, I really don't get it. How does his level of control over you equate to you not caring about me? Were you scared when he pointed the gun at me?"

"Terrified," he replied without hesitation, his brown eyes holding mine and letting me see the bleak darkness in them. "I could *feel* his finger on the trigger, and all I could think was that I was going to *lose* you. That I couldn't imagine any moment without you. But it wasn't *strong* enough."

"Or it didn't matter how strong your feelings were to him. He just had that level of control! That's not your fault!"

Leo frowned. "I know what Grey told you. I know about his offer to..."

"Okay, I am not there yet," I told him, holding up a hand. "Right now, this isn't about Grey. It's about you, and your feelings. He seems to think you do care about me, but I want to hear it from you."

"This is all new to me," he admitted softly. "I'm scared."

"Of what?" I asked, curious about what could be so terrifying that he couldn't tell me how he felt.

"Of losing you. Even before Baldy, even when you didn't want to talk about it, I knew that whatever I felt for you was doomed from the start, because of Grey. Then he woke up and wanted to be aware, and I realized... I was never going to have you. That, plus what happened with Baldy..." He shrugged and looked away. "It seemed like the right thing to do."

I stared at him. "You're right, you are stupid." His head whipped back at me, his mouth dropping open, but I didn't feel sorry for him. "Instead of just owning up to what you felt and what we did, you added to an already emotionally charged situation and made it that much more unbearable for the group. And you jeopardized the health of one of us in the process."

He shut his mouth and cringed. "I know. I'm sorry."

I stared at him for a moment or two longer, and then sighed heavily. "But speaking as regular Liana, instead of leader Liana, I am really happy that it was just you trying to push me away. That I can understand. If you'd told me that you never felt anything for me in the first place, that would've broken my heart."

It hurt to admit it, but I had just finished chastising him about being honest regarding his feelings, and it was time for me to be honest about mine. I stared at him for several seconds, heart in my throat, but he didn't leave me hanging long.

"Come here," he said roughly, holding his arms out to me, and I practically threw myself at him, needing his arms around me more than ever. It had been a long, trying couple of days, and it promised to get harder, but in that moment, for the first time since yesterday, I felt safe.

Even if I was still a little sore with him. "I'm still a little mad at you," I told him.

"Yeah, that's fair. I was a really big jerk."

I laughed against his chest, and then paused, suddenly uncomfortable, knowing the moment was being witnessed by Grey. I sobered, and asked, "How's... Grey handling all this?"

Leo was silent for a second, and then let out a sharp laugh. "Um... I'm not sure you want to hear it. It's not exactly... polite."

I pulled away from him so I could peer into his eyes, instantly suspicious. "How do you mean?" I asked, drawing the question out.

Leo was already blushing, but his smile was broad. "He's dutifully reminding me that it's his hand and insisting that it should be placed lower."

I stared at him for a second, feeling where his hand was still resting against my back, only a few scant inches from my butt, and then laughed. "He really is okay with this?" I asked.

"I think he's going to want some time with you, too," Leo said carefully. "But yes, he is surprisingly accepting. I quite like him, actually. I didn't think I did, when we first met, but I really do now that I understand him a bit more. Now that he understands himself and me a bit more as well. His change is unexpected, and yet he seems satisfied with it. He likes the person he is becoming, more than he liked who he was before. I feel guilty, and yet... not. Is that wrong?"

I bit my lip. Grey's personality shift was a bit alarming, but he didn't seem upset about it. If anything, he somehow felt older and wiser, even if he still wasn't fully restored. I could still sense him, the loving, playful man who had made me feel safe enough around him to share my innermost thoughts and secrets. I trusted him with my heart like no other, in a way that Leo couldn't quite fill. But then again, I trusted Leo with my life in a way that I couldn't quite trust Grey. His calm and patient way had also made me feel safe around him, but in a completely different way. Both men had definitely changed. Leo was growing emotionally, while Grew was more mature, and yet somehow, it only made them more attractive to me.

Did I think Leo should feel guilty? No, not at all. If anything, I thought he should feel proud of his personal development, how Grey had affected him, as well as his influence over Grey. The two complemented each other, like they were meant to be united from the very beginning.

I looked up into Leo's eyes, and offered him a tender smile. "No," I told him. "I think if Grey's okay with it, I'm okay with it. I just want both of you to be happy."

Leo returned the smile, his eyes glowing with love. "I'm always happiest when I'm with you."

The sweetness of his words made me weak, and I lowered myself back down against his chest and snuggled against him. His arms folded tight around me, and he just held me—exactly as I had been needing him to for the past few days—with a strong, steady grip that told me that I was safe and secure. My heart felt lighter than ever, swelling with happiness. Both of them were staying with me. Both of them were willing to make this work. I felt loved and safe and cherished.

But more importantly, I didn't feel alone.

34

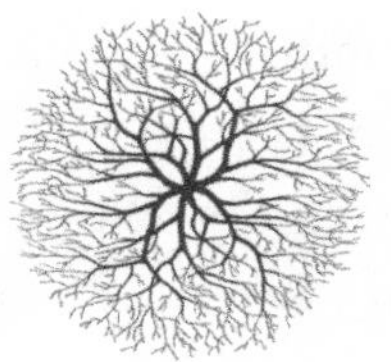

The next morning I found myself winding through the halls of the Medica, Maddox beside me, two cups of a spiced rice drink warm in my hands. We followed the white-clad attendant silently, walking along the pristine surface of the Medica's walls as he led the way to where Sage would be meeting me.

I was nervous, possibly even more nervous than I had been yesterday, but I kept it all behind a pleasant face, while rehearsing in my head my premise for being here. I wanted to talk to him about the upcoming council meeting, and the expulsion chamber vote that was about to be delayed for a second time. I knew it wasn't going to go anywhere, but that was what made it perfect. If I could draw him into an amiable debate, then it might be convincing enough to keep my true purpose—collecting his cup at the end of the meeting—from him. Because if he drank from that cup, I would have some of his genetic material, and could test it against the samples we had gotten from the undocs.

The attendant stopped short of a door with a little green leaf on it, indicating that I was about to enter one of the greenhouses where the Medica grew medicinal plants, and quickly ushered me through as soon as the door opened. I shot a parting glance at Maddox, who mouthed, "Good luck," and then slipped into the room.

The difference between the inside and the outside was like stepping from a freezing shower into a hot bath. The lights in here were warm and yellow, nothing like the antiseptic feeling of the halls outside, and the room was a riot of colors. Green, purple, red, white, orange, lilac—my eyes darted over dozens of different plants hanging from shelves on either side of the aisle the door had deposited me into, drinking in the sight and smell of all the flowers in bloom.

I let myself just look at it for several long seconds, trying to commit the beauty I was seeing to memory, and then started forward, trusting that somewhere in the room, Marcus Sage awaited me.

I once again saw various white-clad individuals doing this and that to the plants. From trimming back some of the leaves to spraying them with chemicals, everyone seemed to be doing their duty. I studied them closely, looking for a sign of the elderly man, but he wasn't in any of the rows that I passed, so I headed deeper.

Like the previous room we'd been in, the shelves came to a stop at the edge of a wide-open space, where numerous metallic-topped tables were set up in long rows, their mirror-like surfaces spotted with pots of plants. Sage was standing in the middle of it all, studying a rather unique flower that was supported by a single stalk. I started toward him, fixing a congenial smile on my face.

He spotted me long before I made it to him, swiveling around to face me as I walked down the row, one eyebrow going up when he spotted the cup in my hand. "Is that for me?" he asked as soon as I drew close enough that we wouldn't be shouting at each other.

"It is," I said, coming to a stop before him and offering him the cup. "It's spiced rice milk." I knew it was his favorite, thanks to Quess. He was Medica-born and knew more about Sage than I did.

"My favorite," Sage exclaimed, a smile growing on his weathered face. "How did you know?"

"Actually, it's *my* favorite," I lied. "And when I went down to get one, I realized it would be rude to show up with no drink for you, so I got you one, too. I hope that's all right."

"Of course it is!" he exclaimed, reaching out to take the cup. "And such a thoughtful gesture on your part. You really didn't have to go through all this trouble for an old man like me."

"It's no bother," I told him. "I'm just glad you like it. Cheers."

The wrinkles in his cheeks and eyes grew more pronounced as his smile broadened, and he quickly touched his cup to mine in good cheer, then took a swig of the sweet, creamy liquid inside. I followed suit, hiding my own smile behind the cup. It was only the first step—I still had to get in and out of this conversation without tipping him off that anything was amiss, and then reclaim his cup before I left—but I felt confident that I could do it.

"Ahhh," he exclaimed, smacking his lips together as he drew the cup away from his mouth. "That's the stuff." He set the cup down and pierced me with a canny look. "Now, I suppose you're up here to explain yourself. Go ahead, I'm ready to hear it."

"Explain myself?" I repeated, the edges of panic starting to roil through me. Scipio help me, had Sage been spying on me? On us? Was he really behind everything, and did he know what we were up to? What if he took the drink because all those people I had passed were legacies, and he knew I wasn't getting out of here?

Had I just stumbled into a trap?

"The DNA samples?" he drew out, giving me an encouraging nod. "The thirty or so samples that didn't come back as matches to anyone in the Tower?"

I blinked in surprise, but it only lasted a few seconds before the horror bled in. Of *course* he knew about the DNA samples. He was the head of the Medica, and all DNA testing happened there. The tech who had performed the tests had likely reported the oddity of all the samples being genetically related and had flagged it in the Medica's system.

But how did Sage know about it? Surely he had better things to do than monitor all flagged genetic specimens. There must have been hundreds of them passing through the Medica on a daily basis. I supposed it was possible he was on the lookout for anything odd that came through his department, but what if it was far more insidious than that? What if he was paranoid because he was a legacy? Hell, we were here to test him for just that.

It was critical that I choose my words carefully. If he was a legacy, then he was trying to pump me for more information on what I was planning, and if this was a trap, getting out of it might depend on my answers. If I made any misstep at all, he would put two and two together, and warn the other legacies.

"I actually wasn't here to talk about that," I told him, putting my cup down on the table and crossing my arms. "Can I ask how you found out about them?"

He gave me a crooked smile. "You think any one of my people wouldn't notify me of proof of undocs, especially in such a great number?" He frowned. "Why did you come here?"

I gave him the prepared story, but quickly readied my next deflection, realizing he had a valid point—the medic who ran the tests would've notified him. "I was here to talk about the expulsion chambers. And the samples you're talking about are part of an ongoing investigation."

"Into what?"

I pressed my lips together into a thin line. "I'm not prepared to make an official statement yet."

"I see." Sage went silent for a few seconds, and then nodded.

"That is sensible, if slightly annoying. But then again, I'm an old man who really doesn't have a lot of patience for these sorts of things. So, let me ask you this: Is the Tower in imminent danger?"

I considered the question. The truth was yes and no, but if he was a legacy, telling him yes would immediately set off alarm bells, because it would indicate to him that I knew more than I should. But if I told him no, he would wonder why I was keeping it a secret. As usual, hedging was the best bet. "Not imminent, no. But yes, some danger does exist."

"And are you doing everything in your power to stop it?"

"Of course," I said, not bothering to lie. "It's kind of the biggest part of my job."

He chuckled and nodded, his head bobbing up and down in duck-like fashion. "It is, at that," he said. "You do realize, of course, that I have to report this to the council, however."

I sucked in a breath. "You do?" I asked, mildly surprised. "Why? I was planning to report it when I had something substantial."

"But you *do* have something substantial. You have proof that there are a considerable number of undocs running around the Tower. At least thirty of them, unless I miss my guess."

I sighed theatrically, trying to blend into my part. "You are not wrong," I told him. "But I had hoped to keep that under wraps until I could round them up. More people knowing about them means more people potentially messing things up for my Knights."

"I understand that," Sage said patiently. "But the fact remains that any proof of undocs roaming around the Tower needs to be brought to the attention of the council! They are a threat to our very way of life and are somehow able to avoid our sensors. That warrants some serious attention, not just from the Knights, but from IT as well."

I could already see where this was going, and realized I needed to stall him. Whatever his intentions—good or bad—it didn't matter. If Sadie found out that I was looking into a large undoc group, she would know I was on to her and the others. It wouldn't take long for her to get them mobilized, and she knew where I lived. In fact, I wouldn't be surprised if they turned around and killed us all to cover their tracks.

"Sir, I appreciate your feelings on this, but I wonder if you could give me some more time. I have a suspicion that someone high up in another department is helping them, and I'd like to avoid embarrassing a department head by publicly exposing one of their direct inferiors if I happen to be right. Can you just give me another day or two to try to figure a few things out? Please?"

Sage gave me a canny look that I wasn't entirely sure how to perceive—like he knew exactly what I was doing—and then sighed and took another sip out of his cup before responding. "Do you really think a citizen of the Tower would help these loathsome creatures?"

"I think it's important not to rule anything out," I replied coolly.

"Wise words. Very well, I will hold off letting the council know until our next meeting, which I believe is in two days. Do you think you will have something concrete by then?"

By then, I hoped to be marching everyone who was a part of the conspiracy into the Council Room to face justice.

"Yes," I replied, feeling light and hopeful. "I really do believe I will."

"Excellent. So now, about these expulsion chambers. What seems to be the problem?"

"No problem, sir, just wanted to see if I could pick your brain about them more. But unfortunately our time is already up. I'm so sorry to come and go, but I've got a debriefing scheduled in about ten minutes."

"Of course, my dear," he replied, waving his hand in the air. "By all means, do not let me get in the way of your duties. I'm just sorry that we didn't get to talk about what you *came* to talk about. Next time, though, eh?"

"Next time," I agreed. "Are you finished with your drink? I can take your cup if you are."

It was risky asking for the cup directly, but given that they weren't disposable, wanting it back wasn't an unreasonable request. I just hoped he didn't do anything crazy, like decide to wash it for me right then and there.

He peered into his mug, eyeing the contents inside, and then lifted it to his lips and took several strong pulls until the cup was empty. "Exceptional," he said, holding the cup out to me. "And thank you for your kindness. You spared me from doing any dishes —my most hated of all chores."

I forced a chuckle of agreement that I did not feel. I actually liked doing the dishes, but he didn't need to know that. Besides, letting him think that I hated the chore as well went a long way to show how generous I was being doing it for him. It would tell him that I wanted his approval and put him more at ease.

He held the cup out to me, and I took it, trying not to look too excited that he was handing me DNA that would prove or disprove his role in the legacies—or at least the undoc army—once and for all. It was hard not to flee from him afterward, propelled by a desire to start processing the test as quickly as possible, but I managed, giving him a polite farewell before heading back the way I had come.

And with that, we had everything we needed to hopefully figure out who had been kidnapping women from the Tower and forcing them to have children to populate their army. Whoever he was, this patriarch of the family, he was controlling things in some way. I was sure of it.

All we needed now was to do this DNA testing without him realizing it, figure out where the undocs were hiding now, and round them up—along with all of Sadie's spies—*without* drawing Sadie's attention, and then present them to the council.

Easy peasy.

35

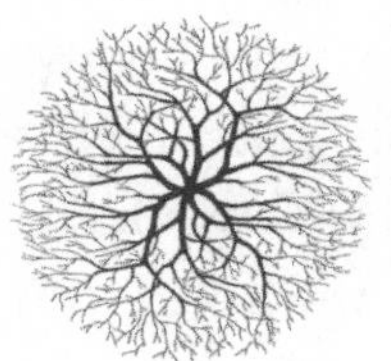

The next meeting I had was with yet another department head, and though I wasn't quite as nervous as I had been with Sage, I was still slightly apprehensive. Because Sage was an unknown, but the danger from Lacey Green was very real.

Lacey was a legacy from a different family, one working to protect Scipio. And our relationship was rocky at best. She had blackmailed me and my friends into protecting her cousin Ambrose, and we had failed. She wanted us to find the men responsible, and every day that passed without us taking anything tangible to her was another day that she lost her patience. She still had evidence that proved we had tampered with Scipio's code to get away with murder, and she was going to use it if I didn't come through for her.

But now I was going to give her what she wanted; it was half the reason I had requested the meeting in person. It just required her to give me something as well—not only by adding her forces to my own so we could arrest every legacy as quickly as possible, but also information about Kurt, the fragment AI her family had stolen in an attempt to save him from the other legacies.

It was risky to confront her on this—she would no doubt kill to keep Kurt's existence a secret—but we didn't have a choice. Bringing a case against not one, but two council members, along with over a hundred people, meant exposing what they had done to both the council and Scipio, and the fragments were essential if we wanted to prove that they were guilty. I hoped that once they started testifying, Scipio would finally be forced to acknowledge the damage to his own code. At which point we could start making progress toward putting the Tower back on track.

I glanced around at the four men and women surrounding Maddox and me—Lacey's escort—and then back at the hall ahead of me, trying to guess at what Lacey's reaction to all this would be. The halls were largely deserted, as Lacey had invited us during the middle of a work shift in this section, and that made the entire sub-level feel oddly imposing. Like it was threatening to engulf us.

I tried to shake the feeling away, reminding myself that we had *good* news for Lacey. We could finally give her the people who had killed her cousin. We had uncovered, in one of Sadie's files, the identities of the six individuals who had attacked him, as well as several others who had caused us problems during the Tourney. A few of them were now safely entrenched in different departments, their faces modified by plastic surgery, but the bulk of them were still with the undoc forces, awaiting plastic surgery before they could be reassigned.

While we didn't have the location for the undocs yet, I was still hopeful that I could get it from Liam. He didn't seem to like the people he was related to any more than we did, and I was praying that I could somehow exploit that to get him to tell us where we could find his family. I didn't want to have to resort to other measures to extract the information from him, like uploading Leo into his brain to find out what he knew.

Maybe we'd catch a break, and Dylan or Eric would find something out while they were following Plancett or Dreyfuss.

Either way, I was going to find the information I needed before I could make this plan a reality, and I was going to need Lacey's and Praetor Strum's help executing it. Which was why I had requested a meeting with Lacey right after my meeting with Sage.

We turned left down one of the side passages and were faced with rows and rows of doors that I knew led to apartments. The halls here were poorly lit compared to the lights of the rest of the Tower, the UV lights flickering periodically, and I frowned when I saw that, wondering why the problem hadn't been fixed yet. Cogstown prided itself on having everything functioning in their department, so it seemed odd and out of place that they would have ignored this.

The lead man stopped at an apartment about halfway down and turned around to face us. "In here," he said with a brusque nod.

"Thanks," I replied dryly. I knew from a previous meeting with Lacey that this wouldn't be her apartment, but one of her workers', borrowed at random so she could host clandestine exchanges such as these. I hit the button on the door, and it opened automatically, skipping the normal security scan.

I stepped through the door into a small hallway, which deposited me into a living area that clearly didn't belong to a family unit. The entire living area was antiseptic, devoid of the small touches that made a place a home. So this was dormitory housing, where young Cogs were placed until they started families of their own.

Lacey was sitting at a table, leafing through an orange Mechanic manual, but she wasn't alone. To my surprise, Strum was here as well, leaning over her shoulder and staring down at the manual she was flipping through.

"It's about time you got here," the woman said, putting the

manual down with a loud slap. "I thought we were going to have to wait forever."

I stared at her, trying not to roll my eyes at the thinly veiled hostility in her voice. Instead, I made a show of pulling back the sleeve of my uniform to reveal the flat black disk of my indicator and swiped it over to the clock function. "Three minutes early," I reported tightly.

Lacey's mouth tightened, but she didn't reply other than to cross her arms and lean back in the chair. "Call me a little suspicious, then. I thought I told you I didn't want any more face-to-face meetings until you caught Ambrose's killers." Her brown eyes widened theatrically as she craned her neck around, searching for people she knew for a fact weren't there. "I don't see them. Are they invisible?"

"Do you want to know why we requested a meeting or not?" Maddox retorted, losing her temper in the face of Lacey's bitterness. "Because we can go and—"

"It's fine, Maddox," I said, interrupting her. I gave her a look that told her there was no point in getting upset, and then turned back to Lacey. "We found them."

"Who?" Lacey asked, her eyebrows coming together. "Ambrose's killers?"

I nodded, and a slow, predatory smile developed on her face. "Where?"

"It's not so simple," I told her, sitting down in a chair across from them. "It's not just Ambrose's killers, but the entire legacy group that you've been after."

Lacey blinked at me several times, her expression wavering between disbelief and eagerness, and it was Strum who took over for her. "How do you know?" he asked.

"Because we broke into Sadie's quarters," I replied. "Speaking of which, I'm going to need both of you to reset your quarters using the virus on this." I reached into a pocket on my sleeve and pulled out a data stick as I spoke, setting it on the table and sliding it toward Lacey. Strum reached out and caught it, his long fingers snapping it up.

"You reset your own quarters?" Lacey asked, and I was amused at the dumbfounded look on her face. "*Wait.* You *broke* into *Sadie's*?" The alarm in her voice and eyes was only rivaled by the impressed look Strum was giving us. "Are you insane? Sadie's assistant—"

"Was knocked offline," I said, cutting her off. I didn't want her to start nitpicking over the details of my plan. We didn't have time. "The virus reset it, covering all the records of our coming and going. So you can relax; she won't know it was me. However, it would be helpful if at least one of you would reset your own quarters, to make sure Sadie buys that the rooms resetting themselves is just an unfortunate glitch."

"Why did you do this?" Strum asked, finally breaking his silence. "What was in Sadie's quarters, and how does doing this relate to Ambrose's killers?"

I took a deep breath and prepared to drop my first truth bomb. "Sadie is a legacy. I'm not sure if she's at the top or if there is someone above her, but we uncovered evidence in her terminal that proves it. She also has a legacy net." Lacey gave me a look that read, 'How do you know that,' and I shrugged and said, "I had to wear it to get access to her quarters."

Lacey's jaw dropped, and then quickly snapped shut. A moment later, she was up and moving, pacing back and forth across a small stretch of floor. "So Sadie's another legacy. I thought we'd weeded them all out of the council with Devon, but... argh!" She stopped suddenly and kicked out a nearby chair, sending it flying into the next room. The violence of it surprised me, and I leaned back, studying her.

"Calm down, Lace," Strum said. "We couldn't have known."

"No, you're right, we couldn't have known! That's the point,

Strum. We never know! We are fighting in absolute darkness! For every one of them we kill, another three move around and get their fingers into something else! When is this ever going to be over? When are we ever going to be done?"

"Soon," I said, giving her an answer that I knew the Praetor couldn't. That brought their attention back to me, and I rolled with it, knowing we had a lot more ground to cover. "I have a list of her entire network, including spies stationed inside the other departments. There are a few details I need to collect before I can act, but once I have them figured out, I'm going to make a move on every single one of them. But I need your help to do it."

"Our help?" Lacey folded her arms across her chest and looked at Strum, seeming to communicate something to him nonverbally. For all I knew, they were communicating using their neural transmitters to have a private conversation while we were here. But honestly, I didn't care. If it helped them come to some sort of consensus sooner, I was all for it. "I suppose we can assist you in executing them," she said.

I blinked. That wasn't exactly what I had been expecting, and it definitely wasn't a good sign. If their first response to the problem was to kill everyone, without even considering a legal option, it meant that they weren't going to take too kindly to the idea when I presented it. If anything, they could deny us the manpower outright, and then we'd be in a little bit of trouble.

But they were just going to have to get over it. My information, my rules. "We're not going to execute them," I informed them. "We're going to arrest them, all of them, and then we're going to hold a special council meeting to try to convict them."

For several long seconds, no one said anything. Then Lacey said, "You're serious?" I nodded, and she suddenly sat down, as if her knees weren't capable of holding her up. "But... can you prove what she's done to Scipio?"

I inhaled and exhaled slowly, and then seized upon the

entrance her words had given me. "Not in the way you think, but definitely, yes. We both can."

"We *both* can?" she repeated, looking confused. "What do you mean?"

"It's simple. I let the fragment AIs I've managed to rescue from Sadie's legacy group testify, and you let Kurt do the same." I watched her closely, worried that I was pressing her too far with the demands today.

Lacey's face paled, her eyes growing wide. "How do you know about that?" she demanded. "How could you possibly—"

I reached up and tapped the back of my neck. "You gave me the net," I told her. "You didn't think I would wonder why I couldn't retain certain memories after they happened?"

"You tampered with the security lock we put on there." Lacey exhaled with a groan. "Of *course* you did. I knew giving you a net was a mistake."

"Mistake or not, it doesn't change the fact that I know about Kurt, nor that I have Jasper and Rose. With them giving testimony about what happened to them, we can—"

"I don't have Kurt," she cut in abruptly, and now it was my turn to frown.

"But the memory..."

"Lacey's great-grandfather, three generations removed, and his sister," Strum said, his face grim. "My family was allied to Lacey's even then, and my ancestors found their bodies thirty-three minutes after they downloaded Kurt—in that same room, where they were murdered. Kurt was never recovered. Presumably he was stolen by the murderers."

I leaned back in my chair, my heart pounding. Lacey didn't have Kurt? Then who did? He wasn't on Sadie's computer—Leo would've found him if he had been. But if he wasn't there, was it possible she was keeping him somewhere else? And if so, how could we find him? If she didn't have him... then who did?

And how were we ever going to learn what happened to him?

I wasn't sure, but it didn't change our course of action. Just having Rose and Jasper should be more than enough to convince Scipio that he had been tampered with, and force Sage—if he wasn't our enemy—to support the arrest of the two council members who were.

"That's disappointing," I said in a gross understatement. "But it changes nothing. I still have two fragment AIs—"

"I didn't say I didn't have one," Lacey interrupted coolly. "I do. It's just not Kurt. It's Tony."

"Tony?" I asked, blinking. "Wait, how did you get Tony? Did you manage to steal him before someone else got him?"

Lacey shook her head. "No," she said softly. "Tony found me. And I do mean *me*. When I was twenty years old, before I ever became Lead Engineer. He somehow managed to break free from Scipio's code in the Core and transferred himself into the Cogs' mainframe, trying to escape the legacies before they took him, too. We started developing all of these glitches, and I was dispatched to figure out what was causing it. To my surprise, it was both a who and a what. But I'm not sure how much his testimony is going to help you. He's... practically a child in his mannerisms."

It took me a moment to respond to her comment, mostly because I had a hard time wrapping my head around the fact that Tony had just shown up in the Cog mainframe. I supposed it was possible that had he feared for himself and figured out a way to disconnect from Scipio to keep the people who were stealing the other fragments from getting him, too.

The fact that he was a child in his mannerisms was a little surprising to me, given what I had read in the report on him. From all accounts, he was Scipio's creativity, but they never mentioned him being childlike. Still, I doubted Scipio would care about that when it came to testimony. Besides, he needed to know what had been done to him. And if Tony only came into Sadie's life twenty years ago, then it stood to reason that he had witnessed every other fragment being taken. He might be the best possible witness.

"He will need to testify," I told her. "His story is just as important as the others."

Lacey gave me a look. "I don't want to risk his safety."

I smiled with what I hoped was more reassurance than dark, bitter humor. "If we manage to grab every single legacy in one night, then we won't be risking anything. They won't be able to control Scipio's response, and we'll have all the evidence."

"Not to mention one of the councilors in handcuffs," Strum said.

"Two," I retorted, earning me a shocked look. "Plancett has been working with Sadie to keep his people out of the expulsion chambers."

"He might've also fathered an undoc army," Maddox added. "Him, Sage, or this old Knight named Jathem Dreyfuss. Someone has been kidnapping women from around the Tower and forcing them to have their children, and we've narrowed it down to three men."

"Based on what parameters?" Lacey asked. "Who is Jathem Dreyfuss?"

I hesitated, and then dismissed the question with a simple "It's not important. What is important is that we need a way of running another blood comparison outside of the Medica, so as not to tip Sage off. I have the DNA from each of those men, but I need a comparison made to the files we have, to figure out who is fathering those undocs." I produced a second data stick from a different pocket and handed it to Strum, while Maddox placed the plastic-wrapped cup, handkerchief, and hair we had taken from the three men on the table. "Can you do it?"

"I can," Strum said. "Which is which?"

"I'm not telling you that," I told him, standing up. "I don't want either of you running off and killing him before I have a chance to arrest him and bring him up on charges. As soon as I have the information I need, and everything's confirmed, I will tell you—but I want him taken alive, along with the rest of them. Is that acceptable to both of you?"

The two were silent for a long time. "It is," Strum said. "If it finally ends all of this once and for all... then it is."

"Good," I said. "Send me the results as soon as you get them. I'll keep you updated as things occur."

"Good," Lacey said. "It's about time you started improving in that area."

I shot her a death glare as I left, but to my surprise, she smiled—and it looked genuine.

I just wished it didn't look quite so bloodthirsty. But I let it go. I had my support, and soon would know which of the three men was responsible for fathering over thirty people. Then I would just need to figure out where the undocs were now.

36

The waiting was the worst part, but luckily Maddox, Leo, Quess, and I still had a lot to do in regard to creating our case against Sadie, which provided us with a productive way to pass the time. We also had our evening check-in with Alex, who was fine, but didn't have anything new to update us on as far as the Patrians were concerned. The next morning found us all planted in the war room, continuing to sift through the files Jasper was still decrypting, trying to collect as much information about Project Prometheus as possible. There was a lot of extraneous data to sort through, even with Jasper pulling the unrelated stuff out. Schematics, blueprints, lists of people, dates, names, times... Not to mention a detailed list of everything they did to Rose to make her revert back to Jang-Mi. Nothing to tell us what their final plan for Scipio was. Nothing to tell us what their ultimate plans for the Tower were.

To make things easier, we had split certain things up. Medical reports from Dr. Smiley went to Quess, so he could figure out what they were about, while Maddox handled schematics and blueprints, trying to identify places and devices that would be perfect for sabotage. Leo handled anything AI-related and was searching through those files to see if he could figure out exactly how the legacies were influencing Scipio's vote. Removal of the fragments wasn't enough; they had to be using something to force him to vote the way they wanted, and we needed to know what that was, so we could make sure to destroy it.

Or at least make Scipio himself aware of it. I was praying that he could break out of it himself, once he understood it was there, but I didn't know for certain. None of us did, really. Not even Jasper.

But we were hoping that understanding would help, which was why Leo was on it. I was helping Maddox with the blueprints, although my goal was slightly different from hers: I was looking for possible locations for the undoc legacies. Tian had told me that she had caught Liam outside of Water Treatment, so I was certain their new home was somewhere in there, and I was betting that in all of these files, there had to be a clue regarding where they were. I wanted to do everything I could to try to find it before I was forced to go in and start questioning Liam.

A momentary pang of regret came over me, and I set the pad down for a second and rubbed my eyes. I really didn't want to have to question a sixteen-year-old boy as to the whereabouts of his family members, but as soon as Lacey got the test results back, she would be on me to know when we were going to make our move against the legacies. And I already had a deadline set in place by Marcus Sage.

Tomorrow. The council meeting wasn't until later in the morning, but it wasn't a lot of time to have everything in place. And if we didn't, then Sadie was going to find out we were after her people and move them again. Which would make Liam's information useless, as he likely wouldn't know where the new place was.

"Liana," Quess said, interrupting my thoughts. I blinked up at him and saw an excited grin on his face.

"What is it?" I asked, leaning forward.

"I think I figured out who Dr. Smiley is," he replied, his smile growing. "And I was right. Looking at the pictures did help."

I cocked my head at him, confused. "I'm going to need a little bit more than that. How did the pictures help?"

"Look, there are over one hundred legacies running around, and excluding those who are too young to be used as spies yet, that left about eighty who had gotten the surgery at one point or another. After compiling the before-and-after pictures to create a record of the changes made, I noticed that there was one person we'd seen before whose picture has never been included."

It took me a second to understand the significance, but when it hit me, I was impressed by Quess's cleverness. Whoever the plastic surgeon was couldn't operate on his own face, so there would be no file for him to send. And if we'd seen him before, then that meant Quess would recognize when he was missing. "Who?" I demanded.

"The other guy who was in the Medica with Devon and Baldy after they took Maddox."

Plain-Face. I had been wondering how he fit into this. "Do we know where he is?"

"Yes," Quess replied. "I fed the pictures into central command's mainframe, and was able to match everyone but the undocs, except for one person. I looked him up, and it's him. His name is Eustice Crowley." He tapped on his pad, and the lights on the holographic table coalesced into a profile, complete with pictures of a creepily plain-looking man whose eyes seemed to be watching me even now. I recognized him instantly, and my hand balled into a fist. "And he's never had any plastic surgery?"

"Not once. But what's more, his file shows that he was Medica-born and bred. He even got into medical school, but transferred out in his third year to go into IT. And he's definitely related to the others. Blood was collected at the scene that matched the other samples taken from the bridge and the legacy house in the Attic."

My lips thinned. He might be placed in IT, but it was only so he could perform the plastic surgery in an environment that Sadie could control. But that also meant we couldn't grab him without alerting Sadie. It was going to take careful planning to get to him and the other legacies she had in IT, but we were one step closer now. "Good work," I told Quess. "That's one down, only a few more to—"

"Sorry to interrupt," Jasper cut in smoothly, and I looked up and over my shoulder at the screen on which his face had appeared. "But you're getting an incoming call from Eric and Zoe. Should I patch them through the speakers?"

I blinked and looked down at my wrist. Sure enough, my indicator was blinking that I had a net call, but now that I had Cornelius, he fielded my calls for me. Which meant Jasper had taken over the job. "Yes," I said. "Go ahead."

There was a burst of static, followed by, "Liana, Dreyfuss just met with someone who I think you fought in the qualifiers of the Tourney." Eric spoke in a low voice, and I blinked in surprise.

"Wait, what? How could you know that?" I asked. We had the pictures of those individuals thanks to the initial investigation conducted by Astrid Felix, but they used plastic surgery to redisguise people after their cover had been blown, making it impossible for them to be recognized.

"I obsessed over those vid files for days," he replied.

"He did," Zoe confirmed a moment later. "He's been looking for a way to make himself more useful to the group and started by practically memorizing everything Astrid gave us, including the vid files from the Tourney, so he might know what he is talking about."

"I do," he said insistently. "I figured plastic surgery was all about modifying faces, but there are identifying marks all over people that make them stand out, including birthmarks and mannerisms. Anyway, one of the guys in your fight had a birthmark shaped like a bee right under his hairline on the back of his neck. Huge purple thing—hard to miss. I was watching Dreyfuss when a guy in a Knight's uniform showed up at his stall, the same damn mark on his neck."

A Knight's uniform? We knew Sadie had legacies in the Knights Department, but had they actually had the audacity to put him *back* inside after he had already committed a crime there? I looked over at Maddox. "Do you have the files on the Knights who were missing after Ambrose's attack?"

She nodded, and quickly tapped a few buttons on her pad. A moment later, several pictures began to form over the table, projected holographically for us all to see. "I'll eliminate the woman, but I can't see their necks. Eric, which one was he?"

"Thompson, I believe," Eric said, and Maddox quickly pulled up his picture, revealing a young man with dark blond hair and muddled hazel eyes. I vaguely remembered him in the fight. I thought Leo had taken him out.

"Did you catch the name he's using?" I asked Eric, hoping he managed to at least get the last name from where it was sewn into our uniforms.

"I did. It's Andrews now."

I looked over at Quess. "Tell me that name matches the one from Sadie's list."

Quess nodded and managed to look even more smug. "And, his name matches one of five aliases and faces he's used, according to Dr. Smiley's pictures. Look." He swiped the screen and four more faces floated up next to the one Maddox had pulled up.

Side by side, I could see the resemblance between each man—the changes that were made to his jaw, lips, eyes, mouth, ears, and nose—growing more and more pronounced with each figure. "Five faces," I said, appalled. "That's horrific."

"He's only twenty-three," Quess added, and I wasn't sure why he had thought to mention it. It certainly didn't help calm the queasy twist of my stomach as I realized just what lengths these people would go to in order to accomplish their goals.

"Eric, when they met—"

"They made an exchange," he said, cutting me off. "I'm not sure of what, but I think it was a net. He left, but I couldn't follow him and leave Dreyfuss alone. Dylan's with Plancett on another level, and I wasn't going to let Zoe follow him without backup."

She snorted, the sound causing a loud static pop in the speakers, but held her tongue, giving me a moment to think.

I considered what he was saying, but realized it probably wasn't a good idea to follow anyone we knew for sure was a legacy, lest they figure out what we were up to. Besides, we were planning to move on them as soon as Lacey finished up the DNA tests. "Let him go," I told Eric. "We know where he's going to be."

Eric was quiet for a moment. "Okay. Any word on the tests?"

"Actually, you've just received a message from Lacey Green, marked priority," Jasper informed us. "Do you want me to read it?"

I looked around the table to where everyone was watching me, their eyes reflecting different degrees of curiosity. "Yup," I told him. "Go ahead and read it."

There was a pause, followed by, "So, it seems that of the three samples you gave her, the hair tested positive as having a paternal relationship with all thirty-four original samples. She informs you that she can have her people ready to mobilize within an hour, followed by what could be construed as a backhanded compliment."

"That sounds like Lacey," Zoe said lightly through the speakers. "So that means Dreyfuss is the father?"

It did. I couldn't help but feel a grim sense of satisfaction that

I'd been right. Dreyfuss was the man who had escalated the legacies' plans twenty-five years ago, when the Patrians unexpectedly showed up at the Tower. The legacies must not have wanted to establish diplomatic relations until *they* had control over the Tower, and they knew that they only had a limited amount of time before other explorers came. Maybe Sparks had been the head then, but I was betting Dreyfuss played a part in the decision and was now helping Sadie carry it through. It made sense. I wasn't sure yet why they were working together as partners exactly, but maybe he just controlled the undoc side of things, while she helped him from the inside. Either way, hiding him under the guise of a retired Knight was the perfect cover for a leader of a terrorist cell.

"Yes," I said. "So that's one of two problems down."

"Hold up," Maddox interjected, waving a hand in the air. "So Sage is *what* in all this? The guy who got away? If you're right, then this Dreyfuss guy had Roark's wife and a whole lot of people killed, but somehow missed Sage, who also knew about the whole thing? What's up with that?"

"You do realize that there have been multiple attempts made on Sage's life, right?" Quess asked, before I could even formulate a response. "People who were upset at him for quarantining sections of departments and letting their family members die of disease, people he's kicked out of the Medica, any of his leads who want to be in charge... The old man has shown a remarkable ability to survive all of them."

I frowned. "I've never heard of there being attempts on Sage's life," I told him. And I suspected that was intentional. Gossip in the Tower had always been manipulated in one way or another by the council, even when certain subjects were supposed to be classified. The expulsion chambers were an example of that. They allowed the gossip because it served their interests to have rumors circulating about them, as it helped keep the populace in line. And by that same token, they wouldn't want anyone to know if one of their own had come under attack.

So how did *Quess* know?

"How do you know that?" I asked.

"My father talked about it a few times," Quess replied. "He isn't the biggest fan of Sage and tended to bemoan the fact that the old man survived all those attempts."

I blinked. Quess had never really talked about his family, let alone told us that his father didn't support Sage. I had been under the impression that the Medica staff grumbled about Sage being in power for nearly eighty years, but it was all in good fun. Now, hearing that actual attempts had been made...

It only furthered my belief that they were targeting him in some way. Maybe they'd targeted him several times, and when that hadn't worked, they had moved on to other means, like slowly setting him up as a fall guy should their ration card or DNA schemes become exposed. Maybe it wouldn't be enough to convict him, but he'd definitely lose the department in the next election, which could've been their plan all along, to try to get more control over the council.

Either way, it meant that every piece of the puzzle was there, save for one.

"I need to go have a chat with Liam," I announced to the others. "I need to see if he can give us the location of the undocs."

"Do you really think he'll tell you anything?" Maddox asked.

I honestly wasn't sure, but I couldn't give him any more time to come around. I also couldn't wait for Dylan and Eric to figure out where their hideout was. If Dreyfuss was smart, he'd maintain as much distance as possible, and I doubted they would entrust the information to Plancett, given that he wasn't related to them. Once I got into that room, I wouldn't be leaving until I had an answer. There had to be some magical combination of words that would reach him, and I just had to find them.

"I don't know. But Sage is going to tell the council that I've uncovered nearly thirty-five undocs, which will prompt Sadie to move her people again. And if she does that, we lose whatever chance of finding them we might have had, and the whole plan goes down the toilet. Unless we have all the legacies, and the people controlling them, this doesn't work. We have to know where they are *now*."

Maddox gave me a doubtful look, but I didn't let it deter me. I stood up, nodded at everyone, and then made my way to Liam's room.

I was halfway there when Leo caught up with me. "Liana, wait," he called, and I stopped and gave him a surprised look.

"For what?" I asked, curiosity burning through me. He'd still been sleeping when I slipped out of bed this morning, and we hadn't had a chance to talk since last night. "Is everything okay?"

"Of course," he said with a lopsided smile. "I just wanted to see if I could help. Or rather, Grey would like to help. He's pretty good with young people, and I know firsthand, from his memories, that he is correct. We figured..." He trailed off and then gave me an embarrassed look. "Sorry," he said. "Grey interrupted me to say that he doesn't need my endorsement. When he says he's good at something, he's good at something."

I was stunned for a heartbeat, confused by the rapid shift in conversation and the fact that I had witnessed an exchange between Grey and Leo that I hadn't been able to overhear. It was then that I decided that of all the hurdles we had to jump through to make any relationship between the three of us work, that was going to be the first one—especially if we ever got into a fight. I was pretty sure the internal conversation between them was going to drive me crazy.

But this wasn't the time to bring it up, so I just nodded. "I'd love to have you and Grey with me. I need all the help I can get with this kid."

He smiled tentatively. "I'll let him take over now."

I nodded, and then, on impulse, kissed him. "See you soon."

His smile brightened even more, and then he closed his eyes. A second later, they were open again, and I could tell it was Grey by the salacious look he gave me. "If Leo gets a kiss goodbye, do I get a kiss hello?" he asked in a husky voice.

"Hey, I thought you were just happy that it was your body," I joked, but I stepped closer to him and went up on my tiptoes to kiss him. Unlike Leo, who accepted the kiss with surprised approval, Grey immediately wrapped his arms around my waist and drew me closer until not a millimeter of space was left between us. I moaned as he drew my lower lip into his mouth and then used the opportunity to slip his tongue over it, tasting me. I shuddered at the invasion and grabbed the back of his neck, my own hunger mounting.

He broke the kiss after a few more skin-sizzling seconds, taking a step back and panting slightly. "See, Leo?" he said, and I gave him a confused look, wondering why he was addressing Leo out loud. "That's how you kiss the girl you're crazy about."

My cheeks flushed, and I gaped at him. "Tell me you are not teaching Leo how to kiss me," I groaned.

"Of course I am. I've got to make sure that when he's behind the wheel, he's at least doing things right."

I shook my head, torn between laughing and smacking him. A laugh finally escaped me, and I rolled my eyes. "You are a piece of work, Grey."

"Yes, but you love me anyway. Sucker."

I laughed at that, enjoying how lighthearted our banter was, but all too soon I remembered what we were doing in the hall, and sobered. "We... um... We should probably get this over with," I said.

"After you," he replied. I hit the button on the door the second we arrived and stepped through the portal as the door slid open.

Liam stood up from the chair he was sitting in, a wary look on his face.

"What do you want?" he demanded, taking a step back as we entered. I caught movement from the side of the room and turned to see Tian sitting cross-legged on the bed, her chin in her hands, watching Liam.

"That's not how you treat guests, Liam," she said imperiously. "You don't just demand to know what they want. You've got to say 'hi' first and ask them how they are."

Liam didn't look at her, but his words acknowledged that he had heard her. "I would, except they are here, and they want something from me."

"That makes you smart," Grey said from beside me. "I'm Grey. And you're Liam. And we're going to talk now."

"Don't want to talk," the boy said sullenly. "I want to leave."

"You know that's not going to happen," I said softly. "I'm sorry, but it can't. Your family has been trying to take down Scipio for several generations, and it ends now."

"So you're going to kill them," Liam retorted. "You're right. I'm *not* stupid."

"Liam, no one is talking about killing them," Grey started, but I put a hand on his shoulder and stopped him before he could go any further.

"Don't lie to him," I said grimly. "It doesn't do us any good. Liam, the truth is that if this goes according to plan, then they will be found guilty, and will likely be put into the expulsion chambers. Maybe not the children, but... you're old enough to be tried as an adult." His face grew pale, so much so that his freckles seemed bright by comparison. He turned away, but I didn't stop speaking. He needed to hear the truth. "We know that they are your family, Liam, and we know that all of you share one single father, but your mothers were kidnapped from Tower society and forced to get pregnant."

"Stop," he said, his shoulders hunching.

"That's not your fault, Liam," I told him, coming around so that we were facing each other. "I'm not trying to say that it is. But you know about it, don't you? And you never said or did anything to stop it."

He cringed, his eyes filling with pain. "That's not fair," he mumbled.

"No, it's not," I said, in perfect agreement. "But it probably wasn't very fair for your mother, either. You didn't have a choice about being born, but you're old enough to decide for yourself—and now it's time to do that. Do you want to protect people like that? Do you want to wage war on a way of life that you've never even gotten the chance to experience, let alone agree with?"

"Scipio is an abomination!" he spat. "He is content to leave humanity to stagnate and rot, making us fat and lazy, with no dreams for the future. He doesn't let us survive; he grinds us down, robbing us of the things that make us *human*! He doesn't deserve to—"

A pillow hit him squarely in the face, and I blinked in surprise as Tian pulled it back and then unleashed another blow at him, cutting off whatever legacy dogma he was about to feed us. He lifted his arms in defense, blocking it, but it didn't stop her from pulling it back over her shoulder again, her face flushed with anger.

"You're so stupid!" she shouted at him, launching another blow with the pillow. "Do you even hear yourself?" Another hit, this time to the solar plexus, forcing him back a few steps. "You let them force women to get pregnant, have babies, and die when it became too much for them!" A shot to his side, partially deflected. I briefly entertained the idea of intervening, but it was only a pillow. Besides, Tian was laying down some serious truth. "You slept on the floor, under dirty blankets made out of old uniforms! You ate food that was made over two hundred years ago! All because you think Scipio is bad for us? Worse than what you were seeing around you? You are a stupid, *stupid* boy." Hit, hit, hit, until suddenly Tian stopped, her chest heaving, her blue eyes filling with tears. "You need to do a good thing right now and tell us how to find them."

Liam's chin quivered, and he looked away, seeming to fold in on himself. I held my breath for several seconds, afraid even an exhalation would cause him to lock up and shut down on us.

"If our mom dies when we come out, we're called runts by the others," he said, his voice hollow, and I knew that his mother had died having him. My heart bled for him, and I longed to wrap my arms around him and give him a hug, but I held off, sensing that he wasn't finished. Not by a long shot. "The others get taken away from theirs when they're old enough." He didn't explain what that meant, and I didn't ask. Somehow, I knew that particular detail would only make it worse. Any age was too young to be taken from your mother. "We aren't raised by a single person, after that. I guess everyone cares for us in their own way, but mainly they leave us alone. As long as we follow the rules, we don't get a whoopin' or thrown off the Tower." He gave me a soulful glance, his eyes shimmering. "I watched them do it twice. Once to a boy who was only six, when he left the main room to explore, and another time to a girl who was sixteen. She'd gone out to meet a boy she was sweet on in the farming department. They killed them. And you expect me to fight against that?"

He made a fair point. "You couldn't, until now," I replied. "But if you tell me where your family is hiding, then I will. I promise you that."

His eyes darted to Tian, questioning.

"Liana keeps her word to the best of her ability," Tian told him with a sage nod, and I shot her an appreciative smile.

"If they find out it was me..." He trailed off, and I knew he didn't need to say anything else. The rest might as well have had a big red neon arrow pointed to the words "They're going to kill me."

"They won't," I reassured him. "Baldy is already dead, so he can't hurt you now anyway. Now, tell me where they are. Please."

He absorbed the news of Baldy's death by growing very still. I couldn't tell how he felt about the news, and for several seconds, he said nothing. "Really?" he asked at last, and I heard the faintest sound of hope curling through his words.

"Really," I confirmed for him. He glanced up at me then back down, clearly considering everything in a new light. I could tell he was hovering on the edge of his decision, and it felt like eternity waiting for him to decide. I couldn't make out much beyond his pensive face, but I felt confident that some of what we said to him had gotten through. Still, the urge to shake him cropped up a half dozen times or so, each one more powerful than the last.

"Our new home is over the hydro-turbines," he finally said. "Hidden between Turbines 2 and 3, in an unused monitoring facility."

I looked over at Tian, who was wearing a satisfied smile on her face, her eyes already seeking and holding my own. "I told you there was a good hiding place over the hydro-turbines," she crowed, her blue eyes sparkling with mischief.

She was right, and while I was happy for her victory, my mind was already whirling. Over the hydro-turbines was perfect; Strum would know how to get in and out of there unnoticed, as the turbines belonged to Water Treatment. We knew who the father of all the undocs was and had enough evidence between Sadie's files and the three AI fragments to sink them all.

Now all we had to do was round every last legacy up before Sadie, Plancett, or Dreyfuss noticed what we were up to.

37

The hours after Eric's call and Lacey's message consisted of a whirlwind of activity, from planning the raid with Lacey and Strum, to meeting all the people who were going to be involved, to finally getting to our starting points and beginning to shift into what would be our final placements before the raid on the undoc stronghold began.

It had taken Lacey and Strum only four hours to formulate a plan of attack, which was impressive, considering the location the undocs had chosen to hide in was damn difficult to get to. The large monitoring station between the hydro-turbines was only accessible from the Tower through doors on the east side of the compartment, and the legacies undoubtedly had guards at those doors. Guards who would buy time for their comrades in the back to escape, and possibly warn Sadie and the others that their cover had been blown.

Meaning a direct assault through the doors was going to be impossible.

Coming at them through the access hatches on the outside was also impractical. The water kicked up there by the hydro-turbines would render the lash beads completely useless, and Quess didn't have any time to make more humidity-resistant lash ends. So that option had been eliminated as well.

That left the ventilation ducts that fed into the section. Which were numerous, as the entire monitoring station held rooms and offices for the Divers who came in to perform inspections and studies on the hydro-turbines, which often took days or weeks. And because of the station's proximity to the river below, the humidity rate was high—and lots of ventilation was required to keep the water from eroding the metal of the Tower.

But it was all we had, considering the plan Lacey and Strum had formulated. Even now, they and their teams were moving into position, hauling large canisters of X-21J—a sleeping agent designed by the Medica and the Knights to help stop large-scale riots should they occur—to dump in the atmospheric processors that led into the rooms. The plan was to flood the place with the gas. It was late at night (or early in the morning), and we were banking on most of the legacies being asleep when the gas started pouring through. But there was every chance that some would be awake. And they would have a small window of opportunity to escape, or call Sadie or Dreyfuss for help. Which was why it was critical for us to be in the vents, ready to enter, then secure and restrain every legacy as soon as the gas started to pour in.

But Scipio help me, I *hated* crawling around in vents.

I shifted slightly in the cramped tube Leo and I were hiding in, trying to relieve some of the pain that had developed in my lower back in the thirty minutes he and I had been here. We were holding position in a junction, listening for Maddox and Quess to confirm troop placement before we proceeded to the next turn.

Because everyone had to be in place before anyone started anything. And in some places, some people had to climb through hundreds of feet of duct before reaching an opening, circumnavigating the entire area. In order to prevent confusion, Maddox was guiding us to our designated placements step by step, but that took time.

Lots and lots of nail-biting, stomach-churning time. It was almost a joy when I finally heard Maddox say, *All right, primary teams, go ahead and move forward to the next junction, and then hold for secondary teams.*

Even though her words meant that Leo and I would be holding our positions again for several minutes, forward motion was good, and I quickly unfolded myself until I was lying on my stomach. My lower back twinged in protest, but I ignored it as I shuffled onto my hands and knees and began to crawl down the dark shaft.

Leo was carrying the light behind me, and out of habit, I kept as far to one side of the tunnel as possible to let light stream past me and illuminate the path ahead. Even though he was supposed to be in front of me, I was smaller and could maneuver more quickly in the tight confines of the room. We would switch eventually, either in the tunnels if the room we were entering was occupied, or in the room itself if it wasn't. I spotted a gap between two bits of duct, indicating a duct heading straight down, and I slowed to a stop, settling in the middle of the tunnel to block the light with my body while signaling for him to kill the light.

I stopped at the edge and peeked over into the room below. Darkness greeted my eyes, telling me the room wasn't being used or was filled with sleeping people, and I quickly crossed over the space, moving as silently as possible. I moved down a few feet and then managed to turn around enough to check on Leo's progress. My heart raced in my chest as he carefully pulled himself over the gap, taking his time. If the room was filled with sleeping people, the slightest sound from either of us might wake them up and warn them of our presence.

The hand light in his grip made the slightest tapping sound as he reached out with that hand to brace his weight, but it was whisper-soft, only loud in my ears. Within seconds, he was securely on the other side of the vent, and I was moving again. There was another forty feet of duct space before the vent dead-ended, and I turned left, remembering my instructions from last time, and then stopped about ten feet in. *Team 2 in position,* I dutifully reported.

Teams 1, 3, 4, 5, 7 are also in position, Maddox's voice buzzed in my ear. *Team 6 is taking a detour due to a damaged duct, and estimating another nine minutes until the secondary teams are in their final positions. Hold tight.*

I tried not to let out an impatient sigh. This was our third round of troop movements, and the secondary teams, the ones hauling the canisters of gas, took the longest time to get into position. Luckily, this was our second to last movement before we were all finally in our final positions, but unluckily, that meant even more waiting. For a long time. A ridiculously long time.

This time I did sigh, and carefully tried to maneuver myself into something resembling a position of comfort. After three rounds, you'd think I'd have the hang of it, but so far, nothing seemed to alleviate the pain in my back or the occasional bout of impatience that struck me as the seconds marched on into minutes.

Truthfully, I had mixed feelings about how long this was taking. On the one hand, it was to be expected; we had over seventy people in the ventilation shafts, a quarter of them wriggling around with large canisters of the sleeping agent to put into the air processing units. The rest of us were stuck waiting, just listening for the order that would send us wriggling forward.

The wait *had* helped burn off some of the excited nervousness I'd had when we first slipped into the shaft, eager to finally start putting an end to the legacy threat, but once it was gone, I was only left with the dark, my nerves, and a highly overactive imagination that kept going over how everything could go wrong.

"Stop," Leo whispered next to me as my shifting weight caused the thin metal beneath us to bend, resulting in a dull thud. I wasn't too concerned—we still had one more junction to go and weren't that close to the room yet—but he was right. I needed to try being quieter. The ducts had a funny way of carrying sound, and while our entry point was supposedly just a storeroom, any legacy who was inside and heard a sound coming through the vents might check it out. And we'd be sunk.

"Sorry," I replied, my voice just as soft. But the pain in my spine intensified in protest at the new position I had just wriggled into, signaling that a vertebra was about to pop out of position. "But I have to do something. My back is killing me."

I looked over at where he was folded up beside me, his features barely lit by the light between us. We had it set to the lowest setting and would shut it off when we got to our entry point, but for now it was the only thing holding back the claustrophobic darkness. "Me too. I have an idea."

I watched as he slowly started to unfold himself, sticking his legs behind him until he was laying on his side. It was a little tight for him—his shoulders were squished between the top and the bottom of the vent—but we were both thin enough that we could lie front to back. That was all it took to convince me, and within seconds I was lying pressed up against him, stretching my legs and lower back out. The relief was immediate, and I couldn't help the small sound of pleasure that slipped through my lips.

Luckily, it wasn't loud enough to carry very far.

"I feel you," he whispered, his breath brushing against the sensitive skin of my earlobe and sending shivers down my spine. "Here, move forward a little?"

Scipio help me, Leo was going to give me a back rub. A part of me wanted to argue; after all, we were just waiting for everyone to get into position before we could move again. We should be alert and ready. At the same time, if I didn't do *something* to pass the time, I was going to go stark raving mad. Besides, Leo and Grey weren't going to do anything to jeopardize the mission. And my back was *hurting*.

I tried to steady myself as I shifted forward a few inches, and then his thumbs were pressing on either side of my lower spine, digging into the aching muscles.

"Oh, that's perfect," I said with a sigh, relaxing further into his hands as he found a particularly sore spot and quickly removed the ache with a few strong rubs of his thumbs. This was okay—a distraction in the form of some much-needed pain relief. Besides, it didn't hurt that he did it so well... Which made me wonder how he knew how to do it in the first place. "Is this Leo or Grey?" I asked, curious.

"One hundred percent human," he replied, and I smiled, realizing I was talking to Grey.

"Hey," I said with a smile. Then I frowned, realizing I hadn't touched base with him once since everything had started to gain momentum. Undoubtedly, he was nervous, considering this would be the first time he and Leo were in a combat situation together since he woke up, and I felt bad that I hadn't taken the time to make sure he was handling it okay. "I haven't had a moment to ask how you were holding up with all of this. Everything came together really fast."

"I'm... nervous," he admitted. "But I know Leo can handle a fight if things get too crazy. Besides, I should be asking you how *you're* holding up. You seem tense."

He hit another stiff muscle, and I bit back a groan as his thumb stroked over it. "And the award for understatement of the year goes to..."

I trailed off and was rewarded by a soft chuckle from Grey. "I suppose you're right. I feel like I was asleep for months, when in reality it was just a couple of weeks. A lot went down without me. And what's worse, you had to do all of it alone. You have every right to be stressed."

"I wasn't alone," I said immediately. "I had the others."

He snorted. "That's not the same, and you know it. You shoulder everything. The responsibility is enormous, and it's all fallen squarely on you. I can only imagine how hard it's been—every step back, every deviation, every loss..."

I sniffled, his words hitting too close to home, touching a nerve that I'd done my best to keep hidden from everyone. Pain flooded me, not only from the idea that I was going to lose the others, but from the sheer amount of stress I had been under for the past few weeks. Grey knew—he *understood*. I hadn't been able to talk about it with anyone else because it didn't seem fair. If I was frustrated with one of them, and started venting to someone else, then it would just create a bad environment. And if I was constantly expressing my doubts and fears to them, it would be toxic to our little group.

But holding it in had been toxic to me. Now Grey was back, and it was like he knew exactly what to say to draw the truth out of me.

"I feel out of my mind half the time," I told him, giving my thoughts freedom. "I worry about *everything* and *everyone*, and... Scipio help me, I've gotten so paranoid not knowing who to trust. There's this one Knight, an old friend of my mother's. I've known her my *entire* life, and I have no idea whose side she's on. I still don't really know if I can trust her!"

I paused, taking a moment to realize what I had just said. Even with a potential end in sight, I was still doubting those around me. We had Sadie's files. We had discovered her conspiracy with Plancett and had DNA evidence confirming Dreyfuss's role in all this, as well as Eric witnessing the exchange between the two of them. I should have been more confident, but all I could feel was anxiety that I was missing someone, something, somewhere. And I couldn't help it as the truth spilled out of me.

"Even now, I can't help but feel like I've missed something or someone important, or that all of this is going to wind up to be a huge setup, somehow. The legacies have been ninety bajillion steps ahead of us the entire time. I just can't seem to believe that this is going to work!"

"Hey," he said, his arms coming around my side to pull me tight to his chest, tethering me to him. "It's okay. I promise you, it's going to be okay. Let's think it through logically and see if maybe you did miss something. I don't think that you did, but maybe it will make you feel better. Let's see... You got all of the information from Sadie's computer on how many were in her legacy group and about... half that group's placements in various departments, right?"

"Right," I agreed, curious as to where he was going. "The spy legacies."

"Yes, well, Sadie could know that you took those, but her lack of action tells me that she bought your cover story. I mean, that was really sensitive information, but given the measures you and Leo took, she has no reason to believe it's been stolen. If she thought it had, surely she would have reacted by now."

I bit my lip. It was a fair point—unless, of course, they somehow knew what we were up to and were using it as a trap to lure us in. What better way to eliminate your enemy than by drawing them in to a fight that could get them killed?

"It could be a trick," I said.

"Maybe, but this didn't just come from Sadie's files. You got the blood tests from both the Medica, and then later from Lacey and Strum. The location for the undoc side of the legacies came from Liam. I mean, it's not like all of it came from Sadie's files. A lot of it, yes, like Dr. Smiley, but you had to fit the pieces together to understand it in its entirety, and much of that information was given by multiple sources. If it's a trick, then it's one that required a lot more foresight then I think they had time for."

My mouth tightened in automatic disbelief. He was right, but I couldn't seem to get my nerves to agree. All I could think was that if we missed even one legacy—if we let one get away—then all of this could start again. He or she could try to rescue their people before they were executed, or finish whatever plan they had for Scipio before we had a chance to fix him. "I don't know... It just feels like... It's so much so fast. I don't trust it."

"Or it's the result of your investigative work finally paying off," he said, and I could hear a tinge of exasperation in his voice. "Look, I'm not going to lie. Is there a chance that you were noticed collecting the DNA, or that Sadie somehow figured out that you stole her files? Absolutely. Of course. But I don't think so. I don't think so, because every move that's taken you closer to them has put them off balance, and forced them to react to you, instead of working on whatever it is they're planning. Every step you've made has been logical, and the risks you took were calculated. There is no reason for you to doubt anything, and doing so is a waste of your beautiful mind."

His words were like a balm to my ravaged soul, and it was only the tight confines of the shaft that prevented me from turning around in his arms and showing him exactly how much better he had made me feel. I was still scared, but finally giving voice to those fears helped tremendously.

"You always know the perfect thing to say," I said, resting my arm over his and threading our fingers together.

"That's because I'm perfect," he shot back, and I bit back a laugh at the pained quality of his voice. "It's my burden to bear."

I snorted. "Scipio help me, I have no idea how you fit both your ego and Leo's in that head of yours."

"Well, it helps that we have similar interests," he replied in a hungry voice, and pleasure curled through me when I realized he—they?—were referring to me. Heat bloomed in my cheeks, and I ducked my head, suddenly feeling weird. It was nice that Grey seemed to have a handle on sharing his body with Leo, but I still wasn't as confident that this could work, even with him insisting that it could. Two minds in one body? It was a recipe for jealousy and pettiness, no matter what Grey or Leo said.

"I still can't get over how at ease you are with all of this," I told him, unable to keep it back. Maddox's voice buzzed in my ear, notifying me that two more teams had gotten into position, and I paused to make sure we weren't about to move.

We weren't, much to my relief.

"If I were you, I'd be hurt and angry."

"You're not me," he interjected softly. "Leo's not me, either, and he's just as confused as you are."

"Well, I'm not confused, just... I have a lot of doubts," I admitted. "How can you not feel betrayed?"

Grey snorted. "Because you didn't betray me! You didn't owe me anything then, and you certainly don't now. And I don't own you—you aren't a possession. You're free to make your own choices and decisions."

"But what if Leo were another man, with another body? Wouldn't you have an issue with that?"

"Maybe, but he's not, and he's not asking me not to be part of your life. Don't get me wrong: I would fight for you if anyone tried to get between us. But Leo doesn't want to get between us. Hell, he almost killed me to prove that point."

I sighed. He kept trying to make me understand, but the reality of it wasn't lost on me. Relationships were hard enough between two people. But between three? "But..."

"But, but, but!" He sighed heavily and pulled me even tighter against his chest, snuggling close. "I love you, Liana Castell. Have pretty much since the day I met you. And maybe you just haven't experienced it before, but love, for me, is unconditional. That means I accept you, no matter what. I stand by you, no matter what. And I accept anyone you choose, no matter what."

My heart swelled at his words, which were so sweet and honest that I felt all of my doubts about the weirdness of the situation start to crumble away. Oh, I had no doubt that we would have problems. But the way that Grey talked about his love for me made me think that maybe, just maybe, I didn't have to say goodbye to either Leo or Grey.

All teams in secondary locations, Maddox declared, her voice interrupting the moment in the worst possible way—by reminding me that we had a job to do.

Then again, that should've been at the forefront of my mind, given our location.

All teams now ordered to move to primary ingress position and await breach orders. No one moves until all teams have reported in. Confirm orders, starting with Team 1.

Crap, we were Team 2, which meant we needed to respond right after Team 1. I craned my neck around to look at Grey and found his face hovering over mine. "We have to—"

"I know," he said, before pressing his mouth against mine for a brief kiss. "Get moving. I'll hand the reins over to Leo. Just be careful."

"I will. And I'll remind Leo to be as well." I turned away and began to pull myself forward. *Team 2, orders confirmed,* I thought, using the neural transmitter to send the message. *Moving to primary position to await breach orders.*

38

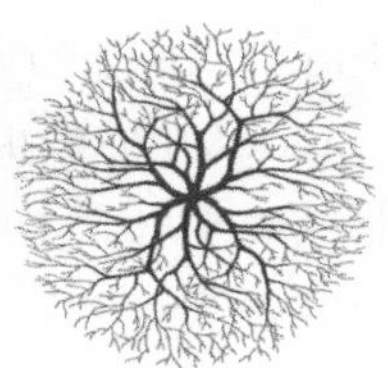

It took an additional seventy-five feet of ventilation shaft for us to get to another junction, and by the time we were there, I was swearing to myself that the next time a mission called for us to go through a vent, I would find a way to be somewhere else.

Like where I had set Maddox and Quess up on the floor above us, giving orders and coordinating the different groups.

I came to a stop just beyond the junction and peeked around the corner, toward the opening that would let us into the maintenance room. The shaft was ten feet long, and I could barely discern the softer colors of the nighttime lighting through the black shapes made by the slats. I held my breath for several seconds, listening for any sound of life, but everything was quiet.

Team 2 in the junction, I reported, ducking back behind the corner. *No lights, and no sounds.*

Roger, Maddox replied. *Waiting on Teams 11, 17, and 20.*

Team 11 is in position, a masculine voice reported—one of Lacey's or Strum's people, I wasn't sure. We had representatives from both departments in our group, to give us the numbers we needed for this mission. *We have lights on in the room ahead and can hear voices. Two—one male, one female. Possibly a guard room.*

Acknowledged, Maddox replied in my ear. Her tone didn't reveal anything, but Team 11's report had made my nervousness return. In just a few moments, we would be slipping on our masks and waiting for the gas to blanket the floor. Only then would we move—and only to get to whoever was still awake, before they managed to make a call. Hopefully most of them would be sleeping when the gas entered and wouldn't wake up. But the matter was complicated by the guards, who were in a position to spot the gas when it started coming in and do something about it.

If they managed to rouse the others or warn Sadie or Dreyfuss, we were sunk.

Waiting on 17 and 20, Maddox muttered into the link.

Don't get your panties in a twist, Lacey growled across the line, responding for Team 17. *This particular bit of shaft isn't exactly the easiest to navigate. We're slipping into the air processing unit now. We need forty-five seconds to hook up the tank.*

Don't rush it, I warned over the net. *Any noise you make in that unit is going to be heard.*

Oh, hey, you want to reiterate that point one more time, Champion Castell, or can I just do my frickin' job up here?

I rolled my eyes and bit my tongue, both physically and mentally. She was right—my warning was unnecessary. I just wasn't used to this. There were so many moving parts, and so many people I had never worked with before. I couldn't help the instinct inside me that wanted to stress how important it was that no one gave away our presence before we could enact the plan.

There were several seconds of dead air, then, and I felt each one as if hours had been compressed into it, hyperaware of my breathing, my heartbeat, and the way my skin tingled like it was drawn just a quarter of an inch too tight.

Team 21 is in position and set up, Strum finally said, and I exhaled. *Apologies for the delay. We had to take down several laser defense grids without activating the monitor station's internal security.*

I gritted my teeth together. Laser defense grids hadn't been mentioned at the meeting, but given that Strum had already deactivated them, I supposed it was a moot point. Likely, he had known about them to begin with, which was why he had been very particular about what group went where during our planning session.

Ready to activate on Command's orders, he finished.

Show off, Lacey transmitted.

More time elapsed, and I struggled to keep my breathing even. Scipio help me, if we didn't start to move soon, I wasn't sure what I was going to do.

Then Lacey was back. *All right, we're hooked up. Ready when you are.*

I felt a finely tuned shiver of fear mixed with anticipation shoot through me, and I forced myself to remain calm, trying not to grow impatient now that the time for attack was *finally* upon us. I knew there were still a few steps between now and when we would push through the grate, and this was not the time to get overexcited about the prospect.

All teams, move to final egress points, Maddox said, and I took a deep, calming breath before easing forward and around the corner, trying to keep my movements spread out and slow so as not to rattle the vent too much.

In position, I reported when my face was still a foot from the grate. I slowed to a stop and leaned forward, peering out between the gaps in the slats. This opening was high off the ground, and from my vantage point, I could see the storeroom, the shelves piled with the silvery foil packets I recognized from the undoc house in the Attic. *I have confirmed evidence of a legacy presence,* I added.

Roger, Maddox replied. *Other teams, check in.*

I waited while the other teams reported in as they reached their entry points. Tension radiated through me as Maddox ordered, *Masks and thermal goggles on.* I pulled out the respirator mask Strum and Lacey had given me during the briefing and slipped the rubbery material over my nose and mouth, and under my chin, using my other hand to twist the hard plastic circle at the front so that it suctioned to my face. I tugged it a few times to make sure it was seated properly, and then twisted around to make sure Leo had his fitted on his face properly, as well.

He pulled at mine while I returned the favor, and we both nodded, confirming the masks were in place, before quickly donning the rose-tinted thermal goggles. I tapped the corner and my entire field of vision changed as the lenses lit up, blossoming into a white blob rimmed in red and orange to my left, where Leo was, and a dark blue and black to my left, where the vent and the room were. The goggles couldn't penetrate walls, but the fog generated by the gas would be so thick that we'd need them in order to see anything. I tilted my head toward the vent and scanned the room to make sure it was free of people, and the lenses only reflected more blue and black. The room was cold and empty—not even a residual trail of heat.

All right, last reminder, people. Do not enter the room until the vapor cloud is obscuring your entry. We do not need them sounding the alarm because someone jumped the gun. Now, on my mark, the gas teams will blow their canisters. Starting on three.

I licked my lips and looked at the vent, mentally preparing myself for what I had to do: kick the grate out, climb down, and clear the next three rooms on our side of the hall, securing any legacies and planting neural scramblers on them in case they had nets. We couldn't afford for them to call anyone. Another team would be working opposite us, so it was important to keep an eye out for them, and not attack them in the process.

Three. Two. One. Mark.

My muscles screamed at me to move, but I held back, knowing that it wasn't time yet. Instead, I focused on the breeze that was increasing behind me, and the voices reporting in my ear.

Air flow has increased by 50 percent, Lacey reported. *Canisters are mixing. Expect vapor cloud soon.*

Sure enough, a white smoke began flooding the room from the vent above, the thermal goggles reflecting the edges and contours of the vapor cloud as it streamed through the slats. It plumed outward, immediately drawn to our vent. I pressed on the slats before it got to us, sealing them up so none of the vapor could get in, and then held up my hand, counting down from five.

Leo's hand brushed my shin in acknowledgement as I hit three, and then, two heartbeats later, my shoulder was pressed against the duct covering and I was shoving. Hard. It popped off on one side first, and a quick push with the palm of my hand on the other side sent it clattering across the small room. I heard it hit something before smacking into the ground, and it must've knocked a few of the MREs off, because they hit the floor with a fluttery metallic sound that I knew from experience.

I was already pushing my way through before they stopped falling, slipping my torso out and planting a hand on a shelf, which showed on my display as a dark outline against the blue. Using it as a brace, I continued to pull myself until my butt was on the shelf and my legs were free. I quickly reached across the narrow aisle for the opposite shelf, to give myself some leverage, and then dropped to the floor and headed for the door.

Leo dropped lightly onto his feet behind me, and within moments I was pressed in the corner, my hand hovering over the control pad, baton in my other hand. *Team 2 at door leading into the hallway,* I reported, trying not to let my nervousness come through. *Entering now.*

Copy that, Maddox replied.

I hit the button, and the door slid up. The vapor, which

showed up almost as an afterimage behind the thermal display, poured through the open portal like a wall being shoved through, holding its shape for several seconds before starting to disperse. I supposed it was beautiful, but I was focused on finding any thermal signatures beyond it.

There were none, and I held back as Leo stepped through first. I counted off a beat so he could clear the space, then slipped through the door after him, using the cloud for cover.

A wash of red caught my eye in the hallway, and I angled down toward it and found my first legacy—a male—lying on the floor. Relief poured through me when I saw him there, as it meant the gas was working. Our plan really did stand a chance.

One down in the hall, I reported, moving toward him, my hand on the restraints on my belt. I pulled them free and knelt down next to him. Taking his hands in my own, I quickly placed them behind his back, connected the two ends of the restraints around his wrists, then produced a scrambler and fitted it on the back of his neck. *Secured,* I transmitted.

Then I turned back toward Leo's heat signature, pausing when I saw two other figures on the opposite end of the hall. The darkened areas over their mouths, noses, and eyes told me they were Team 11—the team that would clear the rooms on the opposite side of the hall—and I quickly dismissed them and turned toward where Leo was waiting by the first door we needed to clear.

I rapidly approached it and took the opposite side of the doorway. He gave me a nod as I swung into position, and I took a deep breath, and then hit the button. It slid up, the gap in the door revealing not one but five red blobs. My heart thumped in my chest as soon as I saw them, expecting movement or an attack, but it never came. All of them were asleep—three in hammocks strung across the room, two splayed out on crude mats on the floor, in conditions that echoed the house we had discovered in the Attic. I hesitated long enough to make sure no one was moving too much, and then set to work gathering them up, tying their hands together, and placing their neural scramblers, before transmitting an update to Maddox.

Leo helped, and in under a minute we were out and moving to the next door. The fog in the hall was going to start dissipating any second, as soon as the canisters were spent, and then we would only have two minutes to restrain them before they started to wake up. I put a little speed in my step, wanting to make sure that we didn't miss opening any door, in case not all of the gas had encompassed the room while it was being piped through the vents.

I hit the button for the next door as soon as Leo signaled he was ready, this time prepared for the shot of red that appeared in the gap that formed as it opened. It was the outline of a hand against the floor, and it soon became an arm, shoulder, torso, and head of a human being, lying outstretched, as if she had been racing for the door when the gas overtook her.

I scanned the room and found six more thermal signatures with the goggles, all of them still in their sleeping positions. I wondered why the girl had been the only one to notice, but it didn't matter, because she was out. Leo and I quickly tied them up, transmitting another status update in the process, and then proceeded to the last and final door.

Maybe it was because every door thus far had been relatively benign in terms of danger, or maybe it was because we'd had two rooms filled with sedated people, but when the third door opened and revealed a woman, alert and crouching over one of her fallen comrades, I froze for a second, surprised to see anyone awake.

She glanced up at us long enough for me to see the black circle around her mouth, which indicated a mask, and then quickly turned back to her comrade. She had cut open his neck to pull out his net, and my eyes widened when I realized that she hadn't been able to call anyone—because she didn't have a net of her own. The mask was a mystery, but maybe she had just happened to have one on hand, recognized what was going on, and got to it before she was affected? It didn't matter. All that mattered was that I stopped her from making any transmission. I sprang into motion, stepping through the door and pressing the button on my baton to charge it.

She shot to her feet and darted away, lifting her hands to the back of her neck, where a small white line in her skin shone brightly against the red glow of her body in the goggles, indicating that she was already bleeding—and was now trying to shove the net in. It was a smart move; she knew that they were under attack, and was trying to reach her people to warn them. It was damned lucky that she didn't seem to have a net of her own, and hadn't been able to net anyone else yet, and I quickly closed the distance between the two of us, my grip tightening.

She finally whirled around to face me, her fingers moving away from the cut on her neck, and I could hear a muffled intake of breath that told me she was getting ready to speak. I swung my baton low, hoping to catch her in the mist, and she leapt back with a muffled, "No!" that was tinged with panic and fear. I could only imagine what she was thinking, but it didn't matter—I had to stop her.

I stepped closer, ducking under a wild haymaker, and brought the baton down on her shoulder. She froze for several seconds, the thermal display in my goggles showing me that her eyes were wide open in surprise as the electrical current locked her in place. I held it for a space of three seconds and then pulled it away, and she dropped to the ground. A quick check of the room told me the other three occupants were fast asleep, although two of them had masks of their own over their mouths that I quickly pulled off. Neither one of them had moved from their hammocks, which told me the girl had put those masks on them, to try to get her comrades up, before donning one of her own. Leo was already quickly pulling them off, but it didn't appear they had worked.

Not in time, at least.

Five more in room three, I reported. *All secured.*

Then that's it, Maddox replied, and I blinked, surprised. *That's fifty-five people in total.*

What about the women? I asked. *Any sign of them?*

Negative, Maddox said, and I could feel her ire through the line. *There's no sign they were ever here. Wherever they are being kept, it has to be somewhere else.* There was a pause, one that I filled with a silent prayer that we would be able to get their location from one of the legacies when we questioned them, and then she said, *Everyone, begin removing nets now, while secondary teams come in to move prisoners to the Citadel. Masks remain on until we get the all-clear from Team 20.*

I swallowed and got to work, but I couldn't shake the sensation that this felt way too easy. I knew it was stupid—it was just as possible that everything had gone according to plan, for once. Maybe I just wasn't accustomed to victory.

We had a good plan and the element of surprise, I told myself as I knelt down to begin collecting the nets. *It worked because we had enough people to make it work. Calm down. You still have a bajillion more arrests to make today, so freaking out now is not going to help.*

The words offered little comfort, even with the fruit of our success lying on the ground in front of us. Somehow, I just hadn't expected it to be this easy.

Then again, how *could* it be easy when we still had to collect Dreyfuss, Salvatore, and the spies embedded in the other departments? Plus Sadie and Plancett?

39

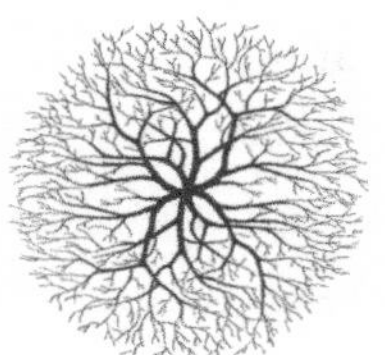

With the first step of our plan completed, and Leo supervising the transfer of our batch of prisoners to the cells in the Citadel using Lacey's tried and true method of laundry bin transportation, it was time to move on to the next step: cleaning our respective departments of the spies that Sadie and Dreyfuss had put there. We couldn't get to the ones in the Medica, IT, or the Farming Department yet, as taking them would undoubtedly draw the attention of the councilors who presided over them, but plans were in motion to capture them as soon as the council meeting was underway. Maddox was already rousing the Knight Commanders we knew we could trust, along with Theo—a boy I used to have a crush on—and debriefing them on the mission, and soon they would be moving against the legacies in the Knights Department.

And I would be joining her, just as soon as I got what I needed from Lacey.

I was in one of the front offices by the gate of the Citadel, waiting—rather impatiently—for the two of them to show up, and I had to remind myself to be calm. A quick check of my watch told me it was 6:15 a.m. There was still plenty of time to get the data to Quess in central command, but I was growing more and more uncomfortable with how everything seemed like it was "hurry up... and wait." I wanted more action than all this endless waiting, but then again, I was about to go after Salvatore, the man who had made a pact with the legacies to win the Tourney and gotten my mother killed.

A flash of blue and orange caught my eye, and I looked up to see Strum and Lacey coming to a halt a few feet from the entrance to the Citadel. I quickly exited the sentry shack and headed down the metal ramp to meet them, waving off the few guards on duty, who were confused by the presence of the heads of both the Water and Mechanics Departments.

"Took you long enough." I huffed when I reached them.

Lacey rolled her eyes, reached into one of the deeper pockets of her toolbelt, and pulled out three pads. "It took Tony a second to figure out the logistics of running three different pads patched with three different feeds from three different departments."

This time, *I* rolled my eyes. "I'm sorry, what were the three different things again?" I asked, unable to keep the sarcasm from my voice.

She growled, but before she could say anything, Strum gave a harsh, "Enough"—and it held a note of command that had an effect even on me. I looked at the bald man, the Diver's marks on his scalp a harsh black under the bright spotlights overhead, and he speared us both with a pointed look. "Now is not the time. We have work that needs to be done before the council meeting starts. Lacey, give her the pad."

Lacey scowled, but shuffled through the three pads and then shoved one at me. "Here. Tony is hacked into the feed of the Citadel, has been since last night. He's kept every single one of them under watch since you gave us their cover identities."

I accepted the pad and turned it on. I was immediately greeted with a split-screen view of four different camera angles. Three of them were thermal sensor readings from the bedrooms, showing the subjects sleeping, while one was monitoring a Knight on sentry duty at one of the rear bridges leading to the shell. I slid a finger across the screen and saw four more thermal viewpoints of subjects asleep—one of them in the Academy dorm rooms, no less, sleeping on the bottom bunk.

It was beyond impressive. Tony was giving us nonstop coverage of our targets—something even the most adept tech would struggle with, given the numerous cameras in the Tower. Never mind using the sensors.

"This is amazing," I said, studying it. "Tony is doing this?"

"He had to learn how to, but yes. He's gotten quite good at it over the years. This is a bit of a nightmare for him, though; he's still monitoring the other three departments, as well."

I couldn't wait to meet him. The way he was handling all this at once told me he was special indeed. I just wished that Lacey had let me do it before we had started moving against the legacies. But she had been adamant about waiting until the council session, and I couldn't blame her. I wouldn't want to expose his location to anyone I didn't fully trust, and I doubted that even Strum knew where he was being housed. I wanted to believe it was as simple as a terminal in her quarters, but knowing how resourceful Lacey could be, I doubted it. Maybe she had him in the Cog server somewhere? It was possible, but then again, I doubted she would be so obvious.

Still, it didn't matter. In a few hours, she would be attending the council session, and would be bringing Tony to testify. Soon, he would be reunited with the others—all except for Kurt and Alice. But hopefully, we would find them too.

I returned my view to the screen and paused when it suddenly dawned on me that Lacey had lied to me a very long time ago, when we had first met. "There was no specialized bacterium, was there?" I asked as she slipped a pad into Strum's hands and clicked it on to reveal his own department. "*Tony* figured out our hiding place under the Menagerie, didn't he? He tracked us like he's tracking the legacies now."

Lacey gave me a smug look. "You never asked yourself how the hell we got hold of a specialized bacterium?" she asked.

I considered it for a second, trying to remember why I hadn't questioned it too hard, and found it all coming back to me. "I just assumed you stole it or something. It made sense, especially if you had spies in other departments. Why not the Medica as well?"

Lacey gave me a thoughtful look. "That is a good conclusion, which was the point. I didn't want anyone knowing about Tony. But we can talk about the old days once they become just that—the old days. For now, let's focus on what we're doing. My department has already started cleaning out the spies."

"Mine as well," Strum said, cracking his neck. "I need to be joining them, but I wanted to wish you both luck."

He was wishing us luck because I was going after Salvatore, while Lacey was going after Dreyfuss. I wasn't happy about Lacey going after Dreyfuss without me or Strum there to make sure she remained in control, but she'd been adamant that he was hers, because she knew how to get in and out of the Farming Department undetected. I didn't like it, but the fact of the matter was that we had to grab as many of their leaders as we could, save for Plancett and Sadie. And that meant grabbing Dreyfuss early, because any one of the uncollected spies might try to contact him if they noticed something was up before we could capture them.

Controlling the leaders meant we could monitor those who tried to contact them and scoop them up before they could reach out to anyone else. And I was already in charge of getting Salvatore.

Letting Lacey go after Dreyfuss had really been my only option.

"Thanks," I said, tucking the pad under my arm. "You as well. Just remember, we need the casualties to be zero—and that goes double for Dreyfuss. We need him taken alive, or our story is going to look less believable to Scipio and Sage. They are going to need someone to punish, and he's the other half of this. He's been fathering the undocs and running the undoc side of things. It'll scream conspiracy if he just up and dies."

Lacey tsked under her breath. "He doesn't deserve to live," she snapped irately.

"Lacey," Strum said, before I could even utter a syllable in response to her vehement and alarming statement. "We agreed on this plan together, and this is what it will take to see it through. Do not jeopardize everything we have managed to accomplish here with your petty need for revenge."

I kept my teeth clenched shut under his wise and calming words, watching Lacey closely. It was on the tip of my tongue to tell her *I* would lead her team in after Dreyfuss, when she sighed, the anger draining out of her in an instant.

"You're right, of course," she said tiredly, rubbing a hand over her forehead. "I'm sorry. I'm just amped up."

I knew the apology wasn't for me, and I could tell that Strum accepted it readily, but I wasn't as convinced. "Lacey, if you think for a moment you are emotionally compromised in this, you need to take a step back. Let Strum go in your place, or even me."

"I'm fine," she said firmly, some of the anger returning. "I will take Dreyfuss alive. I'm not saying he's not going to be a little banged up, but he will be whole and healthy, okay? Now, can we get moving? We are burning some precious time here. The council meeting is happening soon, and we need to get this done."

I kept my mouth shut and didn't argue. I had to trust that Lacey meant what she said and would do what she promised; I had people waiting on the data on the pad, and a raid against Salvatore to carry out.

And only two hours before the council meeting started.

Thirty minutes later, Dylan and I were standing on either side of Salvatore Zale's door, not even a stone's throw from my own father's quarters, and I was trying to distract myself from yet another of the endless waits that seemed to have become my life over the last few hours. She had a tensor placed over the door, the round rubber suction cup holding a very finely tuned receiver that could hear everything happening in the room beyond. It was unnecessary; the pad in my hand *showed* me the two figures of Zale and his wife sleeping in their bed. Of course, the thermal signature didn't translate to sound, so I relied on her to tell me if they were awake and talking, and if so, what they were talking about.

"Anything?" I asked her.

"Two sets of breathing. Deep and even," she reported, before giving me a look and adding, "Same as before. Same as on your screen."

I ignored her jab, knowing that I was probably driving her crazy at this point, and followed my question with another one directed to a different person. *Command, how long before everyone is in position?* Dylan's lips twitched, and I could tell she was fighting back a smile.

I knew I had asked the question before—and more than twice—but, Scipio help me, I wanted to *move.* To get in there and grab Salvatore.

Just relax for a minute, Quess groused in my ear. *I'm waiting on final confirmation that Lacey's and Strum's people are in position, and then I will give the go ahead. I do have an update on the prisoners we collected in Water Treatment. Out of the fifty-five we collected, only thirteen had nets, and only two of those were legacy nets. They're all resting comfortably in the cells above the expulsion chambers, with Zoe and Eric keeping an eye on them. Grey is on his way back to your quarters to start downloading the evidence.*

'Evidence' was code for 'Jasper and Rose'—the real evidence would be transmitted to the council's server after the session began. *Thanks for the update, Quess.*

No problem. Now will you stay off the line and let me do my work?

I suppressed another sigh, attempting to turn it into a fortifying exhalation, and once again tried to summon up a great calm. Hours of preparation would mean nothing once he gave the order to breach the door. No plan ever survived first contact. With everything hinging on us getting the job done in a matter of seconds—before Salvatore and his wife could wake up, or, if they were awake, before they could call anyone still around for help—one slight misstep from any of us could give our enemies the opportunity they needed to slip through our fingers.

If they got a message out before we could stop them, we were sunk. If they somehow managed to escape us and warn the others, then the rest of them would disappear before we could grab them. But I couldn't do anything about any of the other spies being picked up at the moment. I could only focus on my target.

I flexed my hands into fists and then relaxed them, trying to find a way to get rid of this pent-up anxiety. Beside me, Dylan sighed.

"You know," she said conversationally, keeping her voice low enough that it wouldn't carry through the door. "You aren't making it easy to remain calm over here."

"Sorry," I said, relaxing my hands enough to wipe them on my uniform and trying to force myself into something resembling calm.

"It's okay. I don't like this either. I never thought in a million years I would have to arrest Salvatore Zale. Yet here we are, in a joint operation with the Cogs and the Divers, about to grab another thirty-three people who had subversive intentions toward the Tower. It's... weird."

I blew out a breath. Dylan still didn't entirely understand why I had gone to Lacey and Strum before I moved against the legacies, and I couldn't exactly explain that they were also legacies without it getting messy fast. Instead, I told her a version of the truth that might better explain it.

"Lacey was Ambrose's aunt. She approached me after he died to ask me to look into the matter, and I promised her that I'd involve her if and when I found anything out. Besides, arresting Salvatore is going to divide the department—at least until we can explain to everyone why we had to do it. And I can't tell my commanders that without the authorization of the council until after I walk them through all the evidence and convince them of the conspiracy. Hell, I had to exclude at least half of the Commanders from mobilizing on this, because they were in the Academy with Zale at one point or another."

Dylan nodded at my words, her mouth pressed into a thin line. "All very excellent points," she said. She cocked her head at me, giving me a canny look. "I think the Knights chose well when they voted you in. I'm not sure I would've been so circumspect of my Commanders' loyalties like that. But you're right. You can't trust that Salvatore won't prey on his relationship with others to—"

She was cut off by Quess coming over the line. *All teams in position. I repeat: all teams in position. Be ready to breach in ten seconds, on my mark.*

I exchanged a glance with Dylan, and then motioned for her to pack up the tensor. She nodded and quickly detached it.

Ten... nine... eight...

I slipped my baton from the loop in my belt and clicked it on, inhaling deeply and letting my eyes drift closed. From here, I would override the door. Dylan would enter first, sweep the living space, and then proceed to the bedroom, where Salvatore and his wife, Alisha, were lying asleep. Our goal was Salvatore, but Alisha was a seasoned Knight as well, and likely wouldn't let us take her husband without a fight.

Five... four... three...

I opened my eyes and turned to the door, my face tilting toward it.

Two... one... Mark!

"Open door. Arrest mode. Authorization Champion Liana Castell, 25K-05," I commanded toward the door.

"Authorized," the door replied, and a second later, it slid to the side. I held back as Dylan stalked through the entry hall, her baton held out before her in one hand, light in the other. I gave her a three count and then followed, my eyes darting around the dim lighting of the room.

I stopped when Dylan did, letting her sweep the light around a tidy living room and kitchenette area as she searched the shadows for any sign of life. There was none, and she resumed moving forward and crossed the floor into the second hall beyond, her boots barely making a sound. I followed suit, keeping my knees bent to prevent any extraneous noise, uncertain of how lightly either of the married couple slept.

We paused at the door opposite a bathroom, and I waited, nerves tingling with anticipation, while Dylan quickly cleared the bathroom. At her nod, I turned my focus to the bedroom door and took one last deep, calming breath.

"Go," I whispered.

She hit the door control, and the door slid open, the pneumatic hiss harsh in the silence. I pushed through in spite of it, in time to see Alisha sit up, the tall, reed-thin woman's brown eyes wide and searching. She spotted me in an instant and flung the sheets aside with a sharp, "Salvatore!" to the lump beside her.

I bit off a growl as I drew my baton up, intent on hitting her in the shoulder, but she sprang forward off the bed, going low. Her move was unexpected, and my momentum too great, and she drove her shoulder into the center of my chest. The breath exploded from my lungs and I went down, landing hard on my back. My eyes were wide open—wide enough to see her draw a foot back for a kick—and even though I felt I couldn't breathe, I reacted quickly, bringing my hand, my baton still tightly clenched in its grip, up and into the sole of her foot.

She gave a strangled cry, her body trembling, and I heard Salvatore say, "Contact Sadie—" before his voice abruptly cut off. I jerked the baton away, letting Alisha topple over onto the bed, and sat up, one hand going to the spot she'd hit on my chest. I tried to suck in a breath through my frozen lungs, and it came in a sharp wheeze that prompted me to start coughing.

In spite of the crisis of air that had overcome me in the span of a few short seconds, I stood and searched the room for Dylan. I found her hunched over Salvatore's still form on the bed, already pulling out the extraction kit for his net.

"You okay?" she asked.

I nodded. "Alisha always could pack a punch," I wheezed slowly, moving gingerly into a kneeling position over the downed woman and pulling out my own extraction kit. Alisha's loyalties were questionable at best, and I wasn't about to take a chance on anyone being missed.

I paused what I was doing as I listened to the reports flooding through my ear, waiting for my chance to slip in my own update.

...6, target apprehended, net removed.

This is Team 3, target apprehended, net removed.

This is Team 4, target apprehended, net removed.

Team 5, I interjected, grateful that I could transmit orders neurally instead of wasting even more of my breath. *Target apprehended, net removed.*

As if to emphasize my point, Dylan leaned back, a net pinched between two fingers. Black, which meant it wasn't a legacy net. However he'd been working with Sadie, it hadn't been as one of their leaders. Unless, of course, he had taken the legacy net out to keep it hidden, which was possible.

Roger, Quess replied. *Sending collection teams in now. All clear for the Citadel. I repeat, all clear for the Citadel.* Relief poured through me as I realized that all our teams had reported back, but it was premature; we still needed to hear from Lacey's and Strum's people. But we were getting there.

I looked down at Alisha, and then began to roll her over. She was gasping for air like a fish that had been taken from water. I quickly cut her net out and removed it, my hands practiced from having done it five times already today. I hoped it ultimately proved unnecessary, and that Alisha had no knowledge of her husband's activities, but we couldn't take the chance. In fact, the orders we had all agreed upon were taking the legacy spies and all their family members. I already had several rooms and babysitters ready for the youngest members—anyone under fifteen—as they couldn't be held accountable for the actions of their parents. But the adults would be detained in the bottommost cells below—where the expulsion chambers were.

Well, for the first time in a long time, the cells in the Citadel would be teeming with people who actually deserved to be there. I looked up as the secondary team of Knights entered and motioned one of the two men over to carry Alisha. I was still too winded to do it, and besides, it was good to be the boss.

I let him help me up, and then hobbled over to the door. I was halfway there when Quess said, *Strum and Lacey have reported in. All clear. But, Liana, Lacey reported that her target attacked her, and she was forced to kill him in self-defense. Dreyfuss is dead.*

40

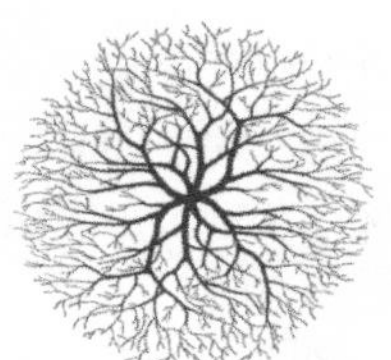

Anger snapped through me, making my skin tight and hot over my muscles. I didn't believe for a single second that Lacey had killed Dreyfuss in self-defense. She had been too eager about going, which told me only one thing: Lacey had gotten revenge for Ambrose's death.

I'd be happy for her, if it weren't so shortsighted. It was going to look mighty damned convenient to Sage and Scipio that he was killed when every other legacy we had grabbed so far had been taken alive. Not to mention the fact that his place in the entire conspiracy made him an essential live target, as he might be the only one who knew where the kidnapped women were being kept.

Thanks for the update, Quess, I thought before disconnecting the line. *Cornelius, contact Lacey right now.*

One moment, Champion.

I used the pause to move away from the others, not wanting my Knights to see anything of the exchange.

It was an accident, her voice buzzed in my ear. My jaw tightened at the irritated quality of her voice.

An accident? I transmitted, knowing my incredulity would come through loud and clear on her end. *I thought it was self-defense. If you're going to feed me a story, Lacey, then you should make sure it is a consistent one.*

Look, I don't really have time for this, and neither do you. You can go ahead and feel free to perform an autopsy and investigate the scene later if you don't believe me.

Oh, I will, I promised her, my fury making me go ice cold. *And if I find out you murdered him, I will drag your ass before Scipio myself.*

You try that, and Strum will release the evidence of you tampering with—

That argument won't hold weight when you hand over Tony, I interrupted her, folding my arms over my chest. *Because I assume that's how you were able to alter Scipio's memories. Tony's creative, right? Can manage any directive you give him, and help you cover your tracks by having Scipio sanction your operations and moves?*

That was war, Lacey seethed. *I did what I had to do to survive, and—*

You're just as guilty as these legacies of influencing Scipio, I said coldly. *Which is why I expect you to bring Tony to the meeting today and surrender him. I'm still going to do my investigation, and if I find out you murdered Dreyfuss, I will come after you with everything I can. Not because you killed the rat bastard, but because you put our entire plan—the plan the three of us agreed to—at risk to get your revenge. If Sage and Scipio refuse to accept our story without him, it's on your head.*

I ended the transmission before she could reply, knowing that she would just continue to defend herself and her actions. And in a way, I could understand. After all, a fragment of my anger was coming from resentment about not getting to confront Dreyfuss myself. I wanted my moment alone with him. I wanted to demand satisfaction. But the bulk of it was that she had put our ability to find those women at risk. There was every chance he hadn't shared their location with any of the other legacies, and now they were likely trapped, alone, and starving—possibly in various stages of pregnancy.

I was sickened to think of what would happen if any of the others didn't know where they were. I doubted Sadie would tell us, even if she knew. If anything, she might hold it back out of spite.

But there was nothing I could do about it now. Dreyfuss was dead, and I had a council meeting in just under an hour. I could figure out a way to locate the women later; start by questioning the prisoners, and work from there. For any of this to work, I had to make it to the council meeting—and I was already at risk of being late, considering I needed to shower and change.

But then again, today was the one day that I could afford to be a little late. Especially when I had such a good excuse.

I tried not to gulp as the familiar white dome of the Council Room loomed closer. I was already five minutes late, and I could feel the pressure accumulating. Still, I somehow managed to keep my entire demeanor cool and confident, if not for me, then for the contingent of Knights that was sweeping down the path behind me, Dylan bringing up the rear.

To ensure that every member of the council would come in person, I had sent a request for a security briefing last night, notifying the council that the issues I had to discuss needed to be delivered in a private, closed-off session. Cornelius and Jasper had both assured me of the protocol, but I couldn't help but wonder if the council would actually show up. They hadn't last time. But then again, this was my first time exercising that little bit of authority. Maybe they'd show up just because they were curious.

No, scratch that. I was worried about what would happen if I arrived, and Sadie and Plancett were missing. If they had somehow been tipped off about all the arrests going down, they would be making their escape even now—going to some unknown fallback position to regroup and plan their next move. If that happened, not only would I be unable to arrest them, I would also be facing an attack from any forces Lacey still had in play.

The only source of comfort I had was the sound of Quess updating me with every legacy spy arrested in one of the three other departments, my group still going even now, when the council was supposed to begin. So far, they had grabbed eighteen of the twenty-one people remaining. The final three groups were just checking in now, as it had taken Lacey's and Strum's people more time to relay the messages.

Teams 13 and 31 have checked in, Quess reported. *Just waiting on 28. How are you doing?*

"I'm almost there," I said out loud, my head aching slightly from all the activity on the net. "Dylan and her team of Knights will be standing at the ready outside, to make the arrests, and I'll notify you when I want you to send them in."

How are Jasper and Rose doing? he asked, and I glanced over my shoulder at Dylan, who was carrying two modified hard drives and their external batteries. It would keep the AIs alive for twenty-four hours, thanks to Quess's ingenuity. However, I doubted we would need them that long. I studied the boxes closely and watched for the blinking lights that told me they were receiving a steady power supply.

They seem fine.

And Dylan has no idea what she's holding?

I smiled. We hadn't told anyone about the AI fragments, but in order to explain why we needed the hard drives, we had convinced her that all of Sadie's files were on them both. She had bought it hook, line, and sinker. *Not a clue.*

Although, I was starting to feel a little bad about leaving her in the dark so much. She had certainly proved herself through and through. Still, I wasn't going to say anything to anyone until I was certain that Sadie and Plancett were in the Council Room, and that we had secured every legacy.

Just got the final report in. We got 'em all, Liana, including Dr. Smiley, the guy in IT. Dinah helped us cover our tracks in and out, so I don't think Sadie has any idea that we got them. You should be good to go for your dramatic reveal.

I smiled at his joke but felt a grim sense of satisfaction as we crossed the final manmade stream via a wooden bridge, our footsteps making heavy clomping noises as we walked across. Dr. Smiley, their plastic surgeon, had been the man accompanying Baldy in the Medica the day we killed Devon—Plain-Face, I had called him. I hadn't suspected him of being their surgeon, but then again, I had only ever seen him once. *That's it, then. And it all comes down to this. Wish me luck.*

Good luck, he replied.

I moved around one of the fountains, barely glancing at the insignias from the departments engraved on each column, and headed for the massive door. I paused just in front of it and glanced toward Dylan. "Be ready for my call," I told her.

She nodded. "We'll be here."

I turned away and slipped through the door, now seven minutes late. I walked around the middle table and to the door, pushing it in and entering the circular chamber.

My eyes immediately darted over to Sadie's position, and I saw, to my imminent relief, that she was sitting there, a displeased scowl on her face. They all were; Lacey and Strum had even beaten me here, and Scipio's holographic projection was represented as sitting, one cheek resting on his fist in abject boredom.

"I apologize for my tardiness," I said, coming to a stop in front of them and offering a respectful nod of my head that was only directed to about half of the group in attendance. "I assure you, it has everything to do with my security briefing, but I believe that is last on the agenda."

"Indeed," Scipio said, leaning forward slightly. "Please take your seat."

I hurried to the door just under the carving of my department, opened it, and climbed up the tight stairwell to the seating area above. Dropping into my chair, I tapped the screen on the terminal, and then gave Scipio a pleasant smile. "Ready when you are."

There were thirteen items on the list, and since my request was the last one in, we wound up going through the other twelve first, most of which were departmental jurisdiction issues. There were only two that I cared about, but just like in the previous session, Sadie requested an extension on the vote to dissolve the expulsion chambers. I voted yes, only this time, there was a savage pleasure in doing it. Sadie's insistence on delaying the vote only meant those chambers would still be in use when she was arrested. If the trial went quickly, Sadie would be executed for her crimes in one of them.

And it would be all her fault.

The second to last issue was Sadie's report on the malfunctioning assistants. Lacey had triggered her quarters to reset the night before last—when I had given her the virus—and Sadie was reporting her findings to the council. With any luck, it would be the last report she gave.

"It's my opinion that the glitch in the assistants is due to a software update that proved to be faulty. We have corrected the problem with Scipio's assistance, and will be sending a new update to the council server within a few hours."

I sat up a little straighter as I realized my security briefing was next and tried to prepare myself mentally.

"Will the update damage or change our assistants in any way?" Sage asked.

"No," Sadie replied with a soft shake of her head. "The patch will just keep the program from ever reading that their council member has died before they actually have. That's all."

"We thank you for your thoroughness," Scipio intoned formally. "I trust this issue is now resolved?"

"Yes," she said. "I yield the floor to the next item of business."

"Which is Champion Castell's security briefing," Scipio said, turning his glowing blue gaze toward me.

I smiled and stood up from my chair, surreptitiously wiping my suddenly sweaty palms on the sides of my hips. "Thank you, Lord Scipio," I said, while simultaneously transmitting, *Enter the room in five seconds,* to Dylan. "Let me begin by ordering the arrests of CEO Sadie Monroe and Head Farmer Emmanuel Plancett."

41

I could've dropped a pin in the silence that followed my statement, and the sound would've been louder than any bell or klaxon. I watched Sadie's face as her jaw dropped, her eyes widening in shock, and felt that savage pleasure again. *We've caught her unaware. Quess was right: she had no idea we were coming. We've got her*. I shifted my gaze to Plancett to confirm, and sure enough, his eyes were practically bulging out of his skull, and I feared one good slap to the back of his head would pop them right out. *We got you too, you rat bastard.*

Suddenly the doors pushed open, and Dylan strode in with the contingent of Knights, jerking Sadie's gaze toward them. Any blood that remained in her face drained completely out, but I could see her already looking around, her eyes calculating. "This is preposterous," she sputtered. "I am a loyal—"

"Yes, but loyal to whom?" I interrupted, unable to keep the smugness out of my voice. "Because I have evidence that proves that it hasn't been to the Tower. And it certainly hasn't been to

Scipio. In fact, you and your family come from a long line of dissidents who have been slowly subverting Scipio's coding for the last two hundred years."

"That's *insane*," Sadie said, standing up and taking a step back as Dylan threw open her door, hard enough to make the wood reverberate. "Lord Scipio, I'm innocent. This is clearly an attempt to—do *not* touch me!" She recoiled from Dylan as if she were a rust hawk and thrust her wrist up. "Scipio knows the truth! He blesses me with a ten because of my service!"

"Actually, he grants you a ten because your predecessor some two or three generations ago ripped out his emotional core and replaced it with a program that ensured that those in the upper echelons of power would remain there—no matter what—while those who weren't privileged enough to earn those positions would fall faster and faster in rank. But we'll get to that." I looked over at where Dylan and Sadie were eyeing each other warily. "Dylan, restrain CEO Monroe. Gag her if she can't remain quiet. I have quite a lot to go through, and it'll go faster without interruptions."

"I stand with Sadie in that this is preposterous!" Plancett declared, finally breaking out of his shock. I glanced at him to see that another Knight was already placing the cuffs on his wrists.

"Can't you see what's happening?" Sadie shouted, and I looked over to see that Dylan had grabbed her and pressed her over the desk, holding her still so she could restrain the struggling woman. "This is nothing short of a coup! The new *Champion* is trying to institute a regime change in our departments so that she can—"

Her shouting quickly became muted as Dylan pressed a metal muffler over her jaw, molding the pliable material against her mouth and cutting off the cries.

"That's better," I said, pressing a finger in my ear. "Now—"

"Champion Castell, explain yourself," Scipio interrupted, his voice an ice-cold vice that promised death should my answers not satisfy him. "CEO Monroe has my endorsement as—"

"You'll forgive me, Lord Scipio, if your endorsement can't possibly hold much weight in this issue," I interjected softly. "CEO Monroe's family is part of a centuries-old terrorist cell, bent on controlling you for their own purposes. And they have been succeeding, sir. Your opinion is suspect, because you are lacking the important elements of your code that you need to make your own determination."

Scipio froze for several long seconds, his face locked in an impassive mask. "I show no degradation of my systems," he said, sneering. "And you are not *qualified* to make such determinations on my coding."

"And yet I have evidence, taken from Sadie Monroe's terminal," I said, trying to maintain my calm. "As well as several parts of your missing code. Parts that Sadie and her family stole."

"And Plancett?" Sage asked, finally breaking his silence. "What is his role in this little melodrama?"

"Conspiracy. Sadie was purchasing Plancett's loyalty and voting power on the council, in exchange for making it more difficult for his workers' ranks to drop and supplying him with ration cards." I paused and tapped on my screen. Sure enough, the file containing all of the pertinent evidence was sitting there waiting for me, sent by Cornelius right after I started speaking. "On the council server, you will each find a message with files recovered from Sadie's terminal. Included among them are messages between her and Plancett, discussing issues like this. The messages were encrypted, but thanks to the bits of Scipio's code we recovered, we were able to decrypt them."

I watched Sage lean forward and tap on the screen, his eyes scanning through his messages. "There are hundreds of files in this," he said. "Thousands. How did you recover them?"

"I broke into her quarters," I admitted. "We knew that she had parts of Scipio's code stored in there and had reason to believe she was planning to use those parts against him."

Sage cocked his head at me for a second, and then his eyes narrowed. "Your quarters resetting. *You* did that?"

I hesitated. I hadn't expected anyone to figure that part out, but Sage was smarter than most. "Yes. It was necessary to cover our movements. You see, Sadie isn't alone in this. She is part of a massive family, half of whom have been infiltrating departments all over. The other half are living as undocs, and soldiers in her war against the Tower. If they had caught on to what I was trying to do, they would've tried harder to kill me and everyone working with me to keep it secret. I have evidence that they did it before, twenty-five years ago. I also have evidence that Sadie was responsible for the sentinel that attacked the contestants in the Tourney, killing Min-Ha Kim and my mother, Holly Castell."

Sage frowned, his bushy brows drawing together. "That is a very long list of some rather serious allegations. And it does nothing to answer Scipio's question. How are you or any of your people qualified to identify Scipio's coding? For that matter, what happened twenty-five years ago that bears any relevance to this matter? I'm sorry, but before I can sign off on you arresting the heads of *two* different departments, I'm going to need to see this evidence."

I swallowed. I had known this moment was coming, and now that it was upon me, the confidence I had been feeling earlier drained out of me. I was about to reveal Jasper, Rose, and Tony to both Sage and Scipio. I had no idea how this was going to go, and that was causing me no small amount of anxiety. Mostly because they weren't sure how he was going to react, either.

"I will answer your questions gladly," I replied. "But first my Knights will need to clear the room. May I have your permission to move Sadie and Plancett to cells in the Citadel, pending the result of this meeting?"

Sage stared at me for several seconds, and then looked up at Scipio. "Lord Scipio?"

"You may remove them to the antechamber," he said after a pause. "I will not allow them to be shuffled out of this room in handcuffs, and marched to the cells, without first having justifiable cause. If the Tower learns that two councilors might have been involved in a plot to overthrow me, there will be a reckoning, and I would like to avoid that in case these allegations prove untrue."

I heard the warning in his voice and got the message loud and clear. If I wasn't able to convince them that I was telling the truth, then *I* would be the one being escorted from the Council Room. It was hard not to make a gulping sound as I swallowed the lump that was my fear. I couldn't fail in this. If I did, there would be nothing to do but run away with everyone, join my brother, and leave the Tower to its fate. Thank Scipio I'd had the foresight to make sure that everyone was ready to go at the first sign of failure. All we would have to do was hide out until my brother and the others arrived.

"As you wish. Knights?"

Dylan finally let Sadie up, hauling her back and then pushing her down the stairs. Sadie struggled, crying out in spite of the muffler over her mouth. I could feel the hatred and spite in her eyes as Dylan shoved her past, the blue of them so dark with anger that they were more black than anything else. Dylan kept her firmly under control, though, and within moments, the Knights had left, leaving the hard drives containing Jasper and Rose on the central dais.

I pushed away from my desk and moved down the stairs, then stepped through the door. "Lord Scipio, does this room have a terminal independent of your own systems available?" I asked, heading for the dais in the middle of the room.

"Yes," he replied. "I trust you need to interface the hard drives to it?"

"Yes," I informed him. "I will also need you to share control of your holographic projectors and speakers."

Scipio blinked at me, and then nodded. I made it to the dais just as a slot opened up from the floor, and a terminal on a table was lifted up from a storage area below. I could see the connection cables waiting, and picked up both hard drives, carrying them over to the table. Setting them down carefully, I plugged Jasper in first. *Here we go,* I said, hitting the button to initialize the download.

"The reason I know that Sadie was responsible for stealing parts of Scipio's code is because the parts she targeted were parts of other AIs, used to enhance Scipio's original programing. They were all candidates for Scipio's position, once, but ultimately weren't selected when their programs failed. However, aspects of their personalities were added to give him extra checks and balances in his decision-making process. Allow me to present the first one: Jasper."

Jasper's download had just finished, and I nervously turned and looked up to where Scipio was sitting on his chair. Seconds later, his form grew less defined as some of the blue beams being emitted by the projectors above shifted, the color changing to an orange hue. Moments later, a ghostly outline of Jasper in his full glory stood next to Scipio, his white hair slicked back and his mustache impeccably groomed.

"Greetings," he said, giving a nod of his head. "It is good to see you, Brother."

Scipio looked up at him... and then back to me. "What is this?" he asked.

I frowned. I had wondered if Scipio had been aware of his loss, and now that he was peering at Jasper like he was an absolute stranger, I was starting to realize that he hadn't been. Hell, watching his face, it was almost like he didn't even remember Jasper in the first place. Disappointment rippled through me as it hit me that Scipio might not be able to help us fix his programming on his own. Especially if he wasn't even aware he was broken.

"That is Jasper. He made up the core of your logic, before he was taken twenty-five years ago."

"That's ridiculous," he said. "I think I would know if my—"

"Are you telling me that you haven't yet deduced that convincing your diagnostic subroutines that you are perfectly well would be the first step any subversive group would take against you?" Jasper asked, and I squinted at him, taking a moment to rephrase his question to Scipio in a way I could understand: You don't think they're smart enough to make you *think* you're okay?

"I..." Scipio faltered, and my heart stopped. I'd never seen the great machine look so flustered, and I suddenly worried about what he might do, now that he was beginning to realize that there was a problem. I prayed he didn't shut down. The last thing we needed was for him to go offline.

"How many of these... parts of Scipio have you collected, Champion Castell?" Sage asked, and I looked back to see the old man standing, his arms crossed over his chest. "I see another hard drive there."

"Three," I said. "I have Rose and Jasper, while Engineer Green has Tony." I paused to look at Lacey and saw her setting a hard drive of her own on the desk in front of her, resting one hand on it and giving me a nod. "There are two more—Kurt and Alice. I know that Kurt was stolen first, over a hundred years ago, but we haven't been able to discover his whereabouts. We have no idea what happened to Alice."

"But they were all stolen?" he asked, spearing me with a look.

"Ye—" I paused, and then shook my head, realizing I was about to lie inadvertently. "I don't know about Alice. All I know is that she is likely missing as well. Tony made his way to Engineer Lacey on his own, when he realized that they would probably be coming after him next. But I haven't questioned him. I am uncertain of his story."

"So that explains it," he muttered. I squinted at him, baffled by his response.

"Sir?" I asked.

Sage blinked owlishly down at me. "Hm? Ah, yes. My apologies."

Apologies for what? I wondered as he unfolded his arms from under his armpits. I started to follow where his hand was pointing, assuming he was about to ask me some sort of question.

Until I saw the object he was gripping, the familiar, matte black L-shape of it barely registering until the first flash of fire erupted from the tip with a violent BANG! Strum jerked in his chair, a red hole forming between his eyes. The back of his skull exploded in a wet mass across the wood of the wall behind him. I stared at it for a second, so shocked that I was unable to fully comprehend what had just happened.

Then Lacey gave a shrill scream of horror. I snapped my head toward her in time to see her standing, staring at where Strum was still sitting, his body still and lifeless. Suddenly another BANG barked from over my shoulder, and I ducked down instinctively, covering my head with my hands. Blood spurted from high up on Lacey's chest, just below her collarbone.

She staggered back, and the next bullet caught her low in the stomach, at which point she disappeared behind the desk. I whirled around, finally breaking through the shock of his attack and already starting to call Dylan, when Sage said, "Scipio, lock down this room and jam all transmissions coming from this building, authorization code Pine, Ezekial 0-1-9-5-1."

"Authorization confirmed," Scipio replied automatically, and I heard the metallic grate of locks being slammed into place and additional security doors being lowered. My breath caught when I realized that I was trapped. Alone.

With a man I feared I had gravely misjudged.

READY FOR THE FINAL BOOK OF LIANA'S STORY?

Dear Reader,

Thank you for reading *The Girl Who Dared to Endure*.

Book 7, **The Girl Who Dared to Fight**, is the **grand finale** of the series!

It releases **May 10th, 2018**.

Order your copy now: www.bellaforrest.net.

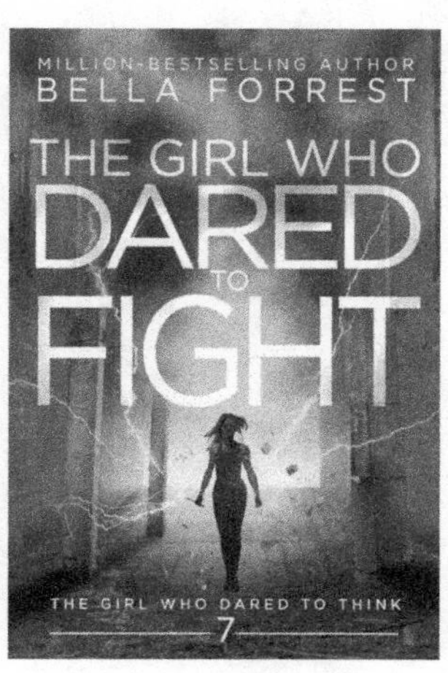

I'll see you again soon, for one final return to the Tower...

Til then,

Bella x

P.S. If you're new to my books or haven't yet read my **Gender Game** series, I suggest you check it out. It is where the Tower's story began and is set in the same world as *The Girl Who Dared* series—the two storylines complement each other.

P.P.S. Sign up to my VIP email list and I'll send you a personal heads up when my next book releases: **www.morebellaforrest.com**

(Your email will be kept 100% private and you can unsubscribe at any time.)

READ MORE BY BELLA FORREST

THE GIRL WHO DARED TO THINK

The Girl Who Dared to Think (Book 1)

The Girl Who Dared to Stand (Book 2)

The Girl Who Dared to Descend (Book 3)

The Girl Who Dared to Rise (Book 4)

The Girl Who Dared to Lead (Book 5)

The Girl Who Dared to Endure (Book 6)

The Girl Who Dared to Fight (Book 7)

THE GENDER GAME

(*Completed series*)

The Gender Game (Book 1)

The Gender Secret (Book 2)

The Gender Lie (Book 3)

The Gender War (Book 4)

The Gender Fall (Book 5)

The Gender Plan (Book 6)

The Gender End (Book 7)

HOTBLOODS

Hotbloods (Book 1)

Coldbloods (Book 2)

Renegades (Book 3)

Venturers (Book 4)

Traitors (Book 5)

A SHADE OF VAMPIRE SERIES

Series 1: Derek & Sofia's story

A Shade of Vampire (Book 1)

A Shade of Blood (Book 2)

A Castle of Sand (Book 3)

A Shadow of Light (Book 4)

A Blaze of Sun (Book 5)

A Gate of Night (Book 6)

A Break of Day (Book 7)

Series 2: Rose & Caleb's story

A Shade of Novak (Book 8)

A Bond of Blood (Book 9)

A Spell of Time (Book 10)

A Chase of Prey (Book 11)

A Shade of Doubt (Book 12)

A Turn of Tides (Book 13)

A Dawn of Strength (Book 14)

A Fall of Secrets (Book 15)

An End of Night (Book 16)

Series 3: The Shade continues with a new hero...

A Wind of Change (Book 17)

A Trail of Echoes (Book 18)

A Soldier of Shadows (Book 19)

A Hero of Realms (Book 20)

A Vial of Life (Book 21)

A Fork of Paths (Book 22)

A Flight of Souls (Book 23)

A Bridge of Stars (Book 24)

Series 4: A Clan of Novaks

A Clan of Novaks (Book 25)

A World of New (Book 26)

A Web of Lies (Book 27)

A Touch of Truth (Book 28)

An Hour of Need (Book 29)

A Game of Risk (Book 30)

A Twist of Fates (Book 31)

A Day of Glory (Book 32)

Series 5: A Dawn of Guardians

A Dawn of Guardians (Book 33)

A Sword of Chance (Book 34)

A Race of Trials (Book 35)

A King of Shadow (Book 36)

An Empire of Stones (Book 37)

A Power of Old (Book 38)

A Rip of Realms (Book 39)

A Throne of Fire (Book 40)

A Tide of War (Book 41)

Series 6: A Gift of Three

A Gift of Three (Book 42)

A House of Mysteries (Book 43)

A Tangle of Hearts (Book 44)

A Meet of Tribes (Book 45)

A Ride of Peril (Book 46)

A Passage of Threats (Book 47)

A Tip of Balance (Book 48)

A Shield of Glass (Book 49)

A Clash of Storms (Book 50)

Series 7: A Call of Vampires

A Call of Vampires (Book 51)

A Valley of Darkness (Book 52)

A Hunt of Fiends (Book 53)

A Den of Tricks (Book 54)

A City of Lies (Book 55)

A League of Exiles (Book 56)

A Charge of Allies (Book 57)

A Snare of Vengeance (Book 58)

A SHADE OF DRAGON TRILOGY

A Shade of Dragon 1

A Shade of Dragon 2

A Shade of Dragon 3

A SHADE OF KIEV TRILOGY

A Shade of Kiev 1

A Shade of Kiev 2

A Shade of Kiev 3

THE SECRET OF SPELLSHADOW MANOR

(Completed series)

The Secret of Spellshadow Manor (Book 1)

The Breaker (Book 2)

The Chain (Book 3)

The Keep (Book 4)

The Test (Book 5)

The Spell (Book 6)

BEAUTIFUL MONSTER DUOLOGY

Beautiful Monster 1

Beautiful Monster 2

DETECTIVE ERIN BOND

(Adult thriller/mystery)

Lights, Camera, GONE

Write, Edit, KILL

For an updated list of Bella's books, please visit her website: www.bellaforrest.net

Join Bella's VIP email list and she'll send you an email reminder as soon as her next book is out: www.morebellaforrest.com

CPSIA information can be obtained
at www.ICGtesting.com
Printed in the USA
LVHW091909250421
685340LV00039B/274